M000206267

IT SHOULD HAVE BEEN ME

SUSAN WILKINS

For Sue Kenyon, who makes it all possible.

PROLOGUE

22 May 2000

She sat slumped at her desk, elbows resting on it, face in her hands. Her head was throbbing fit to burst. How many tequila shots? Too many. The sour after-burn was still fizzing in her gullet. And for what? Some puerile student drinking game. She didn't even like tequila. She glanced at the clock. 1.57am. Now she had to pull an all-nighter just to get the essay done and in on time. She needed more coffee.

The fancy glass cafetière stood empty on her desk, a present from Mum and Dad back in October, when she was a fresher, full of resolutions about how hard she was going to work at uni and how she'd graduate with a First. But in the helter-skelter of the last two terms, her studies had taken a back seat to all the other urgent demands of student life. Bad habits had ambushed her. Now exams were about to start. She'd left her revision to the last minute, and the threat of retakes in the summer loomed, not to mention parental disappointment. And Sarah was the golden child; she didn't disappoint. She'd always been top of the class at school. But uni was different. Everything was way more complicated. All that stupid stuff at the end of the autumn term, but she wasn't going to think about that.

Her fingers hovered over the keyboard. The blue-tinted light from the laptop was drilling into her retinas. Another cigarette would help. She picked up the packet. Smoking kills. Yeah, she got that. But not until you were really old, like maybe sixty. In the meantime, she was relying on the nicotine to help her focus.

The block she lived in was on the edge of campus and faced the dark hillside behind the university. One of the most exciting places in the country to study, or so the prospectus had bragged. Perched on the edge of the South Downs, it had a dreamy quality, an otherworldliness, which appealed to Sarah. She liked to leave her blinds open at night and stare out into the inky blackness. It calmed her and gave her some respite.

Student life had turned out to be way more stressful than she'd expected. There was no let up. You always had to be full on. Clothes, hair, attitude. Everyone was always judging you. The competition was relentless. It was all too easy to get labelled a loser.

She lit the cigarette and inhaled. If she was honest, she hated the acrid taste it left in her mouth. But it did the job. She typed another sentence. Read it over, realised it was crap and deleted it. The font had begun to swim before her eyes. Maybe she needed glasses; that would be a total pain. What she needed was more coffee.

There were eight rooms in the block—she lived at the top —with a shared kitchen on the middle floor. As she padded down the stairs, she felt a whoosh of cold air rushing up from below. Some genius had left the outer door open again!

Ducking into the kitchen she filled the kettle, slotted it on the base and clicked it on. Then she went downstairs to close the door. A motion sensor activated the outside security light, but the nerd—he did mechanical engineering—who lived on the ground floor and went to bed at ten, said it kept him awake, so he'd removed the bulb. Tossing her cigarette into the dark shrubbery, Sarah slammed the outer door shut. With any luck it would wake the nerd up.

She returned to the kitchen, spooned coffee into the cafetière and was filling it with boiling water when she heard footsteps on the stairs. It must be one of her roommates going to the loo. She put her head round the door, intending to scare them. But there was no one there. Then she caught a whiff, chemical and cloying, some kind of cheap body-spray that boys used to make them irresistible. As if.

Carrying the cafetière of coffee, she headed back up to her room. Two more paracetamol plus a couple of mugs of this should finally kick her synapses into gear.

She pushed open the door and he was standing there, arms folded, wearing a Bill Clinton carnival mask. Her heart sank. Could this get any worse? She had an insane deadline, and he was the last person on the planet she wanted to see.

She huffed. 'Oh what! Like I don't know who you are?'

The baby-faced features of the 42nd President of the United States grinned back at her. The fool probably thought he was being amusing.

'You're up late.'

'Really. Well spotted.' She made no attempt to keep the sarcasm out of her voice. 'What do you want?'

'Coffee smells nice.' He was fiddling with the pen on her desk, twiddling it in his tapered fingers.

She grabbed it from him. 'I'm working.'

He pushed the carnival mask up on to his forehead and

smiled. 'Take a break. It'll do you good. Help your concentration.' Not what you'd call a handsome face. Too weaselly. But he had a great body, and he knew it.

'It won't. This will.' She pointed to the coffee.

'That's disappointing.'

'Well, it is what it is. I've got a deadline.'

A standoff. He had his hands on his hips, skinny jeans, tight T-shirt emphasising his biceps. She could feel the pheromones. It was obvious what he wanted. And there was no way.

Picking up the cafetière, she poured herself a mug. 'You need to go.'

He chuckled. 'You think I don't know?'

'Know what?'

'I'm not stupid. I figured it out. Avoiding me is not going to work.'

Their eyes met and she stared him down, but it took effort. He couldn't know, could he? It wasn't possible. She just had to hold it together and get rid of him. Still, his attitude irritated her.

'I'm not avoiding you. But you act as if you've got some kind of right to be here. I've told you I need to work, but no. You want sex and my needs don't matter. It's all about what you want.'

'What I want? That's rich.' He shook his head. He didn't like to be denied, and she could sense the anger bubbling up. He had a temper; she'd glimpsed it before. But she refused to be bullied.

She glared at him. 'I've got work to do. I need you to go.'

He took a step closer. 'Don't pull this feminist shit on me, Sarah. I'm not an idiot. Don't treat me like one. You just want to be in control of everything, don't you? You flick your hair and all the boys coming running. And that's how you like it.' The tone was sneering.

She was determined to stand her ground. 'I've had enough of this. Go, or else.'

'Or else what?'

'You need me to spell it out for you? I'll scream the place down if I have to.'

He tilted his head and laughed. 'You'll say I tried to rape you?'

'Don't tempt me.' She cradled the mug in both hands.

But his eyes narrowed. 'You'd do it too, wouldn't you? If only to spite me.'

She sighed. This was getting uncomfortable. 'Look, I have to write my essay. I just—'

The fist smashed into her face. A move so swift it took her entirely by surprise. The force sent her sprawling backwards, her skull smacking against the wall before she landed spreadeagled on the bed.

And the pain! Head spinning, mouth filling with blood, she stared up at him in total shock.

He leaned over her, face flushed with fury. 'Here's some news for you, Sarah Boden: you don't say no to me. You think you get to choose? You don't get to choose. I'm the one who chooses. Okay?'

She wasn't listening. She had to get up. Hands desperately flailing, she tried to grab the desk for support. Blood oozed from her mouth, dripped from her chin.

He straightened up, shaking his head wearily. 'Now look what you made me do.'

The anger had abated as quickly as it came. The punch had been harder than he'd intended. He slotted his hands in his pockets. 'Look, I'm sorry. That was an accident. I didn't mean to hit you that hard.'

She was dizzy. The door. If she could just get to the door. She wanted to scream, but her mouth wouldn't work. The pain in her jaw was excruciating, and she was choking on her own blood. Focus on the door! She launched herself towards it.

As he watched her, he realized the sad truth: this bitch was about to ruin his life. She wouldn't hesitate, even though it was clearly her fault because she'd provoked him. But who would pay any heed to that? His career prospects, the life he'd meticulously planned, he could lose it all. And he didn't deserve that.

Once she was out of that door, he'd lose control of the situation. She'd backed him into a corner. Once again, she'd robbed him of choice.

Taking a deep breath, he shoved her back down on the bed and placed his knee on her chest. He picked up the pillow, put it over her face, and pressed down with all his strength. Her legs kicked. Her body twitched. But it was all over in seconds. It was unfortunate, but what else could he have done? She'd left him with no alternative.

1

....

January 2017

Detective Constable Jo Boden was crouched in the corner of the surveillance vehicle. Her knees were stiff, her whole body numb with cold; it had been a long night. Sitting in the dark, watching, waiting, this was her least favourite part of the job. Around midnight, a blanket of freezing fog had descended on the city. Peering out, little was visible beyond the sulphurous haze of the street lamps. They were scheduled to go in at 5 a.m. but the chatter on the comms suggested some kind of hiccup.

She'd been partnered with the new bloke, Darryl; he was cocksure and she didn't rate him. But Boden kept her opinions to herself. It wasn't easy. He was pressing all her buttons. She could see that beneath the bravado he was nervous—his first big op on the squad—but when he spoke to her, his gaze strayed to her tits, which was just annoying.

They were in an alley in Catford, tucked round the corner from the target premises. Jo had joined the grandly titled

7

Human Exploitation and Organized Crime Command, part of the Met's Specialist Crime Directorate, the previous spring. She'd spent most of the summer in fuggy vans in London's piss-stinking back allies. Parked up between the bins, the rusting white goods and rotting mattresses in a miasma of dogshit and flies, she was learning that surveillance was a game of patience. And Jo Boden was not patient. She'd taken and passed her sergeant's exams at the earliest opportunity. But promotion depended on vacancies arising. The logjam in the lower ranks showed no signs of easing. Cuts made it worse. So she was stuck; occasionally it was exciting but often she was bored.

The current operation was against Albanian human traffickers who ran a lucrative sideline in underage prostitutes, both male and female. The kids were between twelve and fourteen and had been picked up in the migrant camps of France and lured with the promise of safe passage to the UK. They were then separated from any siblings or friends and kept under lock and key in a number of residential properties across London.

However, the place they were hitting this morning was more than a brothel. It was the ramshackle headquarters of this particular clan. The Kelmendi family had bought the yard and warehouse from a South London removals firm who'd gone bust in the recession of 2008. The signage of the old company, paint peeling, still hung above the roll-up garage doors. A yard, overgrown with weeds and drifts of rubbish, gave it a semi-derelict air. But a tip-off from an informant on the inside had prompted two weeks of visual surveillance and revealed plenty of activity. Fejzi Kelmendi, the nominal head of the family and already subject to a European Arrest Warrant, was thought to be hiding out in North Cyprus. But for the rest of the gang, it seemed to be business as usual.

Jo stretched her long legs out in front of her and clicked her phone on to check the time. For a few seconds Darryl was illuminated in its eerie beam. He had a good physique, lean and muscular, which was always top of her list. If she met him in a bar, she might be tempted. But sex with colleagues was taboo in her book; it always led to trouble and complications.

Being a young and ambitious female officer in an organization which played lip service to equality meant treading a careful path. Office banter, sexist jokes and innuendo obliged her to be a good sport, one of the lads. But there was an unspoken rule that you broke at your peril. Unless you planned to marry him, it was best to never get involved. No officer wanted to say *ma'am* to a boss who everyone regarded as a slag. Better if they assumed you were a dyke. Better still if they simply didn't know.

Audio bugs had been planted by sneaking on to the roof of the building three days previously; since then, they'd been listening in. A tiny camera, positioned precariously on a skylight, had worked at first, but had got shifted out of alignment, probably by roosting pigeons. Going up a second time to fix it had been judged too risky. The Kelmendis ran a tight ship and were vigilant about their security. They always used burners and it had proved impossible to get a trace on any of their phones. So the audio recording was going to be a vital piece of evidence.

Darryl had positioned himself on the stool in front of the monitor at the beginning of their shift and he hadn't budged. He played a lot of computer games and seemed to assume this gave him superior competence with any technical kit. Jo couldn't have cared less, even though she had far more experience. Much of the chat was in Albanian, so the audio feed was being streamed to the ops room where they had translation facilities.

The main reason she was there, besides the need to babysit Darryl, was because the tip-off, which had located this place, had come from Razan. And Razan was her chis—Covert Human Intelligence Source—an eighteen-year-old kid they'd pulled out of the back of a lorry with twenty other Syrians at Clacket Lane services on the M25. But Razan was canny and way too cynical for her years. She spoke passable English and had demanded to speak to the officer in charge. Then she'd offered them a deal. The traffickers still had her little sister, whom she was desperate to find. So for a guarantee of fast-tracked asylum, she'd return to the Kelmendis, put herself on the line and gather information for the police.

Jo had been stunned by the matter-of-fact courage of this unassuming Syrian girl and, as her handler, she was determined to ensure she got out unscathed.

Darryl pulled out one of his earbuds and huffed. 'We're talking about a delay. Some problem with one of the ARVs, maybe a flat.'

One of the Armed Response Vehicles had a flat tyre? Fifteen pre-dawn raids across the capital were being held up because of a flat tyre? Jo gave her head a weary shake. She took a pack of chewing gum out of her pocket and unwrapped a stick.

Darryl grinned. His features were barely discernible in the monitor's glow. 'Don't I get a bit?'

She ignored the tone and offered him the gum. That's when they heard the scream. It was loud enough to make Darryl jump as it leaked from his earbud.

'What the hell?' Jo glared at him. 'Give it to me!'

Darryl fumbled with the earbud. Jo grabbed it and

listened. A low keening, sobs of pain then a pleading female voice. 'Please … please, no! No no.'

The thwack of a fist on flesh was followed by another howl.

'Oh, shit!' Boden clenched her fist. 'Shit! Shit! Shit!'

'Is that your chis?'

'Well, it's not one of the bloody Albanians, is it? Something's gone wrong. What's the ETA now for the armed response team?'

'I don't know.' He sounded as if he might cry.

'Darryl, get a grip. Five minutes? Ten? Ask them.' Jo was on her feet.

'Okay okay.'

'Tell Command we've got a problem—looks like our chis is blown and we need armed backup now. Got it?' She slid open the side door of the van.

'What you going to do? What if they see you?'

What was she going to do? All she knew was she had to do something or Razan could end up dead. Her brain was rapidly calculating. How many of them inside? Since she'd come on shift, there'd been no movement. It would be in the log, but she had no time to check that.

'Don't crap your pants, Darryl. Just do as you're told. Inform Command.'

Jumping out of the van into a slab of moist, freezing air, Boden twisted her shoulder-length blonde hair into a coil and tucked it up under her hood. She zipped her jacket, shoved her hands in her pockets, and let her shoulders settle into a slouch. Even so, it was hard to disguise her height. In a ball-gown she'd have turned heads on any red carpet or catwalk. In a hoodie and jeans, she had to work at becoming invisible. But she'd had plenty of practice.

As she emerged from the alley into the main road, she

broke into a fast trot. Traffic was still sporadic. It was hours before dawn, London was frozen in a dark wintery stillness. Nitrogen oxide laced with soot hung in a toxic smog. It zapped her lungs. She wrapped her scarf round her face and skirted a couple of illegal meat vans belching diesel, arriving to bag a good pitch on the edge of the market. Reaching the pocked concrete yard at the front of the garage, she lowered the scarf and spat out her gum.

Next to the entrance to the building was a metal, half-glazed side door. Jo hesitated, heart pounding, adrenaline pumping; should she wait or go in? She knew what the gold commander's instructions would be: wait for backup. But that could be too late for Razan.

Keeping her head dipped, she rapped on the door. Nothing. She rapped harder until it opened a crack. A scowling pair of eyes rested on her.

She didn't meet his gaze, she just mumbled. 'Need to score, mate. I'm desperate.'

'Fook off!'

'Naaa, please! Know you sell the stuff. I got cash. And I'll give you a blow job. I'm good.'

The door inched open. His hair was shaved up the back and sides, his cheeks pitted with acne, and he looked about fifteen.

'See face?' The accent made him virtually unintelligible.

Lifting her chin, she shot him a timid look. Shoulders hunched, she let her body shake. It wasn't hard—she was chilled to the bone—and it created a passable impersonation of a junkie. He opened the door and beckoned her in.

She found herself in a small office with an inner door to the garage beyond. That door was ajar. She could hear male voices, some kind of discussion. But worryingly the crying had stopped.

The boy was staring at her and unzipping his fly.

'Let's see the stuff first.'

He sneered. 'Stupi' bitch! No drug.' Easing his penis out of his jeans, he gave her a curt nod. 'Now you do.'

Jo smiled. This was turning out to be easier than she'd imagined.

Moving with lightning speed, she grabbed the penis with her left hand and twisted it, while clapping her right palm over his mouth and ramming him back against the wall. He gave a muffled squeal.

Lifting her palm, she splayed her fingers and slammed her right forearm diagonally across his throat, causing him to gag and splutter.

Her voice was a silky whisper in his ear. 'Nice and quiet, butch, or I'll rip your dick off. Understand?' She gave his deflated member a tug. 'Understand? Nod your head.'

Face red, gasping for breath, tears in his eyes, he nodded. He was a gangly teen, the stubble on his upper lip and chin was downy. Fooling the men in the garage would not be so simple.

She released her grip on his manhood, spun him round, yanked his arm behind his back, and jerked it up as far as it would go. Thrusting her index and middle finger into the pressure point under his jawbone, she propelled him forward towards the internal door.

They stopped just short of the threshold. Peering over the boy's shoulder, she counted three men standing over a body on the floor curled into the foetal position: Razan. She wasn't moving.

Jo was hoping for a couple of seconds to assess the situation, but she wasn't in luck. Ardi Kelmendi had already turned towards the door and was staring straight at them with a puzzled look.

'*Çfarë qij?*'

She shoved the lad forward into the garage. Flies gaping, he stumbled over and landed in a heap.

Ardi burst out laughing.

Short and beefy, Jo recognized him from numerous surveillance photos. Plus she'd read his file. The eldest son of Fejzi, he was the de facto boss. For the last five years, he'd been his father's enforcer and was the prime suspect in several gang-related homicides.

A black leather jacket hung on the back of a chair about two metres to the Albanian's left. Looped over it was a belt and a gun in a holster designed for concealed carry.

Ardi folded his arms, both etched from knuckle to elbow with serpentine tattoos. Shaking his head with amusement, he addressed the boy. '*Çfarë po duke luajtur në?*'

The boy was too ashamed to even look up; still on his knees, he mumbled a reply.

The Albanian's chilling black eyes then came to rest on Jo Boden. 'And what the fook are you?'

She met his gaze. The next few seconds would determine the outcome of this encounter, for her and for Razan, who might already be dead. Displaying any kind of fear was not an option. Like a rabid dog the gangster would smell it, see it as an invitation to strike.

Pushing back her hood and standing tall, Jo smiled. 'I'm a police officer.'

Ardi gave a hoot of laughter and placed his hands on his hips. 'A cop? You look more like a whore to me.'

He chuckled, but Jo noticed his glance straying to the holster on the chair. His two thugs also seemed to be enjoying the joke. One was a carbon copy of Ardi, solid muscle but with a sagging gut. The other was bearded and wiry, Asian or possibly Arab, with an intense, angry stare. Jo figured he was the one to watch, some kind of wandering jihadist who'd washed up on the gangster's payroll.

'A lady cop?' Ardi's voice dripped sarcasm. 'And have you come to interview me or just to suck my dick?' Both he and the carbon copy chortled.

'No. I've come to arrest you.' Jo glanced at Razan; still motionless on the floor, she didn't appear to be breathing. 'And here's what you need to consider, Ardi, before you go for the gun and do something stupid. We're recording all this — audio and video.'

He stared at her, then laughed again.

'I don't believe you.'

Jo pointed upwards. 'We drilled holes in the roof.'

The gaze of the two Albanians shot up towards the ceiling. The bearded jihadist continued to glare at her.

'You think I'd walk in here with no backup? You've been under surveillance for some time.'

The Albanian's lizard-eyed stare flicked back to her.

He was hardly two metres away and she could feel the fury erupting from him like a wave.

'*Kurvë trashë!*' He spat the words at her. 'And you think I let some bitch take me?' He drew his index finger across his throat. 'You dead meat. I promise you.'

His tongue skimmed his lower lip and Jo knew what was coming next. He lunged sideways and made a grab for the gun. She threw herself forward. It wasn't brave, more instinctual. *Stop him getting the gun.* She head-butted him in the gut. He didn't even stagger. Ripping the gun from its holster, he whacked her across the face with the side of it. Hard metal cracked into the bridge of her nose, knocking her clean off her feet. As she hit the concrete floor and rolled, a volley of thoughts rattled through her brain—the excruciating pain of the blow, the metallic taste of blood, the mindless stupidity of it all. Why had she done this? Now he'd shoot her. What a futile ending. Would it hurt?

What she heard next was a thunderous bang—*puzzling because you never hear the bullet that kills you*—followed by a blinding flash as the stun grenade exploded. It felt as though her eardrums would shatter, but somewhere out there, beyond the ringing in her head, she could just make out a muffled shout: Armed Police!

2

Jo Boden entered the briefing room to a slow handclap. An hour's wait in A & E had confirmed she had mild concussion and a broken nose. She'd been poked and prodded, but there was too much swelling to decide yet whether she would need corrective surgery. Puffy mauve bags underscored both eyes, and the treatment recommended was frozen peas and paracetamol.

The twenty officers present rose to their feet and burst into song:

Why was she born so beautiful? Why was she born at all?
She's no bloody use to anyone, she's no bloody use at all!

They ended the ditty with whoops and a round of applause.

Jo dipped her head in acknowledgement and gave her colleagues the middle finger. She didn't enjoy being the centre of attention, although she appreciated the gesture.

With a sweep of his arm, Darryl drew out a chair for her. He was basking in her reflected glory. She sat down at the large conference table to slaps on the back and congratulations.

A hush descended as the Chief Superintendent strode in and took his place at the head of the table. Dave Hollingsworth let his gaze travel around the room. His nickname was 'the Undertaker'. A tall, narrow man with vulpine features, he had a naturally mournful manner.

'Well done, everyone. Good team effort all round. We now have ten gang members in custody, including Ardi Kelmendi. And the CPS regards the evidence as solid. So we should see some convictions.'

He glanced at Jo. Was he about to single her out for praise?

'That looks painful, Boden. Has it been looked at?'

'Yes, sir.'

He nodded. It seemed as if he was about to say more, then changed his mind. 'Do we have an update on the Syrian girl?'

Jo didn't know. She'd been driven to hospital in a squad car, while Razan had been whisked away in an ambulance.

A soft female voice whispered from the back. 'She's still—'

'Stand up and speak up, DC Georgiou!'

'Sir.'

Jo craned round to look at a slight raven-haired girl dwarfed between two brawny middle-aged men. She felt for her. She'd been the rookie not so long ago. Now this young DC was a stand-in for Jo Boden.

'She's still in surgery. Some bleeding on the brain from a skull fracture.'

'Do the medics think she'll pull through?'

'Hopefully.' She sounded nervous. 'I think so. She's got a smashed eye socket too. So she could lose an eye. Sir.'

Jo tried to give Georgiou a reassuring look, though she wasn't sure the girl had noticed.

Hollingsworth nodded again. The mood in the room was

upbeat. After the successful conclusion to a lengthy operation, everyone wanted to celebrate, and a couple of the DSs had even taken bets on the chances of the boss cracking a smile. But his face remained grave.

'Let's hope she makes a good recovery. Outstanding paperwork should be completed today. The DCI will be issuing further actions. And there'll be a drink for everyone tonight. Frank's buying.'

The DCI raised two fingers to his forelock in mock salute. This produced a muted cheer.

The boss nodded again, but he was niggled. The truth was, the operation had been a fiasco. Broken-down vehicles, timings gone awry; they'd been lucky to get away with it. And several gang members had escaped.

His eyes scanned the room then his lips turned upwards into a definite smirk. 'We've rescued twenty-six children and young people today and put some seriously nasty villains away. It's a great result. I'm proud of each and every one of you. But it all comes down to teamwork.' Jo got the impression he was deliberately avoiding her eye. 'Thank you.'

Then, as he got to the door, he turned. 'DC Boden, have you got a minute?'

'Sir.'

Jo accompanied him out of the room to winks and grins. DC Debbie Georgiou's dark eyes followed her like a startled fawn. Jo got on with her colleagues, although most regarded her as an enigma. This was the persona she'd cultivated and it provided a protective carapace. She wouldn't even tell them which football team she supported. But the view in the squad was unanimous: she deserved recognition for her audacity. If she hadn't acted, the chis would probably be dead.

Hollingsworth ignored her. He and the DCI set off down the corridor, leaving her to trail behind. The two men chatted about golf. When they reached Hollingsworth's office, he opened the door and nodded to her to enter.

The room was sizeable, with a large window and an eye-level view of the elevated section of the A40(M), wreathed in fog. The ghostly traffic swept by only metres from the building, the double-glazing reducing noise to a background rumble; but Jo didn't notice any of it. All she saw was the person sitting on one of the two sofas. Dark curly hair, foot furiously tapping, it was Ardi Kelmendi's bearded sidekick, the wandering jihadist. She stared at him in disbelief. He shot her a sullen look.

Hollingsworth's expression was impassive. 'This is DC Jabreel Khan.'

'Seriously?' She shook her head. Her nose throbbed.

'Sit down, Boden.'

'I'll stand. Thank you, sir.'

Khan jumped to his feet and jabbed a finger in Jo's face. 'What the fuck were you playing at? You could've blown my cover!'

'How was I supposed to know you were in there? I was trying to protect my chis.'

'Yeah, well, I'd stopped them killing her. Before you came blundering in.'

This was too much for Jo. 'She has a fractured skull and a smashed eye socket. What do you call that? Acceptable collateral damage?'

'These are very dangerous men.'

Jo stepped forward. 'Oh, I get that. They obviously scared you.'

Fists clenching, Khan also stepped forward. 'Who the hell do you think you are? You could've got us all killed. Some grandstanding girl, angling for promotion!'

Hollingsworth raised his palm. 'All right. That's enough.' He glared at Khan. 'Jabreel, enough!'

Folding his arms, the undercover cop shook his head and turned away.

Jo inhaled. The events of the morning were spiralling through her brain: struggling to her feet as the dust settled, surprised to even be alive, cradling Razan as they waited for the paramedics. Her own bloody, swollen face. 'Why am I here, sir?'

'For operational reasons, it's necessary for you to exclude any mention of DC Khan from your notes. I wanted you to understand why.'

Jo was furious. Operational bollocks! They'd had an undercover officer in there all along, and Razan had still been beaten half to death. Now they were covering their arses in case the IPCC came calling.

'Is that an order, sir?'

'It's a request. We've had a good result today. But it's like cutting the head off the hydra. With his son in jail, Fejzi Kelmendi is likely to send others to pick up the reins.'

Khan glared at her. 'Yeah, and while you're getting pissed up and petted by your mates, Boden, I've got to go back out there.'

Jo glanced at Hollingsworth. 'This isn't my cock-up, sir. Surely the first duty of any undercover officer—'

'Don't tell me my job!'

'All right, Jabreel. I think the point's been made.'

The DC took a breath, but his dark eyes continued to bore into Jo. 'Can I go now?'

'Yes, thanks for coming in.'

With a sneer, DC Jabreel Khan pulled up his hood and disappeared out of the door, leaving Jo facing her boss.

During her time on the squad, she'd had little personal contact with Hollingsworth. His approach, like his manner, was distant. He was always ready to praise his officers for teamwork, but was a stickler for protocols and procedures and, Jo suspected, old-fashioned respect for the chain of command.

She waited for him to speak.

'You made a judgement call, Jo. I appreciate that.'

Her brain and body were fizzing with fury. The thumping pain across the bridge of her nose and down her face made it worse. *Keep quiet, just listen.* She couldn't.

'If we had an officer undercover, why was Razan even in there?'

'To gain as much intel as possible. Jabreel couldn't wear a wire, it was too dangerous.'

'But not too dangerous for her.'

His thin lip curled. 'These are strategic decisions, taken with the utmost care.'

'She was a decoy, wasn't she? Ardi finds the wire on her, slaps her around a bit. Then, when he gets nicked, his old man isn't going to be looking for any other plants in the organization. We were using her to protect our undercover officer.'

The words tumbled out of her mouth before she had time to consider. Still pumped with adrenaline, she felt both right and righteous. It was the longest one-to-one exchange she'd ever had with Hollingsworth. And in that moment the prospect of a promotion any time soon had evaporated.

His pallid eyes came to rest on her face, but the expression was impossible to read.

After several seconds, he sighed. 'Jo, this is a difficult job at the best of times. You have to learn not to take these things too personally. As the girl's handler, you did everything you could. So did Jabreel. And ...,' he paused for effect. 'I'm going to recommend you for a Commissioner's commendation.'

Half an hour earlier, Jo would've been delighted. But he was playing politics, she knew that. She was female and photogenic. It would make a great photo-op for the Commissioner. *Our brave young officers out there risking their lives to keep London safe.* It was on the tip of her tongue to tell him where to stuff it.

Instead, she forced a smile, which made her wince. 'Thank you, sir.' She touched the swelling with her fingertip.

They stood for a moment facing each other, in a silent space with only the motorway traffic providing a background hum. Jo didn't know what to do. The meeting seemed to be over. She was merely waiting for some indication that she could go. But the dead-eyed gaze continued to scan her, still assessing and calculating.

'That looks pretty nasty. Have you got painkillers? You should take the rest of the week off. Then we'll see.'

'I'm fine, sir. I'd rather keep busy.'

'It's an order, Boden. Go home.'

'Sir.'

Interview over, she headed back down the corridor and the realization of what had happened began to sink in. *Then we'll see.* See what? Her anger had simply got the better of her; as a result, she'd handled the situation stupidly and naively. Her attempt to rescue Razan had created problems. Still, it had been well-meaning and Hollingsworth might have accepted that, if she hadn't waded in with a direct challenge to his integrity.

All the months of hard work she'd put in, establishing her place in the squad, making sure the bosses knew she was a solid officer who could be relied upon. She'd thrown it all away—and for what? Because she wanted to be right? She was smarter than that. Or she thought she was.

Stopping by the vending machine, she put her hands in her jeans pocket for some change. In the absence of frozen peas, a can of something cold and fizzy would have to do. But her fingers fumbled on the keypad. She missed the correct button, the interior mechanism spun its wheels, clunked and failed to deliver. She thumped the plastic housing with the side of her fist.

'Abuse of government property could be considered a disciplinary offence.'

She spun round to face the speaker.

'DC Boden, isn't it? The girl who tried to nick Ardi Kelmendi single-handed.'

Jo didn't like his tone. But challenging yet another senior officer so soon was probably not politic. She settled for a scowl.

Removing her coins from the reject slot, he fed them back into the machine.

'This stuff rots your teeth and turns you into an obese blob. Which sort do you want?'

'Anything that's cold.'

What was it with blokes and vending machines, Jo wondered? There must be some YouTuber or journo—bushy beard, backside hanging out of his jeans—giving advice about chatting up women. Bullet point three: sidle up to her casually at the office vending machine and say something cool. Jo had a tendency to attract male attention. It was a fact of life, and she usually bought her drinks and snacks in the canteen in order to avoid these not-so-random encounters.

He handed her a can of some sports concoction laced with taurine, but it was cold and dewy.

'Thanks.' She held it against her forehead and waited for him to go away.

He folded his arms. 'I'm Steve Vaizey.'

'I know who you are. Sir.'

Operation Grebe had taken up residence in the adjacent suite of offices about a month earlier. Secretive and special, they were tasked with targeting gun smuggling. Vaizey was in charge, and his reputation preceded him. Young for a Detective Super, not yet forty, he was known for getting results.

Jo had noticed him. Everyone in the squad had noticed him. Getting on a specialist op was the holy grail to success in the Met.

Tall and lean, he fidgeted with his key fob, flicking it back and forth with a restless energy as he looked her up and down. She found the scrutiny uncomfortable, but wasn't about to let him know that.

Finally, he smiled. 'You know, DC Boden, there might be something useful you could do for me. Have you worked much undercover?'

'A bit.'

'Fancy a secondment?'

Jo met his gaze, a hard, flinty stare, impossible to read. Was he being serious?

'Erm, yes.'

'I'll have a chat with Dave Hollingsworth. See if we can borrow you. Is the nose broken?'

Jo nodded.

'Looks painful. Take a couple of days, then come and see me.'

He gave her another smile and sauntered off down the corridor.

Jo wasn't sure whether to be pleased or petrified. Her undercover experience consisted mainly of posing as a potential drug buyer to street pushers with half a brain. She'd done the course. She'd done every course on offer. But role-playing in the classroom hardly prepared you for stepping out into a live operation against organized crime.

Jabreel Khan flashed into her mind, the weary, hunted look he had, the product no doubt of stress and worrying 24/7 that the target might suss you out and shoot you in the head.

But she was being offered an opportunity any one of her colleagues would kill for. The chance to work undercover on a high-profile op. It was a frightening prospect. And she was overjoyed. It was the break she'd been waiting and working for, the chance to step out from the pack and show them what she could do.

3

Nathan Wade believed that all things in life contained a hidden purpose, though it was seldom revealed. He didn't link this to a belief in God in any conventional sense, although his parents had been regular churchgoers. This feeling had emerged gradually, more as a survival mechanism, a hook to grasp and haul his thoughts up from the pit of resentment and despair. In earlier years his rational mind had been attracted to nihilism. He knew this, but he'd seen enough prison inmates turn that into an excuse to embrace monstrous ideologies. No way was he going down that road. There were easier ways to commit suicide.

As always, he'd woken around dawn and sat in a half-lotus on the floor of his cell, focusing on his breathing. Meditation was a daily ritual. Detachment was always his goal; it was the only way to stay sane. Thoughts drifted in and out of his mind. On the surface he was calm, but the nattering irritants that plagued his life knew how to bushwhack him: the ingrained grime on the floor, the greasy Blu Tack stains on the wall, the smell of stale sweat infusing his mattress. He hated these things. Sometimes his temper would erupt and it would require extra discipline to keep it in check. But today he was on an even keel. He could loosen the reins.

The first image that had come into his mind was of Sarah. He often thought of Sarah. The familiar procession of fractured memories kicked in and he knew better than to resist them: getting high; her belligerent mood that night; the row; waking up the next morning with the police kicking down his door and dragging him out of bed; his life imploding in the ensuing nightmare. Then there was the frustration of forever grasping for what he couldn't recall, for the details that were lost.

He'd been charged with her murder twenty-four hours later. It was surreal. He remembered the pain on his mother's face, and the doubt. The police interview had been interminable; one detective pretended to be his friend. He insisted Nathan may have blacked out or forgotten what he'd done. All the dope he'd smoked would've been a factor. He kept going back to the row; what did they argue about? What didn't they argue about? They were always having rows. Followed by sex. Nathan told them he couldn't remember, which was true. But he did remember how beautiful she was.

The trial had passed with him in a daze. His barrister, after consulting with his parents, decided not to put him on the stand. The members of the jury avoided looking him in the eye. The judge called him *a vicious killer who refused to take responsibility for his crime.* A few days short of his twentieth birthday, he was found guilty of murder and given a life sentence with a tariff of sixteen years before he could be considered for release on licence.

At thirty-six he'd seen the inside of a variety of jails. Now he was completing his sentence at Ford Open Prison in West Sussex and working outside during the day to prepare for his release.

Prison had completed his education, though not in the way he'd ever intended. He'd learnt how to survive the brutality of the system, how to play the game, how to tailor his behaviour and words to what the shrinks and offender managers wanted to see and hear and, above all, to express remorse.

Contrition was the box they needed to tick, but getting it right was an art form. The amount of emotion that accompanied expressions of guilt had to be finely judged. Tears certainly, but not often. A surfeit of feeling, any tendency to gorge on self-pity, and they'd whack you on some mind-numbing medication. Their definition of normal behaviour was a narrow one.

Drugs not prescribed were another matter entirely. Jails might be awash with them, but any involvement in either their consumption or trade invited hassle not just from the authorities but from other inmates. They fuelled violence and often ended any chance of early parole.

Maybe all this was obvious, but it took Nathan the first five years of his sentence to work it out. The process was slow and bitter. It wasn't until he joined the addiction programme and his addled brain cleared that he started to face up to the reality of his situation. It took another couple of years for him to morph into a reformed junkie who did online courses and mentored other inmates. There was still the occasional spliff in secret, but in the end, getting clean was a relief. He came to regard any intrusion on his body, from substances, from other people, as unacceptable. He couldn't control much else in his life. All he had was his carcass and the psyche that inhabited it. And he was determined to keep both unsullied.

The minibus left the prison each morning at seven to take inmates to a variety of jobs in the nearby seaside town of

Littlehampton. Nathan's careful years of reflecting back at the prison regime what it wanted to see ensured they regarded him as a model prisoner with a negligible risk of re-offending or being a danger to the public. As a result, he'd wangled one of the better jobs on offer to offenders. It was with a major coffee shop chain, and they'd agreed to train him with the possibility of proper employment once he was released.

Making coffee wasn't a bad job. During his incarceration, he'd done far worse. He found he enjoyed the precision and repetition, not to mention drinking the luxurious non-prison brew. He rapidly became a whiz at all the delectable permutations the shop offered. Fast and meticulous, he kept his work area clean, and Lech, the manager, regarded him as his star barista. Although they had little in common, the gabby Pole and the laconic convict got on. Lech wasn't interested in what crime he'd committed; to him all authority was inherently suspect.

For Nathan this was a novel experience. He'd had no truck with friendship since his conviction. Sixteen years inside had taught him that intimacy was more dangerous than aggression. His reputation as a recluse had protected him. He didn't dislike Lech; he regarded his boss as an innocent, a man who thought well of everyone until he had a reason not to. To Nathan, this was naïve. Nevertheless, Lech was useful. Once he was out, Nathan didn't plan on remaining a barista, so a glowing reference from his good mate might come in handy.

It was seven thirty when the prison minibus deposited the model inmate outside the coffee shop. Lech was helping the delivery driver unload the day's supplies. Nathan pitched in. He hoisted two six-packs, each containing twelve litres of milk, on to his shoulder.

The manager laughed. 'Hey, look at you! Such muscles! That girl, that's why she keep coming back.'

Nathan was lanky but strong. His straggly hair had thinned on top to a monkish tonsure. He walked with a stoop —a habit acquired from years of avoiding eye contact—he knew he was no one's idea of a catch. He smiled, but ignored the tease.

Lech meant well, but he didn't understand. Over the years, Nathan had received plenty of letters from stupid women who'd wanted to befriend him. Some were weirder than others. Murderers seemed especially attractive to these types. When an article of his was published in a small anthology of prisoners' work, he'd received two proposals of marriage from total strangers.

But *that girl* was a rather different problem. Briony Rowe had started to write to him a year previously. He hadn't recognized the name until she reminded him she'd been a close friend of Sarah's. He had some recollection of a dumpy girl, rather shy, who'd been on their course. Sarah loved to give everyone nicknames, usually to torment them, and Briony had been dubbed *Miss Piggy*. He remembered that.

He'd agreed to a visit and in it she'd explained that she was now a freelance journalist and film-maker. She had never believed him capable of her friend's murder, she said, and she was making a film about it. What had happened to Nathan was a miscarriage of justice, and she was determined to expose it. Funding was a problem, but with his cooperation, she was hoping to rectify that.

Nathan was amused then annoyed. The whole thing was a scam. Briony Rowe was awkward and odd; she alluded to unspecified health problems, which had, she told him, affected her career. When questioned about her *many TV credits*, she was vague.

He wrote her a polite letter saying he wasn't interested. But she hadn't given up. She continued to badger him with requests for another visit, and now she'd tracked him down to the coffee shop in Littlehampton.

The previous week, he'd been serving a customer and realized she was filming him through the window on her mobile phone. Lech thought it was a great joke.

But Nathan found it disturbing. The parole board was about to meet to set a date for his release on licence. This was the last thing he needed, some messed-up woman using him to give her failed career a boost. He didn't know what to do. He considered confiding in his probation officer, but if they suspected he'd given her any encouragement or wasn't accepting his guilt, it might affect his release.

The second time she'd put in an appearance, he'd instructed Lech to tell her to go away and leave him alone. His annoyance had turned to bitterness and anger that anyone should presume they could exploit him in this way. He'd served his time. All he wanted was to put the past behind him.

It was the tail end of the morning rush and he was clearing tables when he caught sight of Lech out of the corner of his eye. And here she was again. He couldn't believe it! The two of them were outside the shop having a conversation.

Nathan took a couple of steadying breaths. He had a temper, he knew that, but he couldn't afford to lose it. Not here, not in this situation. His release date was due any day. It was all too easy to get knocked back. He'd seen it happen: some trivial incident and they whacked another six months on your sentence.

He watched them for a few minutes, but all the while he could feel his rage bubbling inside. Lech was nodding his head. Miss Piggy was feeding him some line. Then the Pole glanced in Nathan's direction.

He strode into the shop and clapped his mate on the shoulder. 'She tell me the story, Nathan. Man, you need to listen to her.'

Gripping the edge of the tray he was holding, Nathan shot his boss a savage look. 'That's exactly what it is. A story. She just wants to use me. So she can get her silly film made.'

'Okay. Well, you tell me. You really kill this girl? This Sarah Boden.'

Nathan forced himself to take a deep breath. 'Okay, I know you mean well—'

'She say to me she knows who did it. And it wasn't you.'

Nathan became aware of Briony Rowe. She'd followed Lech into the shop and was standing behind him, twisting the rings on her pudgy fingers.

She edged forward. 'I worked it out years ago.'

'You know what she used to call you? Miss Piggy.'

'Yeah, I know. She had a great sense of humour.'

Nathan glared at her. Her cheeks were damp and red, her eyes startlingly blue, like a deluded little gnome.

'Some might say Sarah was a vicious bitch who got what she deserved.'

'You don't think that.'

'How do you know?' He picked up the tray and walked away. 'You know nothing about me.'

Briony pursued him. 'I know Sarah had a stalker. He was a postgrad. He followed her about, spied on her. She'd gone out with him a couple times at the beginning of the first term, then dumped him.'

'That sounds like Sarah.'

'He wouldn't leave her alone. We used to joke about him.'

Nathan caught Lech's gaze; he was watching the exchange with puzzlement. So were several of the customers.

Their scrutiny, the sad doggy eyes of his Polish friend, made Nathan feel hot and ashamed. He headed for the kitchen.

The gnome followed. 'It's a lot to take in after all this time.'

He opened the dishwasher, unloaded his tray. By focusing his attention on each small action, he suppressed his desire to smash her in the face.

'I only want to help, Nathan. You have to believe that.'

Believe! That was a joke. He didn't need to believe, he knew. She was just like Sarah. A user.

'Did you tell all this to the police?'

She dropped her gaze. 'Well, no. Not at the time. We were all too upset. Later on, I tried to make a statement. They said the case was closed.'

'That's convenient.'

Nathan stared at her. He'd regained some measure of composure. She wore a sack-like dress to cover the bulges. It was a nondescript colour, camouflage, as if she hoped it would help her disappear. But she was smart. He'd give her that; the tale she'd concocted had plausibility.

When she smiled, a small dimple rippled her left cheek, giving her face a lopsided appearance. 'Look, I know I should've done something more, made a fuss. But well, inertia is easier, isn't it? We always find excuses. But I've felt guilty ever since. All I want is to get to the truth. I feel I owe it to Sarah and to you. I know you're innocent, Nathan. And you've paid an awful price. I'm here because I want to help.'

'Do you? Do you really?'

'Absolutely.'

'Then fuck off and leave me in peace!'

4

Jo Boden took the tube to Westminster and headed across the bridge. A watery sun was leaching through the fog, choppy brown waves churned the surface of the river and an icy wind cut into the scurrying pedestrians. It wasn't a day for tourists and photos, although a few hardy souls were attempting the mandatory selfie.

Jo wrapped her scarf round her battered face, put her head down and pressed on. They had transferred Razan to St Thomas' Hospital, which occupied a riverside campus of old and new, tile and glass, opposite the Houses of Parliament. With instructions from Debbie Georgiou, she went in the main entrance and followed signs to the east wing and up to the second floor, where the Intensive Care Unit was located.

She showed her ID to the sister on duty and was escorted to Razan's bedside. Not long out of surgery, the sister explained she was heavily sedated. The next twenty-four hours would be crucial in terms of her prospects of recovery.

Jo had spent plenty of time in and out of A&E during her spell as a fledgling PC. Ferrying drunks, drug addicts, the homeless and victims of violence had formed a substantial part of the work on Response. But the quiet of ICU, the array of monitors, the tangle of tubes and wires, the drips and ventilators, was not an experience of hospitals she was familiar with. Standing beside the bed and gazing down at her chis, she felt awkward.

Razan's face was covered in white dressings; only one eye was visible, the grey lid firmly closed. Ardi Kelmendi had been efficient in his punishment. If a woman's worth was all about appearance—and Jo presumed that's what a thug like Ardi would think—then he'd made sure Razan would be scarred for life, if indeed she lived. Damaged goods that no one would want.

Jo felt angry and responsible. How could Hollingsworth call it a strategic decision to use the girl in this way? She'd been exploited. They'd both been exploited. Even if she accepted the justification of necessity, it felt cold and callous to Jo.

She shifted uneasily from foot to foot and, though her eyes welled, she didn't cry—that would be unprofessional. Going in alone to rescue her chis was reckless, she knew that. Another thirty seconds could've produced a very different outcome. She could've been in that bed herself. Or worse. It was a foolhardy; as a police officer, she had to acknowledge that, yet she couldn't bring herself to regret it.

Unruly thoughts swirled, guilt competing with self-reproach; she could taste the bile rising in her throat as her head and nose throbbed. She had to get out. Walking briskly, she headed for the nearest exit.

She strode out of the hospital into the heavy winter chill and westwards along the riverside walk; her pace didn't slacken until she reached Vauxhall Bridge where she stared over the parapet at the roiling river.

Exercise, indeed any kind of movement, always made her feel better. She found if she kept her body busy, the carping critical chatter in her head trailed off. But it wasn't a day for admiring the view. Sharp needles of rain thrashed across the bridge and soon drove her to seek shelter.

She skirted the front of the giant SIS building at Vauxhall Cross and wondered if her new job would involve working with the security services. The headquarters of MI6 rose up like a mad mash-up of a brutalist car park and an Aztec temple. But she didn't even know if what she'd been offered was a new job. Vaizey had spoken of a secondment, which sounded temporary. Still, it was an opportunity, and she needed to focus on that instead of ruminating on mistakes. Looking back and allowing the past to haunt you had to be resisted at all costs. She knew this only too well.

Finding refuge in a small coffee shop at the southern end of the bridge, she treated herself to a hot chocolate heaped with marshmallows. The sugar hit and two more painkillers helped improve her outlook. Whatever Vaizey wanted her to do, she wouldn't disappoint him. By the time she'd finished her drink, she was imagining the promotion that would result from this.

She visualized it in detail—Vaizey giving her the news, praising her in front of the team. Part of her still felt ridiculous when she did this exercise, but she persevered. Sometimes it worked. She'd spent her teenage years in therapy; twice a week, her parents insisted. She'd hated it, but it had produced one or two useful techniques. She stepped out of the coffee shop on to the rain-slicked pavements, having banished thoughts of Razan from her mind. At least for the time being.

She set off back along Albert Embankment towards Waterloo, where she planned to pick up the tube. This was an area being transformed. The shabby backstreets were full of building sites and skips. Trains rumbled by on the nearby mainline. West of Vauxhall Cross at Nine Elms luxury apartments were sprouting up around the American Embassy. Beyond that, Battersea Power Station was being refashioned into a residential oasis. Foreign wealth would soon replace hard-hats and high viz jackets. Living somewhere like this would never be possible on a copper's wages. But she wasn't envious. London had always been about money and the battle to grab or steal more of it. Anyone with the job of protecting its citizens couldn't fail to be aware of that.

She put on headphones and scrolled through the playlists on her phone to find some upbeat music. But before she could make her selection, the phone buzzed with an incoming call. Glancing at the caller ID, her heart sank: Mum. She let the call ring out and go to voicemail. But she knew what would happen next. Alison Boden would leave a lengthy garbled message and then ring again, and again, more or less continuously, until her daughter responded. It wasn't yet midday, so a little early for her mother to be up and about.

The drizzle had turned into a heavier downpour. Jo took shelter under the cantilevered canopy of a posh new hotel and gave in to the inevitable. The phone buzzed again. This time she answered.

'Morning, Mum. You're up early.'

'Jo, I cannot believe it. I seriously cannot believe it!'

Wincing, Boden clicked down the volume control. Alison was upset, but there was nothing new there.

'What's up?'

'They phoned me. They just phoned me. I was half asleep when I answered. So at first I really didn't believe it.'

'Slow down, Mum. Who phoned you?'

'Victim liaison. Someone—I don't know—some name I didn't recognize. You are not going to believe this, Jo.'

'Well, no. Not until you tell me.' The bored hotel security man—cheap black suit, earpiece—was giving her a suspicious once-over; she must look bedraggled and poor. She gave him a smile.

Her mother's melodramas and the histrionics that accompanied them had been a feature of her life for many years. Calls like these happened on average two or three times a week. A row with a neighbour, an altercation with someone in the supermarket queue, a refusal by the GP's receptionist to give her an emergency appointment with her favourite doctor, the only one who understood her. The difficulties of Alison Boden's life were legion and since her husband left her, when Jo was thirteen, there had been no one but her daughter to sort them out.

Jo didn't resent this. It was simply how it was. She'd learnt to be patient and not to engage. Alison had received various conflicting diagnoses for her condition. Sometimes they'd called it post-traumatic stress disorder, other times clinical depression. She'd seen an army of therapists, and been prescribed enough pills to make her rattle, but the truth was rarely discussed: she'd never recovered from the murder of her eldest daughter, Sarah, when Jo was eleven. Alison soldiered on in her own chaotic fashion and one way or another, they coped.

There was a pause on the other end of the line, punctuated by shuddering gasps.

'Don't cry, Mum. Just tell me. I'm sure we can sort something out.'

'Victim liaison phoned me up to tell me—they're letting him out.'

Jo took a deep breath. She'd been expecting some stupid row. This was genuinely surprising.

'Well, we knew this was on the cards—' She felt her own annoyance rising. If Nathan Wade was being released on licence, why hadn't victim liaison had the good sense to speak to her first? Katie Carr, their original family liaison officer, retired long ago and had since died. Some idiot in the office hadn't taken the trouble to read the case file properly.

'How can they, Jo? His sentence was life imprisonment. So why doesn't life mean life?'

'That's not how the system works. We've talked about this. Did they say when?'

'Shortly. She said they'd phone again once he's out. That bastard goes free, but Sarah's still dead!'

'He's not free exactly. He'll only be released on licence. They'll be keeping a close eye on him.'

'It's just not fair!'

'It's the law, Mum. He's served his time.'

'Sixteen years, eight months and five days since I lost my baby!' She was sobbing now. 'I'm still serving my time, every hour of every single day! When will I be free?'

Jo swallowed hard. She stroked the plaster on her broken nose. 'Listen, I'm going to come over, okay? Make yourself a cup of tea and I'll be there as soon as I can.' She waited for a reply. None came. 'I love you, Mum.'

Wiping away the flecks of rain with her palm, she peered at the screen. But Alison Boden had already hung up.

Jo stood alone on the damp pavement as a cascade of warring emotions engulfed her. Remembering her dead sister could do this, which was why she always resisted it.

There were few traces left of the actual person that Sarah had been. But as a ghost, her presence was huge. Myths and tales, especially Alison's fantasies, had taken over. Jo did her best to ignore these. Becoming a detective had given her a different handle on the world. She'd interviewed enough witnesses to understand that perceptions varied, memories were fallible. Everyone's brain nattered away with its own unique story. Truth was as slippery as an eel. This left only one way to cope as far as Jo could see: hold fast to the evidence. Ignore the rest.

5

10 October 1999
Brighton

Dear Pixie,

I'm really sorry to hear that you don't like the new school. If it's any consolation, I hated it myself for about the first month. But trust me, Pix, things will change. It's a big step going from a little primary school and all the mates you've known since forever to a huge High School. No one wants to be in the babies' class again. But, contrary to what you might think, Mummy and Daddy are not trying to make your life a misery. They want you to be happy and to have all the chances that going to a really good school will bring.

I know some of the girls are snotty and posh, but inside they're as scared as you are. That's why they band together and say all the nasty stuff they do. You just have to ignore them. When you see them coming, pretend in your head that you're Tank Girl and give them the look. Then they'll leave you alone and pick on someone else.

The first week at uni was awesome. When it's your turn, and it will be one day, you are going to love it, I promise. Freshers' Week is basically one long booze fest and an even longer hangover! (Don't tell any of this to the parents!)

We had this three-legged pub crawl in town and I was partnered with this postgrad, much better than some spotty first year with BO! We came third. It was so much fun. He's hot. Plus, he has a car! A CAR! The other girls on my course are green with envy. I know he really likes me. So watch this space!

Well, Pix, I've got to go. I have my first seminar this morning and, despite what you might think, I do intend to do some actual work while I'm here.

I'm going to send you a new tape of all the cool stuff I've collected. Can't neglect your musical education, can we? I hope you've followed my instructions and binned those Spice Girls posters! Geri was the only good thing about them in my humble opinion.

Went to a gig by this awesome new band called Coldplay. Chris Martin is gorgeous. Pin back your ears, Pix, they are gonna be BIG! You heard it here first!

Take care of yourself, my little Pixie. School will get better, I promise. And remember the family motto – DON'T LET THE BASTARDS GRIND YOU DOWN!

Tons of love and hugs,
S xxxxxxxxxxxx

6

Nathan had a well-worn repertoire of tricks, which, used judiciously, usually got him what he needed. Pulling a sickie was one he rarely used and no one thought his stomach complaint was anything other than genuine. A potion was administered by the nurse at the medical centre—her guess was mild food poisoning or a bug—he'd swallowed it and was given permission to remain in his cell for the rest of the day.

The stomach ache and nausea wasn't a total lie. He was nervous with fear and what worried him most was his own reaction to the disruptive events eddying around him. He couldn't afford to get angry. He needed time to steady himself, to think, and to plan. He'd bribed one of the screws to keep him in the loop about when the parole board was due to meet. Would his case be on the agenda at their next meeting?

The moron had been unable to tell him that, even though Nathan had supplied him with some useful information about how one of the jail's major dealers was bringing in large quantities of high-grade skunk by drone. Ford had been an old RAF base, then a Fleet Air Arm station and Nathan wondered how its old denizens, who fought the Battle of Britain, would have regarded the secret comings and goings of these pilotless craft loaded with contraband.

The prison officer had failed to pass the intelligence up the chain. Bought off by the dealer, was Nathan's guess. The result was Nathan was the one shafted, but there was nothing new in that. It was how the system operated; get over it, move on. But it had upset his equilibrium, as had Briony Rowe. And he was still in the dark about his exact release date.

Sitting on his bunk, he pressed his fingernails into his palms until it hurt. Then he tried to focus on the red welts he'd created in his own flesh. Pain helped; pain was cleansing. The craving for drugs continued to niggle, especially when he was feeling stressed. The voice in his head whispered: *Just this once, it won't do any harm.*

Harm? That was a loaded word. Did Briony Rowe have any concept of the harm she'd done him? She wanted to get to the truth, she said. But her truth was another story. And it wasn't a story that would help him. He pondered, struggling to detach his thoughts from any sort of emotion. Maybe all women were users. Perhaps it was a survival mechanism, part of their DNA.

He decided to meditate. For the rest of the afternoon, he sat cross-legged on the floor. The vinyl covering had a cushioned underlay providing insulation; it was also easy to clean. He liked that. Most of the nicks he'd been in were grubby and rank, cold concrete permeated with years of grime and cleaning fluid. But being in an open prison wasn't so bad. He had his own cell, his books; he didn't need anything else. Thinking about the weight of his body pressing down into the soft plastic helped him relax, and he let his thoughts come to rest on his breath.

Sarah had had a stalker. That was the thought that popped up. He attempted to let it go. But it wouldn't. Persistent little bastard. Sarah had a stalker who could've been a postgrad. But how could that be? They didn't know any postgrads. They were first years. Postgrads didn't mix with first years. Back to the breath. His chest felt tight, his stomach muscles rigid with tension. What you resist persists, so said the Zen masters. The thought-stream was a river. You had to let it flow.

He'd noticed Sarah at their very first lecture. It was hard not to. Her hair was golden, an unruly halo framing her face. But it wasn't just the fact she was beautiful; she had a light in her eyes and an unexpectedly dirty laugh. He remembered the first time he'd heard it. After a lecture, they were all filing out, someone made a joke. Sarah tossed back her head and an unrestrained gravelly howl erupted from her perfect lips. He stood rooted to the spot. He felt the vibrations of that sound in his bones, in his belly. In that moment, she'd bewitched him. But for all of that first term, he'd watched her from afar. Girls like that frightened him. Such confidence was unnerving. She seemed to know something he didn't.

He opened his eyes. The wall in front of him was grey and stained from the Blu Tack left by the previous inmate. Nathan had picked off every last speck and scrubbed the wall with a scouring pad, but he could still see a hint of blue residue left by the adhesive. It irritated him deeply. He preferred plainness, no decorations, no distractions, just an expanse of clean plaster.

In the middle of the spring term, she'd bumped into him in the library. He wore sunglasses all the time and she'd commented on it. It was typical Sarah, sarcastic, but accompanied by a provocative look. After that, things moved swiftly. His experience of sex comprised one proper girlfriend when he was at school, and a series of drunken one-night stands. As with everything else, Sarah seemed confident and experienced. She liked to needle him, provoke an argument, and then make up. And making up was always passionate.

Although they never discussed it, they soon became regarded on campus as an item. This brought about a change of status that he'd enjoyed. People who'd previously blanked him sought him out. He was *with Sarah*, which meant he was cool.

Was there envy that she'd chosen him? The police had badgered him about that. Such a beautiful girl, they said. Was he scared he'd lose her? Was he jealous?

He did wonder why she'd picked him, but he'd never come up with an answer. Sometimes she was all over him, playing with his dark corkscrew curls, calling him 'Lord Byron'; other times, she'd ignore him for days. Her moods were as unpredictable as the weather.

If she'd lived, what would she have become? She belonged to the Drama Society and had won the lead role in one of their plays, but after a row with the director, she'd pulled out. He remembered her in the student bar, jabbing her finger in the poor bloke's chest, calling him a sexist bastard. Life had never been quiet around Sarah.

Now, when he sat for some hours, his joints would stiffen and become painful. His body was adept at reminding him that the years were passing. He looked in the mirror as little as possible. His greying hair had become wispy and the stodgy prison diet left his skin prone to eruptions.

He had a strict rule about self-pity. But the imminence of his release had caused speculation. And it was hard to resist. He wondered about his own life. What would have happened to him if malign fate hadn't cast him in the path of Sarah Boden? Perhaps he'd have become a film-maker himself? If a pathetic creature like Miss Piggy could manage it, surely he could have?

She hoped to manipulate him. That was clear. And there was no way he was falling for that. But now his temper had cooled, he considered how the situation might work to his benefit. Maybe he could get something out of her. Money would help. His needs inside had been few. But once he was out, he didn't want to have to survive on coffee-shop wages.

He would need to wait until they confirmed his release date before he made any move. But then, perhaps it might be to his advantage to cooperate with Briony Rowe and her film. It was certainly an option worth considering.

7

As Jo headed eastwards in the driving rain, she felt conflicted. This was what always happened. She would be forced to drop everything and rush to Alison's rescue. But she'd been up all night, in and out of hospital, and was desperate for clean clothes and a shower. She decided to make a detour.

Her current home was an old LCC deck-access block off Southwark Bridge Road, where she shared a flat with another girl. It was central, a five-minute walk to London Bridge, and close to the chic delights of Borough Market. The flat itself was pretty grotty with a tiny ill-equipped kitchen and mould growing on the bathroom wall, but this meant she could afford the rent.

The place belonged to a jovial Nigerian, who, together with his brother, owned half the flats in the block. He wasn't a bad landlord, in comparative terms. He responded complaints and had a bevy of 'cousins' who carried out repairs. The mouldy bathroom got a lick of paint when it got too bad and Adebayo would come round in person to check things over. Each time, he would ask Jo out and make a joke about how he'd love to be handcuffed by her. She always gave him the same reply: she never went out with married men.

When she got home, she was annoyed to find her flat-mate's boyfriend in the shower. Marisa worked shifts—she was an A&E nurse—and was fast asleep. He did very little, as far as Jo could see. He had the radio blaring as he sang along, using up all the hot water that he wasn't paying for. Jo suppressed her anger for the best part of a minute, then hammered on the bathroom door. As a result, it was two o'clock by the time she got to Greenwich.

Since her divorce, Alison Boden had lived in a Victorian terraced house on King George Street. It was small—originally a two-up, two-down—but its location close to Greenwich Park had seen its value accelerate into the stratosphere. A few years back, desperately short of ready cash, Alison got conned by a dubious equity release scheme. She nearly lost her home and Jo had to cajole her father into bailing his ex-wife out.

Letting herself in the front door, Jo was struck by the quiet. Her stomach lurched and her mind flew back to a similar occasion when she'd found her mother collapsed on the bed with an empty bottle of sleeping pills beside her. An avalanche of guilt surged through her. She should've come straight away, jumped in a cab.

The downstairs was open plan, the living area running into a galley kitchen at the back. Jo took the stairs two at a time, but her mother's bedroom was empty, so was the bath-room and the small box bedroom where Jo had spent her miserable teenage years. As she returned to the ground floor, she felt a draught of cold air and noticed the back door was ajar.

The garden was generous by London standards, enclosed by a brick wall at the rear and wooden fences, which in the summer were hung with clematis and honeysuckle, creating a pleasant and secluded refuge. In her better moods, Alison was an enthusiastic gardener. But her other passion was art and she'd built a studio—more an extended shed—at the end of the garden.

Jo followed the short path between dark shrubs, sombre and damp in their winter foliage. The double glass doors to the studio were shut, but she could see her mother inside, sitting on her cane chair.

She opened the door. 'You all right, Mum?'

Alison turned at the sound of her daughter's voice. A small fan heater was blasting out hot air. She had a mug in her hand. 'I'm doing what you said. Having a cup—My God! What's happened to your face?'

Jo did a quick scan. Alison's eyes were red, cheeks pale, but she seemed calm enough. 'An accident, that's all. Sorry I took so long to get here.'

Alison had a look of horror on her face. 'What sort of accident?'

Jo touched her nose gingerly; it still hurt like hell. She told her mother as little as possible about her life. It was easier.

'It's nothing, Mum. Looks worse than it is.'

Jo knew this wasn't true. After her shower, she'd replaced the hospital dressing with a smaller plaster. But both eyes were underscored with huge mauve welts. Even her flatmate Marisa had been shocked.

'Has some man hit you?'

'No!'

'All this online dating! Tinder, whatever it's called. I've

told you before, it's dangerous. You don't know who you're meeting.'

'I don't do Tinder. It was a work thing.'

Alison Boden wasn't listening. 'I couldn't stand it, Jo. If something happened to you as well, it would do for me. You can't tell what kind of man you're dealing with just from a picture. You have got to be so careful.'

'Listen to me, Mum. I was at work. We were arresting a suspect. There was a scuffle. It was an accident. He's under lock and key.'

'Looks broken to me.'

'It's not. Just badly bruised.' Another lie, but necessary.

Her mother gave her a sceptical look, sighed and pointed to the canvas set on an easel in front of her. 'What do you think? I think it's shit, but the gallery wants two more the same.'

The painting comprised abstract shapes set in a symmetrical pattern. The colours were bright with the addition of impasto blobs of gold and silver.

Alison screwed up her nose in disgust. 'Happy pictures that match any décor. I think that's my brand.'

'Why don't you paint something for yourself?'

'This sells at five hundred quid a pop. I need the money. People round here have no taste, if you ask me.'

Putting her mug down, Alison pulled a crumpled pack of Marlboros from the pocket of her long cardigan. She extracted a cigarette and lit up. 'Want one?'

'I told you, I've given up.'

Inhaling, she coughed, a mucousy rumble deep in her chest. She pointed the cigarette at her daughter. 'And don't give me the spiel.'

'I wasn't going to.'

'Bloody vaping! I'm not interested.'

'I didn't say anything.'

'Good. Cause I'm not in the mood today. Injury at work —will you get compensation?'

Jo smiled to herself; for all her craziness, Alison was still sharp as a tack. 'I doubt it.'

Her mother was looking straight at her now. Those startling blue eyes, the cheekbones, the blonde hair fading to silver at the temples. Even now, at fifty-eight, she was a remarkably handsome woman—she'd had a brief modelling career in the seventies before she married—and this striking beauty had been passed on to both her daughters.

'You sure it was a work thing?'

'Yes! So tell me what they said.' Jo settled herself on a stool in the corner of the studio.

Alison drew on her cigarette. 'The parole board have granted him a release date, though they can't tell us what it is. There are all sorts of conditions. He won't be allowed to come anywhere near us. Sarah's dead, but he gets his life back. And they call it justice.'

Jo sighed. 'Well, like it or not, that's the system.'

'Why in God's name did you ever join the bloody police? Accidents at work! The whole thing's an accident, if you ask me.' This abrupt change of subject, the sour anger in her mother's tone, was all too familiar to Jo. Alison was on the attack. It was what she did when she had nowhere else for her feelings to go.

'It's a worthwhile job. I like it.'

'You could've done anything if you'd set your mind to it. Something creative. Or taken a leaf out of your father's book and made some money.'

'This suits me.'

'What? You want to end up like me? Without two pennies

to rub together because I relied on a stupid man! I brought you up to be independent.'

'I am independent.'

Jo could feel her body tensing, although she kept an even tone in her voice. To react with the least hint of annoyance always made things worse. She'd learnt that the hard way.

'On a copper's pay? That's why you live in that squalid little flat.'

'It's a good location. Easy to get to work.'

Alison slumped back in her chair; the drooping tail of ash on the end of her cigarette dropped to the floor. The rant seemed to have drained off some of her bile. Now she stared listlessly into space.

'Sarah wanted to be a theatre director. Did you know that?'

'Yes, Mum. I knew that.'

'I think she would've probably ended up in films. She had a very good visual eye. Like me.'

Jo said nothing.

'I always wanted you girls to be creative. It was different for Carl.'

Everything was different for Carl, Jo thought bitterly, though she still said nothing. Her brother was the middle child, three years younger than Sarah, four years older than her. He'd opted to live with their father.

Both the men in her life had responded to the family tragedy by walking away. In Carl's case, he'd kept on going. He'd won a scholarship to study in the States and had subsequently made his home in Toronto.

Alison stubbed out her cigarette. 'We should call him and tell him. D'you feel like doing it?'

'Not really.' She met her mother's eye. 'But I will.'

Alison didn't mention her ex-husband, and Jo wasn't about to.

Nick Boden took early retirement from his job as an insurance broker in the City. He'd moved to the North Norfolk coast, where he renovated flint cottages and barns, then sold them on to Londoners in search of a chic coastal bolthole, at inflated prices. He'd married a schoolteacher twenty-five years his junior and they had two boys.

After the acrimonious break-up of her parent's marriage, Jo had been left to take care of her mother and in the years since then little had changed.

She painted on a smile. 'Have you eaten anything today?'

Alison shook her head. She could rarely be bothered to cook for herself and subsisted on cheese and crackers and fruit.

'Got any eggs?'

'How should I know? Probably not.'

'I'm going to go out and get a few bits. Make us a nice lunch. What d'you think?'

Her mother responded with a peevish frown. 'Have you put on a bit of weight? You look, I dunno…' She puffed out her cheeks.

'Don't be spiteful, Mum. I'm offering to make you lunch. Just be grateful.'

Seeing the steel in her daughter's eye, Alison shrugged. 'I don't mean to upset you. You know me, I'm a visual person, I notice the details.'

'I'm not upset.'

'You should go to the doctor. You might need surgery to reset that. I'm sure you could get your father to pay. You don't want to end up looking like a rugby player.'

'It's been looked at. It'll be fine.'

Mother and daughter faced each other, as they'd done many times before.

Alison shook her head wearily; tears welled in her eyes. 'I'm sorry. I know I'm being a bitch.'

'No, you're not. I won't be long.'

Leaving her mother in the garden, Jo collected a hessian bag from the hook in the kitchen and an umbrella and headed out. She walked down Royal Hill towards the Sainsbury's Local on Greenwich High Road.

To escape from the house, if only for half an hour, was a blessed relief. She'd known for some time that her sister's killer was coming up for release. Still, she'd dreaded this moment. Intellectually, she understood and accepted the notion of justice and rehabilitation. But emotionally, she harboured the same dark fantasies as her mother; she'd like to have seen the bastard strung up for his crime. She wondered how they were going to get through this.

Grabbing a basket, she zipped round the store, filling it with tomatoes, peppers, leaves, the ingredients for a salad, which she planned to serve with a cheese omelette. Although Alison could be picky and had phases where she insisted she was a vegan, she did like omelettes and had once even admitted her daughter was a decent cook.

Jo was opening an egg carton to check the contents were intact when she became aware of a presence at her elbow. A man, a hoodie, and he was standing far too close. Abruptly, she spun round, putting the wire basket between them. He was probably hoping to grab her bag or extract her purse while she was busy with the eggs.

Facing him, she fixed him with a hostile glare. His dark eyes stared back from under the hood. He had a beard. Then she recognized DC Jabreel Khan.

He glanced around. 'We've got a problem. We need to talk.'

'Are you following me? That is a problem and I'll be taking it up with Hollingsworth.'

Under the shaggy beard, his lips curled into a grin. 'I get it, Boden. You think you're hard. Now can we find somewhere quiet to talk? Cause I've got some important intel that you might want to hear.'

8

While Jo paid for her shopping, Khan waited outside. He had the knack of merging with his surroundings. Melding into the flow of people on the High Road, his eyes were everywhere, scanning, searching out anomalies. He missed nothing. Jo followed several paces behind and he led her towards Greenwich Park.

The day was raw, but the rain had given way to splashes of brightness with enough thin sunshine to bring out the tourists. Once they'd passed through the gates and negotiated the small gaggle of visitors milling around them, they headed up the hill and Jo fell into step beside him. He was narrow across the shoulders, wiry and full of jittery energy. Jo was fit, but as they climbed the steep hill towards the Observatory, he set a blistering pace. She wondered whether he was deliberately trying to challenge her, or was he simply being male?

What would it be like, operating out there in bandit country, living off your wits? Maybe it was the ultimate test. Could you hold on to your identity and retain your moral compass? It placed Vaizey's offer in a different light.

Veering off the main path, Khan headed across the grass

towards a small copse of trees. The turf was sodden underfoot and soon they were well away from the dog walkers and the joggers and any other prying eyes. The trees were stark and bare, resting on a ridge looking out over the baroque splendour of the Old Royal Naval College. He stopped, leant his back against the trunk of the nearest tree and folded his arms.

Jo's trainers were caked in mud. She huffed. 'I haven't got a lot of time. This had better be good.'

He was studying her. 'Nose looks painful.'

'It's fine.' She resented his sympathy.

'Listen, I'm sorry about your chis.'

'Tell that to her.' Jo was searching for a dry enough patch under the trees to put her shopping down.

He pushed back the hood and pulled off his knitted beanie; his dark hair was messy and damp. 'I'm just trying to do my job here. Ardi is an unpredictable psycho. He said nothing about the girl. They turned up with her. I didn't even know why they'd brought her there.'

'Is this why you're following me? Because you want me to absolve your conscience?'

He gave her a sullen look. 'Is that really what you think?'

Jo met his gaze. His eyes were bloodshot. He looked like he hadn't slept. She was being aggressive. Part of her knew it, but she was still aggrieved about Razan.

She shrugged. 'Okay, let's hear it.'

Khan rubbed his face with his palms and sighed. 'It's taken me six months to get an in with the Kelmendis. Everything is tribal with them, anyone outside the family is suspect. They're possibly the biggest gang of traffickers bringing people into the UK. They're certainly the most vicious.'

'I've read the file.'

'Yeah, well, what's not in the file is that they've got an informant of their own inside the Met. Not very high up, probably some disgruntled DC who reckons they can pocket the extra cash and get away with it.'

'Does Hollingsworth know?'

'Yes.'

'Is that why he wanted you airbrushed out of the record?'

'Yes. You have to understand my position.'

'Believe me, I'm trying to.'

'The Kelmendis don't trust me. But they let me stick around because they think I'm a fucked-up jihadist with access to weapons.'

'How do you explain to them the fact that you're still walking around free when Ardi was nicked? Isn't that likely to make them suspicious?'

'Only Ardi and his sidekick know I was there at the bust and they're on ice in Belmarsh. They think I'm in there too.'

'Sounds risky to me. What if they find out?'

'Thank you, Boden! Risky is what I do.'

Although the sarcasm was a rebuke, his tone was weary. She wondered about the pressure on officers with any sort of Arab or Asian background, who could pass as jihadists. Terrorism and organized crime were becoming increasingly enmeshed and he was in the eye of the storm.

She managed a smile. 'I'm sorry. I'm being arsey. It's been a difficult day.' And he didn't know the half of it.

He gave her a jaundiced look. 'So the idea is I hold on for another couple of weeks. With the organization in a mess, Fejzi Kelmendi will have to come over himself to sort things out. Then we nab him.'

Jo studied his face. He made a convincing gangster except for the eyes. There was a softness, a hint of vulnerability. If the Kelmendis ever saw that, he'd be dead.

'I'm sure you didn't track me down just to tell me this.'

'You've been a cop long enough to understand how

villains like this work. They operate on the basis of fear. Violence is a tool and reputation is everything, the idea they can get to anyone. You wrong-footed Ardi, pissed him off.'

'Good.'

'No, not good. When his old man finds out a woman took him down, there'll be hell to pay.'

'I didn't do it on my own.'

'You made yourself very visible, gave them something to focus their anger on. When Ardi threatened you, he meant it. They're targeting you for payback.'

Jo felt her throat constrict as she swallowed. 'Thought you said he was on ice in Belmarsh.'

'He'll have got hold of a mobile. He's sent instructions out to his subordinates. We didn't net them all.'

'Great. Hollingsworth omitted to mention that in his pep talk to the troops.'

Khan shrugged.

'If he's got a phone, doesn't that put you more at risk too?'

'He's been fed a line that I'm in a special unit for suspected terrorists. We're hoping he'll believe that and forget about me. Might give me enough of a window if I'm careful.'

She took a breath. She was tempted to laugh. But that was a knee-jerk reaction. The release of Nathan Wade was enough bad news for one day, even if she ignored her smashed nose and a chis she was supposed to protect but who'd ended up in ICU. And now this.

'Have you told Hollingsworth about me?'

'Yes,' he sighed, 'but he's not convinced yet of the credibility of the intel. Thinks it's gossip, a bit of macho bravado. Y'know, "We're gonna get the bitch", that sort of thing.'

'I see.'

'What I'm hearing is that they're asking their snitch on the inside to find out who you are and where you live, which will not be that difficult.'

'And you don't know who this person is?'

'No. Obviously, we're trying to find out.'

Jo swallowed hard. She didn't want him to see her fear.

His eyes rested on her face. 'I've said to Hollingsworth that we should tuck you up safely somewhere. He thinks that's overkill. If the gossip is true and any officer searches for your details, we've nailed our informant. His argument is that info on you will never get back to the Kelmendis.'

'But Hollingsworth didn't plan to tell me any of this?'

'No. He says it's unnecessary.'

'Another one of his strategic decisions! Excellent.'

Khan sighed and rubbed his finger across the mossy bark of the tree trunk. 'Most likely, it'll be okay. But it's too easy for stuff like this to go pear-shaped. I thought you had a right to know.'

She looked into his tense, dark eyes. 'Thanks, Jabreel.' She hesitated. 'You know I've been offered a secondment to Operation Grebe?'

'I didn't. Doing what?'

'You're going to laugh. Undercover.'

'I've worked for Steve Vaizey myself.'

'What do you make of him?'

'Good boss. Tough. Doesn't suffer fools. But he's smart and he gets the job done.' He smiled. 'I'd take it, if I were you.'

'Would you?'

'Pretending to be someone else is a good way to hide.'

'You saying I should hide?'

'I'm saying you should take sensible precautions. But it shouldn't be for long. We will sort this out.' The expression was earnest. Without the hood up and the scowl, he seemed almost boyish. She could only guess his age, but it was close to her own.

'Is Hollingsworth going to be hacked off with you for telling me this?'

He shrugged. Then he cracked a smile. 'That's his problem.'

9

Nathan received the news officially from a junior member of the offender management team. She was young, still in training. He thought her name was Rachel but couldn't be sure. Too many had come and gone during his sentence. Mostly they were gullible and vapid. There'd been a similar girl on the team before, who'd pretended to like his writing; she was called Rachel, so perhaps he was getting confused with her. But this one seemed genuinely excited for him as she announced that the parole board had ruled on his case. He would be released on a life licence and the board, together with the team supervising his sentence, had agreed on a date. It was happening. She handed over a document to confirm it.

Under his resettlement plan, they would find a place in approved premises for him in the Littlehampton area and he'd continue with his job at the coffee shop. The National Probation Service would take over his supervision, but she couldn't yet tell him who his probation officer would be, because of problems arising from a shortage of qualified staff.

Left alone in his cell to digest all this, Nathan felt odd, a combination of elated and twitchy. This had been the day he'd looked forward to for so long—the light at the end of the tunnel. It also scared him. Now what? He found it hard to keep still, so he forced himself to sit cross-legged on the floor. Close his eyes, breathe. Opening them again, he let his gaze come to rest on an uneven patch of plaster on the grey wall. The faint blue stain. But in less than a week, he would be out of here. No more dirty walls. He'd paint his walls every year, twice a year, if he wanted. He would be a free man.

Well, not totally free. His release was conditional, and it would always be conditional. A life licence meant that if he broke the terms of it, he'd be subject to recall. Banged up straight away on his probation officer's say-so. They drummed this into you, this motley crew of so-called offender managers. It was their mantra. They wanted you to know you were still being judged and you'd always be judged. You remained under surveillance forever. That was the system.

The next morning Nathan returned to work at the coffee shop and his sense of irritation with anything and everything hadn't improved. Lech wasn't due in until lunchtime and the deputy manager, an ineffectual oaf who chewed his finger-nails to the quick, was in charge.

The queue snaked out of the door; the bin was over-flowing and there was milk splashed over the work surfaces and a sink piled with washing up. Daley, the oaf, was in the back skiving and texting his girlfriend, leaving Nathan and a new girl to cope on their own. The new girl was panicking. She didn't know all the products and couldn't find them on the till. Nathan was at the espresso machine, turning out drinks as quickly as he could.

A hatchet-faced woman with a bad blonde dye job shoved her way past the waiting customers and thrust her paper cup at Nathan.

'There's no fucking coffee in this latte.'

'Did you ask for a double shot?'

'I don't have to. It should come with a double shot.'

The cup was small, therefore it came with only one shot. She knew this, but didn't want to pay. She was trying it on. They got this all the time.

Completing two cappuccinos, Nathan placed them on the counter.

'I'm happy to make you another.' He forced a smile as he imagined punching her.

'Pisses me off I gotta ask.'

'I can only apologize.'

The woman fixed him with a spiteful eye; he sensed her suppressed fury. He'd encountered it plenty of times on the inside—all that negative energy with nowhere to go—she was spoiling for a fight. And the queue was getting restive. Someone else pitched in.

'If you didn't ask for a double shot, how's the poor bugger supposed to know?'

She turned on the interloper. Short, paint-spattered trackies and builder's boots. He had a big order for the site down the road. She glared at him. 'Why don't you mind your own fucking business?'

'Cause I'm stood here waiting for my coffee, love, and you already got yours. Plus, you've drunk most of it, so you ain't that bothered.'

As Nathan watched them, a wave of contempt washed over him. These were his fellow citizens, members of the society he was finally being allowed to rejoin. Did they always follow the rules? Had they ever crossed the line? Were they better people than him? No. Just luckier.

The blonde dye-job fronted up to the builder, her face red

and crumpled like a furious toddler. 'I hope you fucking die of cancer!'

'Charming!'

She hurled her cup and the remaining coffee across the floor and stormed out.

The builder shrugged and turned to Nathan. 'Stupid cow.'

Nathan turned on his heel and walked away. He headed for the kitchen. Daley was rocking back on a chair, talking on his phone.

He waggled a finger at Nathan. 'This is a private conversation, mate.'

In a single fluid movement, Nathan seized the back leg of the chair and flipped it, tipping Daley on to the floor. Their eyes met. Nathan didn't speak. Taking a deep breath, he counted to ten.

Daley scrabbled to his feet. Then Lech appeared in the doorway.

The deputy manager spluttered. 'He's gone fucking mental! Fucking convict scum! No way I'm working with him no more.'

Lech gave him an equable smile. 'I agree. It's better if you leave. Then I can get someone in who maybe wants to do a day's work.'

Daley glared, but he was backing away. 'You lot. You all stick together. You're all scum.'

'Write a letter of complaint to the company.'

'I fucking will.'

Retrieving his phone, Daley slunk out of the door.

Lech turned to Nathan and grinned. 'He won't. Couldn't even fill in the form by himself when he applied for the job.'

Nathan took a long, slow breath. 'I'm sorry. I lost it there for a bit.'

The Polish manager shrugged. 'You got a lot going on.'

'They've given me a release date.'

'Yeah? Whoo-hoo! We need to celebrate!'

Nathan took another deep breath. His heart thumped against his ribcage. 'I've been thinking. Have you got a number for Briony Rowe?'

'The telly woman, yeah. She leave me her card. You gonna do it?'

'I've been giving it some thought. Could you call her for me? Say I'm sorry I was rude. And I've changed my mind about her film.'

Lech clapped him on the shoulder. 'Hey, that's great! Double celebration, my friend! We're gonna clear your name.'

10

The swelling across Jo's cheekbones had subsided and closer examination of her nose in the bathroom mirror reassured her it was straight. An operation would be unnecessary. It was still painful. Her whole face felt taut, as if it had been shrink-wrapped. But she was useless at doing nothing. Inactivity depressed her, so she decided to take a couple of co-codamol and return to work. She opted for a suit with a skirt, hair up in a French twist, a discreet amount of make-up. She wanted to create the right impression at Operation Grebe. But she set off early intending to make a stop at St Thomas' first to visit Razan.

The weekend had been odd. She'd walked away from her encounter with Jabreel Khan, brain and body reeling. A gangster wanted to kill her? As a police officer, she was used to risk. Any nutter on the street could come at you with a knife, but this still felt unreal.

Before returning to her mother's house she'd scraped the mud off her shoes, then taken a turn around the park, wandering past the formal flowerbeds of winter pansies and the children's playground—beacons of safe everyday life—as she let this information percolate through her consciousness. Like him or hate him, Khan was an experienced officer and he had nothing to gain, as far as she could see, by ignoring Hollingsworth and tracking her down to give her this warning. If he thought the Kelmendis were out to get her, he was probably right. She wasn't taking any chances.

Her mother had been nonplussed by the news that she wanted to come and stay and did her best to resist it.

'I don't need a babysitter. I'm not going to do anything stupid.'

'I might do something stupid.'

Jo was finally serving the promised cheese omelette, dividing it between two plates.

Alison shoved the food away. 'I'm not hungry.'

Covering her mother's clenched fist with her palm, Jo's chin quivered. 'Mum, maybe I need you. Can I come and stay? Please.'

Alison glared at her daughter. 'What the hell's going on?'

'Nothing.'

'I don't believe that for one minute.'

Early next morning Jo had gone home to her flat in Lant Street, packed a suitcase, told Marisa she was taking a holiday, a last-minute deal—two weeks' skiing in Meribel—and returned to Greenwich by a circuitous route. She walked to London Bridge, took the Northern Line to Moorgate, where she got out and made a beeline for the nearest coffee shop.

The Saturday-morning City was quiet, with many places closed; she bought a coffee and a croissant and sat at the back of the shop, monitoring the comings and goings. Once she'd registered every face, stored them in her memory for future retrieval, she got up and headed for the door. She paused outside the shop, on the pretext of retying her scarf, but continued scanning the street for anyone who appeared to be hanging about without purpose. On such a frigid day, most people were in a hurry.

She walked round the block using windows and reflective surfaces to check if she was being followed. Satisfied that she had no obvious tail, she set off in the direction of Liverpool Street, jumped on the Central Line to Mile End, switched to the District Line and rode one stop to Bow Road.

All the while she was on high alert—checking faces, anyone who'd been in the coffee shop, anyone she'd passed on the street. This was what Jabreel Khan spent his life doing and, it was hard work. Early in her career as a DC, she'd done three months as a watcher on a surveillance team, so she knew the drill. But it felt different when you were out there on your own, when you were the potential quarry.

She took the DLR to Greenwich and edged into the trickle of tourists meandering out of the station. There were others like her, towing their cases on wheels, visitors from Asia and China shivering in newly acquired bobble hats. She let herself be carried along in the slipstream of sightseers until she got to the park, then she cut through into Crooms Hill. No one followed, as far as she could see. Confident that she was off the grid, she turned the corner onto her mother's road.

Alison had adjusted to her presence and Jo even got the impression that it had cheered her up. She'd cooked a chicken casserole for Sunday lunch, which her mother ate. They lit the wood burner and spent a cosy afternoon on the sofa watching *Bridget Jones's Diary*.

After giving the matter some thought, Jo explained to Alison that she had a new job, a secondment to a special operation. She hoped it would lead to promotion and wanted to get it right. The problem: her flatmate's boyfriend was a total dick, and she needed peace and quiet until she could arrange to move. It wasn't the truth, nor was it a total lie, but her mother had bought it.

On her arrival at the hospital, Jo threaded her way through the bustle of a busy Monday morning. People arriving early for outpatients appointments. Staff getting coffees, chatting about their weekends as they prepared to tackle the working week.

Making her way up to the quiet oasis of the ICU, Jo found Razan awake. They had taken her off the ventilator. A staff nurse explained that she was doing well and would be transferred to a high-dependency unit later in the morning.

Jo sat down beside the bed. She painted on a smile. Half the girl's face was bandaged, but one dark eye roved over Jo, then the lips moved. Jo leaned in to hear, but the words were inaudible.

She glanced towards the staff nurse. 'Do you know what she's saying?'

'Something in Syrian. And a name, I think. Amira?'

Amira was Razan's sister. She wanted to know if they'd found Amira. That was Jo's guess.

Razan's hand trembled, and Jo cradled it in her own. 'We're looking for Amira and we will find her.'

'Amira?' She whispered the name, followed by a dry sob.

'Razan, you need to concentrate on getting better. We have officers out there looking for your sister.' Jo hoped this was true. Hollingsworth had assigned Georgiou to follow up.

Still, she felt responsible. Maybe she shouldn't have accepted Vaizey's offer when there was still work to do here? Or perhaps her old boss was right: you couldn't take these things too personally. You just did what you could.

'I'm going to make a phone call, do some chasing.' She smiled and patted Razan's hand. There was also the asylum question. Hopefully, Georgiou or someone would be talking to the Home Office.

Razan's fingers clutched at her hand. 'I promise my father. I promise take care of Amira.'

Razan's father had lost both legs in a car bombing in Homs. He'd given his daughters a body-belt of US dollars and ordered them to leave him. This much the police had gleaned when they first interviewed Razan. One war story among many. Jo wondered how she would've coped in such a situation, but then she pushed that question firmly away. There was no benefit to her or anyone else in thinking about that.

'I know you promised your father. And you've done your best. He would be proud of you. Your job now is to rest.'

Razan turned her head away. Jo could hardly catch the words. 'No. Should be me. Me, not Amira.'

11

14 November 1999
  Brighton

Dear Pixie,

Glad to hear things are looking up at school. And the junior school hockey team, wow, that's awesome! Hockey was always my favourite at school. Make sure you get some good shin pads, though. I've still got a dent in my leg from a bad tackle when I was in Year 10!

Uni, things are a bit different when it comes to extra-curricular. You have to make choices. I probably belong to too many societies already—drama is taking up a lot of my time—so sport will have to take a back seat. At least until I'm old and fat and have to get down the gym to avoid turning into Mister Blobby!

I hope you've made some new friends. Though I would say it's a good idea to be picky. You don't want to get lumbered. Someone you randomly meet at the beginning of term and you think is really great can turn out to be a complete pain. You then have to spend the rest of the year trying to avoid them. Trust me, it happens!

I'm making a new tape for you and it will be in the post asap. Craig David! Check it out! (This is actually a joke, which you will get when you listen to him.)

I know you want to come down one weekend and that would be awesome. There's so much I want to show you, Pix, and tell you about. Don't want to put it down on paper though, in case you-know-who snoops through your drawers!

But I've got a bit of catching up to do work wise, so it'll probably have to be after Christmas.

This term seems to be going really quickly. One minute you're a fresher, the next everyone's stressing about exams. I have to say, looking back now, school seemed much easier. Enjoy it while you can! At least you don't have to do your own washing! My radiator is always covered in knickers. Granny B would not approve!

Really looking forward to coming home for Christmas and seeing you all. I might even let Carl win at Monopoly.

Ttfn,

Tons of love and hugs,

S xxxxxxxxx

12

Jo left a sharp message for Debbie Georgiou. By the time she reached the office, she'd also given herself a stern talking to. There was only so much you could do. Then you had to move on. And she was moving on, definitely.

Detective Superintendent Vaizey's door stood open. She tapped on it. He was on his feet pacing as he talked on the phone; he beckoned her in. His shirt sleeves were rolled up, his tie loose. Jo found it difficult to guess his age. It must be late thirties, but he had the lean broad-shouldered frame of a man who worked hard to keep fit.

Vaizey pointed to a chair. Jo sat down while he continued his call. As she watched him speak, she noticed a fizz of sexual desire prickling at the edge of consciousness and producing a tension in her belly. She was annoyed with herself. He wasn't even that good-looking. Older men, father figures—it was such a cliché, given her history. She focused her attention out of the window: a brick wall and rusting pipework dangling from a corroded bracket. He was almost certainly married.

'Yeah, well, all right, mate. Don't worry. We'll sort something out. I'll let you know. Yeah. You too.'

Hanging up, his gaze zoned in on her. 'Didn't expect to see you this soon. Are you sure you're fit for duty?'

The look was challenging; she forced herself to meet it. It almost felt as though he'd changed his mind.

'I wouldn't be here if I wasn't, sir.'

'Okay. Well, I can only take you at your word. You'd better come and meet DS Foley.'

He was out of the door and halfway down the corridor before Jo caught up. She wondered at his response; it was as if her arrival had irritated him, or maybe he was just busy.

Operation Grebe had a large office suite at one end of the building. They processed a good deal of sensitive intelligence, and there was a keypad lock on the door.

Vaizey reeled off the six-digit code and Jo got the distinct feeling this was a test. But she'd never had much of a problem remembering numbers or facts and figures. Regurgitating details in exams had always proved easy for her. Her brain liked facts. What it resisted were feelings.

Foley had a corner desk, littered with coffee cups and files. He was halfway through a bacon roll, which he put down, dusting off his fingers as he saw Vaizey approach.

'Morning, boss.' He stood up. Matching Vaizey in height but with a barrel chest. He was twice the size.

'Cal, this is Jo Boden. I mentioned her to you.'

Foley wiped his palm on his trousers and then held it out to shake. 'Y'alright.'

Jo's hand was swamped by his meaty paw. 'Sarge. Really pleased to be joining the team.'

Foley shot his superior officer a quizzical glance and then smirked.

Vaizey had his hands on hips. He looked eager to be off. 'Do you own your own place?'

Jo shook her head.

'Never bought a property?'

'You are joking.'

'You'll soon pick it up. Cal'll fill you in on the target.' He gave them a curt nod, then he was gone.

Foley picked up his roll and demolished it in two more bites. 'Grab a pew.'

Jo rolled an adjacent desk chair over and sat down. Foley plonked back in his own chair and scanned her from head to toe. He made no attempt to disguise his scrutiny.

If he hadn't been wearing a laundered pink shirt and a silk tie with a gold pin, he might have passed for a thug. The bulk was muscle, his bull head was razored to jet black stubble, a narrow sculpted beard traced the contour of his jaw and upper lip. And the ebony eyes never left her face.

He smiled. 'Quite a smack you got there. Must smart.'

Jo shrugged. 'I'll live.'

Foley smiled again, turned to his computer screen, tapped the keypad and brought up a file. 'Right, well, this is our target. Ivan Rossi.' Several surveillance shots of a young man in his twenties danced across the screen. 'No previous. Works in an estate agent's in Shepherd's Bush. London boy, Dad's Italian, Mum's Belarusian. And it's Mum's family that's interesting. She has a brother, known to Interpol, who's a big supporter of Lukashenko, and runs Russian guns, it's thought with the approval of the regime, out of Grodno.'

'You think the nephew's involved in trying to bring them into the UK?'

'That's the theory. And we're talking about serious arma-ments here. Assault weapons and semi-automatic rifles of the sort we do not want to fall into the hands of some teenage gangster or wannabe jihadist.'

'So I'm going to pose as a client. Get him to show me a few properties?'

'The last girl didn't gel with him at all. We reckoned she was pretty enough. But maybe he's picky.'

Jo tilted her head. 'What are you saying, Sarge? This is a honey-trap?'

Foley chuckled. 'Call me Cal. Everyone else does. I hate Sarge. My old mum, she's a woman of faith. Church every Sunday without fail. Called me Calvin and my brother Luther. Strong names for Jesus's army, that's her theory.'

Jo smiled back, but she wasn't about to be deflected. She already had the feeling that Foley didn't like her. 'Aren't honey-traps illegal?'

'Are you going to be difficult about this, Jo Boden?'

'No. I just want to understand what I'm being asked to do.'

He laughed again, but the eyes remained cold and hard. 'You're being asked to work undercover, to cultivate a target and to use your discretion. I'm not asking you to give him a blow job, if that's what you want to know.'

Jo found his hostility unnerving. But he changed tack and grinned. 'You know how much pressure we're under here?'

'Yeah, of course I do. And I'm not trying to be difficult. All I want is to be clear about the parameters.'

'Fair enough. If I was you, with a nice shiny gong in the offing and my eye on an early promotion, I'd be watching my step too.'

'Meaning what?'

He smiled and rocked back in his chair. 'Actually, the boss has a plan. Lateral thinking, he calls it. His speciality. You look like you've been smacked about a bit, so we're going to appeal to Ivan's better nature. I'll be playing the role of your abusive boyfriend. The big nasty black bastard – you get the picture? And you're trying to find yourself a flat to escape me. You desperately need Ivan's help and will use your injury to win his sympathy and then his trust.'

'You think he'll be amenable to that?'

'Don't know till we try, do we? That's the job, Boden. If you're up for it.'

13

Briony Rowe borrowed a Canon XF305 from a mate who was a freelance cameraman. They helped each other out from time to time and he owed her a favour. She'd edited his latest showreel for him, producing a seamless sequence, showcasing every brilliant shot. But, as an editor, that's what you did: made everyone else's work look fantastic. Very few people watched a show on the box or walked out of a movie going, Wow, didn't you just love that editing? Editors were the unsung heroes, holed up in dingy edit suites, eating too many biscuits and putting on weight. Briony had done it for ten years, she knew all about it and she'd had enough. Now her name was going above the title. She was a film-maker.

Having spent a year on the research, she knew her project was a winner. She had a hot topic—miscarriages of justice. There was drama, there was emotion and then there was that little sine qua non that cracked it with the broadcasters: this was real. Lives would be changed because of this film. She'd already rehearsed the acceptance speech she'd make on the podium at BAFTA. Unfortunately, it all hinged on the cooperation of Nathan Wade.

She'd met Nathan all those years ago in that faraway first year at uni. She'd noticed him in the library, wearing sunglasses as he browsed the poetry shelves. He looked dreamy and inscrutable, with dark flowing locks like one of Georgette Heyer's Regency bucks. She fell in love with him on the spot. Then she discovered they were all on the same course.

She was the one who'd introduced him to Sarah, and they'd giggled over the sunglasses. Sarah joked that he probably thought he was Lord Byron, but she was being sarcastic. What Briony had never admitted to her friend was that to her, he was the embodiment of all her teenage romantic fantasies: Lord Worth.

Sarah teased her about fancying him. Then, out of the blue it seemed, Nathan and Sarah became an item. Sarah could've had anyone, blokes trailed her like a bitch on heat, so it was more than a little galling when she picked Nathan.

Watching them from afar was exquisite torture for Briony. She imagined their more intimate moments and, in an odd way, she was glad to have someone as gorgeous as Sarah as her proxy. He loved her madly and extravagantly. That was obvious to Briony, and she came to regard it as fitting. The notion that he could've murdered her was absurd. It was a dreadful mistake, a police blunder of monumental proportions. And Briony Rowe always imagined, in the secret recesses of her heart, that one day she'd be the one to set it straight and rescue Nathan.

In order to get the film made, Briony needed at least some interest from a reputable production company. She had a couple in mind; she knew a few of the key players because they used the facilities house where she'd trained and worked as an editor. But to get money on the table and secure a commission, she was making a short trailer. This would be her pitch.

For budgetary reasons—she had no budget—she was opting to shoot guerrilla style. The crew comprised herself, on camera, and her assistant, a nineteen-year-old film student intern called Kayleigh, lugging the tripod and keeping a lookout. At a later stage, she was hoping to inveigle her cameraman buddy into lending her a steadicam rig. But for now, they were managing pretty well.

She'd also just received a piece of very welcome news. The Polish bloke who ran the coffee shop where Nathan worked had rung and said that, having given the matter some thought, Nathan had decided he was interested in taking part. This was the breakthrough she needed and a real boost to her flagging self-confidence. On the back of it, she'd borrowed the camera, called Kayleigh, loaded her Mini Clubman and headed for Shooters Hill.

Greenwich Cemetery was located on rising ground beside the South Circular, between Woolwich and Eltham. Briony had visited it before to search out Sarah Boden's grave. The marble headstone was plain and carved with her name and dates plus the innocuous phrase: *rest in perfect peace*. The Bodens were not a religious family, nor, it seemed, did they favour florid sentimentality to advertise their tragic loss. But the dates—1982–2000—spoke for themselves. Sarah Jane Boden was a few months short of her nineteenth birthday when she died.

Briony found it interesting that they'd opted for burial rather than cremation. Maybe they needed something tangible to hang on to, a memorial they could visit. She hadn't attended the funeral, which was a private family affair.

But Sarah's murder and the subsequent arrest of Nathan had

created a feverish maelstrom on campus. Rapists and murderers were seen to be lurking around every corner. The university authorities had moved swiftly to contain the hysteria and panic, and counselling was offered. Briony was so upset that her tutor advised her to go home immediately, which she did. It was the news that they had charged Nathan Wade with murder that precipitated her breakdown. Her world imploded. She didn't emerge from her room for months. Only later did her failure to speak up come to haunt her. But by then it was too late.

Briony returned to university a year later and completed her degree on antidepressants. Her experience of university and indeed her subsequent career had never lived up to her youthful expectations. She was thirty-five, single, and had become accustomed to disappointment. But she'd also learnt to get on with things. Her nature was optimistic and she was currently doing an online course with an inspiring American guru on how to access your mind at the quantum level and reprogram it for success.

The Mini Clubman drove through the cemetery gates after they opened at nine. On a bitter January day, the place was completely deserted, but Briony had a plan, should anyone challenge them. The cemetery contained a number of fallen servicemen from both world wars. Her cover story was that she was making a historical documentary on them and had the permission of the Commonwealth War Graves Commission to film.

In the event, no one bothered them. They set up the camera and got some fantastic general shots down towards the river; it was a bright morning with a chilly blue sky. A change in wind direction had blown away the smog and air pollution that had plagued the London basin for weeks. There was enough breeze to shake the skeletal trees, which, together with the spiky towers of the City hedging the skyline, provided the perfect backdrop. The graveyard itself was a quiet enclave full of crumbling Gothic angels, tilting crosses and various other funereal monstrosities, which Briony shot at alarming angles. They'd make a great montage.

Once they moved on to the actual grave, Briony framed a series of carefully composed shots. Later, once she'd secured his cooperation, she would film Nathan against a green screen and slot him into the graveside sequences in the edit. This would be the trailer that would sell the project — the pilgrimage of an innocent man to his murdered lover's grave.

She would cut in some emotional close-ups of Nathan's face. The years had not been kind to him; the handsome boy he once was had disappeared. He was thirty-five, like her, but looked much older. His hair was grey and balding, thinning strands replacing youthful curls. His eyes had a watchful stare, and his cheeks were gaunt. A life destroyed by a terrible injustice; those eyes would look perfect on a nice big poster at tube stations.

The grave itself was well-tended and planted with pink and white hellebores now in full winter bloom. Briony was crouched right down beside it, panning across from an individual pure white petal to the cold marble headstone, which was why she didn't see Alison Boden approaching.

Kayleigh coughed. 'Briony.'

'Hang on a sec.'

Alison was carrying a hessian shopping bag containing a small fork, a trowel and her gardening gloves.

She stared in disbelief. 'Who the bloody hell are you?'

Taken by surprise, Briony tried to jump up, but her bulk impeded her. Instead, she rolled on to her side. Alison loomed over her.

'What are you doing?'

It took Briony a moment to recognize her. She'd only ever seen pictures and some old news footage from the trial.

'Mrs Boden? Oh my God! I'm Briony Rowe. I was a friend of Sarah's.'

'What?' Alison wore a baseball cap, a waxed Barbour and wellies; she wouldn't have looked out of place on a country dog walk. 'Who gave you permission to do this?'

Briony struggled into a sitting position. The camera was beside her, clamped to the tripod. 'I'm a documentary film-maker. I wrote to you several months ago.'

'What?'

'I asked you for an interview. Don't you remember?'

It was hard to read Alison's expression under the brim of the cap.

With a helping hand from Kayleigh, Briony scrambled to her feet and painted on what she hoped was a confident smile. 'We're taking a fresh look at the evidence and circumstances surrounding the terrible tragedy of Sarah's—'

Without warning, Alison pulled the trowel from the bag and swung it with lightning speed at the camera, cracking into the side of it. The legs of the tripod were splayed wide, holding it low and firm. It rocked slightly. Kayleigh's jaw slackened, Briony raised a pleading hand and wailed. 'Mrs Boden, please—'

Alison lifted her arm and brought the full force of the steel trowel down on the camera. The lens splintered with a sickening crunch.

Briony tried to grab her arm. 'For fuck's sake! That's worth thousands of pounds!'

Swinging round, Alison brandished the sharp end of the trowel at her. 'Yeah, I got your letter. In fact, I read it very carefully and I'm not stupid. He's being let out and you want to say he didn't do it, don't you? At least tell the bloody truth. This is for him. You're here for him.'

Tears welled in Briony's eyes as she stared at the smashed lens. 'You mad bitch! Look what you've done! How am I going to pay for this?'

Alison Boden pushed back her cap. 'You dare to come here and desecrate my daughter's grave. You're lucky I don't whack you right in your smug little face!'

14

....

After her briefing with Foley, Jo had to wait for her cover story to be put in place. It was hard not to feel excited despite her reservations about the DS and his combative attitude. And however you spun it, it was a honey-trap. Scandals followed by investigations and recriminations had produced policy on this. But Jo was only too well aware of the reality she was dealing with here. Male officers preying on female targets may be taboo now. The other way round, though? That remained a grey area.

Foley had made it clear that she had a choice. She could say no and go back to her old squad or she could take a risk. She'd got the impression he'd prefer her to bottle out. But if she wanted to work at the sharp end, for a boss like Vaizey, who carried about him the aura and rumour of a future Commissioner, then she needed to be pragmatic. London was a febrile city. No one wanted to see more guns added to the mix. The Met was woefully under-resourced and political clout depended on results. It was a complex problem, whether or not you chose to bend the rules. This was her chance to be part of the solution, and she wanted that.

Jo was settled at a computer terminal in the Grebe office, going through the file on Rossi and mulling over how to reel him in, when her phone buzzed. Alison was trying to call her. It went to voicemail. Jo felt irritated. Staying with her mother was far from easy at the best of times. But the news of Wade's imminent release had set Alison off on one of her downers.

Over the weekend, she'd dragged out all the old photo albums and spread them across the sitting room floor. Baby Sarah in the arms of her joyful parents, her first steps, her first trike. It had always seemed to Jo that the family archive contained more pictures of her sister than anyone else. Sarah was the golden child, feted and adored from day one and as Jo had grown up, her looks, her mannerisms, every egg-and-spoon race she'd won or exam she'd passed were compared to the previous achievements of her big sister. Carl was treated differently. He was the boy. But even before her sister's demise, Jo had lived in the shadow of Sarah. She didn't resent it. It was just how it had always been.

She'd promised Alison that she'd call her brother but had been putting it off. It was breakfast time in Toronto, so a good time to catch him before he went to work. Stretching, she got up from her desk and headed off down the corridor to find a quiet corner where she could make the call undisturbed. But she checked the voicemail first. Ignoring Alison when she was in a state was never sensible.

The message was short, the tone sorrowful. 'I've been arrested. I'm at Lewisham police station.' Her voice cracked with tears. 'I don't know what to do.' There was a snuffle-filled pause. 'I'm really sorry.'

Jo took a cab to Lewisham. Going AWOL on her first day wasn't ideal, but she hoped her absence wouldn't be noticed. The office was busy. She'd probably get away with it.

When she got to the station, she showed her ID and asked to speak to the custody sergeant. He was friendly and amenable; he explained there had been an altercation at the cemetery and the charges were threatening behaviour and criminal damage. He made a call and one of the young PCs who'd arrested Alison appeared.

She gave Jo a summary of the facts: a damaged camera, threats with an offensive weapon, namely a steel trowel, abusive language to the police when they arrived. She and her colleagues seemed to take the view that Alison could have mental health problems. They'd called the duty medic to make an assessment. Meanwhile they had her under observation in a cell, where she was sitting obsessively unravelling a loose thread on her gardening gloves. The woman PC's partner was in the process of taking a full statement from the complainant, Briony Rowe.

Jo frowned. The name was familiar, though she couldn't quite place it. Alison hadn't mentioned that she'd planned to visit the cemetery that morning, although she knew her mother went there frequently to tend the grave. And who was this Briony Rowe? Somebody? Nobody? Alison had a habit of getting into rows with random strangers. This one had a camera, so what was she filming and why?

Jo smiled at the PC. 'Can I speak to the complainant? I know it's not proper procedure. But, here's the thing. My mother went to the cemetery to visit my sister's grave. My sister was murdered sixteen years ago and we've just learnt that the man convicted is about to be released from jail.'

The PC puffed out her cheeks. 'I see.' She was young, still a probationer, and more used to dealing with drunks and homeless people.

Jo shrugged. She didn't want to be too pushy. 'You're absolutely correct in identifying my mother's mental state as fragile. For the reasons I've explained. I don't know what's happened here, but I may be able to help sort this out.'

The PC nodded and went away to consult.

Ten minutes later, a uniformed sergeant appeared, introduced himself and invited Jo to accompany him.

As they entered the interview room, Briony Rowe shot a nervous glance at Jo. Her face was red and sweaty. She was seated at the table with a younger woman beside her. Jo read her guilt in a nanosecond—she'd been up to no good—followed by what seemed to be a flicker of shock.

The sergeant made the introductions, but Jo had already decided to take charge.

She smiled and stepped forward. 'I'm very sorry about your camera. We will, of course, pay for it.'

But the colour was draining from Briony Rowe's cheeks. Shaking her head in disbelief, she spluttered, 'Oh my god! You look exactly like Sarah.'

15

They all ended up standing on the pavement outside the police station, like revellers from a nightclub expelled into an inhospitable dawn. Briony Rowe had tried to argue that she didn't know she needed permission to film. She'd explained her project to the police in the vaguest terms and agreed to drop the charges. But Jo had also remembered the letter her mother had received and why the name rang a bell. A film about Sarah's murder, that's what this nonsense was all about.

Alison was subdued, clutching her baseball cap and her hessian bag to her chest like an abandoned child, although her daughter knew this was the result of the diazepam the police doctor had prescribed rather than any sense of contrition. She'd been released with a caution for threatening a police officer with a trowel.

Jo checked her phone: nothing from work. With any luck, she could take her mother home and get back without being missed.

Briony Rowe was hovering at her elbow. 'Believe me, I never intended to upset anyone.'

She had the look of a hopeful puppy. Jo wished she'd go away. 'Really? You've got my email address. Send me a bill for the camera.'

'I'd rather we talked.'

This was rich.

'What? You offering me a deal? A conversation for the price of the camera?'

'Jo, you have to understand. I'm doing this for Sarah.'

'That is the biggest pack of lies I ever heard.'

'What if he didn't do it?'

Briony's beringed hand pawed her arm. Jo shoved her away.

'Okay, my mother had no right to damage your camera. That's the law. So we'll pay for it. Equally, you have no right to harass us or invade our privacy. And you have no permission to film my sister's grave. I shall be speaking to the council about that. Any further infringements, we will take legal action against you.'

'Don't you want to know who killed her?'

'I already know.'

Jo glanced up and down the busy High Street for a cab. She was feeling frazzled. Alison seemed listless; Jo took her arm and steered her along the pavement.

Briony followed. 'You're a police officer. Miscarriages of justice happen, you know that.'

'How do you know I'm a police officer?'

'So you are!' A mischievous smile swept over Briony's features. 'I kind of guessed because their attitude changed completely once you rocked up. It was clear you had leverage. They only do that for other cops.'

Jo felt a surge of anger. How the hell had she let this sweaty little person wrong-foot her? She should be at work, preparing for her first encounter with the target, not dealing with this.

A bus pulled up, blocking her view of the road. Why were there no cabs? She manoeuvred Alison round the queue waiting to board the bus.

But Briony was still on their heels. 'Over two per cent of the cases referred to the Criminal Cases Review Commission result in convictions being quashed.'

'That's sounds a pretty low figure to me.'

'Not if you apply it to a prison population of 95,000. That means potentially nearly 2,000 innocent people are behind bars.'

Marooned on the kerb, another Routemaster bearing down on them, Jo took a deep breath. She wasn't having this. Briony Rowe was like an annoying gnat that needed swatting. She turned on her.

'Are you as crap at film-making as you are with statistics? Two per cent of the cases considered by the CCRC is not the same as two per cent of all the people in jail. To get a case reviewed, you need new evidence.'

'Maybe we've got that?'

'Yeah? If Wade's innocent, why has he waited sixteen years to try to prove it?'

'Wouldn't you like to ask him that yourself?'

'No, I wouldn't.'

Jo felt her mother's fingers digging into her arm. Alison turned her head slowly. Her brain seemed to be playing catch-up. 'Is there evidence?'

'Mum, she's just full of bullshit.'

'I was there, Mrs Boden. Sarah was my friend.'

As the second Routemaster pulled away, a black cab appeared in the slow-moving stream of traffic. Jo waved her arm furiously. The cabbie pulled over and drew up beside them.

Stepping off the kerb, she opened the back door and shepherded Alison towards the cab.

Briony grabbed hold of the door. 'She had a stalker. Only a few of us knew about it. Sarah made a joke of it. But she was scared of him. Her killer's still out there, Mrs Boden.'

'A stalker? Really? I think if she had, she'd have told someone in authority about it. My sister was no shrinking violet.'

Alison blinked, a startled fawn caught in the crosshairs. 'Why's she saying all this, Jo?'

Seizing her mother by the shoulders, Jo propelled her into the cab. Then she got in, gave the cabbie the address, and slammed the door shut behind them.

Alison began to weep. 'Do you think it's true?'

'No. Absolutely not.'

As the taxi pulled out into the crawling traffic, the phone in Jo's pocket pinged with an incoming message. Thinking it might be Foley, she glanced at it and was puzzled to find a text from Darryl. Perhaps there was some news about Razan's sister? He and Georgiou could be working on it together?

Clicking on the text, she read:

Hi Jo, congrats on secondment to Grebe. Onwards and upwards, eh! They've given me your desk. Found some personal stuff in the drawer. Text me your address and I'll send it on. Darryl x

Stuff, what stuff? Possibly a packet of painkillers and a box of tampons. And all she'd done was move down the corridor. Jo glanced at Alison, then the realization hit her like a freight train. Her address. *Probably a disgruntled DC*, isn't that what Jabreel Khan said?

Darryl? Her brain was reeling. Could it be Darryl? How many hours had she spent with him in the back of that stinking van, listening to his lame jokes? They were fellow officers, colleagues, and he'd sell her out to a bunch of Albanian gangsters without a second thought. She felt sick.

16

Once Alison was installed in a cosy armchair with a cup of tea and instructions to call if she needed anything, Jo headed back to the office. For most of her teenage years, her mother had been on some form of antidepressant or anti-anxiety medication. The drugs spaced her out, depending on the dose, and left her suspended, not waving or drowning, just bobbing along on the surface in mental limbo. They were both used to it; for many years she'd left her mother like this and gone off to school or college. It had been their everyday survival mode.

Jo took the DLR to Canary Wharf, where she picked up the Jubilee Line, rode it to Baker Street, then switched to the Circle Line for the last three stops to Royal Oak. The afternoon had become overcast, a heavy slate-grey sky threatening rain. She had no umbrella, so she quickened her pace. The offices were situated in a drab seventies block sandwiched between Westway and the railway line.

Since receiving Darryl's text, she hadn't been as worried about the Kelmendis. If they were relying on him for an address, they hadn't tracked her down—yet. But she remained alert, in watcher mode, searching out anomalies, checking faces.

As for the stupid film-maker and her nonsense about Sarah, she dismissed it out of hand. A stalker? When Sarah was still at school, a scuzzy boy who lived in their street had tried to sneak some photos of her sunbathing. She went ballistic and the ensuing ruckus stuck in Jo's memory because Sarah chased him down the drive in her bikini, brandishing the garden broom. If there had been a stalker, Jo was certain her sister would've given him short shrift.

She ran up the stairs two at a time and headed for her old team's office. The room was stuffy and overheated. The rusting radiators had two modes: red hot or stone cold. Glancing towards the familiar desk, she saw Georgiou sitting there, chin propped in her hand, a glazed expression as she stared at the screen.

'Found the Syrian girl yet?'

Jumping out of her skin, Georgiou shot Jo a startled look. 'Ardi sold her to a bloke in Manchester. We think.'

'Then why aren't you in Manchester?'

The appearance of Darryl, carrying two mugs of coffee, saved Georgiou from the need to come up with a response.

'Jo! Missing us already?' He plonked a mug in front of his new partner. 'I gave Debs your desk in the end, since she's the new you.'

The two women exchanged looks; neither seemed impressed by the notion.

Jo folded her arms. This wasn't going to be easy. 'I got your text.'

Darryl sipped his drink, scalding his tongue. He winced. 'Oh yeah. I could've posted it.'

'It? Why? I'm only down the corridor.' No way he was wriggling out of this.

'Yeah, don't we know it? You hear about the barney Hollingsworth and Vaizey had over you?'

'When?'

'Just before lunch.'

When she'd sloped off to Lewisham to rescue her mother? 'I was out.' She rubbed her nose. 'Had a doctor's appointment.'

'Still looks pretty painful that, you poor old thing.'

Moving towards her, he reached out to pat her arm. Jo stepped back. 'Did you hear this row?'

'Happened in Hollingsworth's office. We knew he was pissed off that Vaizey had poached you. Said they'd never discussed it and he'd never agreed to it. He took it to the Assistant Commissioner, apparently. And that's why Vaizey blew a fuse.'

'Vaizey blew a fuse?' This was an interesting insight into her new boss's character. He seemed very chilled.

'According to my spies, he told Dave it was time he took his pension, fucked off and left the Met to those who actually had the balls to get the job done.'

Jo couldn't help smiling, even though she'd been deflected from her purpose. Vaizey must have a deal of confidence, not to mention arrogance, to speak to another senior officer, indeed a more experienced officer, like that. Or perhaps just political clout.

Darryl laughed. 'Sounds like my kind of boss. Can you put in a word for me?'

'You've only been here five minutes, Darryl.' She gave him a pointed look. 'But maybe you're impatient.'

He smiled and shrugged. There was a lazy confidence about him, the smug entitlement of a young man who'd never had to try too hard. And now she'd learnt something else about Darryl Tanner: he was two-faced.

'So, you wanted my address?'

'Yeah.' He gave her a sheepish smile. 'I thought, well, I wasn't sure—'

'Sure of what?'

He seemed embarrassed. 'I didn't want to upset you.'

His jacket was slung on the back of a chair. He reached into the inside pocket. 'Well, there was just this one thing. But I thought you'd want it.' He pulled out a passport-sized photo. 'I found it wedged right in the back of the drawer.'

The photo was dog-eared and creased. Taking it between thumb and index finger, Jo stared down at it: two gurning girly faces filled the tiny frame. Her stomach flipped.

'Looks like you when you were a kid.'

Taken in Cornwall at Easter, when Jo was nearly eleven and Sarah eighteen, this was their last family holiday together, a frozen moment of happiness before Jo's childhood crashed and burned.

She swallowed hard, took a deep breath. 'Yeah. Me and my sister.'

'I…er, heard the story. About…well, y'know, what happened to her. So I assumed you'd want it back.'

He'd heard the story! How? She never spoke of it. But somehow this was common knowledge? That disturbed her. As she tucked the photo away in her bag, she realized her hand was shaking.

'Thanks.' Her voice was a croak. 'Thought I'd lost it.'

17

5 December 1999
  Brighton

Dear Pixie,

I know you're upset Dad came down to see me and didn't tell you. But he had a work thing, a meeting with a client in Brighton, which was arranged at the last minute, so he literally popped in. I know that Mummy's told you that spring half-term is the best time for you to visit, and I absolutely promise you it will happen.

Also, it means you can come in the week, which is a far better way to see what life as a student is really like.

I'll tell you a secret, but you must promise not to blab. I'm going to try and change courses to American Literature. That will mean I get to go and study at an American university for a year. How awesome is that! I quite fancy Berkeley, that's in California.

I don't know why I didn't think of it before. But when you're at school, you get all this advice from teachers. And really all they want is for you to get an A grade and do their subject at uni so they can look good. So, whatever the teachers tell you, Pix — and the parents, for that matter — do your research and make up your own mind. Be who you want to be. Choose something different, something a bit crazy. If I could do it all again, I certainly would.

Don't expect there are too many boys on your horizon just yet. But here's another word of advice: don't believe everything they say. Boys lie. Some of them are like big fat spiders trying to draw you into their web. Don't fall for it! Stay in charge of your own life. Sounds easy, I know, but sometimes it isn't. Stuff gets messy.

But if in doubt, run like hell. Sometimes it's the best thing to do. In many ways, I envy you. You get to learn from all my stupid mistakes.

Tons and tons of love and hugs, little Pixie,

S XXxxxxx

18

The frontage of the café was tucked under the lofty glass canopy of Greenwich Market. Briony Rowe tried to peer through the small bullseye windowpanes into the wood-panelled interior. It looked like some brand designer's vision of a French patisserie crossed with the Old Curiosity Shop, aimed at the tourist trade. A bell tinkled as she opened the door. She hesitated on the threshold, then she saw Alison Boden seated behind a small table at the back, staring into space.

The text she'd received that morning was curt: *2pm café next to gallery 10 in greenwich market.* It was two days since the debacle at Lewisham police station. Was it a summons in order to heap more abuse on her? It seemed unlikely in such a public place, although anything was possible with Alison Boden. Grief had unhinged her. That was Briony's conclusion. But then, could anyone be expected to recover from the murder of their child?

Briony approached the table with a nervous grin. 'Mrs Boden. I got your text.'

Alison gazed up at her. It took a moment for recognition to dawn. Then her brain seemed to click into gear.

'I want to hear about this stalker.' Her eyes had a vacancy, her fingers a slight tremor.

Reassured that no attack was imminent, Briony plonked her bag down on a chair.

She'd wolfed enough benzos in her time to recognize the effects of the medication. Alison Boden was zoned out; she wouldn't be thumping anyone today. Jo Boden had agreed to pay for the smashed lens, although Briony had already persuaded her cameraman buddy to claim on his insurance.

'I'm happy to share everything I know with you. Can I get you some more tea? What you've got looks a bit cold.'

Alison's eyes drifted to her half-empty cup. 'Yes, thank you.'

Briony went to the counter, ordered a large pot of English breakfast tea, considered a meringue—they looked delicious —but resisted.

She returned to the table and sat down, by which time Alison seemed to have gathered her thoughts.

'The idea that she was frightened of some man. I can't stand that.'

'Well, she treated it as a bit of a joke.'

'A joke?'

'She gave him a nickname. Bruce.'

The crease between Alison's brows deepened. 'The evidence in court. Such…viciousness—'

'That's why I've never believed it was Nathan, Mrs Boden. He adored Sarah. Even if they'd had a row, and they fell out quite often, he would never have done that to her.'

'But surely…I mean, how could the police make such a mistake?'

Briony Rowe smiled. Now she was on solid ground.

She'd studied and researched miscarriages of justice. Over the past month, she'd been writing and firing off pitches to various television production companies and her command of the subject was impressive.

'It happens. The police were under tremendous pressure to charge someone. More often than not, the boyfriend or partner is the culprit. But not always. It's easy for them to jump to conclusions. Then negative bias comes into play. They only look for the evidence that supports their assumptions.'

Alison's chin was quivering.

The tea arrived in a heavy brown pot with a knitted cosy and two delicate china cups. Briony glanced at the cake-laden counter and resolved to be strong. She knew she'd hooked Alison, got her questioning the verdict, or they wouldn't be sitting there. But she didn't want to overplay her hand.

Pouring the tea, she placed a steaming cup in front of Alison. 'Milk?'

Alison shook her head. She was frowning, trying, Briony suspected, to process this new information in her drug-addled brain.

'If you knew about this stalker—'

'You're right, Mrs Boden. I should've spoken up. I've spent years feeling guilty. If only I could turn back the clock. But, as a young person, I wasn't very confident. Not an excuse, just an explanation.'

Alison said nothing. She picked up a teaspoon and, with a shaking hand, scooped three sugars into her tea.

Briony watched. In her head, she was already framing the shot. Alison would be brilliant on camera. Her faded beauty, the sorrow etched in every line of her face. If she could put her and Nathan together, even if they said little, it would be cinematic dynamite.

The phone in the top of her bag buzzed. She slipped her hand in to retrieve it and took a quick glance. Alison didn't seem to notice, obsessively stirring her tea, she was lost in some musings of her own.

Clicking on the text, Briony's pulse quickened. Gordon Kramer's company had agreed to a meeting. After all these months of work, things were moving in the right direction.

Xtraordinary Productions were a smallish outfit, but they had huge credibility. Gordon Kramer was a broadcasting heavyweight, ex BBC, he'd done *Panorama*, *Newsnight*, he'd reported on wars and humanitarian disasters and he'd won a shedload of awards. A bit old now, but his much younger wife, Tania Jones, ran the company. She was the one Briony would have to convince.

Tilting her head, as if a new notion had just occurred to her, she gave Alison a smile. 'Of course, the fact that Jo's a police officer might make things much easier.'

'Why?'

'If she met Nathan—'

'I don't want to meet him.' A shudder ran through Alison. 'I remember him in the dock. He kept staring at us. You'd think he'd have been too ashamed.'

'You wouldn't have to meet him. But as an experienced police officer, Jo could interview him herself and weigh the evidence.'

Briony had spent a sleepless night in a state of high excitement. The discovery that Sarah Boden's little sister was the spitting image of her and was a cop to boot had sent her imagination into overdrive.

The film had morphed into a sister's quest to find the truth. Combine that with an innocent man's crusade to clear his name and she would have something unique. And if she could present the idea that they were working together, that would be magic.

The film-maker took a sip of her tea. 'What does Jo think about you talking to me?'

For the first time, a hint of a smile crossed Alison's face. 'She doesn't know.' Briony had suspected as much. 'My daughter is, well, a very different character to her sister.'

'In what way?'

'She can be rather…difficult. Obstinate. Even as a baby, she cried all the time. Would never sleep.'

Briony slipped her phone on to the table between them. 'You don't mind if I…I've got a brain like a sieve.' With quick jabs of her index finger, she clicked to record.

Alison seemed oblivious, engulfed in memories. 'Why on earth she joined the police is a complete mystery to me. No one in the family has ever done anything like that before. My side, we've always been creative. And Sarah took after me. She probably would've become a film-maker herself, you know.'

'Oh absolutely.' Briony nodded. 'We talked about movies all the time. She had an amazing visual eye.'

Alison smiled wistfully. 'You're right. She did.'

'At the beginning of term, we joined the film society together. I remember going to see all these great old films. Sarah was a real movie buff.'

'In the winter, even when the kids were quite small, we always rented a video on a Sunday afternoon.'

'She told me that!'

Alison's face softened. 'Did she? Really?'

'It's where her love of film started, I'm sure.'

Alison sighed, her eyes welling up. 'Such a waste.'

They sat in silence for several moments.

But Briony realized she'd never have a better opportunity, and it would be foolish not to exploit it.

'You see, Mrs Boden, that's why I believe this film would be such a tribute to Sarah. I sort of imagine it as the film she would've made if she could've done it herself. And who knows, maybe her spirit is out there in the ether somewhere, guiding me.'

Alison Boden ran her middle fingers under both eyes to wipe away the tears, and Briony wondered for a guilty second if she'd pushed it a tad too far.

But then the older woman's gaze came to rest on her and she smiled. 'Yes, you might be right. It is the sort of thing that Sarah would've approved of.'

19

Jo Boden stood across the road studying the estate agents from a distance. It was part of an upmarket chain with offices throughout London, and Ivan Rossi was assistant manager of the Shepherd's Bush branch. The shop occupied corner premises on the Hammersmith side of the Green. It had taken a couple of days for Foley to make the arrangements. She needed some ID and bank details to establish her bona fides as a serious potential client. Jo used the time to focus and to distance herself from the distractions swirling around her new deployment.

Darryl's unearthing of the photo-booth picture had upset her more than she cared to admit. For years it was hidden away behind the credit cards in her wallet; she rarely looked at it. She didn't know how it ended up in the desk drawer.

The only other memorabilia she'd kept were three letters and a couple of glittery birthday cards, which Sarah made for her while she was still at school. The letters were written in Sarah's first weeks at university, after which all correspondence ceased. Jo never understood why. Maybe her sister became too enmeshed with her new student life and couldn't be bothered with her family. Jo had no memory of how she'd reacted to this rejection. The shock of subsequent events wiped it out. But she kept the letters and never told her parents about this private trove because everything else that had ever belonged to her sister—from the one-armed Barbie she'd handed on to Jo to the sellotaped Spice Girls posters—had been purloined by Alison after Sarah's death.

The scrap between Vaizey and Hollingsworth remained office gossip, although neither of them spoke to her directly. Did they discuss the fact she was still a target of the Kelmendis? No one talked to her about that either. Her only contact was with Foley, and he treated her with a lack of interest bordering on dislike. She'd heard nothing from Jabreel Khan.

The encounter with Darryl had been uncomfortable, although she'd jumped to the wrong conclusion about him. There was no evidence to suggest he was the informant. In the end, she decided to get on with the job and hope for the best. As Jabreel had already pointed out, adopting a false identity was as good a way as any to lie low.

But why on earth had they come up with the name Charlotte? Jo neither felt like a Charlotte nor, in her opinion, looked like one. It had been chosen by an anonymous researcher somewhere in the bowels of MI5; they were providing her legend and the documentation to support it. Foley said it emphasized her Englishness. She was an English rose with golden hair, which may well appeal to Rossi. Jo got the impression he was being sarcastic. That seemed to be his default mode.

Nevertheless, she was approaching the job with professionalism and gave careful thought to her outfit and appearance. The most expensive item in her wardrobe was a grey jersey shift dress from Whistles. It was simple and elegant.

With a short leather biker jacket and medium-heeled ankle boots, it emphasized her figure and her long legs. She pinched a gold bangle and a silk scarf from her mother's bedroom to complete the look.

She also created a backstory in her own mind to embellish the legend. Her feeling was they needed something that matched the aspirations of a man like Rossi. They wanted to arouse his sympathy, certainly. But Jo was astute enough to understand that, whatever the official line, this was a seduction, even if it would never be consummated. The skill was to hook him and play him for long enough to gather the intel they needed.

As she cast around for ideas, a random notion popped into her head. The summer before she'd gone to university, her sister, Sarah, did some modelling for an agency. An old friend of Alison's arranged the job and was keen to persuade Sarah to continue during her studies. But Nick Boden had put his foot down and a family argument ensued, with Sarah pleading with her father to let her do both and Alison tacitly supporting her with the proviso that her university work must not suffer.

Jo had sided with her sister. The world of modelling seemed impossibly glamorous to an eleven-year-old. But having spent three weeks from dawn until dusk at the shoot, putting clothes on, taking them off and posing, endlessly posing, Sarah had confessed to her little sister that the whole thing was tedious and hard work, and not what she'd expected at all. Jo was disappointed, too. She'd shared her sister's thrill vicariously. But what she remembered in particular, and what had puzzled her at the time, was Sarah's stubborn refusal to admit to their father that he'd been right. She still kept arguing and harassing him for permission to continue her modelling career.

Was Sarah stubborn, wilful even? Jo couldn't remember. She liked to get her own way. She often flounced into her room, slamming the door after some row with their parents.

Jo tried not to think about the past. And she didn't want to think about it now. But the photo, Wade's release, her mother's hysteria were churning it all up.

Pretending to be someone she wasn't, in circumstances that could be construed as risky, would have appealed to Sarah. Jo hadn't thought about it for years, but as she stood on the corner of Shepherd's Bush Green psyching herself up to morph into Charlotte, a long forgotten memory of Sarah popped into her head. It seemed to come from nowhere, a clear image of her sister, once again in a bikini.

They were on holiday in the Caribbean. The exotic holidays and the moneyed existence of her childhood was something that rarely strayed into Jo's adult consciousness. It belonged to a time labelled *before*, when the Bodens were a family; it was a lost world.

But Sarah was on a sun lounger with Jo deputed to rub sun cream into her back. A group of rich, preppy American college boys had been playing in the pool. Jo found them boisterous and intimidating. One of them tried to chat up Sarah, and she pretended to be French. She spoke to them in a mixture of heavily accented English and proper French, and within five minutes, the entire group was mesmerized. They sat round in a circle, ordering drinks, smoking and paying court to Sarah. Jo's role was to answer her sister's occasional question with a *oui* or *non*. At nine years old, she'd managed her part with aplomb and Sarah later rewarded her with a Knickerbocker Glory.

Crossing the road to the estate agents, Jo tossed back her head, loosened her honey-blonde hair and lengthened her stride as she slipped into the mindset of the character she was creating. Charlotte, she told herself, was the kind of girl who would've spent her holidays as a teenager tormenting gullible boys. Like Sarah, she'd done some modelling but discovered it was tedious. She had family money, obviously. But things had gone awry for her; she'd hooked up with the wrong bloke. Now she was intent on escaping by finding a new flat. Was she going to follow instructions and make a direct appeal to his sympathy? That would be too obvious. The target had to be captivated first, before he could be turned into a white knight. He could see her injuries for himself. Only later would she bring Foley into the mix.

As she pushed open the shop door, Ivan Rossi looked up from his screen. Then he beamed, jumped up, buttoned his jacket and stepped forward to greet her.

20

To prepare for his actual release, Nathan Wade was given a ROTL—release on a temporary licence. He'd had a couple of these before to check just how ready he was to return to society.

The first time out alone, he'd taken a train and visited his old hometown only to find his parents' bungalow had been knocked down and replaced by two semis crammed onto the narrow site. He'd stood in the rain and remembered his mother dead-heading the roses in what had been her immaculate front garden.

But for this outing, Lech had invited him to stay for a couple of days. It seemed bizarre to Nathan that this was his first sleepover at a mate's since schooldays. He also found the prospect nerve-racking.

The Pole lived in the rented basement flat of a large Victorian property close to the seafront in Littlehampton. He shared it with his cousin Mateusz and Mateusz's girlfriend. They'd cleared out the tiny storage room, installed a camp bed and put a vase of freesias on the windowsill to make it look cheery.

Lech and Nathan walked back from the coffee shop after work and as they clattered down the metal staircase to the front door, they were assailed by the robust meaty aroma of a large pot of Bigos stewing on the hob. Danuta had made it in honour of Nathan's visit before going off to teach a boxercise class at the gym where she worked.

Opening the fridge, Lech pulled out two beers, flipped off the caps and handed one to his friend.

'*Twoje zdrowie!*'

They chinked. Mateusz was gabbling in Polish. Danuta had given him some specific instructions about stirring the pot, adding the veg and not letting it burn.

Nathan held the dewy bottle like an exotic gift and watched his hosts jostling round each other in the narrow galley kitchen as they chopped cabbage to add to the pan. The normality of it all and their good-natured hospitality left him feeling awkward. It was a harsh reminder. Prison had robbed him of experiences like this. He couldn't remember the last time he'd cooked for his mates or been invited to dinner. He turned away to hide his resentment and took a slug of beer.

Briony Rowe arrived shortly after seven. She was red-faced and flustered, having driven down from London. A wodge of documents spilled out of her wicker basket and Nathan picked them up for her. They faced each other with self-conscious smiles.

Briony held out her bejewelled hand. 'Thank you for agreeing to this.'

He took her clammy palm. 'Well, I suppose… I dunno.'

He'd made the decision to exploit the situation in the privacy of his cell. Carrying it through was another matter. He couldn't think of anything to say.

Lech stepped in. 'A beer, Briony?'

She extracted a bottle of red wine from the depths of her basket and offered it to Lech.

He examined the label. 'Hey, the good stuff! You want some?'

'It's for you guys. Just the one beer is fine. I'm driving.'

You guys. Nathan hadn't heard anyone say that for years. It was a feminine phrase of the sort that would never feature in prison lingo. It was yet another reminder of how isolated he'd been, how shut away from the scurry and scamper of ordinary life. And from women.

He still felt desire and fantasized often. He looked at porn and gave himself physical relief, but that depressed him. Occasionally, he allowed himself to watch some of the female prison officers; they weren't all dykes or crones. There were a couple of young ones who took particular pleasure in tantalizing the inmates. It was subtle, a special smile, a lingering look. The bitches enjoyed the power. Nathan was certain of that. But he was careful. He refused to give them the satisfaction of seeing they'd hooked him.

The Bigos was served with boiled potatoes. The four of them sat squashed round the narrow table, but it was a jolly meal. Lech and Mateusz made sure of that. Mateusz told tales of his life on English construction sites; he was a jack-of-all-trades, though he'd studied at art college and trained to be a graphic designer. He hoped to go back to it one day.

Nathan realized how little he knew about Lech. They were a similar age. Lech was a good manager, he knew that. But his Polish friend rarely revealed anything personal about himself. This was one of the main things Nathan liked about him.

Mateusz teased his cousin about a girl back home, but Lech dismissed the conversation and poured more wine.

Nathan found himself niggled by memories that he'd

suppressed. In his last year at school, he had started to drink red wine; as a poet, he'd felt it incumbent on him to cultivate sophisticated tastes. But he hadn't touched it since. The flavour seemed odd to him now, lacking in the sweetness of the fizzy drinks that were his usual tipple. The fact he didn't much like the taste made it easier to sip. He didn't want to get drunk. Staying on an even keel, keeping control of his emotions seemed essential.

The dessert was ice cream, which Briony refused, leaving Nathan a double helping. Then the Polish cousins cleared away the dishes. They retreated to the kitchen to make coffee and do the washing up.

Nathan had reflected long and hard on how to deal with Briony Rowe and turn the situation to his advantage, but somehow it all seemed to have slithered out of his brain. Playing the prison system was one thing. This required another approach. Patience, finesse even. It was a different kind of con. He scanned her; up close, he could feel how nervy she was.

'Listen, Nathan.' Her smile was tentative. 'I know none of this is easy for you.'

He shrugged. 'I think I've just blocked a lot of things out.' The evasion was deliberate. It was going to take him some time to get used to her. She had a curious smell, some kind of pungent perfume. Expensive, no doubt. It wasn't attractive.

She was nodding like a robotic little dog 'That's understandable. Have you got anything you'd like to ask me?'

'How much money'll be in it?' The question came out more abruptly than he'd intended. But then, what was the point beating about the bush?

'Money? For you?' She gave a nervous chuckle.

'I've got sixteen years of lost earnings to make up.'

'Surely the priority is to clear your name?'

'You think that's possible? How?'

Reaching down to the bundle of documents stuffed in her basket, Briony adopted a brisk manner. 'I've talked to the Free Representation Unit. If we can interest them in your case, we should be able to get someone pro bono. But what we need in order to go to the Criminal Cases Review Commission is fresh evidence.'

'What if there is no fresh evidence?'

'At the moment, we don't know that. There might be something in the trial documents that's been overlooked. And the whole field of forensics has moved on hugely. DNA collected at the scene may have been too difficult to read sixteen years ago, but they may be able to do something with it now.'

'It all sounds very complicated.'

'It is complicated. Lots of hoops to jump through. But we also have an alternative suspect, if we can track him down. The stalker.'

'You really remember him?'

'Yes.'

'But not his name?'

'Sarah called him Bruce. Remember the *Die Hard* films? Bruce Willis running round in his vest to show off his muscles?'

'A postgrad? Let me guess, he had a car.'

'Possibly.'

'I always thought she was having a thing with that theatre bloke, the American.'

Briony chuckled. 'Oh, God, no! She was faithful to you, Nathan.'

He gave her a sour look. 'What planet are you living on? We're talking about Sarah Boden here.'

'You shouldn't speak about her like that.'

'Why not? She's the reason my life is fucked.'

'No, Bruce is the reason your life is fucked.'

Nathan stared down at his fingernails, ragged and work-worn. This was their first skirmish, the first of many he suspected. But she had to know that he wasn't a sucker.

'Don't films make money? I mean, let's be honest, Briony, you're not doing this for nothing.'

She looked offended. 'I'm not doing this just for the money. We'll need a production company who can take it to a broadcaster and get it commissioned. Then there'll be the actual cost of production. It'll be a long way down the road before we see any profit.'

He smiled. 'But without me, you've got nothing. That's the bottom line, isn't it?'

21

Jo's initial interview with Rossi went well. He seemed ordinary: an M&S suit, a G-Shock watch, the kind of young bloke you might find propping up any bar from Hoxton Square to Brixton. He had a salesman's easy banter and it would be hard to suspect any link between this estate agent with a cheeky smile and Belarusian gun-runners. Was the intel on his family even correct? Jo wondered.

She registered with the agency, discussed her property requirements, laughed at his jokes and gave him plenty of coy eye contact. It wasn't that hard to make him fancy her. And, concealed behind the mask of Charlotte, she found the process of flirtation and seduction much easier.

The bruising under her eyes was fading, but still notice-able. His gaze kept coming back to it. He wanted to ask. She sensed it, but he needed a little encouragement. She stroked the bridge of her nose gingerly with her middle finger and frowned.

Unconsciously, he mirrored her, rubbing his own nose. 'What happened? I don't mean to be rude, but it looks painful.'

'Oh, skiing. My family goes every year.' She let her eyes drift nervously towards the window, enough to tell him she was lying.

He got it immediately. 'I tried snowboarding one year. Sprained my ankle. But we had a laugh. Went with some mates.'

The hook was in, the moment of vulnerability creating a more personal connection. A soft smugness crept into his face and Jo could see that the role of rescuer was an ego-trip that appealed to him.

'So, hey, let me show you this new place that's just come on. It's over in Battersea. But you are gonna love it.'

'I need somewhere fairly quickly. My situation is…' Dropping her gaze, she swallowed and let him glimpse the anxiety. 'Well, it's complicated.'

He gave a gentle nod. 'Yes, I understand.'

They moved on to a discussion of properties. But he was watching her all the time, speculating, calculating. Beauty in distress, men love it, Foley was right about that. When she left the office after three quarters of an hour, he gazed into her eyes, gave her hand a comforting squeeze and held the door open for her. He was going to set up some appointments and call her.

Jo knew she'd made a good start. There was not the least whiff of suspicion on his part. If he was alert to any potential surveillance, she was confident she'd slipped under his radar.

Even though it was raining, walking across Shepherd's Bush Green towards the tube, she felt more light-hearted than she had for some days. She could report back to Foley and Vaizey with confidence. The recording she'd made of the encounter on her phone was clear proof she was up to the job.

She'd always had an inkling that working undercover might suit her temperament, and her encounter with Jabreel

Khan had reinforced that feeling. Despite the initial hostility between them, she had a sense they were kindred spirits, happiest keeping a low profile, watching covertly from the sidelines. She'd concluded that he must feel the connection too; why else would he have tracked her down to warn her about the Kelmendis? He'd gone to a lot of trouble for someone he didn't even know.

And if she was honest, secretiveness had always felt exciting. Years before Sarah's death, when she was still small, some instinctual intuition led her to conceal her thoughts and fears from Alison. There was always a whirlwind of anxiety around her mother, nothing solid you could rely on. Afterwards, Alison's frequent floods of anger and paranoia could inundate everyone in its path and insulating herself from this became Jo's priority.

At school too, she'd faced a deluge of concern. Teachers and counsellors were always keeping a watchful eye and writing reports on her. She didn't want to be the girl whose sister was murdered. She hated being singled out. Being *special* was a term of abuse; the special needs kids were the ones with problems. Avoiding unwanted attention became her priority. Always appearing compliant, she discovered, was the way to keep the intrusion at bay. She became expert at knowing how to evade questions and the right lies to tell. The hidden power of the deception gave her a buzz; it made her feel smart and, more important, it gave her the armour to protect herself.

Her parents had never liked the idea of her joining the police. Nick Boden had tried to persuade his daughter to become a lawyer instead. He found that more acceptable, arguing it was safer. But Jo had detected the snobbery in his attitude. He didn't want his privately educated daughter out on the street dealing with drug dealers, pimps, the violent and the homeless. That was a job for someone else and the pay reflected it. Their disapproval galvanized her.

Jo was never an obvious rebel, and taking care of Alison had made her teenage years sober and staid. There were few opportunities to get drunk and hang out with her mates, because of the need to get home and check on her mad mother. She went to university in London and lived at home. Alison wouldn't countenance her going away and risk a repeat of what happened to her sister. It wasn't until she joined the Met that Jo had found her escape route.

The person who'd had the most influence on her choice of career was Katie Carr, the family liaison officer, who'd spent months practically living in their house. She was always professional, but her calm presence gave Jo something to cling to while her parents imploded with grief and then tore each other apart. Jo adored Katie and wanted to be like her. They kept in touch for years, exchanging Christmas cards. Katie encouraged her ambition to join the police. When Jo received a round-robin email from some niece, announcing that Katie had died of cervical cancer, she cried buckets.

Zipping into Shepherd's Bush tube station, Jo shook the rain from her umbrella and, swiping through the ticket barrier, she joined the stream of damp travellers scurrying and slipping over the rain-slicked tiles towards the escalators.

It was mid morning, a drizzly January day, but that hadn't deterred the hordes of Westfield shoppers bustling along with their bags. Jo got shoved by a couple of bedraggled Chinese tourists, but she gave them a benevolent smile. They were in her city spending their money. She wasn't going to be unfriendly.

At the top of the bank of escalators, she edged into line and joined the queue. Each of the moving staircases had two lanes: standing on the right, walking on the left. There was something quite British about the process, but foreign visitors seemed to get the idea.

Jo went for the left-hand lane of the far escalator, the fast lane. Stepping on to the flat treads, the moving belt carried her forward and then down into the vertiginous chasm of the underground.

She walked, scooting past the passengers riding on the right. The young lad in front of her had speeded to a trot and was clearing the path. She was thinking over the report she'd send to Foley and feeling upbeat. He could be as snippy as he liked, but he would have to acknowledge that she'd made progress.

The sensation of someone close behind her, propelling her forwards, was subtle at first. There was nothing unusual about being jostled or even shoved on the tube. But her intuition flashed warnings to her brain. She'd heard of a colleague who got stabbed on an escalator. Was she being paranoid? The Kelmendis were out to harm her. But could this be the prelude to an attack? She had seconds to decide and take evasive action.

Speeding up, she got two-thirds of the way down the moving staircase, but he kept pace. Then she stopped dead and braced herself. He ran straight into the back of her, hard enough to knock the wind out of her. She made a grab for the handrail and for a panic-stricken moment, it seemed they both might pitch forward and downwards. A man standing to her right grabbed her arm and steadied her.

'All right, love?' He was burly, his grip firm.

Jo gasped for breath. 'Thanks. Sorry.'

Then she turned to get a look at her potential assailant. Young and rough-looking, with dark angry eyes under a tight black hoodie.

He glared at her and mumbled. It might've been an apology.

Jo's rescuer faced him. 'Need to slow down, mate.'

No reply. He bulldozed between them and barged the people in front aside.

'Oi! Watch it!' The hoodie ploughed on, ignoring them all.

As the escalator carried Jo to the bottom, he scurried off, disappearing down a tunnel. She was shaken and a little dizzy.

The bloke who'd helped her shook his head. In his fifties, the Italian wool overcoat and cashmere scarf didn't match the cockney accent. 'Bloody London, eh? Love it and hate it! You okay, love?'

Her heart was thumping in her chest, but Jo painted on a smile. 'I'm fine. Thank you.'

22

Had she been targeted? Jo walked along the underground platform scanning the sea of faces. He could still be lurking, though she told herself that was unlikely. She walked close to the wall, giving the edge of the platform a wide berth. Her head had started to throb. The splinters of light bouncing off the tiled walls seemed dazzling. They seared her retinas. Her shoulders were tense, her neck rigid, and she was developing a migraine.

Her plan had been to return to the office, but she was hardly in a fit state to deal with Foley. She headed back up the escalators and out on to the street.

Jo was prone to migraines, often brought on by stress. Rummaging in her bag, she found some painkillers and popped a couple. Fortunately, it only took a few minutes to hail a cab. She gave the driver her mother's address, sank into the back seat and closed her eyes.

The cabbie regarded her in the rear-view mirror. 'You all right, love?' He was probably worried she was going to throw up.

'Headache. Nothing really.'

Like the man on the escalator who'd grabbed her, he too had concern in his face. It did exist, good people were out there. She tried to remind herself of that.

The journey from Shepherd's Bush to Greenwich was long and expensive. But, as the shock of the encounter subsided and the medication kicked in, it gave her time to replay the incident and consider it from every angle. Had the hoodie been planning to push her down the escalator? Was he carrying a knife? He'd been aggressive and keen to escape. On the other hand, it could've been a piece of random hostility from an angry lout.

If this thug had been sent by the Kelmendis, how did he know where to find her? In order to follow her, they would've needed to know where to look. Had they picked her up as she left the office? But then, how did they know she'd be going out this afternoon? The informant? They would've needed to watch the building closely, and that seemed too well organized. She'd walked out of the estate agents feeling smug, guard down and proving the DS wrong was all that had been on her mind. Was this payback for her hubris?

She used a credit card for the fare, and as she stood beside the cab's open window, she noticed her hand was shaking. The cabbie gave her a smile and advised her to take care before driving off, red tail-lights blinking, into the early encroaching wintery darkness.

Jo had to rest her bag on the garden wall to search for her front-door key. The afternoon rain had cleared and eddies of freezing fog were drifting down the road, creating a sulphurous glow around the Victorian streetlamps.

Suddenly, from nowhere, a dark shape launched itself at her. She leapt back, fear shooting up through her body and seizing her by the throat, the contents of her bag spilling out on to the pavement. Perched on the wall next to her, the sinuous shadow raised its tail and meowed.

It was the fat old ginger moggie that lived next door. Jo took a deep breath. Her nerves were still jangling. Relief flooded through her, causing her hands to tremble even more. To calm herself, as much as the cat, she stroked his head. He was a friendly old thing and rubbed his nose against the side of her hand and purred.

'You should be tucked up indoors, buddy. We both should.'

Collecting up her things, she found her keys and unlocked the front door. As she stepped over the threshold, delicious cooking smells assailed her. Alison was in the kitchen at the back, apron on, stirring a large orange Le Creuset pot, which Jo hadn't seen in use for years.

'You're back early. I'm making ratatouille. I thought we'd have it with some pasta and cheese.' She sounded positively jaunty.

Dumping her bag by the door, Jo joined her mother in the kitchen. The last thing she wanted was to tell her what had happened.

'Nice.'

'Don't sound so surprised. I know how to cook.' She raised her wooden spoon from the pot, blew on it and tasted, nodding in approval. 'Yeah, not bad.'

'What's brought this on?'

'You work hard. You need a decent meal when you get in.' Alison peered at her daughter. 'I have to say, darling, you look like shit. White as a sheet.'

'Bit of a migraine.' She opened the fridge and found a bottle of wine in the door. She lifted it out. 'Top up?'

Alison picked up her glass and held it out. 'You sure you want to drink with a migraine?'

Jo poured. 'Yes.' Taking a glass from the cupboard, she filled it for herself as she scanned her mother.

The volatility of Alison's moods was nothing new. There'd been some discussion with her GP a few years previously about whether she was bipolar. He was reluctant to make a diagnosis and she'd refused to accept the label or the drugs that went with it.

Now she was all smiles though, definitely up, beaming at her daughter. 'What shall we drink to?'

'How about confusion to the enemy?' The toast slipped into Jo's head from nowhere in particular. Then she remembered it was a favourite of her father's.

But Alison ignored this. 'What about truth?' She had a wistful look on her face. Jo had given up trying to interpret her mother's emotional states. Now she rode the rollercoaster and hoped for a soft landing.

'What do you mean, truth?'

'You're a police officer. Surely truth matters.'

Jo chinked her glass. She hadn't the strength to argue. 'Okay then, truth.'

She took a large swallow of wine. It was quite a good Sauvignon Blanc, but it could've been anything. A couple more glasses tonight should do the trick. Calm her down and chill her out.

Alison was twisting the stem of her glass, and Jo sensed her anticipation. Something was going on.

Her mother took a sip, smiled. 'What if Nathan Wade didn't kill Sarah?'

'Fucking hell, Mum! Who have you been talking to? Has that bloody woman been hassling you?'

'I called her.' Alison was trying to sound casual.

'Why?'

'Because…well, it's never felt quite right.'

Jo plonked her glass down on the counter. 'You can't allow her to get inside your head.'

'I don't think I am. I've always had a feeling—'

'Mum, feelings aren't evidence. The prosecution case was rock solid.'

'Jo, you were only eleven.' Her eyes narrowed. 'If you ask me, you get way too many migraines. Too much stress.'

'I'll be fine.'

Alison gave her a sceptical look and shook her head. 'Your father was right. It's a horrible job. You shouldn't be doing it.'

'I remember enough. I was twelve by the time it came to trial. The verdict was unanimous.'

'You didn't sit in that courtroom day after day.'

'Whatever she's told you about miscarriages of justice — okay, they happen. But you have to ask yourself, why's she doing this now? Is it coming from him? Is he now saying he's innocent?'

'I remember him in the dock. Such a boy. And when they went through—' She swallowed hard. 'Well, how she was hit, then choked, all that. He looked so shocked. And Briony says he really loved her.'

'Briony says! Yeah, I'll bet she does. But ask yourself this, Mum, why didn't she say it sixteen years ago to the police?'

'You're upset, Jo.'

'I'm not upset. I'm angry. And you should be too. You're being manipulated.'

'It doesn't feel like that.'

'That's because—' Jo cast around for the right words. 'Because she's telling you a story you want to hear.'

The image of Ivan Rossi flitted into Jo's mind. Lies and

manipulation. But that was different. It was her job and he wasn't an innocent dupe like her mother.

'I've agreed to meet him. Then I think I'll know.'

'You won't. Psychopaths can be charming and very manipulative.'

'I don't think he's ever been diagnosed as a psychopath. I remember the psychiatrist who gave evidence. She said she didn't think he was that.'

'Why are you even thinking about this? And why are you so pleased about it?'

'Because it explains.'

'Explains what?'

'Why I've never been able to let it go.'

'That doesn't mean he's innocent. It means…'

Alison had tears welling in her eyes. 'That I'm some crazy person who can't cope?'

She put her glass down and pulled her cardigan around her. Jo took a step forward and coiled her arms round her mother.

'Oh, Mum—'

Alison accepted the hug, but only for a second, then she wriggled free.

'I know how you see me, Jo. Mad mother, who you have to keep an eye on.'

'Grief does weird things to people.' It was a lame cliché, but all Jo could manage.

'That's for sure. It turned your father into an angry stranger who decided he hated me.'

'He doesn't hate you.'

'He brought the shutters down. Froze me out, like it was somehow my fault.'

'He froze us all out, not just you.'

Jo didn't want to think about her father. He was the ghost

in her life. She maintained polite relations with him and his new wife. They sent her a gift voucher at Christmas and periodic invitations to visit, which she usually declined.

'Okay, let's try to look at all this objectively.' Jo picked up her glass, took another sip. 'This Briony whatever-she's-called, comes out of the woodwork and she wants to make a film.'

'She was a friend of Sarah's.'

'So she says. How do we know that?'

'She's said things about Sarah that ring true.'

'Even so, she's seen an opportunity. Have you looked her up on the net? What kind of film-maker is she? Does she have a track record?'

'What does that matter? I think she's had a guilty conscience for years and now she wants to make things right.'

Jo shook her head, took another slug of wine.

Alison reached out, touched her daughter's sleeve. 'Jo, if you'd only talk to her. All the stuff you're saying, it may be right.'

'I know it's right.'

'No you don't. You think you know. And Briony says there's evidence.'

'And you believe her?'

'I don't know. But you're in a much better position than me to assess it.'

'It's a waste of time.'

'If the man who so brutally killed your sister is still out there, is still walking round free—' Alison pressed the side of her clenched fist to her lips to hold back the tears. 'I can't stand that. Even the possibility of that. Please, Jo, I'm begging you. Talk to her. Listen to what she's got to say.'

'Okay! If that will settle this for you, I'll talk to her.'

'And you'll listen?'

'Yes, Mum, I'll listen.'

Mother and daughter stared at each other, relief on both sides.

Alison nodded, then she smiled. 'Okay, then. Now I hope you're hungry. Because there's a mountain of ratatouille here.'

23

Nathan Wade got off the train at Victoria. The journey up from Littlehampton had taken an hour and three quarters. Mostly he'd gazed out of the window at the bare fields and spectral trees shrouded in morning mist. The rumble and rattle of the train as it sped through the landscape was a novelty. He felt like a kid on an outing. The only other trip of this length that he'd made since his conviction was a depressing and fleeting visit to his old hometown. But today he was putting thoughts of the deadening years of imprisonment behind him. Resentment took up too much energy, now he was moving on. Now it was payback time.

As the train trundled through the suburban outskirts of the city, he'd felt a little tense. It was so many years since he'd been to London and stepping down from the carriage and joining the press of passengers hurrying towards the automatic ticket barriers, he became more aware of how odd it all felt. He seemed to have lost the skill of weaving effortlessly through crowds. People en masse made him uncomfortable. Long periods of incarceration could make you agoraphobic. He'd read that somewhere and with no ankle bracelet tracking

his movements he felt naked. Being free was more complicated than he'd expected. As he puzzled over where to insert
his ticket in the barrier, Briony Rowe appeared.

They smiled at each other awkwardly.

She was out of breath. 'Good journey?'

'It was okay.' He had no intention of sharing the novelty
of it, nor his trepidation with her.

Dressed in black—black coat, black leggings, a sable
cashmere wrap—she seemed older and more sophisticated,
which was possibly her aim. He considered his own shabby
outfit: cheap trainers, threadbare jeans, a thin grey hoodie and
ratty scarf. He smelt of prison and looked more like an overgrown teen, which didn't please him. Inside, clothes and
appearance hadn't mattered to him. But now he was out in the
world again, he felt self-conscious.

The offices of Xtraordinary Productions were off
Tottenham Court Road, so she proposed they take the
Victoria Line to Warren Street; it was, she explained, only
three stops. He nodded; he'd hoped they would take a cab,
had imagined being whisked up to the door and stepping out
on to the pavement. If he was about to become a TV star, that
seemed a more appropriate arrival. Still, he'd resolved to be
patient. Briony would realize soon enough that she couldn't
take him for granted.

Xtraordinary occupied the second floor of a brick-fronted
building of media businesses in Whitfield Street. Briony
could claim an acquaintance with Gordon Kramer and his
company, having done some editing work for them in the
past. But this would be her first visit in her new capacity as a
creative.

Gordon's wife, Tania Jones, was the real boss and it had
taken a couple of difficult phone conversations to secure a
meeting. Gordon may have the awards and the reputation but

it was Tania, at least twenty years his junior, who had the business nous to keep the place afloat in the choppy waters of independent television production.

She had given Briony quite a grilling on the phone: was there a realistic chance of getting the case reviewed? She was interested in the possibility of Alison's involvement. But before she'd commit to anything, she insisted on seeing Nathan for herself. This was an audition to check whether he would make a plausible and sympathetic protagonist. Briony hadn't explained it to Nathan in these terms, but she was realizing that she didn't need to. He was proving far more astute than she'd expected.

The reception area contained several low leather sofas and was divided from the main office by an opaque glass panel. Hung next to this were half a dozen BAFTA awards, a large glossy photograph of Gordon Kramer riding into Baghdad on an American tank and a smaller, more grainy print of his younger, long-haired self with an old-fashioned mic standing beside broken chunks of the Berlin Wall.

Nathan stood looking at this shot for some time. He never watched any television news. The horrors of the contemporary world had passed him by. But he had a keen sense of history. He remembered the Wall coming down—he was only eight years old—but his father had been excited, telling him that everything would be different and Nathan would grow up with a better life in a better world. That seemed ironic now, given how things had turned out.

Briony whispered in his ear: 'He's such a legend.'

'Must've been interesting to be there.'

'You should ask him about it.'

Tania Jones didn't keep them waiting. She was a woman with a schedule and she believed in sticking to it. They were ushered into the conference room by an enthusiastic intern, who offered them coffee, tea and four kinds of herbal infusions.

Tania threw her arms around Briony Rowe and air-kissed her cheek. 'Briony! It's been way too long. How are you? You're looking great.'

'I'm good. And so psyched about this project. But let me introduce you to Nathan Wade.'

Nathan knew without prompting that he had to impress this woman. That's why they were here. Shrewd dark eyes under a severe fringe scrutinized him as she offered her hand to shake. He found it difficult to guess her age. Briony had said she must be forty-five but a lean runner's frame and bags of restless energy made her seem much younger.

'Nathan! Thanks so much for coming in today.' Holding on to his hand, she covered it with her left palm and squeezed. 'It's great to meet you.'

His instinct was to pull away. He wasn't used to this kind of physical contact with women. Forcing himself to hold her gaze, he smiled.

'I'm incredibly grateful that you're interested in my case.'

She let go of his hand, which was a relief, and they all sat down at the table.

'Obviously Briony's told me about it. But, really, I'd like to hear about what happened from your point of view.'

Briony Rowe held her breath. The next few minutes were crucial. Would he make the right impression? She had no idea. He could be difficult and obtuse, she was well aware of that. His reticence wasn't so much of a problem. Shyness made him more sympathetic. But if he was glib or, God forbid, mentioned money, that wouldn't play at all.

Nathan shrugged. 'It's hard to explain. I've spent years trying to understand it myself. I was a student in my first year at uni, still a kid, and I fell in love with a girl. She was…well, the most amazing person I'd ever met. We were having so much fun. One night we got pissed, as students do. I went back to my room and the next morning the police were hammering at the door. They told me she was dead and arrested me for her murder.'

The tone was sad but not self-pitying. Briony felt a lump in her throat, which was a good sign. She glanced at Tania, but her face was inscrutable.

'You have no memory of what happened?'

'No. I remember going home. I didn't live on campus so I caught the train back into town.'

'Were you sleeping together?'

'Yes.'

'So why didn't you stay?'

'Exams were starting and she had an essay to finish. We both had to revise. I must admit, I got home and fell asleep.'

'Who was more drunk, you or her?'

'Probably me. She made a big pot of coffee to sober herself up. And she told me to go. She said I'd be a distraction.'

'The police didn't believe you.'

'The shock of her death completely threw me. When they arrested me, I don't think I could string a sentence together. I was a total mess. They interviewed me for what seemed like hours and hours. They said I might've blacked out, just not remembered what I'd done. And in the end I believed them.'

'Why?'

'I don't know. I suppose it was because they were the police.'

'You think they manipulated you?'

'I was eighteen and I was petrified. I was a good kid, bit of a swot, I'd never been in any kind of trouble.'

Tania Jones nodded her head slowly. Her eyes had never left Nathan's face. Briony dared to hope.

The producer laced her fingers and took a breath. 'Well —'

But she didn't get a chance to say more. The door opened and Gordon Kramer came wandering in with a mug of coffee in his hand. A large man in his middle sixties, he had the red, rumpled face of too much sunburn acquired in foreign climes.

Tania snapped into action, giving her husband a brisk smile. 'Darling, you remember Briony Rowe. Did some brilliant editing for us a few years back.'

'Absolutely. Great to see you, Briony.' He seized her hand in his chunky paw.

'And this is Nathan Wade. He's been the victim of the most atrocious miscarriage of justice.'

Briony's heart soared.

Gordon nodded sagely as he shook hands. 'Judicial system's a fucking mess. And as for the prisons! You can't expect to keep people on lockdown twenty-four hours a day and act surprised when all they want to do is take drugs. I think if we can get a couple of hidden cameras in there—'

'That's a different project, Gordon.'

'Oh—'

'Nathan's not actually in prison any more.'

'Oh.' The big man blinked a couple of times and took a slug of coffee. His eyes were a watery blue, with girlish lashes, and gave the impression that he was staring towards some far-flung horizon.

Briony felt nervous. The atmosphere in the room had changed, and she sensed the momentum ebbing.

She had to do something. 'Well, he's only just been released and—' And what? She hesitated.

Help came from an unexpected quarter. 'I haven't been released officially yet. I'm on a ROTL.'

'A what?' Kramer's restless gaze swivelled to focus on Nathan.

'Release on a temporary licence. If you're a lifer, they let you out for a bit, sort of see if you can be trusted. Then you go back, get assessed, wait for reports. And you're right, all that's a nightmare nowadays, because they haven't got the staff. Everything's been privatized and cut to the bone.'

Kramer nodded. 'How long have you been in?'

'Sixteen years.'

'You must've seen the prison estate change.'

'Oh yeah. Loads.'

The veteran reporter nodded again, but Briony got the impression he was bored.

Tania Jones stood up abruptly. 'The really exciting thing here, Gordon, is Nathan's personal story.' She strolled over to the side table where the intern had laid out coffee.

He frowned. 'Yeah, but we need to be challenging these bastards. And the politics—'

'Are important, obviously, darling. But the viewer needs a prism through which to access them. Emotional engagement is key. And we have more than one issue in play here. Don't we, Briony?'

'Absolutely. Prisons, but also the whole judicial system. Miscarriages of justice are becoming more common.'

Briony had no evidence for this assertion, but it sounded good and had the desired effect of hooking Gordon Kramer's wandering attention.

'Fair enough, but proper investigative journalism requires that we back up the argument with analysis. You know my views, Tania. We're not going soft.'

'There's nothing soft about a man who's spent most of his

adult life in jail for a murder he didn't commit.' She sounded tetchy.

Nathan watched the couple slugging it out. It felt as though they were talking about someone else, a stranger, not him.

Kramer dumped his coffee mug on the table with a decided snap. 'Don't tell me about what the broadcasters will buy.'

Tania sighed. 'I'm not telling you anything you don't already know.'

'There's not one bloody commissioning editor out there with the cojones to stick their neck out. And as for the bloody BBC! They've got their nose so far up the government's arse. I'll give them emotional bloody engagement!'

He shook his head sorrowfully, then seemed to notice there were two other people in the room.

'Good luck, mate. Hope it works out for you.' A brisk handshake with Nathan and he disappeared out of the door.

Briony turned towards Tania Jones with a sinking feeling. Was that it? A thumbs down?

But the producer exhaled and gave them her best professional smile. 'I've got a couple of excellent young researchers I want to work with you on this. Show them all the material and we can put together an outline. As Gordon says, something punchy. And moving. We'll also need to consider a trailer.'

Briony tried not to look surprised. 'I'm already working on that.'

'Excellent.'

Tania glanced at her phone. She had a lunch at Sky and needed to wrap this up.

But Briony was emboldened. 'I want to retain creative control. For Nathan's sake.'

The producer shrugged. 'You direct, we produce. I'm sure we can agree that we both have Nathan's best interests at heart. And if we're going to put up development money…'

Briony's eyes lit up. It also had the desired effect of shutting her up.

Nathan smiled to himself. He knew Briony had been trying to fob him off. No money for ages until the film was out there and made a profit! That had clearly been a lie.

Gordon Kramer may be a legend and an angry old warhorse, but Nathan quite liked him; at least he said what he thought. Tania Jones was a far more shifty proposition. Despite the placatory tone she used with her husband, it was obvious that she called the shots.

She'd become preoccupied with scrolling through the messages on her phone. Nathan suspected this was a ploy. Abruptly, she flashed them a smile and sighed. 'I'm so sorry, I'm being terribly rude here, but we've got rather a lot on the slate at the moment. And it's quite a juggling act keeping all the balls in the air.'

Briony responded by grinning like the cat who'd got the cream. 'Obviously, Nathan's priority is to clear his name, so I've been talking to the Free Representation Unit about getting someone pro-bono.'

'Excellent. A serious and credible lawyer will help. Plus, the faster we can move things along…'

Nathan didn't give a monkey's about clearing his name. That was water under the bridge. Being out was all that mattered. And getting some cash. He'd had more than enough truck with lawyers and courts to last a lifetime. But he decided not to mention that.

'Getting an application into the CCRC is what will take the time.' Briony sounded like an expert.

'Obviously. And the Boden family?'

'The mother's on board. I'm working on the sister.'

The remark was casual; it hit Nathan like a sucker-punch. He shot the film-maker an incredulous look. It was news to him that Briony had even contacted Sarah's family.

'You plan to involve the Bodens?'

'Well, yes. Of course.' She frowned at him and turned back to Tania, beaming like a conjurer about to produce the rabbit. 'But here's something you're going to love. I've only just found out. The sister is a police officer. An actual detective in the Met.'

This was enough to drag Tania Jones' attention from her phone. 'Seriously?'

Briony gave a modest shrug.

Nathan stared at them both in disbelief. She'd never mentioned involving the Bodens. He needed time to think.

Tania seized his hand, did the awful double hand-clasp again and told him how great it was to meet him. Moments later they were back out on the pavement.

Briony was thoughtful. She patted his arm. 'You did well, Nathan.'

He nodded, but continued to look glum.

Briony scanned him. 'You okay?'

'I need some new clothes.'

'Clothes?' She seemed surprised.

'Yeah. I think we should go shopping.'

24

For her second encounter with Ivan Rossi, Jo chose skinny jeans and a silky top with a plunging neckline under her leather jacket. As soon as she walked into the estate agent's shop on Shepherd's Bush Green, he was on his feet, wreathed in smiles.

She'd left it a couple of days, ignoring his phone calls. Then she'd sent him a brief text, agreeing to some viewings. Her feigned ambivalence had paid off. He was more than delighted to see her.

The downtime she'd spent in the office looking at the skimpy intel they had on his family. The Belarusian connection on his mother's side was short on detail and there was no concrete evidence of a close relationship with his uncle or even if they'd ever met. But she had a useful chat with Sandra, the civilian analyst on the team, on what they knew about the European end of the smuggling operation. The arms probably came through Poland, and then by various routes to the Channel ports.

Vaizey had passed her in the corridor; he'd seemed preoccupied and had given her a curt nod.

A strategy discussion with Foley had gone better than she'd expected. They'd formulated a plan. He'd read her report and listened to the audio—Jo wondered if he'd passed it up to the boss—she couldn't tell from his non-committal comments. But she was determined not to display any insecurity or lack of confidence, so she didn't ask.

Dealing with Foley had turned into a bit of a game. Acting tough and disinterested had the effect of making him dial down the sarcasm and aggression, which Jo began to think was a mask for his own hang-ups. He wasn't the first male officer she'd encountered who found it problematic working with younger female colleagues. She'd done a short stint on an MIT, where the lad culture and sexist jibes had bordered on harassment. You couldn't challenge it, you had to play along or you were dubbed a humourless bitch. It was essential to never show any hint of vulnerability. Whatever the official policy at the top, in the lower reaches, the hidden regressive corners of many large organizations, it was still how you survived. This was particularly true in the Met.

But feeling she'd got the measure of Foley had improved her mood. The incident on the tube still niggled, but she'd put it aside. Living in a city like London occasionally exposed you to such ugly behaviour. But if she was to continue to function as a cop and do her job effectively, she couldn't afford to take it to heart or get paranoid. Her priority was to keep a clear head, not to mention her nerve. She'd heard nothing from Jabreel Khan and presumed that something was being done about the Kelmendis and their threats. Maybe the encounter on the tube was related, maybe not. She couldn't be sure either way.

Ivan Rossi took her to a coffee shop round the corner from his office, set up his laptop on the table and tried to wow her with a series of luxury apartments, none of which had a price tag of less than two million pounds.

Jo hummed and hawed. What interested her was the laptop. So she downed her espresso in two gulps and he offered to get her another. While he went to the counter to queue, she scrolled through the various sets of property details. She had little expectation that a work computer would contain anything incriminating—she had no time for a proper look—what she was hoping for was some kind of small personal detail that might prove useful. But she didn't want to make him suspicious.

As he approached with her coffee, she leant back in her chair and smiled at him. 'Thank you. I need this.' That much at least was true.

He grinned. 'I'm no good until my third. Brain doesn't function.'

'I know what you mean.' She let her skittish gaze rest on him a moment longer than necessary.

He gave her a bashful smile. There was something winsome and chirpy about him that was hard not to find appealing.

'So, you're looking for a place on your own? I don't want to pry, but a single woman, I think security needs to be high on the list. Secure underground parking, twenty-four/seven concierge—'

Jo threw him a nervous look. 'I'm not actually single.'

'Oh. Sorry, I didn't mean to presume. A girl like you! Why would you be single?' He chuckled to cover the fact he was being disingenuous. It was clear he'd guessed and made his own deductions from the line she'd fed him at their first meeting.

'Can I tell you a secret, Ivan?'

'Of course.'

'My boyfriend. He doesn't know I'm looking for a place. I'm trying to get away from him.'

'I see.' Another edgy chuckle.

'He'll go ballistic when he finds out.'

'Well, you can rely on my absolute discretion.' He puffed out his chest.

Jo swallowed hard and blinked her eyes. She didn't manage to produce any tears, but she gave a reasonable impression of holding them back as she whispered. 'You're so sweet.'

'It's a brave thing you're doing, Charlotte. You don't have to put up with stuff.' He was staring at the yellowing bruise across the bridge of her nose. 'No woman should.'

'I know. But it's hard.' Placing a hand over her mouth, she turned away.

'My dad's Italian. Bit macho. But he taught me this: a man who raises his hand to a woman is not a man.' There was vehemence in his tone and Jo rewarded him with a sad smile.

She hunched her shoulders and changed the subject. 'Ivan's not a very Italian name. Shouldn't you be called Fabio or something like that?'

'It's after my grandfather on the other side. Mum's from Belarus. Her dad was Russian. I'm a complete mongrel.'

'Do you speak Italian? Or even Belarusian?'

He laughed. 'Mate, it takes me all my time to speak English! My mum hates it, she's very big on family.'

Jo's wandering gaze strayed to the screensaver that had popped up on Ivan's laptop and there it was, the nugget she was looking for: a series of pictures of boats. As each image dissolved and the pixels reconfigured, she realized it was the same boat, a sizeable cabin cruiser.

'Nice boat! I love the water.'

He folded his arms, gave her a swaggering smile. 'Actually, it's mine.'

'No kidding! You own a boat!'

He responded with a modest nod.

'I adore boats. When I was a kid, my dad had a forty-foot cruiser, kept it in Cornwall on the Helford River.' She was improvising now, adrenaline pumping, monitoring his reaction beat by beat. But the flakey, fragile Charlotte act seemed to be doing the trick. His eyes were intense, there was a whiff of desire. He was hooked. 'Every summer we went down there. Until they got divorced.' She frowned and looped her tumbling hair behind her ear with one finger. 'I miss it.'

'Hey, I could take you out on my boat sometime.'

She shook her head. 'No, I couldn't—'

'Why not?' He reached across the table and put his hand on hers. 'Charlotte, you don't have to be scared.'

'You don't know him. What he's capable of.' Pulling her hand away, she hesitated. 'And he knows people, if you get what I mean.'

A sly smile spread over Ivan's features. 'Yeah, well, I'm not the sort of guy who's easily intimidated. And I know a few people myself.'

'I can't involve you in my problems.'

'Why not?'

Right on cue, her phone chirruped. She glanced at it, scanned the text. 'Oh shit! I told him I was going shopping at Westfield. He wants to pick me up.'

'We're going to find you a flat and you're going to get away from him.'

She leapt to her feet, shot him an agitated look. 'He mustn't see me with you. He gets so jealous. I'm sorry, we'll have to do the viewings another day.'

'You know, I can help you. And I don't just mean sell you a flat.'

'Take me out on your boat? I'd love that.' Jo gave him a wistful smile. 'I'd love to go back to Cornwall, in and out of all those little estuaries.'

'My boat's a bit nearer to home, moored off Southampton Water. But it's in a river estuary too, so it's pretty similar. You'd like it.'

Her phone buzzed again. Jo gave it a panicky glance and grabbed her bag. 'Sorry, Ivan, I've got to go.'

He got up. 'You've got my number. Anytime, Charlotte. If you need somewhere. I mean it.'

Ignoring him, Jo scooped up the phone and ran out of the door. She scooted across the road, dodging the traffic. She didn't look back. There was no need to. She knew he was watching.

On the corner of the Green, at the spot they'd prearranged, Foley pulled up in a dark unmarked BMW. Jo opened the passenger door and jumped in. They drove off up Goldhawk Road, passing Ivan Rossi, who was standing on the pavement, laptop tucked under his arm.

Foley turned to her. 'Is he watching? Has he seen me?'

She glanced over her shoulder out of the tinted back window. 'Oh yeah.'

25

At Nathan's insistence, he and Briony took a detour to Oxford Street. He had little brand awareness but still gravitated to the more expensive shops. He refused Briony's suggestion of a cheap suit. Suit, he argued, was not the right image. He'd look like an old lag. He opted instead for well-cut black jeans, a charcoal grey sports jacket and a Ted Baker shirt.

Briony tried not to dwell on the burden this added to one of her many over-extended credit cards. She had to admit he looked much better, a glimpse of the old Nathan, the boy who once stole her heart. She considered suggesting a haircut and a return to the aviator shades. But then realized she was getting carried away. This wasn't about turning back the clock, much as that appealed. The motif for the film was waste, the lost years, the gaunt cheeks, the haunted eyes. A complete makeover certainly needed to be resisted.

While he was trying on shirts, she called the lawyer and he agreed to join them for lunch at an Indian vegetarian restaurant in Rathbone Street.

To someone who'd been living on prison grub and coffee shop muffins, the Keralan menu was exotic and confusing for

Nathan. Briony took charge and ordered several starters while they waited for the barrister to arrive.

Nathan watched her tuck in. 'So they're going to make your film?'

'They'll pitch it.'

'I thought that's what we were doing.'

'They'll pitch it to a broadcaster.'

'Then what?'

Briony wiped her lips. 'We get a commission and we make the film.' No mention of the development money, Nathan noted.

'So "we" is us and Tania and Gordon?'

'They'll produce, I'll direct. But we'll have creative control.'

'Did she say that?' This was one part of the conversation Nathan had understood. Tania Jones had fudged it.

The film-maker shrugged. 'You've just got to trust me on this, Nathan. No one's going to sell you down the river.'

He said nothing. He was thinking about the development money and how to get a 50:50 split. Picking up a vegetable samosa, he took a bite.

Briony grinned at him. 'Aren't they great?'

He nodded. 'You probably think I'm stupid, but to an outsider it's difficult to figure out what's going on.'

She reached across the table and covered his hand with her own. 'That's why you've got me.'

He couldn't help noticing the oily sheen on her fingers.

'I'll be honest with you, Briony, all this clearing my name stuff seems like a lot of effort for nothing. What will I gain? I'm already out.'

'For a start, they won't be able to revoke your licence and send you back.'

'True enough, but I don't intend getting in any trouble.'

'Nathan, this is a miscarriage of justice. Going to the CCRC, overturning your conviction, that's your quest. It's what it's all about.'

'I know but—' He sounded peevish.

Briony gave him a speculative look. 'And if it succeeds, of course there'll be compensation.' She watched the sulky protruding bottom lip loosen. She was learning which buttons to press. 'Wrongful conviction, sixteen years inside, could be a tidy sum.'

'I never thought of that.'

'Why would you? You're not a mercenary sort of bloke. I understand how fed up you must be with the judicial process. It's let you down. Chewed you up and spat you out. But one last push, eh? Surely it's worth it?'

He was staring at the cuffs on his new shirt. The underside was paisley and contrasted with the fine blue line on the rest of the shirt.

He frowned. 'Not sure about these cuffs.'

Briony watched him, a tetchy boy, turned middle-aged and disappointed before his time. 'Fashions change. There are a lot of things for you to get used to, Nathan. And it's not easy, I know that.'

Nathan shot her a surly glance. He preferred it when she was hustling him. He didn't want her sympathy, still less her pity. 'So what's the deal with this bloody lawyer?'

Briony accepted the rebuff with a smile. 'Okay, this is how it works. To get the lawyer to work for nothing, we have to offer him something he wants.'

'You said this unit was pro bono? Isn't that the idea? They do it for nothing?'

'Well, yes.' She sighed. 'But to get someone good, and persuade them to spend time on your case, we need them to think it's worth their while. The legal aid budget's gone down the toilet, so there are loads of people who want their help, deserving people. How do they choose?'

He nodded. 'But if they get to go on television that boosts their profile and helps their career?'

'Exactly. You do get it. It's basic psychology.'

'How do you know the one you've got is good?'

'I've checked him out. Very high-profile chambers, so he's got smart people who'll help him out. Dad's a QC, ditto. First from Oxford. But most of all, he'll want to be the guy who proved, when he was only twenty-five, that Nathan Wade was innocent.'

'Twenty-five? Jesus wept! Don't we need someone more experienced?'

'Experience is expensive.'

'Can't we ask Tania to pay for it?'

'No, Nathan! She can't interfere with the case. That would be unethical.'

Nathan pondered this as he munched on his samosa. That seemed ridiculous. What had ethics to do with any of this? It was the same as in the nick, a trading game. In order to get people to help you, you had to give them something they wanted. Everything came with a price tag. He thought of his friend, Lech. And Mateusz and Danuta. They'd offered him their friendship and asked nothing in return. But then this was why they were stuck in Littlehampton doing the shit jobs no one else wanted. Nathan knew one thing, he wasn't ending up like that.

Briony beamed at him. 'Don't look so down in the mouth. This is all good.' She glanced at the door and waved. 'Ah, here he is!'

Henry McNair-Phillips came scooting round the tables towards them like a young puppy, full of exuberance, who hadn't yet learnt how to avoid bumping into things. He had an over-stuffed backpack, a wayward tie, and a six-foot-six rake-thin frame he had trouble controlling, causing him to have to apologize to several other diners before he made it to their table.

Briony had known the moment she'd set eyes on him he'd be perfect. His chaotic energy, the unruly hair, the glasses, created enough of an impression of a certain popular boy wizard. Which was good because his job was to come up with the magic to set poor Nathan free.

Plonking down his backpack, the lawyer held out his hand. 'Harry McNair-Phillips. Terrific to meet you, Nathan.'

The day had already provided Nathan with enough challenging experiences—he was trying hard not to think about the Bodens—so the arrival of his new legal champion wasn't as much of a shock as it might've been. He managed a smile and a handshake. Then he sat back as Briony took over.

'Fantastic meeting with Gordon and Tania. They're definitely up for it.'

'Excellent.'

'Miscarriages of justice are a hot topic. I don't think it'll take long to get a broadcaster on board.'

'Great PR for the pro bono unit. Thanks for choosing me.'

Having sat down, the lawyer was rooting around in his backpack. He extracted an iPad. 'Now, let me see. Where is it?' He opened the tablet and scrolled. 'Right, now I've been through the list of trial documents, and guess what I've found?'

Briony and Nathan glanced at each other.

Harry read from the screen. 'Item ten: CCTV from station, no ID possible.'

Briony nodded as if she understood.

Nathan frowned. 'What does that mean?'

Harry beamed. 'Well, it means that in the case file, which

the police will have in storage, there is recorded CCTV footage from the railway station. And you said in your statement that on the night in question you ran across campus and got to the station just in time to catch the last train back into town. Am I right?'

'Yeah. But my lawyers said we couldn't prove it.'

'There's a chance that now we can. We get hold of that CCTV.' He held up the iPad, pointing to the screen. 'Look here, according to the record, they've still got it. Then we get it re-examined by some shit-hot techies. They've got all kinds of digital kit nowadays that can take old CCTV and get an image, where it was too blurry before. So, my friend, if they come up with a picture of you getting on that train, then that's the new evidence we need to get through the door and persuade the CCRC to review your case.'

Nathan stared at them. It took him a few moments to absorb what the lawyer was saying. In recent years, he had given little serious thought to what had happened that night, or even what he could remember of it. There was no point. The ghost of Sarah was always floating around somewhere, teasing and taunting him as she always had. But the sequence of events had ossified into a tale that had hardened with repetition.

Sixteen years later, it was impossible for him to sort fact from fiction. That night he'd had a lot of dope, quite high-grade stuff he'd got from a dealer in town. He'd also been selling it on to his mates to chill the pre-exam nerves. But he didn't mention any of this to the police; he was worried if he ratted, the dealer would get pissed off. That seemed absurd now. Blood tests had revealed both alcohol and cannabis in his system. He insisted he'd only smoked a couple of spliffs and had stuck to that line.

The train he remembered. Someone had puked in the

carriage and the acrid reek of it had almost made him throw up himself. Then he'd fallen asleep.

What would any court make of it all now? The argument for the defence had always been that if he'd caught the last train, he couldn't have killed her. The jury hadn't bought it then and Nathan doubted that any high-tech wizardry was about to change that.

The Crown Prosecution Service, the police, the media, the family, the university, everyone had needed a result. Didn't much matter if it was the right result. The system had to be seen to work. In Nathan's view, that was the only truth you could rely on.

26

There were a dozen people in the room for the briefing; Jo sat at the back, tucked away. She found it odd, hearing her own disembodied voice. It sounded simpering and girly, which made her squirm, but everyone else listened attentively to the recording. The quality was excellent, considering she'd made it on a phone dumped on the table with all the background rumpus of a busy coffee shop.

It ended abruptly when she'd jumped up, grabbed the phone and left. Ivan Rossi's last words: *If you need some-where. I mean it*—were quite distinct, his tone heartfelt, but hearing them again, in this impersonal context, left her with an uneasy feeling. The ploy of exploiting his sympathies hadn't been her idea, but she'd executed it. Listening to the recording now, it felt devious. She had to remind herself that there were much larger issues at stake here and the fact he was nice to *Charlotte* didn't mean he wasn't a criminal. Gun smugglers were the worst kind of scumbags, so why was she even doubting the strategy? The end certainly justified the means.

Steve Vaizey lounged at the head of the conference table,

twizzling a gel pen round and round between his fingers. 'Slick work, DC Boden. Well done.'

Slick. Yes, this was her role, to be professional and detached and to serve the greater good. A couple of envious glances strayed in her direction, but she'd deliberately placed herself out of Vaizey's sight line.

He got up. 'Okay, what about this boat? Sandra?'

The analyst was a matronly figure with an exploding mop of frizzed grey hair and half-moon glasses. She'd been doing the job for aeons longer than the steady stream of warranted officers, who came and went on an operation like Grebe, and commanded respect. She drank coffee from an outsized mug and to get in her good books, Jo had soon discovered, required Krispy Kreme doughnuts.

With a raspy smoker's cough, the analyst cleared her throat. 'Quite a few marinas and moorings off Southampton Water. We're working through them. Some have a more formal registration process than others. But, from the description, it's a biggish boat, forty-footer, so it would probably require a pontoon mooring, which should make tracing it marginally easier.'

Vaizey was pacing, he rarely stood still. He shot a glance at Jo. 'Anything else you can give us?'

Colleagues craned their necks. Suddenly all eyes were on her. Foley had already berated her over her failure to get an actual picture of Ivan's boat.

In their drive from Shepherd's Bush back to the office, she'd filled him in on what she'd discovered. His response, as on previous occasions, was hyper-critical. She was still trying to decide if always undermining her was a reflex action or a conscious tactic on his part. Either way, it was becoming a major pain in the neck.

Her reaction had been to keep her head down until she

could find an effective way to combat him.

But with Vaizey addressing her directly, she had to take the bull by the horns.

She stood up. 'I'm sorry I didn't get a shot of it, boss. It was too risky. But I've got a good mental picture and Sandra and I have already identified some close parallels.'

They'd also come up with another lead, but Jo decided to hold on to that for the time being. She wasn't giving any hostages to fortune. Her gaze met Foley's across the table. He was staring at her blankly, a simmering anger behind his black eyes. Jo wondered what that was all about. It felt personal. But why? What had she ever done to him?

Vaizey went on to issue some further instructions about setting up liaisons with the coastguard, Border Force, and Hampshire Police. If Ivan's boat turned out to be the one used for smuggling arms, they would all be needed. The meeting finished shortly after five o'clock.

Jo was gathering up her notebook and peripherals when Vaizey came over, flanked by Foley.

The boss grinned. 'Well, you two seem to make a good team.'

Foley's smile looked more like a baring of fangs to Jo as he placed his hand on her shoulder. But his tone was chummy. 'She's a fast learner, aren't you, kiddo?'

She felt the weight of his palm; his height—well over six foot—seemed to pin her down. She forced a smile.

Vaizey stroked his chin and nodded. 'I leave it to you two to decide how and when we go back to Rossi.'

Foley responded immediately, the hand still heavy on her shoulder. 'I'm sure Jo would agree with me, the sooner the better. We need to ramp up the pressure.'

Easing herself free of his grasp, Jo stepped back and focused on Vaizey. 'Actually, sir, I think we should give him some space. Find the boat. Then a phone call before another visit. We don't want to spook him.'

'Okay.' He glanced at Foley. 'Cal?'

The DS shrugged. She could see he hated being contradicted. 'Clock's ticking. As long as we don't forget that.'

His eyes had narrowed and Jo felt triumphant. If the bastard thought he could bully her, he needed to think again.

He painted on a smile. 'You coming for a drink, Jo? Celebrate our small victory. My shout.' He beamed at her, his new best friend.

But it was clear that this whole performance was for Vaizey's benefit. Jo smiled. She had the measure of him now and was ready for his tricks. 'No, thanks, mate. I've got a few bits I need to do.'

Foley chuckled and turned to Vaizey. 'You're my witness, boss. I offered to pay.' He chuckled. The hollowness of it reverberated through Jo but strengthened her resolve.

Vaizey patted his shoulder. 'Can't say fairer than that. Have a good evening, Cal.'

Foley had little option but to join the stream of officers already filing out and dispersing. Jo watched him go; she'd won the skirmish, but it was only the first tussle in what she suspected would be a long campaign. The thought wearied her.

Vaizey was about to follow but hesitated and gave her a quizzical look. 'Everything all right?'

The room was emptying and there was a gentleness and genuine concern in his tone, which slipped seductively under her guard. He was inviting her confidence, maybe even offering protection. How she'd love to be protected by him.

Foley's attitude to her was weird. Plus, he was a bully. But she didn't want to come over as weak or unprofessional to her new boss.

She shrugged and smiled. 'Absolutely fine. I'm just think-ing. I've got a theory about the boat I want to test out.'

One of the support staff was unplugging the laptop used for the PowerPoint presentation. Everyone else had left the room.

Vaizey slotted his pen into the breast pocket of his shirt. 'Don't let Cal unnerve you. He's over-enthusiastic at times, and a bit gauche, especially with women, but an excellent DS.'

'He doesn't bother me, sir.' She sounded ultra cool and collected, which was a relief.

'Well, that's good. I always had a hunch you'd be tough. And that's what this job demands. Not for the faint-hearted.'

His gaze was hard to decipher. The eyes were grey with a bluish tinge. They had an uncompromising directness and she suspected he used the rimless glasses to make himself seem more urbane. The look held her for hardly a second, but Jo felt a flicker of desire. With an awkward smile, he immedi-ately turned away.

He seemed embarrassed. 'I should get on.'

'Yeah, me too.'

He stood back for her to go first. She walked out of the room and down the corridor without a backward glance. But the scent of something expensive and masculine drifted past her.

He was such a contrast to Foley. None of that drive to sublimate because she was a woman who triggered some uncomfortable carnal desires. Office politics were only ever about two things: competition and sex. Both were traps for the unwary.

Jo settled back at her desk and spent the next hour chasing round the internet trying to pin down a connection between Ivan Rossi—possibly in the form of a directorship—and one of the many small companies with vessels registered on moorings around Southampton Water. It was a laborious task that Sandra had already begun before she'd gone home to feed her teenage brood. The theory that the two women had developed was that the boat would be registered through a front company, but that, somewhere in the small print, Rossi's name would appear.

By six thirty the open-plan office was deserted. Outside it was already pitch-black and icy slivers of sleet streaked the windows. Working had always been Jo's way of transmuting unruly thoughts or feelings. It grounded her. Being a police officer, and consumed by the job, was the very thing that had rescued her from the desolation of her teenage years. She often wished that her mother could understand that. But she didn't.

Leaning back from the screen, Jo eased the crease between her brows with her index finger. A young woman was strolling across the room towards her. A pang of guilt over Razan caught her off guard, because this girl also wore a hijab. They hadn't been introduced, but Jo recognized her as one of the admin support staff.

She stopped beside Jo's desk and smiled. 'The Detective Super's told me to call you a cab and put it on the account. There's a storm forecast. He says you should go home.'

Steve Vaizey was thinking about her. He was taking care of her. Should she read anything personal into it? No, definitely not. That would be stupid. He was her boss, possibly ten years older than her, and he wore a platinum wedding ring.

Still, as she switched off her screen and gathered her things, she couldn't help wondering about the frisson that had passed between them earlier. Something or nothing? She couldn't be sure.

27

Jo rarely splashed out on taxi rides across London, but two in less than a week was a luxury she could get used to. Settled in the back, with a brand-new people carrier to herself, she had time to reflect and maybe even dream.

Traffic on the Embankment was creeping through the mizzle. But as the temperature plummeted, the rain thickened into a deluge of fat icy crystals. The river itself was a churning torrent. The road ahead became a wall of sleet and the windscreen wipers clacked as they struggled to clear the cascade beating down on the cab.

Forced to slow to a crawl, the driver raised his hand from the wheel. 'Look at it! I'd call this a blizzard. They put out an amber weather warning on the radio. Don't make no difference. Everything still grinds to a bloody halt.'

Jo had been oblivious. The ice storm had engulfed them without her realizing. She'd been miles away. Thinking about what? A man she couldn't have?

The driver was obviously waiting for a response. She smiled. 'Yeah, it's awful.'

'This is gonna take a while, love. I'm sorry. I was gonna

do Lambeth Bridge, down to the Elephant, then the Old Kent Road.'

'Don't worry. It's not a problem.'

And it wasn't. Being cocooned in the capsule of the cab suited her mood. The tempest was out there, but she was safe and dry. It could snow all it liked.

When they finally got to Greenwich, the cloudburst had eased. The snow had turned back to rain, but it was still slushy underfoot.

The streetlamp across the road from her mother's house was out, but Jo made a dash from the taxi to the front door and let herself in. The house was in darkness. She flicked the light on and jumped out of her skin when she saw Alison sitting there on the sofa, clutching a large glass of white wine. It didn't look like her first.

'Mum! What are you doing sitting in the dark?'

'Didn't you get my message?'

Jo didn't want to admit she'd been ignoring her phone. 'I've been a bit busy. Sorry.'

'I've been scared out of my wits, Jo. So I kept the lights off. I don't understand what's going on.'

'Why? What's happened?'

Alison stood up, and Jo could see she was shaking. Putting the wine glass down, she walked, shoulders hunched, towards the back door and unlocked it. 'There. See for yourself.'

There was a black bin bag outside the door in an icy puddle on the paved patio.

'What is it?'

Alison was close to tears. 'It was on the front step. I had to pick it up.'

Jo opened the top of the bag and peered in. The smell that assailed her was both metallic and feral. Blood? Excrement?

All she could see was a tuft of ginger fur. It looked like some sort of dead animal.

Alison put a hand over her mouth and suppressed a sob. 'Someone hammered on the door in the middle of the storm. Sounded urgent, so I went to answer. He was just dumped there, throat cut, covered in blood. Don't you recognize him? It's next-door's cat.'

28

Two phone calls and a slew of late-night texts went unanswered, so it surprised Jo when Jabreel Khan turned up on the doorstep at eight the next morning. She was still in her pyjamas, having spent half the night trying to calm her mother down. Alison had drunk too much wine and refused to go to bed. They'd had a ridiculous conversation about what to say to the next-door neighbours.

The Kempsons were an elderly couple. She went out rarely. He struggled down to the shops with a stick. They had a daughter living somewhere on the south coast. Alison shopped for them occasionally, but they were proud people, unwilling to ask for help. The cat was an amiable old tom called Marmalade. His regular perch was Alison's front wall, so he could've been mistaken for their cat.

Jo's strategy was to tell them that the cat had been run over. She'd found it and would dispose of it for them. Alison argued with this. What if they wanted to see it? Bury it in the garden? Jo thought it unlikely. They went round in circles, trying to second-guess the Kempsons' reaction for what seemed like hours.

It was Saturday morning and a watery sun was struggling to break through when Jo opened the door to Khan. She hardly recognized him. The dirty hoodie was gone and the beard shaved. He was wearing a blue polo shirt, a soft leather jacket and chinos.

Alison was still upstairs in bed. Jo took him straight out into the damp garden and showed him the dead cat.

'I'm sorry about all the texts. My mum got a bit hysterical about the whole thing. And I didn't want to involve the local force in case it complicated the issue.'

Jabreel was peering into the bin bag. 'Thank you for that. Your cat?'

'No. Next-door's. But he always sat on our wall.'

He shook his head and exhaled. 'Well, Fejzi Kelmendi was arrested on Thursday. He left North Cyprus, went down to Limassol and got into a fight in a bar. The Cypriot authorities are happy to act on the European Arrest Warrant and hand him over to us. They want rid of him.'

'So you're off the case?'

'There are some loose ends.' He sounded evasive. 'But it was decided that I was too compromised.'

'Bet you're relieved.'

Jo was fishing, hoping for more details. Although his appearance had changed, he still looked bone-weary, with deep shadows under his eyes.

But he ignored the comment. 'As regards you, we think the Kelmendis subcontracted the job out to a street gang from Peckham.'

'And this is their handiwork?'

'We think so. But don't worry, we know who they are.'

He was trying to sound reassuring even though his gaze zigzagged nervously round the room. He grasped the door handle to control the tremor in his hands. Jo watched with concern. DC Khan wasn't even running on adrenaline any more; he was completely burnt out.

Jo knew she should probably be having this conversation with her old boss, Dave Hollingsworth. But he hadn't even wanted her to be told that she was being targeted.

She sighed. 'There was something else that happened. It could be related, but I'm not sure.'

'What?'

'A kid came up behind me on the escalator on the tube. It felt threatening. I thought he was going to push me.'

Jabreel frowned. 'When? You should've called me.'

'Couple of days ago. But I'm probably being paranoid.'

'Did he look like a gang member?'

'He was young and black and wore a hoodie. But I don't want to jump to any conclusions. Most likely it was just random.'

He squinted into the bag at the dead cat. His whole body was jittery. He couldn't meet her gaze. Jo continued to scan him.

'You think the two things are connected?'

He shrugged.

She'd been part of the team that had taken down the Kelmendis, but there were aspects of the operation she simply didn't know about, and it seemed unlikely that Jabreel would fill her in.

Lying awake most of the night, hyper-vigilant and listening for any unusual sounds, the questions had crowded in on her. If it was Ardi Kelmendi's intention to terrorize her as a punishment, he'd succeeded.

'Jabreel, how did they even know I was here?'

'We're looking into that.'

'How could an informant on the inside, in the office even, come up with my mother's address?'

'You may have been followed?'

'I've got a teenage gang from Peckham stalking me? Is that what you're saying?'

'Jo, we are handling this. It's all under control, I promise you.'

The day was raw, the garden a mass of dank foliage. But beads of sweat had formed on his forehead.

'Why don't I feel reassured?'

He shrugged and picked up the bin bag. 'Want me to get rid of this for you?'

She nodded. They went back into the house. He carried the dripping bag through to the front door and rested it on the bristled coir mat.

Jo raked her fingers through her hair. Exasperation engulfed her. 'So if I go to Hollingsworth about this, you're in trouble for telling me?'

He heaved a sigh. 'I've been stood down, sent on leave. So, yeah, probably. But, end of day, it's up to you.'

'What the hell am I supposed to do, Jabreel?'

'Look, there's a team on it. Warrants have been issued. It will be all right, Jo. You have my word.' His dark eyes seemed feverish.

She was about to reply when Alison appeared on the stairs. As she came down, Jo wondered if her mother had heard the tail end of this. But she smiled. She was dressed up in a skirt and her best silk blouse.

'Mum, this is Jabreel. He's a colleague. He's come to sort Marmalade out.'

Alison gave him a calm and regal smile and Jo realized that she was zoned out. A double dose of benzodiazepine usually had this effect.

She held out her hand. 'That's very kind, Jabreel.'

'No problem, Mrs Boden.' He shot a glance at Jo. 'I

should be off. And don't worry. You won't be bothered any more.'

Jo opened the front door for him. There was little she could say. 'Thanks for coming round.'

She watched him carry the bin liner containing the dead creature to a parked Ford Focus. He opened the boot, put it inside, and gave her a nod. Jo suspected it was the last she'd ever see of him.

As she stepped back into the house, she found Alison had picked up her handbag and appeared to be waiting. Her zombielike manner confirmed Jo's worst fears.

'Mum, what have you taken? You can't just double up the dose because you're feeling stressed.'

'You need to get ready. We'll be late.'

'Late for what?'

'We're going out to lunch.'

'I haven't even had breakfast.'

'I sent you a text. We agreed to meet Briony, the film-maker. And have lunch.'

'What? You're kidding. Not today?'

'You said maybe this weekend.'

'I'm sure I didn't.'

'Well, I've arranged it. Lunch. Today.'

'No, Mum, no way!'

29

The restaurant was in Soho and not what either of them had expected. Jo's refusal had been met with a well-aimed guilt trip from her mother. The medication did have the effect of calming Alison and making her more rational. Her argument was that Jo had agreed to meet Briony Rowe and after the brutal murder of Marmalade, which she had in no way explained, it was the least she could do. In the end, Jo caved in. It seemed simpler than answering a barrage of questions about who had killed the cat and why.

They walked down Greek Street until they found the place. It was French, situated in an elegant Georgian building, and struck Jo as being far too expensive for a struggling film-maker.

As they mounted the steps to the entrance, Alison gave her daughter a ghostly smile. 'You see, it just goes to show.'

'Goes to show what?'

'That these people are serious.'

Jo shook her head. A dose of her mother's snobbery was the last thing she needed.

A narrow, panelled corridor led to the reception desk.

Alison gave Briony's name and a smart young woman escorted them through into an elegant old-fashioned dining room.

The high ceiling was decorated with ornate cornices and hung with crystal chandeliers. The style was classic—starched white linen with heavy silver cutlery—and half of the diners were Chinese tourists. The only ones who could afford a place like this, Jo reflected sourly.

Briony was seated at a round table in the corner. She got up as they approached, as did her two companions.

'Alison, I'm so glad you could come.'

'Sorry if we're a bit late.'

Jo hung back. Her mother's attitude was annoying. It would take more than a posh restaurant to get her to take this farrago seriously.

The film-maker was grinning from ear to ear. 'Let me introduce Tania Jones, who's going to be our producer. And Harry McNair-Phillips, Nathan's lawyer.'

Handshakes were exchanged and Jo found herself imprisoned in Tania Jones's double-handed clasp. 'I'm so glad you decided to come, Jo. I know you have reservations about all this. So did I, initially.'

Jo gave her a curt nod, and they all sat down.

The business of menus and drinks orders took up the next five minutes and gave Jo a chance to get the measure of the situation.

Tania Jones played hostess and presumably she was footing the bill. Harry was a pretty typical young barrister; Jo had encountered his type in court. Glib, bags of confidence and, given his obvious youth, there because getting his face on the telly would be a huge career boost.

Alcohol and benzos were not a good combination, nevertheless Alison was soon knocking back the wine. Jo let her mother run on—how difficult it had been, what a clever, talented and amazing person her dead daughter was.

Jo sat back and watched as she became all too aware that she herself was being scrutinized. Tania Jones's eyes hardly left her face. Briony Rowe shot the producer the odd surreptitious glance. It felt like they were plotting.

Finally, Tania interrupted Alison's monologue. 'The thing I'm amazed by is the family resemblance here. Sarah was so beautiful—of course I've only seen photographs—but she clearly gets her looks from you, Alison.'

Jo watched her mother down another slug of wine. 'Everyone's always said how much she took after me. Jo's got the look of her father.'

Tania's calculating gaze came to rest on Jo. 'Oh, I don't know. I think both your daughters look very much like you.'

Jo stared right back at the producer. She'd spent enough of her life being a stand-in for her sister. If that was their agenda, they could stuff it.

She'd ordered a gin and tonic and took a small sip. 'I thought we were here to talk about evidence. If you reckon Nathan Wade was wrongly convicted, where's the proof?'

Briony beamed. 'Cut to the chase. You can tell she's a detective!'

Jo gave the film-maker an icy stare.

But Harry McNair-Phillips, who'd been quietly demolishing a bowl of olives, piped up. 'Well, I've got the transcript of the trial from Nathan's old lawyers and two things stick out. First, the CCTV footage from the station.'

'Which is relevant how?' Jo had no intention of giving them an inch. They could try to charm her with their expertise, but she refused to be suckered.

Harry grinned. 'Well, as a police officer, you'll be well aware that many cold case convictions turn on the forensics.

The advances of the last ten years mean that evidence gathered at the time can be re-examined—'

'That wasn't my question. I don't need a lesson in forensics.'

'Sorry. Okay. The post-mortem established a time of death that was after 2 a.m. The defence argument was that Nathan left campus and took the last train back into town at 11.55. Even allowing for a margin of error on the PM, that would exclude him. The CCTV from the station shows passengers boarding that train. The defence argued that a young man in a brown anorak, similar to one owned by Nathan Wade, was indeed him. But the quality of the footage made proper identification impossible. However, if that footage is digitally re-mastered now, there's a good chance they could use facial recognition software to make an identification.'

'Well, yeah. Some CCTV footage can be improved a bit. And there are several techie outfits who claim to have clever software that works miracles. But I know of cases in the Met recently where crap CCTV has been re-examined and is still crap CCTV. On top of that, it could still turn out to be someone else.'

She lounged back in her chair and smoothed her napkin. If this was what they had, then her suspicions were confirmed. It was all a scam.

'True.' Harry fortified himself with a large mouthful of wine. Tania Jones was watching the exchange with a sly smile.

Alison gave her daughter a peevish look. 'It could be him. Why do you have to be so dogmatic about all this?'

Jo shook her head. 'Because, Mum, that's the role they want me to play here.' She shot an accusing look at Tania.

'Isn't it? You want me to be the dogged detective, don't you? That's my part in your little tale.'

Tania smiled. She seemed unfazed by her guest's rudeness. 'How old were you, Jo, when this terrible thing happened?'

'Eleven.'

'Have you ever reviewed the evidence?'

'No, why would I?'

'Exactly. But that's all we're asking you to do. Have an open mind. After all, you're the real expert here. You know the police. You know how it works and the enormous pressure to make an arrest and get a result. If you look at everything and you tell me you're satisfied beyond reasonable doubt that Nathan Wade murdered your sister, then we'll go away and leave you in peace. You have my word.'

Tania Jones was a shrewd operator, Jo had to admit that. The subtle flattery, plus the apparent abdication of control, were designed to gently reel her in. But it was still nonsense.

Jo glanced at her mother. Alison was blinking away a tear —she was wallowing in her usual mix of prescription drugs laced with booze and sentimentality.

'You said two things stand out. What's the second?'

Harry turned to Briony Rowe. 'We have here a witness who, for various reasons, was never interviewed by the police at the time. And it raises the possibility of an alternative suspect.'

'The stalker theory. Yeah, I've heard Briony's line. And I have to say it sounds to me like a scam. Where's the proof? Apart from Briony's say-so, is there any?'

'Oh yes.' The lawyer smiled. 'Your sister's journal of the time would appear to confirm it.'

'My sister's journal?' Jo glanced at her mother. Journal?

Did Sarah keep a journal? No one had ever mentioned this before.

Tania Jones tilted her head. She had the look of a jackal closing in on its prey. 'I presume you didn't know about this, Jo?'

Jo took a sip of her drink and lied. 'I recall she was always scribbling away in some kind of notebook.'

Alison's eyes swam with tears. 'She wrote such wonderful poetry. Don't you remember, Jo?'

'Of course I remember.' What flashed into Jo's mind was a smutty limerick her sister used to chant as the two girls jumped up and down on the bed.

Harry reached into his backpack and pulled out an iPad. 'There are short extracts from the journal in the trial transcript, but presumably the original was returned to you with all Sarah's other effects.'

Alison nodded. 'Oh yes, I've kept all her journals.'

All? There were more? The trial had included some kind of testimony from Sarah in her own words? This was a complete shock to Jo. Why didn't she know this? With Tania Jones's eagle-eyed gaze fixed on her, she struggled to mask her surprise.

The lawyer was scrolling. 'Here we go. The date is three days before she died. It's part of a whole passage full of details about what she'd been doing that day. Sounds innocuous in itself: *I walked out of the lecture theatre and there's bloody Bruce hanging around again! Has he got nothing better to do? Being a postgrad is clearly a doss. Why can't he just get the message?*'

Jo looked across the table at Briony Rowe. The filmmaker was looking uncomfortable. 'Bruce? What was his surname?'

'It wasn't his real name. It's what she called him.'

Jo continued to stare. 'What d'you mean?'

'It was a nickname. He wore a vest to show off his muscles. You know, like Bruce Willis in *Die Hard.*'

'Why did the police never search for him?'

Briony shrugged. She was sweating. She dabbed her lip with her napkin. 'Maybe no one told them about him. I don't think anyone else knew.' Her nervous gaze met Jo's.

'So this is some other bloke she knew? And you reckon you can turn him into an alternative suspect?'

'She went out with him at the beginning of the first term. Long before Nathan. And he kept hassling her.'

'According to you. But it's taken sixteen years for you to decide this is relevant.'

'I'm sorry. I know I should've spoken up—I'm really sorry.'

'Sorry?'

'I'm doing this because I want to make things right.'

'Bullshit!' Jo's pulse was thumping. Hearing her sister's words, out of the blue, from the mouth of some poncey lawyer, had sent her emotions into a tailspin. The chandelier above the table glittered; for an instant, it seemed to Jo that it was about to come crashing down on their heads. She had to escape.

'You know what I think? I think you read the transcript, saw something you could home in on and made up a story to fit it.'

'That's not true, Jo—' Briony's chin quivered.

'You don't even know his name.'

'Sarah gave everyone nicknames. It was her thing.'

'You were no friend of my sister.' Jo threw her napkin on the table and stood up. 'I've met some con artists in my time, but you lot take the biscuit.' She held out her hand to Alison.

'Come on, Mum. You asked me to listen to them. Well, I've listened.'

'But, Jo—' Alison's eyes were brimming with tears.

'An angry, controlling boyfriend attacked her, probably because she wouldn't do or give him what he wanted. Or he was drunk. Or she made him feel inadequate. Or jealous. Or all those things. Happens all the time, Mum. Nathan Wade killed Sarah. That's the banal truth. But that's no good to them because they can't make a film out of that.'

Tania dabbed the corners of her mouth with her own napkin. 'That's a very good analysis, Jo. And could be true in many ways. But what if Nathan was on that train and they just got the wrong boyfriend?'

30

Jo balanced on the top bar of the short stepladder and slid back the hatch to the loft. Alison held the ladder.

'I think maybe it's all on the right-hand side.'

'Yeah, but where's the light, Mum?'

'The bulb went ages ago. I've never replaced it.'

Jo stuck her head and shoulders up into the dark loft space and used her arms to hoist herself into a sitting position, legs dangling down through the hatch.

'Give me the torch.'

Alison handed it up to her. 'Can you see them?'

Jo shone the beam of the flashlight around the loft. It smelt musty, a combination of dry wood, decaying cardboard and fibreglass insulation, which scratched her hand. More than a dozen boxes were heaped in a jumble on the narrow boarding that spanned the roof joists.

'It's a bit of a mess up here. Did you write anything on the boxes?'

'I can't remember. Your father put it all up there for me.'

Jo had little recollection of her father ever doing anything for them, especially after the divorce. To her mind, he'd just disappeared.

She trained the torch beam on the sides of the boxes. She could make out a few random letters in faded felt-tip. With effort, she could touch some of the boxes if she stretched out her arm. It made her realize that to retrieve them, she would have to stand up. She reached out and grabbed one of the cross beams to haul herself up.

'Be careful, Jo.' Her mother's anxious voice drifted up from below. Careful? That was rich.

For the entire journey home, Alison had alternated between dry sobs and sulking. When she was thwarted, it was like dealing with a petulant child. On the Jubilee Line to North Greenwich, they'd attracted some critical glances. But the restaurant encounter had made Jo too angry to care.

Did her eleven-year-old self know that her sister was such a prolific diarist? She'd lied to rebuff Tania Jones, but like so many other things about Sarah, Jo couldn't remember.

For years Alison had been the jealous guardian of her murdered daughter's memory, shutting everyone else out. Jo had grown up immersed in her mother's version of Sarah to the extent that her own fragmented recollections and Alison's stories had melded in her mind. But since she'd learnt of the existence of the journals, her brain had been nattering with questions. Now here was an opportunity to get a glimpse of the real Sarah for herself.

It took the best part of half an hour to locate all the relevant boxes and to lower them through the hatch. Jo climbed down after them, hands and face filmed in dust. The crumpled cartons filled the narrow upstairs landing.

Each box was wound tightly with brown tape and had numbers: *S1, S2* all the way up to *S12* scrawled on the side. It didn't look like her mother's handwriting. As she heaved and hauled them downstairs, one by one, Jo concluded her father had efficiently boxed up his daughter's effects along with his feelings, his marriage and everything else.

They ended up with a large cardboard pyramid at one end of the sitting room. Mother and daughter stood side by side, staring at the stack. Then Alison went to fetch a Stanley knife from the kitchen.

Kneeling down beside *S1*, Jo glanced up at her mother. Her temper had had time to cool. 'You sure you're going to be okay with this?'

'Just open them.' Alison handed her the knife.

She sliced through the tape and ripped back the lid. The contents were all neatly wrapped in layers of soft tissue paper.

Alison put her hand to her mouth as the tears welled up. Jo shot her a concerned look.

Alison wiped her nose on her cardigan sleeve. 'It's okay.'

It wasn't. That was obvious.

Alison sniffed. 'I was remembering how your dad took such care wrapping everything up. As if he was wrapping her up, making his little girl safe and cosy again.'

Jo sat back on her heels. 'I can do this on my own if you like.'

Her mother sank down on the sofa. 'No, I'll be fine. We need to find out about Bruce.'

Jo still didn't buy Briony Rowe's ludicrous tale, but she wasn't about to argue the point. She had a mission of her own: to find out all she could about the real Sarah.

Lifting out each individual item, Jo placed them in order on the floor until she'd unpacked the first box.

It was a random selection of articles, many of which could've been found in any teenage girl's bedroom.

Alison picked up two cuddly toys—a black sheep and a white sheep. 'Remember these two?'

Jo smiled. 'Oh yeah. Ebb and Flo!' They'd sat on her sister's bed ever since she could remember.

'You see, she was so clever with words, even as a kid.'

Jo unwrapped the first few journals. There were half a dozen in the box. The one at the top was different to the rest —a shiny hardback and black. The others were multicoloured with embossed covers, some even had metal clasps. Alison reached down and picked up the black book. 'This is the one the police took. The last one from uni.'

Jo opened it. The paper smelt fusty, but her sister's large rounded girly handwriting crossed the unlined pages in mainly straight lines. Each entry was preceded by the date in capital letters. It was about two-thirds full, the remaining pages were blank.

'They weren't interested in any of these others?'

Alison picked up a fancy gold and red book with a wrap-over flap. She stroked the moulded surface with her finger-tips. 'These go right back to her early teens. All the years when she was at school. You probably don't remember, she always used to ask for a new book for Christmas or birthdays. When she was younger, she preferred the elaborate ones and bright colours.'

She was right, Jo didn't remember.

'I think your father must have slipped this one in later. It was months before we got it back. She decided all the other colours she'd had before weren't cool. She wanted plain black to go to uni.' Alison swallowed hard. 'We even bought her a black duvet cover, but we never got that back.'

Reaching out, Jo patted her hand. 'This is going to be a long job. Why don't you make us a nice cup of tea, eh?'

Alison nodded and after they'd drunk the tea, she went

upstairs to lie down. For the next half hour Jo unpacked the boxes and separated the journals from the toys, teddies and other items, including a random selection of coloured markers, watercolour paints and a zipped make-up pouch full of crumbling eyeshadows and dried up mascara. She returned these items to the boxes.

This left her with five neat stacks, each over a foot high, books of varying thicknesses and dimensions arranged in chronological order. They covered an eight-year period. These were her sister's journals. All handwritten, some sketches, a few photos, and pictures cut out from magazines. Jo hadn't known of their existence, or if she once did, a combination of shock, grief and time had wiped that memory. But now here it was: Sarah's testament in her own words.

As Jo looked at the careful arrangement she'd created, a shiver ran up her spine. Did she even want to go there? How much pain would be involved? The fact the journals existed had been enough of a bombshell. Digging up the past was something she'd always resisted. No good would come of it. That was her intuition.

Her life worked, after a fashion. She battled with frustrations and regrets, but didn't everyone? She prided herself on being a realist. She'd never win the lottery or get swept off her feet by a passing billionaire in a Lear jet. But that didn't matter. The woes of Alison's existence provided an object lesson in the perils of self-delusion.

Walking away from trouble was common sense. And in terms of Sarah, she'd always tried to be sensible. At the very least, reading the journals would be disturbing. But what if they did cast doubt on Wade's conviction?

Had a full account of what had led to her sister's death come out in court? Probably not. A court case was a joust between competing and partial versions of the truth. Wade killed Sarah. She was still convinced of that. But it wouldn't be the whole story. Getting inside her sister's head might be alarming. Did she really need to do it?

In death, Sarah had dominated Jo's life far more than she would ever have done if she'd lived. Her murder robbed Jo of the upbringing she should've had, and, if she was honest, Jo resented that deeply. Perhaps even to the extent of blaming her sister for getting murdered? Was this the terrible, guilty secret that her mind wanted to keep shut away? The idea it was all Sarah's fault. Was that why her brain stonewalled and refused to look back?

But she wasn't an aggrieved teenager anymore. Now she was DC Boden, a police officer, who understood the wider reality. She knew women get blamed all the time for the violence they suffer. Her skirt was too short, her manner was too provocative. She also knew Sarah didn't deserve or cause what happened to her. No woman does.

Jo studied the five tidy piles she'd created. However uncomfortable it made her feel, she knew it was time she confronted her family's tragic past head on, and examined the truth about her sister.

31

---

26 September 1999

Only a week to go now! I can hardly wait!!! The pixie is being especially annoying, keeps asking when she can come and stay. It'll be such a relief to get away from her, the parents and Mowgli—I swear that boy never washes. This family shit is doing my head in. They are all sooo boring! So predictable! Mum insists we have a family picnic before I go. It will undoubtedly rain. Pix and Mowgli will fight over the Frisbee. And I wonder why I can't wait to leave. Feels like I'll finally be FREE and my life can actually begin.

Everything will be different now, I just know it. But I'm not going to go crazy and get wasted every night. That's stupid. University offers so many opportunities. You succeed there, you can succeed anywhere. I read that in Cosmo. You CAN HAVE IT ALL, if you're smart enough.

Some girls, Becky T for instance, seem to regard uni as a place to hang out and find the right husband. But then she always has been a moron. All that extra private tuition and she still only got two Bs and a C! Jules and I watched her old man's face when she opened her results. He looked like he might have a coronary there and then, poor old sod. She ended up having to go through clearing. If that had happened to me, I'd be mortified!

I'll miss Jules, of course. I'm sure we'll always be friends. In twenty years' time we'll be middle-aged ladies who lunch and bitch about our boring (but rich, obviously) husbands. I'm not sure about her doing law. Of course, it's great that she got into King's and all that. But I can't help feeling she's only doing it because it's what her dad expects. Just because he's a QC doesn't mean it'll suit her. I don't think it will. Only time will tell.

Only time will tell? It was this banal assumption of a future that tipped Jo over the edge. As she read, she'd been telling herself it was okay, she could do this. Now, suddenly and from nowhere, it seemed, the tears were coursing down her cheeks.

She was reading by the light of an anglepoise lamp positioned on the coffee table. It was past four o'clock and winter darkness had descended. Out of the back window, a sliver of orange from the streetlamp in the road behind the house bisected the garden. She wiped her face with her sleeve.

The thing that struck her was how young her sister sounded—eighteen, ten years younger than Jo was now—such a mixture of arrogance and naivety. By the time Jo had reached her eighteenth birthday, all that middle-class privilege had been stripped from her life. Her parents were divorced, she had a part-time job in a burger bar and a full-time occupation taking care of her mother.

Should she be jealous of her sister? Ridiculous in the circumstances. But for all their adolescent immaturity, Sarah's words were compelling. They called up her ghost and for the first time since her death; she was a presence that Jo could imagine, standing there in the room, speaking in her own voice.

It would take hours and hours to do it properly, but Jo already knew she would have to read the lot, every word. She was still adjusting to the impact of it, to the raw emotion that had risen up and ambushed her, when Alison came down the stairs. Her mother was wearing bed-socks and her favourite cardigan, but she didn't seem at all rested.

'Jo! People can see in.' The tone was testy as she headed straight for the front window and pulled the curtains. 'Have you found him yet?'

Fortunately, Alison was too preoccupied to notice she was upset.

'No. I got a bit carried away reading.'

'Couldn't you flick through until you find his name? You don't have to read everything.'

'Have you read any of it?'

'No. I started to. But…I just…' She sighed. 'Your dad said we shouldn't upset ourselves more than we had to. So we put it all away.'

'I'd forgotten that she used to call me Pixie.'

'It was a silly nickname.'

'Where did it come from?'

'Oh God, I don't remember.' Alison pressed her fingers into the sides of her temples. 'I've got an awful headache.'

The wine at lunch, on top of the medication, it was predictable. Jo studied her. Painkillers would only make things worse. She could see Alison was suffering, but as was often the case, there was nothing she could do, nothing either of them could do except wait for it to pass.

'When I joined the Brownies—'

'You can hardly say you joined, Jo. You went for about

four weeks, then suddenly announced you hated it and refused to go again.'

Jo gave her mother a wistful smile. 'Perhaps that was it? Because I think maybe I was in the Pixies—and didn't Sarah rib me about it?'

'She never bullied you or your brother. I would never have tolerated anything like that in my children.'

'But she did like to tease.'

'That's quite natural between sisters.'

'You never had a sister. How do you know?' Jo didn't intend to be provocative, but it slipped out. It was a mistake. She knew it immediately.

Alison pulled her cardigan around her, went into the kitchen and filled the kettle. Her face was tight and pinched.

Jo wondered if deflection would work. 'Well, it's interesting to read all this now.'

'Oh, is it? Is it really? Well, I'm glad it's interesting for you.' Alison's anger was surfacing. She slotted the kettle on to its base, flicked the switch and got two mugs from the cupboard.

'Mum, I didn't mean that as a criticism—'

'Oh, I know you, Jo. Your little zingers! Do you hate me that much?'

'Don't be daft. I don't hate you at all.'

'Then how could you be so bloody rude? I was so embarrassed.'

'Rude to who? Briony Rowe?'

'There's no excuse for such behaviour.'

'I think there is.'

'She's a friend of your sister's. Someone who is concerned with the truth. Unlike you, it seems.'

'That's unfair.'

'Is it? I don't think joining the police has done you any good at all. I've never thought so. This proves it.'

'What's that supposed to mean? Because I'm a police officer, I make judgements based on evidence, not feelings?'

Alison jabbed her finger toward the piled-up journals. 'The evidence could be there! Right there.' She was shouting now. 'But you don't want to find it, do you?'

'That's not true.'

'You're so stuck in your prejudices. Full of your own bloody righteousness. That's what being in the police has done for you. If you cared the least bit about your sister, about me, you'd be going through and finding every mention of Bruce.'

'And what do you think that would prove?'

'I don't know.' The kettle was hissing. Alison reached for the teabags, then changed her mind. Raising the back of her hand, she swept the mugs off the worktop and on to the tiled floor. They landed with a resounding crack, the handle snapping off one, the other smashing into pieces. She gazed down at the shattered crockery. 'But nor do you.'

Jo put the shiny black book down, went to Alison, and drew her into a hug.

She felt her mother's bony shoulders and the tears wet on the side of her neck. 'Why did this happen to us, Jo? Why couldn't our lives have stayed normal?'

'What's normal?'

Alison was sobbing now. 'When will this ever be over? I don't think I can bear it.'

32

22 May 2000

Nathan is being a total and utter dick! Exams proper start tomorrow with the first sit-down and the Poetry essay has to be in by 9. He's probably finished his, competitive little prick that he is, though he didn't say. Thinks that by coming round and hassling me, he'll put me off my stride. Last essay I got 68% and he only got 60. He was livid. So it's payback time. That's probably how he sees it. That's blokes for you.

Still, once exams are over, we can all go home for the summer. Thank God for that! I have so had it with this place. And him. I just want to sit in the garden on a sun lounger and do NOTHING.

Jo turned over the page. There were tiny red dots at the beginning and end of the passage. This was one of the pieces the prosecution had relied on in court to support their contention that Sarah and Nathan had argued that night. It was also the last entry in her last journal, written possibly only hours before her death.

Re-reading, Jo tried to tease out the underlying meaning. Was it written after she'd sent Nathan away? Yes, that was clear enough. He'd been there, they rowed, and she sent him packing. She wrote about it in her journal because she was upset. But what happened next? He was angry with her too and he came back? That was the argument presented in court and the one the jury accepted.

But in the end, that was pure speculation. It was equally possible they rowed and he didn't come back. There was no conclusive proof to confirm he did.

Jo was sitting cross-legged on the battered old leather sofa. This was where she'd done her homework in her teenage years. It had an interesting smell—dried milk, red wine, an acrid cleaning product—but familiarity made it comforting. Alison had spent a couple of hours curled up there beside her while they watched some trash television. Finally, and to Jo's relief, her mother had retreated to bed.

Looking at the case in detail was what Tania Jones had challenged Jo to do and the main reason she'd resisted was that she knew there would be doubt; there always was. But was it *beyond reasonable doubt?* That was a judgement for a jury made up of twelve ordinary men and women. They decided, not the police, not CPS, not the judge. And although Jo was loath to admit it, certainly to Alison, she'd witnessed enough trials where the only explanation for the jury's decision was their emotional response to the case.

Under common law and the adversarial system, two competing stories were presented to them in court and they made a choice which to believe. Considerable skill and expertise went into creating those stories. Jo wondered about her sister's old school friend, Jules. Was Sarah right about her or had she made it through her law degree and inherited her dad's horsehair wig?

But, whichever way you looked at it, the system wasn't foolproof and juries were fickle. Anyone who'd spent any time in court knew that.

Jo flicked back the pages to an earlier passage, also marked with dots. This was the piece Harry, the hot-shot lawyer, had quoted from. He'd obtained a set of legal documents relating to the case, which included a full transcript of the trial. There would've been boxes and boxes of that too.

19 May 2000

Such a glorious day! We sunbathed on the grass for a bit. But then I forced myself to go to the library. Saw that dick-head director who wanted me to strip off—for purely creative reasons, I don't think!—in his wanky play. Next year I'm going to DramaSoc with my own proposal. All these silly boys think they know so much better how to do these things. But I've come to the conclusion they don't. It's all testosterone-driven bullshit! All you need is a bit of confidence to stand up and say your piece. And I think I've got that now. So all the stupid crap that happened last year hasn't been a total waste. But I'm not dwelling on that. What doesn't kill you makes you stronger! Nietzsche was right. I only managed a few pages of Ecco Homo. Strikes me he was a bit of a twat.

I'm still finding it hard to keep all the balls in the air—work, socializing, acting. But this term I have done better on the work front. Haven't missed any seminars. Haven't got drunk in the week. Have made it to most of my lectures. Well, except the ones at 9 o'clock! I mean, I'm not a medic or an engineer!

The last two lectures were yesterday morning and I made both. Unlike Nathan. I'm beginning to think I should dump him. He wants us to go inter-railing together this summer. Dire or what? I walked out of the lecture theatre and there's bloody Bruce hanging around again! Has he got nothing better to do? Being a postgrad is clearly a doss. Why can't he just get the message?

Had this boy stalked her sister? She sounded more annoyed than scared of him. But: *all the stupid crap that happened last year*—what did that mean? The usual melodramas of student life or something more serious?

Going back to the books she'd stacked into five neat piles, Jo sorted through until she found the second journal that covered the period from mid October through November and December 1999, the autumn and her sister's first term at university. Had the murder investigation examined these? Possibly. She'd have to check the trial transcript to find out if any extracts were submitted in evidence. Although, if there were no red dots marking the original, it was a fair assumption they weren't.

She got a notebook and pen from her bag. The process that would've been carried out by the enquiry was familiar enough. A couple of DCs would have been given the task of trawling through the stack of journals for clues. The pressure would have been on to skim through and abstract anything of relevance as quickly as possible. Working with the knowledge that seven months later this young woman would be dead, brutally murdered, hopes and dreams extinguished, shouldn't have affected their attitude or the professionalism with which they approached the task. But Jo knew from her own experience that it would have. Inexperience, a lack of empathy for the victim, or too much, could have all resulted in potentially significant things being skated over.

Jo began her search in the first week of term. And there he was at a Freshers' club night. *He's hot even though he dances like Bruce Willis on speed.* There were no red dots.

Sifting through the text, she came up with six mentions in October and two in early November. No red dots on any of those, either. Her colleagues hadn't been interested in Bruce. Maybe Nathan Wade was already in custody by the time they looked at this. If so, it would have taken something very obvious to prompt going to the SIO and suggesting a different line of enquiry.

Searching for further entries on Bruce, she discovered an odd thing. Towards the end of the first book, five pages had been removed. It looked as though scissors had been used to cut them out. Only narrow stubs remained close to the spine.

Was this Sarah's handiwork? It must be. Jo rubbed her finger along the jagged edge. All that remained of the excised pages. What had Sarah written about at the end of November in that first term that she felt she had to remove? And remove with some care. There were crossings out and revisions in earlier passages. But this was something more. *All the stupid crap that happened last year.* Did Sarah have a secret she wanted to hide?

33

On Sunday morning, Alison Boden didn't get out of bed. Jo took her a cup of tea, which, when she came back half an hour later, was untouched. Jo had witnessed this before, her mother's descent into some dark private place of torment. There was nothing to be done, except keep a watchful eye on her.

Jo had woken up on the sofa, chilled to the bone and with a stiff neck. She'd sat up most of the night, reading and re-reading passages in the journals. As a result, she had a list of questions, no answers and a dilemma about what to do next. Maybe she should do nothing. But she wasn't good at that. Her head was buzzing and she was wired even before she drank a cafetière of coffee.

She found Briony Rowe impossible to like. If Sarah had been a close friend, then her failure to speak up at the time of her murder was, to Jo's mind, unforgivable. On top of that was the undeniable self-interest in her attempt to raise the issue now. The combination of her and Tania Jones left a bad taste. They were like vultures wheeling high above a carcass, waiting for the chance to swoop in and scavenge the remains.

With the day stretching out before her, and Alison sequestered in her room, Jo had time to herself and a chance to take stock. She wanted to go for a walk. A glance out of the window told her it was bright and frosty. But some instinct made her hesitate.

Jabreel Khan had assured her she had nothing more to worry about. Did she believe him? He was a man at the end of his tether on an operation stretched to breaking point. Meaning well was not the same as delivering a result. In her view, Hollingsworth was old-fashioned, inefficient and by the book. Could he be relied on to act swiftly and decisively, or would he worry more about how it looked and his overtime budget? Jo had never rated him, especially when she compared him to her new boss, Steve Vaizey.

She was making some toast and giving herself a stern lecture on how irrational she was being—it was Greenwich on a Sunday morning and she was a police officer, of course she should go out—when the doorbell rang, making her start. Her immediate reaction was to ignore it. This, she told herself, was gutless. She was turning into Alison.

Through the spyhole in the door she discovered Mr Kempson, their neighbour, on the doorstep with a bunch of tulips. Feeling a fool, she opened the door.

The old man was leaning heavily on his stick and refused an invitation to come in. The flowers were to thank Jo and her mother for *seeing to* poor Marmalade.

'Raised in a hothouse, but they're a bit of spring. Always heartening.' He gave Jo a raffish grin.

According to Alison, he was well over ninety. It was hard not to feel guilty for lying about the cat. Jo smiled, accepted the flowers and watched him totter down the path, skilfully avoiding an icy patch. He was rheumy-eyed and stooped but bright as a button and she found his cheerfulness chastening. How could anyone reach such an age with their optimism intact? But maybe her mother was right. Some people were luckier, their lives more normal.

She ate the buttered toast while pacing the room, then went up to check on Alison and found her fast asleep. Watching her papery eyelids flutter, Jo hoped her dreams were peaceful. When her mother was on a downer, she often stayed in bed for days at a time.

Too antsy to remain in the house, Jo grabbed her jacket and scarf and headed out. Reading her sister's journals had been disturbing, as she'd known it would be. She'd tried to be cautious, but the more she delved, the more emotionally entangled she'd become. The big sister she'd both loved and hated was back in her life with a vengeance.

Avoiding Greenwich Park, awash with Sunday tourists, she headed up the hill on to Blackheath. The frost-laden turf crunched underfoot as she marched across it, the exertion calming her febrile brain.

She walked for the best part of an hour, did a circuit of the heath and felt better. Returning to the house, she piled kindling and fire-lighters in the wood burner and lit it. As she watched the dry sticks crackle and catch, she came to a decision.

Her mother's handbag was a Prada knock-off she'd bought years ago in the market. When she was at home, it lived at the foot of the stairs.

Jo picked it up and rifled through it until she found what she'd guessed would be there: Briony Rowe's business card. She sent the film-maker a curt text. She made no apology for her earlier hostility. She didn't think Rowe deserved any encouragement. The truth was she hadn't changed her opinion that much. Nathan Wade still seemed to be the most likely culprit for her sister's murder. But the detective in her couldn't let this rest. Doing nothing wasn't an option. She needed to find out more, and there seemed to be only one way to do that.

34

Nathan Wade had spent the weekend alone in his cell, apart from mealtimes and a visit to the medical centre to be checked over prior to his release. This was scheduled for Monday morning. And he'd been glad of the solitude; he'd needed it to compose himself and to deal with the fear. After the long years of loneliness and the daily battle to resist the drugs and stay clean, his dream was becoming reality: he was being granted his freedom. But like all dreams and desires, its fulfilment was unlikely to bring him satisfaction. That was the nature of desire. He needed to manage his expectations. Change was hard. He also knew his limbic brain would resist and rebel. Things could get hairy. He had to stay mindful. But at the same time he had to be practical and ensure that he didn't end up like most lifers on release: a zero-hours contract if he was lucky and the choice of living in a hostel or on the streets.

Briony Rowe had come to meet him. She was waiting at the prison gate with a camera, a tripod and her assistant, Kayleigh, whom she'd introduced. He'd walked out, with a small holdall and a plastic carrier, then gone back and repeated the action three times so Briony could get the angles she needed and a close-up of his face.

By the time they'd loaded the gear and all piled into Briony's Mini, he'd started to find some amusement in the absurdity of the situation.

Briony drove him to the hostel in Littlehampton and there was more of the same palaver: filming him going in from behind, then resetting, placing the camera inside and getting a shot of him opening the door. The manager greeted him; he seemed awkwardly polite. They shook hands, twice. Did he roll out the welcome mat like this for all new arrivals? Nathan doubted it. It took twenty minutes to get up the stairs, down the corridor, and into his new room.

What seemed a mystery to Nathan was why anyone would choose to be an actor. To spend your days on this continual rinse-and-repeat cycle struck him as boring. Briony explained that it all had to look natural and seamless, although it was a complete pretence. Smiling at the sight of his new room had become hard work after the fourth take. Kayleigh was scurrying around and standing on the bed with a reflector to balance out the poor light from the window.

As he'd unpacked his possessions from the holdall, Briony wanted him to place the photograph of his parents beside the bed. He argued he wouldn't do this because it would be in the way and could get knocked off and broken. But Briony wanted to create the impression that he woke up every morning and gazed at it. He'd replied that he kept the photograph in a drawer and looked at it rarely. At this point, the film-maker had declared it was time to wrap for lunch. She didn't want an argument and was trying to be sensitive to his feelings, which, Nathan reflected, had to be a step in the right direction.

Over burger and chips at a greasy spoon round the corner,

she'd presented him with a brand-new smartphone. This was to celebrate his release, she said. Presumably Tania had provided it, but, as with everything, there was an ulterior motive; they needed him to be contactable.

During his incarceration, black-market phones had been readily available. He'd never bothered with them because he'd had no one to call. The bloke in the next cell at Ford, a fraudster called Nwabueze, who preferred to be known as Ned, did a roaring trade in smuggled mobiles. His USP was that all his devices were 'confectionary jobs'—they were especially small devices, which had been brought in concealed in hollowed-out Mars Bars. They sold at a premium because they came with a guarantee that they'd never been wrapped in clingfilm and hidden in any bodily orifice. More discerning clients were prepared to pay for this luxury.

The hostel room was basic, but that suited Nathan. Attachment to things created suffering. That was the philosophy he'd espoused. It had proved a successful survival mechanism in jail because it meant that the prison regime, which could turn over your cell or move you at the drop of a hat, had no psychological leverage. Nor did the contraband gangs, who wanted to get you in their debt. On the inside, emotional detachment was the only freedom available. But that was then.

As he sat in his new room that evening, curtains drawn to keep him snug, trying out the many elaborate functions of his phone, he'd contemplated the possibility of a different future. He accidentally clicked a button and took a picture of his left foot, complete with its tatty trainer. It made him smile.

The new outfit bought on his shopping trip with Briony was hanging in the tiny wardrobe. She hadn't wanted him to wear it for the initial filming. Her explanation was that his narrative arc had to be reflected in the visual image. As he journeyed towards freedom and the clearing of his name, so his appearance could improve. Optimism symbolized by a colourful new shirt.

This had started him thinking about all the frivolous preoccupations of his youth. Hairstyles, the image you wanted to project, these were things that had once taken up much time and attention. He remembered his obsession with sunglasses. He would need a new pair. Ray-Bans were his favourite. In prison, it was easy to not care about how you looked. In fact, being unremarkable was safer.

But spending a day having a camera shoved in his face had made him realize he was not without vanity. Did he want to appear on film looking like a defeated old lag, a man of thirty-five going on fifty? Was that necessary?

Briony had been brimming with enthusiasm all day and was more than happy to explain the tricks of the trade. Learning from her shtick was easy. He'd plied her with questions and found out loads. She loved displaying her expertise. In the end, what she was doing didn't seem that hard to Nathan.

This raised the question: did he even need her? Probably not. Kayleigh could handle the camera well enough. The relationship with Tania and Gordon's production company was the one that mattered. Harry could deal with the legal bit. He'd seen enough of Tania to guess she wouldn't be too bothered if Briony was cut out of the loop. She might even prefer it. All he had to do was bide his time and wait for an opportunity to make his move. After all, this was his story, not Briony's. Getting rid of her made sense. More money for him.

35

Jo was driving. Alison Boden owned an ancient Vauxhall Astra, which she kept in a rented mews garage two streets away from the house. She never used it in London and rarely went anywhere else. Jo borrowed the car whenever she needed to drive and arranged for it to be serviced, which her mother considered an extraneous expense. She also kept it taxed and insured.

On Monday morning, Jo had been in touch with Sandra at the office. Ivan Rossi's boat had been traced and a full surveillance operation was being put in place. There wasn't anything particular for Jo to do. She'd bypassed Foley and emailed admin support to ask Vaizey for a day off for family reasons. It wasn't a complete lie.

They drove along Shooters Hill Road against the flow of morning rush-hour traffic and headed out of town on the A2 to pick up the M25 for the journey south, stopping only for a tank of petrol and takeaway coffees. Alison's mood was despondent but improved as they clocked up the miles. The sky had cleared, the wintery sun was out and they were going to the seaside.

Glancing across at her mother, Jo hoped she'd made the right decision. She'd communicated with Briony Rowe by text because she'd wanted to avoid any discussion on the phone. The reply she'd received was bursting with grinning emojis, a gesture confirming her view that the film-maker was a halfwit.

Briony had also emailed her the full transcript of Nathan Wade's trial. An evening had been just about enough for Jo to skim through it, but not to study it in detail. She'd evaded Alison's questions and insisted that she hadn't had a change of heart. Bruce did exist, although this proved nothing.

The decision to confront her sister's convicted killer face-to-face was a considered one; this was what Jo had told herself. She'd offered to do it alone, which would've been her preference. But Alison wouldn't hear of it.

The postcode that Briony had provided for the satnav turned out to be a caravan park on the outskirts of Littlehampton. Jo drove through the gates and pulled up outside the office. This was even more bizarre than she'd expected. At first sight, it looked to be shut up for the winter, but a woman in a woolly hat emerged and gave them directions. Apparently the caravanning community was hardy. Following the serpentine concrete road past mainly empty pitches, they passed half a dozen caravans and motorhomes until they arrived at Briony's. An awning had been erected on one side of the VW campervan and Briony Rowe sat under it, wrapped in a tartan rug. There was no sign of Nathan Wade.

As the Astra drew up, Briony leapt to her feet and waved. Jo shot her mother an anxious glance as she got out of the car. For the last ten miles she'd had the creeping realization that they were about to make a huge mistake. Behind the calm and capable exterior of the police officer, Jo had a tendency to act rashly. She knew this about herself. If the choice was do nothing or act, then action always won out, which was why she'd contacted Briony.

The result was a stupid decision. Standing in the middle of a freezing caravan park and watching the film-maker erupting in glee made that clear to her. On top of this, she should never have brought Alison. Her mother was fragile enough before. Who knew what this would do to her?

Briony launched into an enthusiastic welcome explaining that the VW wasn't hers, it was borrowed, but was the ideal base when she was on the road filming. Hotels were expensive and self-catering was a better option.

Jo cut her short. 'Where the hell is he?'

'He should be here shortly. My assistant, Kayleigh, has gone to collect him.'

'We agreed one o'clock.'

'Can I get you some hot chocolate?' Briony held up her mug. 'It's rather good.'

Jo was seething, though her anger was with herself. 'We're not hanging around.'

Alison had got out of the car and was wandering aimlessly.

'Perhaps your mother would like to sit down?' Briony offered Alison her rug. 'It is a bit chilly.'

Jo checked her watch. 'This is ridiculous. We should never've come. Get back in the car, Mum.'

'Please, Jo. He'll be here. But you have to understand, it's hard for him too.'

'Is it? Have you ever considered just how full of shite you sound?'

A flicker of amusement crossed Briony's face. 'Yeah, it's been mentioned before. I gush a bit, I know. It's nerves.'

Jo shook her head in disbelief. The last thing she needed was to feel sorry for Briony Rowe. But as she opened the door of the Astra to leave, a bright orange Mini Clubman, driven by Kayleigh, appeared round the bend.

It pulled up in front of them and Jo got her first look at Nathan Wade. He was nothing like the startled boy in his police mugshot, but she'd hardly expected him to be.

Tall, he uncoiled himself from the low passenger seat and climbed out.

The smile was nervous. His eyes flicked from Jo to Alison and back. 'I'm sorry. I went to the barber's. Trying to smarten myself up. I didn't know there'd be such a queue.'

Jo looked him up and down. His greying hair had been clipped, but he had the weak, hangdog, pity-me manner of every criminal she'd seen shuffle through the custody suite.

Then abruptly the expression changed. Before their eyes the convict morphed into someone else. He pulled back his shoulders, straightened his spine and held out his hand to shake.

He tilted his head and gave Jo a sly smile. 'I don't expect you remember me. But I remember you, Pixie.'

36

Dear Jo,

I couldn't believe it when I saw you. Thought I'd seen a ghost. I was so confused. The same bright halo of hair and that taunting look you always had. It couldn't be. It wasn't possible, and yet…I'm going to be totally honest here. The arousal was instant. My body knows it's you even if my reason questions it, and I still want you. Oh yes. That much is clear.

But can we turn back the clock? Can we correct the mistakes of our youth? Surely that would be true mastery?

I suppose the first thing I need you to understand is that I am not to blame. I never meant to hurt her. You thought she was great, your amazing big sister, and she was. Of course she was. But it wasn't the whole story. I'm not suggesting she deserved to die. I'd never say that. But sometimes situations develop, relationships develop—and we understand this once we become fully adult—which are fated to lead to tragedy.

Once the wheels start turning and gather speed, the momentum becomes unstoppable, the crash inevitable. No one person alone is to blame, but we must all take some responsibility. It was like that with me and Sarah. Rows and reconciliations. And great sex. But you probably don't want to know about that.

What you need to know is I loved her. And that's never really stopped with her death. It just becomes a different sort of love, a love that's always tinged with pain and regret.

I don't mean to sound flowery. How Sarah would laugh at that. She had a built-in bullshit detector, your sister. It was one of the many things I admired about her.

Seeing you, imagine how that feels. You must know how much you look like her. I'm sure plenty of people have told you and I'm sure it's deeply annoying. But there it is. Fate, yet again.

How old are you now? Twenty-eight, maybe? When I look at you, the thing that strikes me is this: Sarah was still a girl when she died. A teenager. Not quite nineteen. All that promise unfulfilled. But here's the woman she could've become. A grown-up version of Sarah. And even more beautiful. I can't stop thinking about you, Jo. You're my second chance.

You belong to me, you always have. But this time it will be different.

37

In Jo Boden's experience as a police officer, the average villain wasn't too bright. Chaotic lives and poor coping skills led to bad choices and violence. Often they were drug- or alcohol-dependent, and many had mental health issues. Kids from poor or difficult backgrounds were swept up in the gang culture with the lure of easy money and a way out. Then there was organized crime and that was a business, which attracted a different class of rule-breaker. These two categories posed distinct challenges for law enforcement and Jo knew which she found easier to deal with emotionally. The professional criminal was harder to catch, but less disruptive personally. At least this had been her belief until she came up against the Kelmendis.

She'd done her time on the streets dealing with the outcasts and casualties who took up so much police time. As a detective, she'd served in various specialist squads and had a broad range of experience, including some high-profile murder investigations. But as she watched Nathan Wade, she was puzzled. He didn't remind her of anything she'd encountered before, which was disturbing.

There was an air of plausibility about him. He could manage eye contact, but not all the time. His anxiety was under control, but only just. The tale he told was not without gaps and contradictions. If this was a performance aimed at deceiving them, he was very good. But then some psychopaths had got appearing normal down to a fine art.

Eleven-year-old Jo had finally got her wish and visited her sister at February half-term. And Wade was right, she didn't remember meeting him back then. Sarah's group of friends had seemed cool and amazing to little Jo. In her memory, the visit was a whirlwind of people and music and bars and her first taste of alcohol.

She wondered if referring to this as his opening gambit was a ploy on Wade's part to unnerve her. Yet as soon as he saw her surprise, he'd backed off. Authentic or devious?

They sat in a circle under the awning. He leaned forward in his seat, elbows resting on his knees. Alison sat opposite him, stock still, face pale, brow creased, wrapped in a blanket Briony had provided. He spoke in quiet sentences and, as he recounted the story of his relationship with Sarah, Jo mentally checked it against what she'd read in her sister's journals. And the two accounts matched.

So did this boy lose his temper? Did a lover's tiff turn into a drunken fight, which spiralled out of control?

As Jo listened, she deliberately slowed her breathing and focused on small visual details: his restless hands, the long fingers with ragged nails; this helped her become more detached. She knew she had to retreat into detective mode, treat the man in front of her as a stranger, which he was, and no different to any other suspect. It was important for her to bring no baggage to her assessment. This would've been easier before she'd read the journals, but she had an eerie sense of her sister beside her, standing at her shoulder. And she too wanted answers.

Jo glanced at her mother. Alison's narrow shoulders were hunched, her bony hands clasped in her lap, her eyes vacant. She didn't even look as though she was breathing. She was there but not there, like a frozen wraith, and it was impossible to tell what impact this was having on her.

Briony remained quiet. She sat on Nathan's left, was keyed-up, but had the good sense to keep her mouth shut. Kayleigh squatted silently on the step of the van.

It occurred to Jo that now they were face to face she had the power, if she cared to use it. Crossing her long legs, she fixed Wade with a hard stare. 'Mind if I ask some questions?'

He looked apprehensive—again, was that for show?—but shrugged. 'Of course.'

'You say you argued with Sarah, stormed out and walked to the train station? Is that correct?'

'Yes. I walked part of the way and then I ran when I realized the time. I knew the last train was just before midnight.'

'How did you realize the time? Did you look at your watch?'

He frowned. 'I didn't wear a watch.'

'So how did you know? Did you have a phone?'

'I had an old Nokia that had belonged to my dad. But I didn't take it out much because the battery was always going flat.'

'How did you know the time, then?'

'Well, I think I knew roughly. Or I guessed.'

'You said I walked, then I ran when I realized the time. Sounds like you made a decision to run. Based on what?'

Nathan put his head in his hands. 'I'm not sure.'

'Have you ever retraced the route you took?'

He shook his head.

'Did you see anyone? Around midnight on campus, there could've still been people about. Other students heading for the station?'

'I was wound up. I didn't really notice anyone.'

'Okay, so you caught the train. How many other passengers got on?'

Nathan was pressing his forehead as if the physical force could prise open his recalcitrant memory. Then his eyes lit up. 'I asked the time. Yeah, I remember now. I passed a couple of people. And I knew one of them, sort of vaguely. A girl from my course.'

Jo studied him. This was the first element in his account that struck her as disingenuous. A lightbulb moment, after all these years? Surely, he'd have replayed this scenario in his mind many times. She decided to see where he was trying to lead them.

'You know her name?'

He shook his head, puffed out his cheeks with frustration.

'Visualize her. What did she look like?'

'She was sort of funky and alternative. Charity shop clothes. And she had her hair braided into long dreads, but she was white with gingerish hair.'

'She told you the time?'

'Not her. The bloke that was with her. He wore a watch.'

'Just two of them?'

'Yeah, I think so.'

'Cyn!' Briony wagged her finger triumphantly. 'Cynthia! But she called herself Cyn.' Jumping up, she grabbed her phone and scrolled.

Jo scanned the film-maker. There was a small cynical voice in her head telling her this was all a bit neat. She was being played. 'You recognize the description?'

'Yeah. She was on our course, a real snotbag. Wanted to be an actress. Sarah hated her.' Briony held out her phone. 'That's her. We're friends on Facebook.'

Nathan took the phone and peered at it. He frowned and rubbed his eyes. 'I don't know. Could be her.'

The dreads were long gone. The profile picture showed a smiling woman with a neat blonde bob.

'I could get in touch with her and ask her.'

'If you didn't like her, how come you're Facebook friends?'

Briony inclined her head. 'Well, I'm friends with all sorts of people now. We've all grown up a bit.' She retrieved the phone from Nathan. Her excitement was obvious. 'Shall I message her?'

Jo raised her palm. 'No.'

The harsh tone stopped Briony in her tracks. She waggled the phone. 'Don't worry, Jo. I'm not that stupid. I wouldn't say anything, y'know, blatant. I'd…well, whatever.' She seemed deflated.

Jo folded her arms. She had an uncanny sense of being on the cusp of an insight. If only she could grasp it. She glanced at Nathan. He was too much of an enigma to read with any accuracy and her default mode was suspicion. Something about him wasn't right. She felt it in her gut, still she wanted to know more.

Her instincts as a detective were propelling her forward. Questions, theories, were nattering away in her brain. Were they feeding her a story? Had this all been rehearsed? But if this person existed and had spoken to Nathan that night, why hadn't she come forward at the time?

She went on the attack. 'Okay, this woman may or may not be significant. But we need to be systematic.' She fixed Briony with a chilly stare. 'Can you identify Bruce?'

'Well, no, I don't know his real name. I never did.' The film-maker was squirming, as Jo had expected she would once her little tale was subjected to scrutiny.

'So you never actually knew him?'

'I knew him. But I only knew him as Bruce. I met him once with Sarah, but I saw him hanging around, talking to her.'

'Could you identify him from a photograph?'

'I'm not sure. Probably. Did Sarah have one?' She sounded nervous now her bluff was being called.

Jo's gaze was unremitting. 'If he was a postgrad, the university would have his details in their archives, including a mugshot.'

'Oh yeah. But would they let us look?'

'Persuade them, Briony. Tell them you're making a film.'

'Wouldn't it be better if you asked them, as a police officer?'

'I have no authority to do that in this case. You want me to take what you're saying seriously?'

'Well, yeah.' She glanced at Nathan. 'We want you to believe that Nathan could be innocent.'

'What I'll believe is evidence. You get me Bruce's real name. Show me an alternative suspect who can be questioned. Then I might consider taking what you're saying seriously.'

Briony grinned. 'It's a test, isn't it?'

'Call it what you like.'

'But it means you've read the journals and you believe he exists.'

Ignoring this assertion, Jo turned to Nathan. 'What do you say?'

Throughout the exchange, his eyes hadn't left her face,

but the look behind them remained aloof. It seemed to Jo that he had an agenda of his own and she was wondering more and more what that might be. But her intuition was clear. She didn't trust him. No way.

He shrugged and smiled. 'Yeah, go for it.'

38

They drove back to London in silence. Alison gazed out of the window. The afternoon was dry, traffic on the motorway cruising easily. Jo sensed that her mother had relaxed, but it was impossible to tell what she was thinking. She'd encased herself in an invisible bubble, which repelled all attempts at communication.

When they pulled into Clacket Lane services on the M25, Jo thought of Razan. This was where she and twenty other frightened kids, mostly Syrians, had been rescued from the back of a Dutch lorry transporting flowers. She felt guilt bubbling up. Had DC Georgiou found the little sister, Amira, yet? She doubted it. She should go back and visit Razan. But what good would that do? She had to let go; it was no longer her job.

As they strolled across the car park, a snatch of birdsong drifted from the nearby trees. Alison pulled a packet of cigarettes out of her pocket and lit up. Turning away from Jo, she hunched her shoulders to show she was in no mood for recriminations about her smoking.

Jo ignored her and walked towards the building. People

were milling about, hands clasped round hot drinks, chatting, laughing. It seemed such a benign and friendly place, a welcoming pit-stop for weary travellers.

It occurred to Jo that the drivers getting out of their cars, stretching their legs or scurrying to the loo, were totally unaware of the numbers of desperate illegal migrants who also passed through this place. The phantoms no one wanted to see. It was one of the motorway stops favoured by the people traffickers as a transit point. Close but not too close to the Channel Tunnel and the ferry crossings, they used it to trans-ship their human cargo from large lorries to smaller vehicles. Surveillance and raids took place regularly, but the police knew they only intercepted a fraction of the trade.

Emerging from the building with some tea and packaged sandwiches, Jo found that her mother had settled herself at a picnic table on the grass. She was chatting to an amiable old lady with a dog; a small Jack Russell, which enjoyed the fuss.

The old lady and her companion wandered off. Alison stubbed out her cigarette and gazed up at her daughter. 'I might get a dog. Don't you think that would be nice? I could take it for walks in the park.'

Jo handed her a cardboard cup. 'You'd spend all your time picking up its poop.'

'You always see the negative in everything, don't you?'

'I was only saying that's what you'd have to do.'

'Maybe that's why you're in the police? You prefer to deal with the unpleasant side of life. You find that easier.'

Every conversation they'd had lately, this was what Alison would harp on. The job. She seemed to have become obsessed with it as an explanation for all the things about her daughter that she didn't like.

Jo let it pass. Whenever her mother couldn't cope, her spitefulness made an appearance.

She sat down, unwrapped her egg sandwich and looked at it. It was rather soggy and unappealing. 'Okay, let's talk about Nathan Wade. What do you think?'

'I don't know. What do you think?'

'Mum, why are you being like this? You wanted to meet him. Now what?'

Alison removed the lid from her cup. 'Well, presumably you're going to talk to this woman.'

'I want to know what you think about him.'

'I'm not sure. I thought I'd know, but I don't.' Her chin quivered. 'He seems…well, rather sad.'

'He's just spent sixteen years in prison.'

'It's not that bad. They have television and everything nowadays.'

Jo scanned her mother. She was retreating into herself and all her old nonsense. Had it scared her that much, this encounter with her daughter's convicted killer? Jo had worried that meeting Nathan Wade in person would be too much for her mother and it looked like she was right.

The only response that ever worked in this situation was if Jo held her temper and didn't rise to the bait. She bit into her sandwich. Not that great, but she hadn't eaten since breakfast and was too hungry to care. Perhaps Alison needed time to process her feelings. It was pointless to push her.

Alison took a sniff at her sandwich, then broke it into pieces and toss it to the birds. She soon had a flock of greedy pigeons strutting around her.

'You need the loo before we go, Mum?'

Alison shook her head.

'I'm going. Won't be long.'

As Jo strolled back into the building, her phone chirruped. A brief glance at the screen revealed the face of an older man. Stopping, she exhaled. What did he want?

She hesitated, then answered. 'Hey, Dad.'

'What the hell's going on, Jo?'

'What d'you mean?'

Nick Boden was the opposite of his ex-wife. Even-tempered and laid-back, very little seemed to faze him. But he sounded aggravated.

'I've just received an email. From this damned film-maker who's been harassing me. Briony Rowe? You know her?'

'Yeah.'

'According to her, you and your mother have met with Nathan Wade and are cooperating in some bloody miscarriage of justice film to prove his innocence.'

'Hang on, Dad, that's only partly true.'

'Which part? Have you met him or not?'

'Well, yes, but—'

'Your mother's met him? Are you mad? How on earth did you agree to this? Have you any idea what effect this could have?'

The hectoring tone, the accusation, was too much for Jo. 'Yeah. More than you, actually. Because I'm the one that's here with her. And it was her idea to talk to the film people, as a matter of fact.'

'She doesn't know what she's doing half the time. Why didn't you call me and discuss this?'

'Why?' Jo took a breath to calm herself. She glanced back at her mother, still feeding the birds. 'You know what? I don't have to discuss anything I do with you.'

'Jo, listen to me—'

With a brisk tap of her thumb, Jo ended the call. She switched her phone to silent, slipped it into her bag and marched towards the toilets.

39

It was already getting dark when they arrived back in Greenwich in the late afternoon. Alison hadn't spoken throughout the journey, and Jo had filled the void by turning on the radio. The bland pop intercut with vacuous banter between the presenter and his sidekick washed over Jo and gradually her fury at her father abated.

By the time they got back, she'd decided. Both she and her mother could do with some space and time to reflect. The Kelmendis, or their informant, had known where to find her. The butchering of Marmalade demonstrated that. So there was little point staying in Greenwich. She announced she was going home to her own flat and Alison didn't object. She retreated to her garden studio with a glass of wine.

Jo packed her case, slotting her sister's university journals in the top, and returned to Lant Street. As she turned her key in the lock and opened the front door, the aroma of stale Thai curry assailed her. But the kitchen was clean, no washing up. Marisa's door was ajar. Jo peeped in and saw her flatmate sleeping. She must be on a late shift this week.

Her own room smelt fusty. Quietly closing the door, she

threw up the sash window and let cold air flood in. The room was small and dominated by her main luxury, a Queen-sized handmade Shaker bed. The frame was solid oak. She'd paid two hundred and fifty pounds for it in a sale, the duvet and pillows were stuffed with white goose down. It was comforter and her refuge. Whenever life gave her a clobbering, she would escape and curl up in her soft-feathered nest. She realized how much she'd been missing it.

Unpacking her case, she put her clothes away in the narrow corner cupboard and placed her laptop and Sarah's journals on the desk that doubled as a dressing table. As she plugged her phone into the charger, she noted three missed calls from her father followed by a text:

Sorry if I've upset you. We need to talk. I've been in touch with my lawyer to find out what we can do to stop this nonsense. Call me. Please. Dad xx

There was a second text from Briony Rowe:

Thanks so much for coming. Know how hard it was for you. Have talked to an admin person at uni and in theory there'll be a pic of Bruce on file. Am chasing it up. Will keep you posted. B.

Kicking off her shoes, Jo flopped down on to the bed and closed her eyes. She must've fallen asleep immediately because she awoke in darkness, an icy current of air rippling across her face and a figure looming over her. Instinct kicked in; she rolled sideways away from her assailant and threw up her arm to protect her head. How did they even get in? The window! She should never've opened the window.

'Welcome home.' Marisa's voice drifted to her through the blackness. 'I brought you a cup of tea.'

Jo sat up. Her pulse was racing, adrenaline screeching through her veins.

'Shall I put the light on?' The voice was full of concern.

'Yeah. Thanks.'

Marisa flicked the switch and the low-energy bulb cast a sepia glow over the room. She studied Jo. 'Sorry, babe, didn't mean to give you a fright.'

'Just a bad dream.' Jo raked a hand through her hair, got up, and shut the window.

'How was Meribel? I wanna hear all about it.'

Meribel? Jo's mind was blank for about ten seconds before she remembered that this was the lie she'd spun her flatmate when she'd learnt the Kelmendis were targeting her and she'd escaped to what she had thought would be the safety of her mother's house.

She looked at Marisa and felt guilty. Too many lies. And Marisa didn't deserve it. She was straightforward and kind. She was also the closest thing Jo had to a best friend. They went clubbing together and had shared plenty of regretful hangovers.

Jo met her gaze. 'I haven't been skiing.'

'Oh.' Marisa frowned. 'So, is it because of Tom? Are you planning to move out?'

'Tom? Christ, no!'

'I know he pisses you off—'

'It was a work thing. Not Tom.'

'Actually, we've split.'

'Really? I'm sorry.'

Marisa laughed, a deep gurgling chortle. 'No, you're not. Don't lie, Jo.'

Jo couldn't help smiling.

'Are you about to go to work?'

'No, I've done a double shift. We had a big RTA and we were already short-staffed so I stayed. That's why I've been asleep most of the day. Totally blitzed.'

'Fancy getting a takeaway?'

'Yeah. Good plan. But not Thai. I seem to have been living on Thai lately.'

'Your choice. I'm happy with whatever.' Jo swung her legs over the side of the bed.

Marisa gave her a quizzical look. 'Are you okay? Has your mum been giving you grief?'

'It's a long story. Let's order, then I'll fill you in.'

40

Dear Jo,

According to the latest neuroscience, the prefrontal cortex of the brain doesn't finish developing fully until around the age of twenty-five. Until then, impulse control is not complete. It's why kids do stupid things and it's why I lashed out that night. It's not about willpower or lack of it, it's simple biology. That punch was far harder than I intended. I was a boy who didn't appreciate his own strength. I wasn't in the habit of hitting people. More than one life was irrevocably altered that night, Jo, that's for sure. But I can't be held solely responsible.

I'm not sure why I'm writing all this down now. I suppose it brings me some relief. I doubt you'll ever read it. I want you to understand how it happened. Of course I do. But that in itself is a risk.

Will we ever be able to have this conversation face to face? That's my fantasy. I'm not asking for forgiveness. That implies guilt. I don't feel guilty. And, as I've already explained, your sister bears her share of the responsibility.

She thought she could lie to me and get away with it. Lies are pernicious. If you knew what she was capable of, then I think you might have some sympathy for my point of view.

When you and I met, it took me a moment to realize that I had seen you before. You were only a little kid and you came to visit her. She didn't want me anywhere near you. When the mood took her, she could be a real bitch. And trust me, that happened quite a lot.

I think you were eleven, just started high school. You were skinny and gangly, tall for your age but clumsy, like a foal learning to run and tripping over its own feet. And you worshipped Sarah. She was a bit naughty with you, took you into the campus bar and gave you half a pint of cider. I'm sure your parents would've disapproved. But you loved it. Loved getting pissed like a proper student. Even when you puked everywhere, you weren't that upset. Sarah patted you on the head, told you it was an initiation. But she looked after you. I think we all wish we had a big sister like that.

41

An evening spent with Marisa was the tonic Jo needed. They ate Italian — spaghetti alla carbonara — from a little Italian place in Borough Market, delivered within fifteen minutes of ordering by a boy on an electric bike.

They discussed Marisa's break-up with her boyfriend. He'd been on a team-building exercise at some fancy hotel and spa with work. In the Jacuzzi, he and a colleague discovered their mutual attraction. One thing led to another and he'd sent Marisa a text the next day informing her he needed *space to sort his head out.* He came round to pick up his stuff and Marisa realized it wasn't his head that was the problem.

She'd shed a few tears. Then a new junior doctor in A&E, where she worked, had asked her to go for a drink. A few days later, Tom had texted her, suggesting they meet up and talk. She'd told him to get lost.

Jo found her flatmate's resilience heartening. Marisa had optimism written into her DNA. Nothing ever seemed to upset her for long. She was also one of the few people Jo knew who could listen.

After their second glass of Pinot Grigio, Jo showed Sarah's journals to her flatmate.

'You never knew these existed?'

'Well, I suppose I did. I must've done. But I'd sort of forgotten.'

'Makes sense. You were only eleven.'

Jo refilled their glasses, emptying the bottle. 'Does it? I feel… I dunno—'

'Guilty? That makes sense too. Survivor's guilt.'

'But it was all so long ago. Okay, she was my sister. But, to be honest, I don't think about her that much.'

Marisa picked up the black shiny book. 'Until now?'

'I don't know what I should do. My mum thinks that if the wrong person was convicted, this somehow explains why she could never come to terms with Sarah's murder.'

'Post-Traumatic Stress Disorder, untreated for years and over-medication with a cocktail of drugs is probably a more accurate explanation.'

Jo sighed. 'I know that.'

'What d'you want to do?'

'Run away? But I can't.'

'Can't you?'

'That's what my dad and my brother did.'

Marisa shrugged. 'Men are often better at prioritizing their own needs.'

'Knowing that doesn't help.'

'Maybe it does. The past is, well, past. It makes no difference to Sarah whether or not the right man went to jail.'

'Matters to me, though.'

Marisa chuckled. 'Then there's your answer, kiddo.'

42

Jo got to the office early and found Sandra already at her desk.

The analyst invited her to come and inspect the image on her screen. Jo peered at it. 'Ivan Rossi's boat?'

The forty-foot cabin cruiser was sleek and white, with a sharp prow and wrap-around tinted glass to protect the helmsman in the cockpit. It was not the sort of vessel that the average assistant manager in an estate agents could afford.

Jo nodded. 'Looks like a pretty good match to me. Where is it?'

'A marina on the Beaulieu River down in Hampshire. We've tracked the company that owns it and made the connection back to Rossi.'

'So what's next?'

Sandra was about to answer, but Foley pre-empted her.

He strolled over, hands in pockets, wreathed in smiles. 'We're putting a surveillance UAV up. Should be online and sending us some lovely live pictures within the hour.'

A drone watching the boat, because of the intel she'd

gathered. No wonder Foley had decided to be nice. 'So, are we still hanging fire on Rossi?'

'Yeah, boss thinks that's best. Until he makes a move.' Foley gave no hint of his previous opposition to this course of action. His sunny smile made Jo suspicious.

But she returned it. 'Sounds great.'

Hands on his hips, he was scanning her, too closely maybe? It was creepy. 'You're on standby in case we need you to call him. A little twitch on the thread? But we'll see how things progress.' He hadn't given up his line completely.

'Okay. Fine.'

The DS wandered off, and Jo realized Sandra was studying her.

She pushed her glasses back into the mass of grey curls. 'Whad'you reckon?'

'About the op? Seems to be going well.'

'About Foley?'

'Foley?' Jo frowned.

'He's in a right old spin about you. Been trying to pluck up the courage to ask you out.'

'What? You're kidding! He hates me.'

'He tried to find out from your old crew if you're with anyone.'

Jo stared at the analyst in disbelief. 'Y'know how much grief he's been giving me? Everything I've done, he's pulled apart.'

'Yeah, that's Cal. Gets confused, goes for the jugular. But he's been running round like a scalded cat ever since you arrived. When you didn't come in yesterday, he was worried you'd gone back to your old squad. Immediately went down the corridor to find you and tell them what for.'

'I took a day off. Personal stuff.'

The look of horror on Jo's face prompted a wry smile

from the analyst. 'Surely you've come across blokes like him before?'

'No.'

'Oh well. If you're not interested, watch your back then.'

'I'm definitely not interested.'

Jo retreated to her desk. Overtures from Foley—that was the last thing she needed. She glanced across the room in his direction and wondered if Sandra was right. It seemed bizarre. Why be so unpleasant if he fancied her?

For the rest of the morning, Jo kept a low profile. She sloped out for coffee when she saw him busy talking to some other members of the team.

The rest of the time, she sat at her desk. Sandra sent her a link and she watched the live-feed from the drone. Down below through the eddying mist, the cabin cruiser bobbed gently at its mooring. There was no one about. A couple of moorhens glided by.

Secreted behind her computer screen, Jo pulled out her sister's journals. The issue that had kept her awake half the night was the missing pages. Five pages cut out? Why? What had happened that Sarah had written about, then felt the need to erase even from her own private record?

The only other items of her sister's she possessed, that were personal to her, were three letters Sarah had sent her. Jo had dug them out of a shoebox in the bottom of her cupboard. All written in the autumn term, the last one was dated 21 November.

There were two other entries in the journal on 22 and 24 November, then the pages had been removed. It was a week before Sarah wrote her next entry. And it was short:

Christmas vacation soon and I'm looking forward to it. Still pretty wiped out, but I hope that will pass. Now I've had a chance to think about it, I don't mind dropping out of Much

Ado. I still think I should've played Beatrice, not Hero. And anyway, who wants to see another bloody version of another bloody Shakespeare play? Rumour has it that Cyn's been cast in my place, which just goes to prove what a crap director he is.

Jo re-read the passage a couple of times. Had Sarah been ill and therefore forced to withdraw from a student drama production? It sounded like that. But the thing that hooked her attention was the mention of *Cyn.* Briony identified this person as someone on their course, *the snotbag* who Sarah didn't like. And the journal entry seemed to confirm that.

Mulling this over, Jo found her thoughts drifting on to Nathan Wade. It did matter to her that the right man had been convicted. But was there any reason to think it wasn't him? She didn't like him, she knew that. He gave her the creeps. However, that didn't make him a murderer.

Her phone buzzed with an incoming text. She sighed as she read it.

I'm downstairs. Let me buy you lunch. We need to talk. Dad x

43

Briony Rowe had been a painfully shy teenager and her student years had been a struggle. But once she'd emerged from her twenties and accepted she'd never be a size ten, her life had improved. She had an excellent visual eye and an obsession for detail. Her career as a video editor blossomed. Producers sought her out. She helped to turn many a director's incompetent mash-up into a sharp and coherent narrative. She earned the respect of her peers and was always in demand.

Becoming a film-maker in her own right had always been a distant dream. Unfortunately, a reputation as an editor didn't persuade those who controlled the purse strings you were on the same creative level as them. Documentary commissions were hard to come by and there was a wariness of a techie who didn't know her place.

But Briony was a terrier. She never gave up. She believed in hard work and persistence, virtues she possessed in abundance. Ten-hour shifts in a dingy basement edit suite had hardened her resolve to succeed.

Thanks to Briony's coaxing, Jo Boden was moving from

hostile to spiky but curious. She'd set Briony a challenge: go to the university archive and find a picture of Bruce. Briony knew Jo believed the whole thing was a fiction and she wouldn't be able to recognize him. But the cop was wrong about that. Briony had an appointment with someone in the registrar's department and was confident that within days she'd have a result. And a name.

Underneath the cuddly carapace, Briony was still shy. But on social media, she was in her element with her slick videos and clever quips. She had eight hundred friends on Facebook alone, loads more on Instagram, she was regularly on TikTok, and spent most evenings chatting and posting. In recent years, Cynthia Fenton-Wright had popped up on her timeline occasionally. Like many old friends who'd never really been friends, they'd embraced the concept of networking and exchanged a few polite comments and likes.

But putting a name to Bruce's face was stage one in the campaign to get DC Boden onside. Stage two was Cyn.

The restaurant was in Clerkenwell; it boasted a Michelin star and when Briony arrived, slightly late, at 1.15., it was packed with City suits.

Cynthia was already at the table, thinner and blonder than Briony remembered, the dreads replaced by a sharp A-line cut, but her manner hadn't changed. She had the same effortless superiority, but it was no longer quite so intimidating. She rose from her seat for air-kissing and polite greetings, then they settled with the menus. The invitation had been Briony's, but Old Cyn took charge.

'Are you drinking? I don't at lunchtime.' Cynthia gave her a condescending smile.

'I'll have a gin and tonic.' Briony glanced at the server. 'Sipsmith, if you've got it.' A little dutch courage wouldn't go amiss.

Cynthia laced her fingers neatly in front of her. 'It's been way too long. We should've done this ages ago.'

'Busy lives.'

'Indeed. And you're a film-maker now. How exciting!'

'It was always my ambition.'

'I didn't know that.' The tone implied surprise at such a notion. 'Shall we order?'

Briony picked the most expensive starter and filet of beef. She hoped her credit card could bear it. Cynthia had chosen the restaurant, but Briony had no intention of giving the impression she wasn't used to this kind of venue. Her dining companion opted for sea bream and salad.

The menus were removed and they faced each other across the table. Briony was feeling a lot more relaxed than she'd expected. She noted with satisfaction that Cynthia seemed a little tense.

'You mentioned you're making a film about Sarah Boden. How on earth did that come about?'

'I don't think Nathan Wade did it.'

'That's a bold assertion after all these years.'

'I never believed he was guilty. He adored Sarah.'

'Didn't everyone?' There was a sourness in Cynthia's tone. 'Of course, the whole thing was awful. Such a lovely girl.'

Briony beamed. She was enjoying herself. The gin arrived in a large bulbous glass beaded with moisture.

Cynthia gazed at it. 'I'm starting to wish I'd ordered one of those.'

The film-maker took a mouthful and licked her lips. 'It's delicious. Let me get you one—'

'No no! I couldn't possibly. I've got a client flying in from New York this afternoon.'

Briony took another sip. 'What made you decide to go into branding?'

'Mainly the intellectual challenge.' Her brow puckered as if to emphasize the seriousness of the decision. 'We're a branding *and* digital design agency, so what we do is pretty cutting edge. I suppose I concluded that acting wasn't for me. Being ordered around by some silly director. I like to be the one in charge. And business is more creative than most people think. Especially when you're the CEO.'

'You were always very well organized.'

'Was I?' Cynthia laughed. 'Fancy you remembering that.' She gave her companion a considered look. 'So, do you think the case will be re-opened?'

'I hope so. Otherwise I haven't got much of a film.'

'You genuinely believe he didn't do it?'

'There was such a lot of fuss when it happened. I'm sure you remember.'

'Oh, it was horrible. I was scared to leave my room.'

'The pressure was on the police to make an arrest. The boyfriend did it. That's the usual assumption, isn't it?'

'If not Nathan Wade, then who?'

Briony shrugged. 'There are various theories.'

'Such as?'

'I shouldn't really say. I'm working closely with Nathan's new lawyers.'

The gin level in her glass was sinking, and the delectable spirit was filling her with warmth and confidence. Cynthia Fenton-Wright was such a bitch, she always had been. But Briony had promised herself that all she was going to do today was rattle her cage. Very gently.

'What I can tell you is that we've discovered some potential witnesses who weren't interviewed at the time. Nathan met them on the way to the station.'

The shock that passed through Cynthia was barely perceptible. She covered it by pressing her napkin to her lips and coughing. She returned the napkin to her lap and smoothed it out. 'Which is relevant how?'

Briony pretended not to notice. 'If Nathan caught the train as he says, he couldn't have committed the murder. They saw him. Talked to him.'

Cynthia was rescued by two servers bringing and explaining their starters: a salad with a quail's egg on the top and a wild mushroom risotto.

Sliding her fork into the risotto, Briony savoured her first mouthful. 'I'm so pleased you suggested this place. This is amazing.'

'It's a favourite of mine.' If Briony's bolt from the blue had unnerved her, there was no longer any sign of it. 'We always come here for a treat. So I did hope you'd like it.'

'I'm definitely putting it on my list.' It would join Nandos and Pizza Hut, but Briony didn't mention that.

Cynthia painted on a smile. 'And have the lawyers tracked down any of these potential witnesses?'

'Y'know, I'm not sure. I think perhaps they've got some addresses they're following up. There's been some talk of a private investigator.'

Briony had to rein herself in. Exaggeration was fair enough, but that was a total lie. She shouldn't go there. It wasn't necessary.

Cynthia prodded her quail's egg. 'And are you...involved with any of that?'

'No.' Briony scooped up the last forkful of risotto. 'Not at all.'

She should stop there, leave it at that. Outright lying was stupid. And unethical. She'd already succeeded in throwing Cynthia off balance. But another seductive thought snaked into her mind. She wouldn't lie. But couldn't she brag a little? Where was the harm in that?

'Actually, the witness thing is only part of it. I've got a meeting at the university the day after tomorrow. Our old alma mater has agreed to let me trawl through its archives.'

'Really? What do you hope to find?'

'The boyfriend theory isn't entirely wrong. We think the police just got the wrong boyfriend.'

'You mean Sarah was going out with someone else?'

'It was a fling she had at the very beginning of the autumn term. With a postgrad. He was a sleaze, so she dumped him. Then he started to stalk her.'

'Wow! You know who he is?'

'Not by name. But I'd certainly recognize him. His mugshot'll be somewhere in the records. Once I find him, we can put a name to the face. Then we can nail him.'

44

'I think maybe they do food here.' As Jo pushed open the heavy glass-panelled door, an aroma of burnt fat and stale beer assailed them.

The pub was cavernous, a tackily refurbished Victorian monstrosity round the corner from her office. It was the sort of place she knew Nick Boden would hate, which was why she'd chosen it.

Following her in, he wrinkled his nose but said nothing.

She walked across the room to the long wooden bar. Two young guys perched on stools looked her up and down and scuttled off. They were drug dealers who could smell a cop.

Jo turned and gave her father a chilly smile. 'What can I get you?'

Tall and rangy, Nick Boden looked far younger than his sixty-two years. His grey hair was receding only slightly and the salt-and-pepper sculpted beard gave him, his wife assured him, a rakish air.

He tilted his head and smiled. 'I take your point, Jo. Now, can we go somewhere decent?'

'Such as where? I don't have a lot of time.'

He sighed, pulled out his wallet and gave the barman a nod. 'Half of...I dunno—' he scanned the pumps 'Bud Light, and...?' He glanced at his daughter.

'Sparkling water.'

'Sparkling water it is.'

The drinks were served and paid for, and they settled themselves at a rickety table in the far corner of the room.

Nick shook his head wearily. 'First, I'm sorry. I've handled this badly.'

'This being what, exactly?'

He was wearing a Canadian goose down jacket and a cashmere scarf. Taking the jacket off, he slotted it on the back of his chair.

'What do I have to do to get beyond your hostility, Jo?'

'I'm not hostile, Dad. I'm simply not interested.'

'If I could wind back the clock, don't you think I would? I'm only trying to protect you and your mother.'

Jo shrugged. Dealing with him had always made her both belligerent and uncomfortable. This had been true as far back as she could remember, but, in reality, probably dated from the time of her sister's death.

Nick Boden had chucked in his City job in insurance and walked away from his mad, grieving wife and the ghost of his murdered daughter. He'd been on some epic journey of self-discovery. Jo didn't know the details and didn't want to. When he'd surfaced a year later, thinner, fitter and with a tropical tan, her brother, Carl, had gone to live with him. She'd refused to leave Alison.

They'd moved to Norfolk and he'd started converting barns. After he'd run out of barns, he'd become a full-blown developer. His projects were upscale and bristling with the latest ecological design features. He'd made a ton of money, although Jo doubted any of it would ever come her way. He had a wife twenty-five years his junior and two little boys, her half-brothers, whom she hardly knew.

'How are Emily and the boys?'

'Good, thank you. You should come up. They'd love to see you.'

He pulled a phone out of his pocket, brought up a snapshot, and handed it to Jo.

Two beaming faces gazed at the camera. She realized she could almost be having a polite chat and admiring the family photos of a colleague at work or some other casual acquaintance. 'How old are they now? I lose track.'

Leaning over, her father pointed. 'Jack's nearly nine. Oscar's seven.'

She forced a smile, as she returned the phone.

'It would be good for them to know their sister and, you never know, it might be good for her too.' He smiled.

Jo met his gaze. They shared the same slate-grey eyes. 'What have your lawyers got to say about all this, then? Presumably you're in London to see them.'

Nick crossed his legs and leant back in his chair. 'I was upset. I went off at a bit of a tangent. When this woman got in touch, this wretched film-maker, I should've come to you. After all, you're the detective.'

Now he was trying to flatter her into submission.

She sighed. 'Dad—'

'Hear me out, Jo. All I want is for us to discuss this and come to a consensus as a family.'

A family? They'd ceased to be that long ago.

'Are you planning to involve Mum in this discussion?'

'If you think that would be at all possible, yes.'

Jo picked up her glass of fizzy water. She was wishing she'd opted for something stronger. She thought about the cardboard boxes of her sister's journals and the care with which he'd wrapped them up in tissue paper and put them away.

'I've been reading Sarah's journals. We got them out of the loft.'

He raised his eyebrows. 'Wow! You've got more courage than me.'

'Why courage?'

'I don't know. Perhaps because I fear finding out how much I'm to blame.'

'How can you be to blame?'

'A man should be able to protect his own daughter. She was so young. Eighteen years old. Little more than a child. I should've—' The back of his hand brushed his mouth. 'I'm sorry.'

Jo found his self-pity annoying.

'Why didn't you get some kind of proper treatment for Mum?'

'My God, Jo, you think I'd didn't try? The GP suggested having her sectioned. I thought that would only make things worse. Grief isn't a mental illness, it's part of life, a normal process.'

'Having your child murdered isn't normal.'

'I thought we'd somehow get through it together. I didn't understand, at the time, what was happening to her. Or to me. It was all so drawn out. Well, you know how long these things take. Waiting for the trial. Sitting in court every day, it was torture. After it was over, I think we both just went off the deep end in our different ways.'

Jo was watching and listening to him, but curiously she felt nothing. She could empathize with a Syrian refugee, or an elderly neighbour. She could even shed a tear over a dead cat. But faced with her own father's pain, she felt cynical and detached.

What had happened to her? This wasn't normal. She knew that. But in his grief over Sarah, Jo was the daughter he abandoned. He'd tried later and at various times to come back into her life, but she'd always resisted. Her anger with him was implacable. But where did it come from? Jo could remember little from the period of the trial. When it was over, he just disappeared. All she was left with now was a sense of emptiness tinged with resentment.

She sighed. 'Listen, Dad, I don't think there's a straightforward way you're going to be able to shut these people down. An injunction? On what grounds? Nathan Wade has every right to ask for a review of his conviction. I've talked to the producer. She says if I look at the evidence and remain convinced that the conviction is sound, then they'll walk away.'

'And you believe her?'

'In the absence of any other practical alternative, I'm giving her the benefit of the doubt.'

Nick Boden had his hands clasped together, almost in an attitude of prayer. 'Will you keep me in the loop?'

'Of course.' Even as she said it, Jo knew she was lying.

45

It was still dark when Calvin Foley collected Jo from her flat in an unmarked police car. The Met had the lead because she'd gathered the intel and they'd built the case. But within days, the remit to seize illegal arms had morphed into a major operation with the UK Border Agency, Hampshire Police and the National Crime Agency. Ivan Rossi's boat had slipped its mooring at high tide the previous day and been tracked across the North Sea to the Dutch port of Zierikzee, fifty miles south of Rotterdam. Rossi himself had been on board and was now under surveillance by the Dutch police.

By 7 a.m. Foley and Boden were on the M3, heading south. Their destination was the New Forest and the tidal reaches of the Beaulieu River around the medieval ship-building village of Buckler's Hard.

Driving into the forest, as pallid shafts of sun leached through the morning mist, gave Jo a sense of eerie detachment. Overnight, there had been a thick dusting of snow. The boughs of the overhanging canopy dripped with a white frosting, creating a magical tunnel through the trees. It reinforced the sensation of leaving everyday reality behind.

Once they turned on to the byroads, the snow was several centimetres deep. Their route crossed patches of open heathland clothed in a fresh white mantle. It forced Foley to slow right down, follow the tyre tracks and keep an eagle eye out for the wandering ponies that appeared like spectres in the mist.

The DS had made several attempts at conversation during the journey, but Jo had closed her eyes and pretended to doze. Knowing he fancied her didn't help. She had plenty to think about, and the job was the least of it. Fortunately, Foley left her alone; he tuned into Classic FM—a surprising choice for him, she thought—and let it play in the background.

They drove into Buckler's Hard to find the village deserted. Boats bobbed at their moorings shrouded in mist. The row of neatly preserved redbrick Georgian cottages was blanketed in snow and water lapped at a slipway crusted in ice.

Foley parked in a puddle of slush outside the hotel. Opening her car door, Jo peered gingerly out. Snow rarely settled in London and she was wearing ordinary shoes. She hadn't thought this through.

But from the boot of the car, the DS produced two pairs of green wellies.

He offered one to Jo. 'Had to guess your size.'

'I've got big feet. Size seven.'

'Yeah, that was my guess.'

The boots fitted, she got out of the car and they sauntered about. The brief was to pose as tourists.

He took a couple of photos with his phone, but he seemed genuinely excited. 'Can you imagine what it used to be like? From defeating the Spanish Armada to Nelson beating Napoleon's fleet, several centuries of British naval power started right here. *Euryalus*, *Swiftsure* and *Agamemnon*, great wooden ships of the line. They were all built here. *Agamemnon* was Nelson's favourite.'

Foley bursting with boyish enthusiasm; this was another side to him Jo wasn't expecting.

She wrapped her scarf round her neck and pulled on her gloves. 'How do you know all this stuff?' He'd probably just looked it up on the net so he could play the smartarse.

'Came here as a kid. My mum insisted on taking us to all sorts of places. Country walks too. She was always wanting to get out of Peckham.'

Jo smiled, but she was envious. Parents who showed you things and took you places, so you learnt about history. Family outings. An ordinary upbringing. How different her life could've been.

They headed for the hotel. A discreet mobile comms unit was up and running in a suite of river-facing rooms on the first floor. It was manned by two colleagues from Operation Grebe, but there was no backup or uniforms in evidence. The priority was to maintain a low profile for as long as possible.

The SIO, they were told, was down on the quay in the tiny Harbour Master's office; it was more of a shed but commanded a good view of the river.

Crunching through the crisp snow and taking a few more snaps on the way, they discovered Steve Vaizey consuming a bacon sandwich and chatting to the Harbour Master.

He seemed relaxed, given the size and complexity of the operation. 'You two are bright and early. White-out in the Channel last night but this morning a calmer sea, so if I were them I'd be tempted to give it a go.'

Foley nodded. 'What d'you want us to do?'

Vaizey glanced at Jo. 'It would be useful if we could get some idea of his plans. What do you reckon?'

'I can try calling him. He's left me a couple of messages, wondering why I haven't been in touch.'

'Okay. But, y'know…'

'Don't worry, boss. I won't spook him.'

Vaizey nodded and turned straight back to the Harbour Master.

Jo didn't mind his curtness. He was focused on the job and she admired that.

She and Foley strolled back towards the hotel. The sun had broken through and there were patches of blue sky.

Foley smirked, scooped up a handful of snow, and patted it into a ball.

Jo wagged a gloved finger at him. 'Don't even think about it!'

'Aww, don't be a spoilsport. Just getting into the role.'

'Yeah, right.'

He shrugged and tossed the snowball away, in a long overarm cricketer's throw; it plopped into the river. A moorhen squawked and took flight.

'See, you're frightening the ducks.'

'Moorhens.'

She shot him a baleful look.

He smiled. 'Sometimes I get the impression you're not my biggest fan.'

'I wonder why.'

He hesitated, shoved his hands in his pockets. His bashful tone surprised her. 'I don't know why. But I think it's a pity. I like you, Jo. And, for the record, I think you're doing a great job.'

Her heart sank. Was Foley about to make a declaration? In the middle of all this? Surely not.

But his gaze had strayed to the river. Perhaps Sandra was

right. It was all about male insecurity and now he was trying to make friends? He smiled. 'You ever done any sailing?'

'Boating. On holiday as a little kid.'

'I used to do it competitively. Finn dinghies. I was pretty good as a junior.'

Jo couldn't decide if he was boasting again or making conversation or a bit of both.

She batted it back at him. 'Where did you sail? On the south coast?'

'Brighton. Even went to uni down there so I could carry on.'

'You went to uni in Brighton?'

The flicker of surprise in her voice didn't escape him.

He laughed. 'Okay, so I look like a meathead and sometimes I act like one. I'll admit it. But I do have a degree. History, as a matter of fact. Not that surprising, is it?'

She shook her head and smiled.

But it was the mention of Brighton that had thrown Jo off balance. Her sister had gone to uni there and never come back. Thoughts stampeded through her brain. Foley was a student there too? When? Could he have known her? He was about the right age. Even thinking it was absurd.

Reading her sister's journals had unmoored her. They'd filled her with regret and sadness for the life she'd lost. And it was affecting and distorting everything.

She stopped and pulled out her phone. 'Okay, if I'm going to do this, I need some space.'

He nodded. 'Yeah, of course. I'll wait for you in the hotel bar?'

'Yeah.'

Glad of an excuse to escape him, Jo picked her way down the icy slipway towards the water's edge. The tide was still ebbing, exposing a narrow band of coarse shingle, which gave way to slabs of brown river mud. Squatting down on her heels, she scrolled her phone to find Ivan Rossi's number.

Before clicking on it, she paused to compose her thoughts. The last few days had been an odd time. Throughout her police career, the job had been a refuge from the complications of her family and the past. But even now, in the midst of a major operation, when her mind definitely should be on the task at hand, her thoughts were jumbled. She couldn't concentrate. Seeing her dad hadn't helped.

Here she was, with the biggest opportunity of her career, a chance to prove what she could do, and her brain was in a spin.

She'd lied to her father, but did she even have a plan? Since that encounter, she'd been consumed with listlessness. It was hard to accomplish even mundane things. She hadn't spoken to Alison; she had no idea what state her mother was in.

Now, as she stared down at the phone screen, something inside ruptured, desolation flooded out, tears flowed and she couldn't stop them.

She pressed the call button. It rang twice, then he answered.

'Hey, Charlotte. I was hoping you'd ring.'

Jo sobbed. It came from a deep well and it was for real.

'My God, are you okay? What's happened? What has that bastard done to you? Charlotte?'

'I'm sorry! I'm so sorry—'

'No, you were right to call.'

'I didn't know what else—'

'Where are you? At home?'

'I've run away.'

'That's good. That's smart.'

'I don't know what to do, Ivan.'

'Listen to me, you can come and stay with me. I'm out of town at the moment. But I'll call my sister and get her to let you in.'

'No, I don't want to bother anyone. And not your sister. I'm at a friend's. But he'll be looking for me.'

'I'm going to be back in London tonight. Seven o'clock at the latest. Will you meet me then?'

'I don't know.'

'Let me help you, Charlotte. I want to help you. Are you safe at your friend's for now?'

'I think so.'

'Meet me at seven.'

'You will be there?'

'I promise. I'll text you the address right now.'

'I don't know what I'd do without you.'

'Hey, not all blokes are like him, y'know.'

'I'll see you later. And thank you.'

She hung up. Her cheeks were wet. She pulled out a tissue and blew her nose. Standing up, she felt light-headed and for a moment. She thought she might throw up.

She took several deep breaths. The freezing air zapped her lungs but helped clear her head. She walked slowly back to the hotel. Foley was standing on the steps of the main entrance, rubbing his hands.

'You okay?'

She glanced around to check no one was in earshot. 'I've arranged to meet him in London at seven o'clock tonight.' Her voice sounded tiny and seemed to echo in her head.

'That means he must be coming back on the afternoon tide.' Foley clenched his fist and muttered under his breath. 'Yes! We've got the bastard. Great work, Jo. I'll let the boss know.'

Turning away, he disappeared into the hotel. Jo watched him go. She felt spent. How much of that was an act and how much real? She didn't know. She brushed a crust of ice off the wall and sat down. For the next quarter of an hour, she watched her breath condensing in the frigid air.

46

By early afternoon, the mist was gone and the snow was melting. Jo and Foley had a sandwich in the hotel bar. Their chat was innocuous. It was very much a live operation; they remained in their undercover roles and on the lookout for any accomplices of Rossi who could well be hanging around. But there were few people about; a couple of sprightly retirees in walking boots were the only others having lunch.

Posing as tourists, the two cops had taken covert snaps of everyone they encountered in their wanderings, mainly the few guests and staff around the hotel. These had been sent to the control room in London and checked against the national database. Nothing was flagged up.

As surveillance jobs went, loafing around a four-star country hotel wasn't that onerous. Jo's skittering thoughts became calmer. Foley could be a pain, but she couldn't fault his professionalism. His eyes were everywhere, his conversation bland and undemanding.

However, as the afternoon wore on, Jo started to worry. Her histrionics on the phone to Rossi seemed to have worked. But was it all a bit too easy? He seemed such an ordinary young bloke, yet how could he be? What if he had played her and not the other way round? What if her phone call had alerted the gang to the fact the police were waiting for them?

High tide was around four o'clock. It came and there was no sign of his boat. Jo announced she was going for a walk on her own. Foley didn't object.

As she strolled along the quay, a small dingy with an outboard puttered towards her. Vaizey sat in the bow with a rod leaning against his shoulder, surrounded by fishing tackle. The other fisherman with his hand on the tiller, she recognized as a colleague from Operation Grebe.

The boat came alongside and Vaizey jumped out on to the pontoon. He looked damp and cold and had a sour expression. 'Y'know what I think, Jo. I think we're blown.'

'No sign of anything?' She felt unaccountably guilty.

'Tide's ebbing. It'll be dark within half an hour.'

He tied a line from the boat to a post on the jetty. He rubbed his hands to warm them up. His companion unloaded the fishing tackle. Vaizey turned to him. 'A large Scotch for you in the bar when you've finished, Alan.'

'Cheers, boss.'

Vaizey and Boden walked back towards the hotel. His manner was subdued, but she could feel his suppressed anger. He wasn't a man who liked to lose.

'I'm sorry, boss.'

'These things don't always go to plan.'

'I thought I had him. I really did.'

'May not be you. If his gang's used this place before, then they'll have eyes and ears. Possibly even someone local or even working at the hotel to tip them off. Hampshire have got officers staked out in the boatyard pretending to work there. Could be that.'

'Shall I try to call him again?'

'No. Let's see if he comes back to you. Then we'll know if your cover's blown.'

They walked on in silence. When they got halfway up the slipway, he turned and gazed out at the river. The light was already fading. The sky was louring, but the rippling water had a mercurial sheen.

Turning to face her, his smile was wistful. 'Beautiful spot, eh? Maybe I should take up fishing for real.'

There was a softness in his eyes that she'd not seen before and suddenly the notion of him being defeated, of suffering, irked her. If this operation turned out to be an expensive failure—as it likely would—he'd have to shoulder the blame. She wanted him to know that she was on his side completely.

'Y'know, maybe Rossi's smarter than we thought. Some girl walks into his shop? He could've made me, fed me a line—'

He raised his index finger and placed it gently on her shoulder. 'I appreciate the offer. But I don't need you to take the fall.'

His touch was so light, but its effect was electric. She just wanted him to kiss her.

But he stepped back. 'Come on, I'll buy you a drink.'

It was disappointing but also a relief. Her head was in enough of a muddle. She didn't need to make it worse. He was a married man with a family. And did she want to commit career suicide? Absolutely not.

The phone in her jacket pocket buzzed. Pulling it out, she glanced at the screen, then stopped dead. 'It's him!'

Vaizey turned to face her, a wry smile hovering on his lips, as if he'd known, he'd always known.

He gave her a nod. 'Okay then.'

Jo took a breath and answered the call. 'Hey, Ivan?'

47

Jo positioned herself at the back of the room. The image on the screen was bleached of colour. It was almost dark but with enough reflected light from the river and patches of snow to make it possible to see what was happening.

In the hotel suite there were four monitors lined up on portable tables, each showing live-feed from a separate camera. But attention was focused on the far-left screen. Camera one.

Looming in the twilight was a motor cruiser gliding towards a mooring post out in the channel; it was sleek, white and glittered in the dusk. Most of the surrounding vessels were smaller: sailing boats and skiffs, so it stood out. It was upriver, well away from the marina and the Harbour Master's office.

In the call Ivan Rossi made to Jo, he'd been astonishingly candid. He'd explained that he was doing a favour for a family friend and had gone out on his boat. But engine problems had slowed them down and he was late getting back. He insisted he would still meet her in London by nine.

The sympathy and anxiety in his voice, his trust in her, had made Jo uncomfortable.

'Listen to me, Charlotte, I will be back. I made you a promise and I intend to keep it.'

As she'd listened to him, she'd reflected ruefully that, like her, his mind wasn't on the job in hand. He was oblivious to the fact he was walking into a trap. She had to remind herself that this was good. But a small part of her felt sorry for him.

The hotel's largest suite had been turned into a comfortable mobile command centre. Vaizey was on his feet, pacing as he directed operations, and Foley was at his side. The tension and excitement in the room was palpable. Jo watched from the back, keeping out of the way. She'd played her part; her job was done.

Camera one zoomed in on the cruiser. There appeared to be three men on board, all wearing heavy waterproof sailing jackets with the hoods up and tightly fastened to conceal most of their faces. The tide was receding fast. They'd left it too late to tie up to the jetty. Or perhaps it was always their intention to use one of the mooring posts further out in the main channel.

Their jackets were fluoro-yellow, so even in the fading light the men were easy to pick out. They worked swiftly and efficiently, launching a small inflatable with an outboard motor. One of them got into the dinghy, the others returned to the cabin. They made four trips, carrying a bulky holdall each time, which they passed to the man in the boat. Then they boarded the tiny vessel, too.

Foley folded his arms. 'If they're not careful, they'll sink it.'

Vaizey smiled. 'I'm guessing this isn't the first time they've done this.'

The action moved to camera two and the point of view

changed. Loaded down, the inflatable was ploughing towards the shore, where it beached on a patch of hard sand. The camera panned to take in a black Mercedes panel van parked on the grass close to the shoreline, behind it, black trees and dark woods. A man in a hoodie got out. The transfer of the holdalls from the boat to the van took less than a minute. One of the sailors stripped off his jacket, joined the hoodie in the van and it drove off.

As the dingy was being pushed back into the water, half a dozen armed police swarmed from the trees and the two sailors were surrounded up to their knees in water. They raised their hands in surrender. The sound on the footage was muffled, only the shout *Armed Police!* was audible.

Gaze fixed on the screens, Vaizey nodded to himself. The comms officer seated in front of the monitors punched the air with his fist.

Foley was on his phone, finger pressed to his other ear. He turned to Vaizey. 'We've got two drones on the van, boss. And as soon as they hit the main road, ANPR will pick them up.'

Camera three wobbled and turned. A bright light was being shone on the two sailors as they were hauled out of the river and cuffed. The officers arresting them pulled their hoods back and the camera zoomed in on their faces.

Ivan Rossi looked wet and cold and in shock. His companion was older and sullen, but then Rossi seemed to gather himself. He started speaking to the armed police, arresting him. The words were impossible to decipher, but the tone was pleading.

Vaizey tapped the comms officer on the shoulder. 'Ask them what he's saying?'

The comms officer relayed the question through his headset. The answer came back almost immediately.

'He wants to call his girlfriend. Says she's expecting him and if he doesn't show, she'll be upset.'

Foley gave a hoot of laughter and swivelled round to face Jo. 'You've completely suckered him. What a numbskull! You're the business, Jo Boden. A real femme fatale.'

Everyone in the room was looking at her. Jo felt uncomfortable. She managed a smile, aware of Vaizey and that chilly, unremitting stare resting on her. Then he nodded. 'Yes, DC Boden. Well done.'

48

Jo was at a loose end. The comedown after a successful op was a strange time. Alcohol was almost always involved.

The mobile comms unit was being dismantled and packed into crates when reports came through from the team tracking the van. It had joined the M6 and speculation was its destination was Manchester or Liverpool. After a day hanging around, Foley had been champing at the bit, so Vaizey had allowed him to join the pursuit; Jo was left to drive their unmarked pool car back to London.

The cruiser had been searched and impounded. The two gun smugglers transferred to cells in Southampton. Vaizey had ordered up several bottles of Scotch and toasted the DI from Hampshire and his officers. This was a good result for everyone.

The call from Foley came at around 11 p.m. Vaizey put his phone on loudspeaker so the team remaining from the Met could listen in.

There were sirens in the background and Foley sounded wired. 'We tracked the van to a small industrial estate in Stockport. The buyers are a well-known Manchester crime family. Ten arrests, the guys in the van plus eight armed thugs at the warehouse.'

'How many weapons?' Despite several whiskies, Vaizey was very much in control.

'I'll send you the video of the preliminary exam. Looks like two bags of Skorpion machine pistols, possibly twenty units. Ten Russian assault rifles, all AK 47s. One of the bags is ammo. Plus, there's a selection of handguns. It's a fucking arsenal, all right!'

'Any problems?'

'We took them completely by surprise. We thought they might try to shoot their way out. But when they saw what they were up against, they thought better of it. SIO here is extremely chuffed. Dream come true for him catching one of their leading local mobsters red-handed with a pile of guns. He asked me to pass on his compliments to you.'

'Give him mine, Cal. And tell the rest of the team well done from me. Textbook operation.'

'Will do, boss.'

Vaizey clicked the phone off, turned to Jo and smiled. 'Top-up?'

She was lounging on the sofa and allowed him to pour an inch of whisky into her glass. Her plan had been to leave several hours ago. But that hadn't happened for reasons she couldn't quite pin down. She wasn't drunk, but she was probably over the limit.

The atmosphere in the room was one of tired relief. Any further coordination through the night would be handled from the London control centre. The comms officers were running through their checklist, making sure nothing got left behind.

One of them turned to Vaizey. 'Mind if we get off, boss?'

'Yeah, you go. Thanks.' He hesitated, then added. 'That

other vehicle we're tracking? Mark it so the notifications are sent straight through to me.'

'No problem.'

Jo put her glass down without touching it. 'I should go too. Long drive.'

Vaizey gave her a stern look. It reminded her of her father, which wasn't good. 'Aren't you somewhat over the limit? We've got this entire suite until tomorrow. Plenty of space to crash.'

His tone was casual, and it would be hard to read anything into it. She looked at him. That chilly penetrating gaze scanned her, but only for a moment.

He picked up his glass and drained it. 'Me, I was up at four. So I shall be out like a light as soon as my head hits the pillow.'

Jo got up slowly. She couldn't help feeling like a gawky teenager trying to appear cool and in control.

This was the operational life, long hours of boredom, then a burst of excitement. Euphoria at a successful result laced with alcohol. She'd been in this situation before, in the back-wash, mellow with drink. It was easy to forget that life existed outside the job. This is where affairs began and marriages ended.

She gave him what she hoped was a disinterested nod. 'Yeah, you're right. Thanks, boss. I'm fine with the sofa.' Kicking off her shoes, she plonked down and started to get comfortable.

The comms officers carried the last of their gear out and closed the door behind them.

Steve Vaizey hesitated and then put his hands on his hips. 'You know I'm married, don't you?'

Now they were alone, the tone of voice was less matter-of-fact. He tilted his head and gave her a quizzical smile. Jo stared at him. She didn't get it. His abrupt change of manner had wrong-footed her again.

'Meaning what?'

'Meaning I intend to stay married, but that doesn't mean to say that I don't want to sleep with you.'

She felt both annoyed and manipulated. This was hardly the hot-blooded passion she'd hoped for. His attitude puzzled her.

'What about what I want?'

He shrugged. 'Okay, well, I guess that answers the question.' He turned and headed for the bedroom. 'Sleep tight.'

As he walked away, she felt a rush of regret.

'Hang on.' She spoke without thinking.

He turned back to face her and she could feel her pulse racing.

His smile was sardonic. 'So what do you want, Jo Boden? Do you even know?'

49

She woke in the morning with a fuggy head—whisky had never been her drink—to find herself alone. The king-sized bed occupied the main bedroom in the suite. She couldn't remember getting into it. The large soft duvet was hardly rumpled. Then she remembered the sex; it had taken place on the sofa in the other room, awkward and perfunctory. He couldn't maintain an erection. He'd apologized, and said again how tired he was. So why hadn't he stayed? Probably because he was embarrassed. The state of the bed suggested she'd slept there by herself.

Getting up, she wandered through the suite. Her clothes were arranged in a neat pile on the chair, which was not where they'd landed when she'd pulled them off. There was no sign of Vaizey and no note. His bag, his laptop, his jacket were all gone.

She pulled back the heavy drapes and white icy light flooded the room. It sent a lonely chill through her. Whatever romantic illusions she'd harboured about Steve Vaizey had turned out to be just that. It was like bad-first-date sex, the result of alcohol and inertia tinged with the vague hope that this time would be different.

She felt used, but she'd allowed it. He was the SIO and after a successful and tense operation, he probably regarded sex with a silly and available DC as a perk of the job. By hanging around and having a drink with the team, hadn't she issued an invitation? Or perhaps he'd confused her with Charlotte? Either way, she felt like a slut.

As she stood under the shower, soothing herself with hot water and complimentary toiletries, she discovered a couple of tiny finger-mark bruises on her left bicep. A man who didn't realize his own strength? Or, more likely, didn't think that a girl like her would object if he was a bit rough.

Standing alone and naked in front of the broad illuminated mirror and double sink vanity unit, Jo looked herself up and down. And she didn't much care for what she saw. She was tall; her damp shoulder-length hair was naturally blonde; she wasn't carrying any excess fat. But the penetrating LED lights emphasized the whorish pallor of her skin. Was this what Steve Vaizey had seen? The kind of twenty-something girl, adrift between relationships, who wouldn't say no because the big three O was looming, and she was feeling a little desperate. *What do you want* and *do you even know?* There had been a hint of disdain in his voice, but she'd chosen to ignore it. Now she wondered why.

She dressed, collected her belongings, and headed downstairs. The girl behind the reception desk had a seen-it-all hotel smile and a Slovakian accent.

Jo placed the key card in front of her. 'Did any of my colleagues come down for breakfast?' She had a residual wisp of hope that maybe he'd left her to sleep and was still around.

The receptionist shook her head. 'No, madam. You are the last. Everyone else has left.'

Eating breakfast alone in the dining room didn't appeal, and Jo considered just leaving. But she was hungry, she had a nagging headache and wasn't that sure what she should do. The car had to be driven back to London. There'd be reports to write, but she saw no urgency. She'd done her job, so officially her secondment to Grebe was probably over. Maybe Vaizey had already decided that, which would explain his cavalier attitude last night. He didn't expect to be facing her in the office.

She went into the bar, ordered a large black Americano and a croissant, then settled herself in a window seat while she waited for it to arrive.

The coffee should help kick her sluggish brain into action. She gave herself a stern lecture: okay, she'd made a mistake, but there was no point dwelling on it. He'd drunk far more than her. Her dignity was damaged, but his poor performance meant he was unlikely to brag about it, so her reputation would survive.

Rummaging in her bag, she unearthed her phone, which had been set on vibrate only. She found six missed calls. She felt a flutter of expectation ripple through her.

He'd been trying to call her. Of course he had! He was on the road. He'd want to be present when the various gang members were interviewed. This was still very much a live operation. He may even be headed for Manchester. Assembling a body of evidence, liaising with the CPS, the bust was only the beginning of the process.

Relief flooded through her. Waking up alone had fed the demons of self-doubt, but it was paranoia. Then she saw the calls weren't from him, they were from an unknown number. That didn't make sense. Was there a reason he wouldn't be calling from his own phone? There could be several. She knew he carried more than one handset. She'd seen them.

The coffee and croissant arrived. She thanked the server and took a sip. Should she call him back on this other number? She was puzzling it out when the handset vibrated.

Same number. Anticipation surged as she clicked to answer. 'Hello?'

The voice was female and impatient. 'Finally! You're a difficult woman to get hold of. This is Tania Jones.'

Tania Jones? The television producer.

'I'm sorry. This is not a good time. I'm working.'

'I'm afraid this is important. It's Briony.'

Jo felt a ripple of her anger. She wasn't about to be hassled. 'Look, I've explained, I can't—'

'Briony's killed herself.'

'What?'

'It happened early this morning, we think. She threw herself under a train.'

50

The drive to Littlehampton from the New Forest took Jo an hour and a half. Leaving the icy sepulchral stillness of the heathland behind, she hit the damp morning rush-hour around Southampton where she picked up the M27. The busy coast road was a steady stream of traffic crammed between sea and Downs. But she switched to autopilot, found a local radio station with nineties pop and inane chit-chat, which soothed her journey and helped her stop thinking about Briony Rowe and why she might've killed herself.

Jo's strategy with the film-maker had been to force her into a corner and call her bluff. Had it succeeded beyond her expectations? What if Briony couldn't face the shame of being found out? In her belly, Jo had a queasy sense of guilt.

She stopped for petrol outside Chichester, and checked her phone. No missed calls, no texts, nothing at all from Vaizey. But then, why would he call? He'd made it clear it was a casual encounter, what Alison would've called a one-night-stand. That was the deal and Jo had bought it.

After some thought, she opted for a circumspect

approach. She sent a text to Foley asking him to call and update her.

She was in the garage shop buying coffee and chocolate when the phone buzzed.

'How's it going, Boden? I knew you must be missing me.' He sounded as if he'd been up all night.

'Not as much as you think. What's the latest?'

'We're getting "no comment, no comment". But we've got it all recorded, them receiving the guns, examining them.'

'What does the boss think?'

'Haven't spoken to him this morning.'

'Oh. He left early. I presumed he was headed for Manchester.'

'Cosy evening then, just the two of you?'

'Oh, fuck off, Foley!'

'Sorry.' He did sound contrite, which surprised Jo. His voice softened. 'Maybe I'm jealous.'

'Let me be clear. Vaizey is my married boss. You are the DS and a colleague. My personal life and professional life do not overlap in any way.' In essence, this was true.

'Okay—'

'I'm assuming my secondment is over.'

'I dunno. You need to check that with Steve. I think he's in London. They're tracking the money. Our Manchester gang boss sent a text to his accountant authorizing a money transfer to an offshore account in the BVI right after he'd examined the goods. That's the last piece of the puzzle. CPS reckons once we put it all together, they'll be going down for a lengthy stretch.'

'Good result all round then. If I'm not needed today, I thought I'd take the scenic route back.'

'Fine by me. Listen, Jo, I know I can be a bit, well y'know—'

'Apology accepted. See you back in the office.' She'd hung up.

Foley, the Neanderthal bully she could handle; at least in that role, he was predictable. But Foley trying to play the emotional modern male and coming on to her was just creepy. And why had he suddenly changed his tune? Or was it sudden? Lust didn't seem enough of an explanation. The experience was unnerving, but Jo didn't have the mental space to figure out Foley.

Her headache was worsening, and she concluded she'd had it with him and his boss. Going back to work for a boring old school copper like Dave Hollingsworth would be a relief. And now, on top of all this, she had to face the fact that she could be responsible for driving Briony Rowe to suicide?

She drove into Littlehampton and found the police station, which was where she'd arranged to meet Tania Jones. She discovered the TV producer at the front desk giving a perplexed young PC a piece of her mind.

'Thank goodness you're here. I can't seem to get any information.'

Jo showed her ID and asked to speak to the duty sergeant.

As they waited, Jo faced Tania. Her sophisticated carapace was showing definite cracks. Streaked mascara, hastily wiped away, showed she'd been crying.

'I just—it makes no sense—'

Jo shepherded her to a chair. 'Start at the beginning. Tell me what you know.'

'Kayleigh, Briony's assistant—you might remember her.'

Jo had a fleeting image of a sullen girl with dyed hair.

'She called me this morning. Poor girl was hysterical. She said Briony had driven back from London, parked her Mini by a level crossing outside the town and walked in front of a train.'

'How did Kayleigh know?'

'The police got in touch. Hers was the last number dialled on Briony's phone. They found it beside the track. I mean, can you imagine it? What a horrendous way to die!'

Jo didn't want to imagine it.

'Do you know anything about Briony's state of mind?'

'She phoned me yesterday morning, and she was excited. She was on a roll. The last thing she was is suicidal. The university had agreed to let her look for Bruce in the archives. She had an appointment and was convinced she'd be able to identify him.'

'Has it occurred to you, Tania, that this may have all been a line? A story she invented.'

'I don't think so.'

'When she came to you, how desperate was she to get this film made?'

Tania wiped her face with her palm. 'I'm not stupid, Jo. I've been in this business a long time. I can read people pretty well. Briony had been looking for a break for years. She knew she'd only have one chance to get it right. She had to deliver on this, and she believed she could. The two things she needed were Nathan on board and putting a name to an alternative suspect. That was the film: Nathan's innocent, Bruce did it.'

Jo studied the producer. She knew Briony well enough and she sounded convincing. Jo's thoughts skipped back to her sister's journals. If she'd been given this as a cold case to review, wouldn't this have been an alternative line of enquiry?

'Okay, well, who else knew that she reckoned she was about to ID him?'

'That's the thing she told me on the phone. Yesterday she was having lunch with Cynthia Fenton-Wright.'

'You mean the girl that Nathan says he could've met on the way to the station?'

'Yes. You're the detective, Jo. You tell me, isn't that a bit too much of a coincidence?'

Jo felt an eerie sense of foreboding slithering through her. Anger and her reluctance to look at the past had blinkered her. The investigation into Sarah's murder had the hallmarks of a bodged job. This had been her intuition since she started reading the journals, but until now, she hadn't wanted to admit it.

51

Nathan Wade wasn't used to taking care of anyone except himself. But he could see Kayleigh was distraught. Walking beside him, along the riverside walk in Littlehampton, she was tiny. An elfin figure bundled up against the February chill; a spiky blue quiff of hair stuck out at an erratic angle from under her bobble hat. He glanced across at her. Her cheeks and nose were still blotchy and red from crying. It was all rather awkward.

Kayleigh never had much to say, but Nathan had gleaned a few things about her. She was a film student. Nineteen. She was an intern, which meant she worked for Briony for nothing. He wasn't sure how she managed that. Stan and Olly, it was hard to be around the two of them without noticing the comic potential of their contrasting appearances.

Tania had instructed him to keep an eye on Kayleigh while she tried to find out more details about what had happened. But he would've done it anyway. It had been his suggestion that they go for a walk. The day was bleak, a whited-out sky, snow showers and a biting wind off the sea; as they reached the mouth of the narrow estuary, choppy waves were rolling in, creating turbulence as they hit the tidal flow of the river.

Nathan found it hard to feel anything other than contempt for Briony Rowe. She was devious and manipulative. All she'd ever done was try to use him. But now she was gone, Tania and Gordon might let him take charge of his own project. Even if the film never got made, he could learn a lot from them in the meantime. It was a better start to his new life than a job in a coffee shop.

He glanced at Kayleigh. Perhaps she'd seen a different side of Briony. Hard to imagine, but it was possible. Except Kayleigh wasn't being paid either, so Briony was using her too.

'You okay?'

Nathan knew this was a redundant question, but it was the sort of thing people said when they were trying to be sympathetic and couldn't stand the silence. He would have preferred silence, but maybe that's not what Kayleigh needed.

She looked up at him. 'She was a brilliant film-maker, y'know. She could make the camera see inside people's heads.'

'Could she?' Nathan found such a notion disturbing. The last thing he'd have wanted was a camera ogling his private thoughts.

She wiped the back of her glove across a damp nose. 'The police piss me off. They're so fucking smug. "Oh well," they said, "it's that time of year. Suicide rate always goes up." I mean, get a fucking grip! This woman was not suicidal. I told them that. I told them they needed to preserve the scene. Too late, they said. The train company was hassling them. They had to reopen the line.'

Rage was whirling off her tiny frame. It made her curiously attractive, a pint-sized Valkyrie. And he was drawn to her all the more. Or perhaps it was just that he'd been in jail a long time.

'You don't think she was prone to depression?'

Kayleigh laughed. 'Briony? She'd been dumped on her whole life, including by you. She figured there was a choice: give up or get over it. She chose the latter. I learnt so much from her. Not just about film-making. She got it. She understood how this world works, how people treat one another. And what it takes to make it.' This was the most Nathan had ever heard her say.

'When did I dump on her?' He frowned. This was unfair.

'When you were students.'

'I hardly knew her.'

'She was in love with you, Nathan. The boy poet who wore his sunglasses in the library. And you picked her mate.'

He took a deep breath and shook his head. 'I had no idea.' This was certainly true. Briony in love with him? The notion was alarming.

Kayleigh gave him a scathing look. 'Yeah, but you were a complete idiot back then, weren't you? Which is how you ended up getting fitted up for Sarah Boden's murder.'

Nathan smiled at her. The mouse had roared. Who would've guessed?

The phone in his pocket buzzed. He pulled it out and read the text. 'It's Tania. She wants us to meet her.' His face fell. 'Seems Jo Boden's turned up.'

'Lucky for you.'

'What d'you mean?'

Kayleigh took a deep breath and exhaled. 'Briony always said: the key to this is Jo Boden. When Jo decides to find out what happened to her sister, then we'll have a case.'

Nathan wasn't sure he liked the sound of this. The Bodens had been weird when they'd met up. They hadn't given the impression that they were likely to cooperate. The mother had stared at him. She seemed borderline deranged, but it was Jo, now the image of her sister, who'd unnerved him.

It was like meeting Sarah's ghost and that had thrown him completely. But not only the physical resemblance. Jo had her dead sister's manner; her chin slightly raised as she gazed at you, giving the impression of a critical and superior attitude. Nathan had felt judged. And also turned on. He needed more time to adjust before another encounter. He wanted to be ready for her. And he wasn't.

'You sure you want the hassle of a load of questions? It won't bring Briony back. Why don't we just go to the pub?'

52

Dear Jo,

I must admit, this isn't going to plan. Things are getting out of control, and you have to take your share of the blame. You've let me down. Just when I was beginning to think I could trust you.

Do you have any idea how tough it is to be a bloke nowadays? We don't know what's expected of us. What women expect. Oh, I know what to say, how to tell you the things you want to hear. What we all assume you want to hear. But, let's face it, we're only skating over the surface.

At a deeper level, we're all dissatisfied. We're all just animals. Our primal wants and cravings don't get wiped out by a hundred-odd years of so-called enlightened Western values. Equality may be a nice idea. But homo sapiens killed off the other hominids because they could. Empathy doesn't extend beyond our own tribe. Maybe we're living in a historical bubble that's about to burst.

A mother needs to know that she and her offspring will be

protected from predators and that they'll eat. She has to pick the right man for that. It's got little to do with desire and a lot to do with need. Safety comes before satisfaction if you want to survive. Traditional roles haven't been all bad. And girls like you and Sarah need to understand that.

Okay, I'll admit I've my own biases. We're all moulded by our background. I like order and organization. I like to do things my way and that means I prefer to be in charge. For me, it's easier. And some women let you assume they want that too. Then you realize that you're being managed and they're using you.

I watched my mum and dad as I was growing up. She was so much smarter than him. She played the housewife and mother, pretended to be the meek woman, but she had him wrapped round her little finger. He drove his bus and brought home his wages. Never had the final say about anything in our family. He thought he did, poor bastard, but she was in control. She always got to choose.

And your sister was the same: an ace manipulator. The difference was, she didn't even bother to disguise it. She was arrogant enough to assume she could do as she liked. She didn't tell me what she was doing. She thought she could lie and I wouldn't find out. But it should've been me, Jo. It should've been me, not her. I should've been the one to decide. I should've been the one to choose. That's the natural order. It would've been better for everyone. You have to understand that.

But I've got my eye on you, Jo Boden. And know this. I won't be fooled twice.

53

Jo met up with Tania's crew in the coffee shop where Nathan worked. Lech, the manager, arranged a couple of tables for them at the back. Curious locals gave them covert glances, which turned into blatant gawping when Gordon Kramer and his sidekicks turned up.

Gordon was dressed for action, olive green combat jacket with matching scarf and aviator shades. He strode into the shop, Phil the cameraman following in his wake, steadicam rig strapped to his body, filming the veteran reporter from behind. A researcher juggling three bags and an iPad brought up the rear.

Kayleigh had refused to go to the pub, as Nathan suggested. They sat in a corner. She turned to him with a sad smile. 'Briony would love all this.'

But he ignored her. He had an envious look on his face. He smiled at Kramer. 'Cool sunglasses, man. I need a pair like that.'

Jo Boden watched in disbelief. It was left to Tania Jones to take control of the situation. She told Phil to take a break, the researcher to get more coffees, introduced her husband to Jo and instructed him to sit down.

He removed the coveted Ray-Bans and he frowned at Jo. 'We've got some footage of the level crossing and the track. Terrible business.' He shook his head, though he seemed far from sad. 'But you have to admit that it goes some way to proving poor Briony's argument. Your sister's murderer is probably still out there.'

'It raises some questions, that's all.'

Gordon gave her a knowing flicker of a smile. Tragedies and disasters. He was in his element. This was what fuelled his fire. 'Important questions though, that's why we're all here, isn't it?'

Jo responded with a chilly glare. She was beginning to understand the term *media circus* because that's what Gordon Kramer brought with him. If you ignored the expensive camera and kit, they were a travelling band of mischief-makers. And Gordon was the ringmaster. He could take any tale, fillet it and serve it up in bite-sized chunks for the fickle channel-hopping viewer.

Allowing them to turn her sister's death into TV fodder was something Jo planned to resist. But on the other hand Kramer was right. The questions raised by the film-maker's so-called suicide were too big to ignore.

The discussion Jo had had with the uniformed sergeant at the local police station had been annoying and brief. He was surly and suspicious. He scrutinized her ID and then homed in on why the Met was interested in the dead woman. Jo got round this by saying that she was a personal friend, which aggravated him even more. As far as he was concerned, the incident had been squared away and Jo knew she'd have to go over his head to get anywhere, which could be complicated.

Her thoughts flitted to Steve Vaizey. A call from him to

Sussex CID would get them looking at it again properly. But how could she ask him now? More hurdles. Jo felt irritated and nervous. This was uncharted territory on too many fronts.

And they were all looking at her expectantly. She reached into her bag and pulled out a notebook and pen. If she looked like a detective, it might help her feel more like one.

'Let's see if we can pin down Briony's movements in the forty-eight hours before she died. Who can tell me about this lunch?'

'She knew Cynthia was a witness and was hiding something. So she decided to tackle her.' Kayleigh's voice was small but vehement.

'How did she know? It's an assumption she's hiding something.'

'It's obvious.'

Jo nodded. 'With all due respect, it's a potential line of enquiry. Nothing's obvious.'

'What about her car? Her Mini.' The intern was glaring at her.

'What about it?'

'Fucking cops have towed it away. Impounded it or something, so we can't get to it.'

'If Briony's dead, they would need to establish who the rightful owner is.'

Kayleigh leapt to her feet. 'It's got a dash-cam, a fucking dash-cam. Whatever happened, it could all be there. Recorded. But no one's interested in that.' She grabbed her bobble hat and headed for the door.

Tania shrugged apologetically. 'She's very upset.'

Jo sighed. 'Understandable.'

Retreating into detective mode and adopting an attitude of professional detachment was helping her get a handle on her unruly thoughts. What she needed was time to think and analyse. Somehow, she had to wrap this up and escape.

Then something caught her eye. Nathan Wade was sitting slightly apart, watching, with the hint of a smile playing round his mouth. It was only Jo's second encounter with him, but she knew one thing for sure: she didn't like him. He exuded the passive-aggressive cynicism of the ex-con.

She folded her arms and turned abruptly to face him. 'Where were you last night and early this morning, Nathan?'

The intention had been to catch him off guard and it succeeded. He blushed as all eyes turned to him. 'In bed.'

'In bed where?'

'The hostel.'

'Alone?'

He laughed. 'What the hell is this?'

'Simple enough question.'

'I didn't kill Briony.'

'Who says Briony was killed?'

Gordon Kramer's gaze strayed in the direction of Phil, who had his camera balanced on his knee; the red light winked, indicating he was filming.

Nathan stood up and his anger erupted. 'Kayleigh's right. You cops, you're rubbish. And you can twist anything. That's what you're doing. And that's what they did to me over Sarah. Trick questions to make me look stupid and guilty. But we're all sitting here thinking Briony was killed. Even you, DC Boden. Isn't that why you're here? Why can't you be honest? I'm sick of the lot of you—you and your fucking games.'

Scooping up his jacket, Nathan stormed out.

Kramer turned to Jo. 'You rattled his cage.'

'So it would seem.'

'You don't seriously think he shoved Briony under a train?'

'Hadn't thought that until now.'

'But why on earth would he? She was helping him.'

Jo shrugged. 'Perhaps he doesn't see it that way.'

54

Jo finally escaped, drove back to London, returned the car to the pool and made it home to her Lant Street flat by early evening. She'd resisted the impulse to pop into the office. Bumping into Steve Vaizey in a corridor wasn't something she was ready to cope with—not yet. There was a team debriefing scheduled and she'd already decided to leave it until then. She needed to put their relationship back on a proper professional footing.

She made herself cheese on toast and retreated to her solitary cell and the comfort of her bed. Opening her notebook to a blank double page, she stared at it as she ate. Nathan Wade was right about one thing. She was operating on the assumption that Briony didn't commit suicide. A bizarre accident seemed unlikely; her car was several meters from train tracks. She was killed by person or persons unknown.

She wrote across the top of the left-hand page: *Who killed Briony? Why? Is it connected to Sarah's murder?*

The last question was easiest to answer. Briony Rowe didn't seem to be the sort of person to have acquired that many enemies in her life and, even if she had, what were the chances of one of them randomly striking at her now? It had to be connected to her film project. That left *who* and *why*, two questions that were related.

Briony had set out to prove Nathan innocent. Why would he not welcome that? Again, the easy answer was because he was guilty. He'd served his sentence, was released on licence. What would he have to gain? In which case, why hadn't he just refused to cooperate?

Jo could think of several reasons for that, but what she wrote was: *Narcissism?* She had a strong feeling that he was clever and had a hidden agenda. If celebrity appealed to him, which it might, that could be lucrative. A jail sentence was no obstacle to creating a popular media persona. Reformed gangsters were always attractive to the public, but a wrongly convicted murderer would have even more appeal.

She drew four parallel lines, which she formed into two rectangles. She coloured these in. *Celebrity = MONEY.* Perhaps he regarded Briony as an impediment to that. There might be financial spin-offs from the film, which he didn't want to share. Perhaps he was just greedy?

Across the top of the right-hand page she wrote: *Bruce—who is he? Why would he kill Sarah? Why would he kill Briony? To protect his identity? Who could've told Bruce that Briony was a threat—Cynthia?*

Jo took her plate to the kitchen and washed it up. She made herself a mug of camomile tea, which she hoped might help her relax and loosen her headache. What she needed was sleep, but her mind was jittery and refused to rest.

She hadn't heard from Alison in days, which was never a good sign. When they returned from the initial encounter with Nathan Wade, her mother had seemed to be shutting down and slipping into one of her downers. Jo assumed this was what had happened, and she felt guilty for not having gone round. She thought about phoning but, if she was right, Alison wouldn't answer.

There was also the question of Briony's death. Who knew what impact news of that would have on Alison? Jo didn't want her to hear about it from anyone else.

The idea of trekking to Greenwich on a freezing February evening had little appeal, so Jo tried the phone. Her first attempt rang out. She tried again. On her third go, Alison picked up.

'Hello.'

'Hey, Mum. How you doing?'

'Well, I'm not dead, if that's what you're wondering.' Scratchy but combative; not as bad as Jo feared.

'Sorry it's been a couple of days. I've been working. And…I've been to Littlehampton again.'

'To see him?' A definite spark of interest.

'Partly. There's something I need to tell you about. It might be a bit of a shock.'

'You found Bruce.'

'No. Briony's dead.'

'Dead? What do you mean?'

'They found her body on the railway line, near a level crossing.'

'On my god! Some kind of accident? They're so danger-ous, these unmanned crossings.'

'The local police are treating it as suicide.'

Silence on the other end of the line.

'Suicide?'

'Yeah.'

Alison heaved an audible sigh. 'Poor Briony. Well, just goes to show, doesn't it?'

'Goes to show what, Mum?'

'You never can tell about anyone.'

'Are you okay?'

Alison didn't reply. Jo could discern the snap of the lighter as her mother lit a cigarette. She needed to change the subject.

'Anyway, I've been reading more of Sarah's journals and there's something I wanted to ask you.'

'Funny, isn't it? It's the ones you least expect. She seemed quite…I dunno, jolly?'

'Yeah. Well, I was wondering about the time Dad went down to visit Sarah on his own. In the first term, in November.'

'I don't remember that. We always went together.'

'Yeah, but he might've been down there on business and popped in to see her.'

'No. He never did that.'

'Are you sure? Maybe you've forgotten?'

'What? Now, not only d'you think I'm crackers, you also think I've got dementia! You've got no heart, Jo. That poor woman's killed herself, and you're asking your stupid questions.'

'C'mon, that's not fair.'

'You think I don't remember every single time we saw her, every visit we made in those months she was there? You went at February half-term.'

'Yeah, I know. But did Dad—'

'No! Absolutely not!' The phone went dead. Her mother often hung up when she was annoyed. Jo ignored it.

But why was Alison so vehement in her denial? She tended to get upset when her version of the Sarah story was challenged. Jo decided to go back to the source.

She opened the drawer in her desk and took out the envelope containing her sister's three letters.

The second one was dated 14 November and was a chatty

mixture of advice and scandal that sounded like the big sister Jo remembered. But in the third letter, dated 5 December, the tone had changed. And there it was in black and white:

I know you're upset that Dad came down to see me and didn't tell you. But he had a work thing, a meeting with a client in Brighton, which was arranged at the last minute, so he literally just popped in. I know that Mummy's told you that spring half-term is the best time for you to visit and I absolutely promise you that it will happen.

Had Alison forgotten? It was entirely possible. When she and Nick broke up in a welter of toxic grief, did she block out the separate relationship he'd had with his daughter? Over the years, Alison's recollections of her had ossified into her version of saintly Sarah. Anything less than flattering had been redacted from the record.

Jo skimmed through the rest of the letter: Sarah's wish to change course and her plan to apply for a year abroad at a university in America. It ended in a different vein to all their previous correspondence. These were the last words her sister wrote to her:

There's nothing wrong with wanting to run away. Sometimes it's the best thing to do. In many ways, I envy you. You get to learn from all my stupid mistakes.

Run away from what? She'd seen Sarah subsequently. At Christmas. The half-term visit, which was fun. But Jo couldn't recall any sisterly tête-à-têtes. If anything, Sarah was more distant. But surely this was natural—two girls growing up and growing apart. It would've happened anyway. They would've ended up in different places with different lives and a few shared memories to be giggled over at family gatherings when they dragged out the old photo albums.

Jo wondered what sort of life she might've had if tragedy hadn't intervened. Perhaps they'd be living on separate continents, connecting on the Net and meeting every few years when one of them could afford to make the trip. This was the relationship Jo had with their brother, Carl. And she knew less about him than she did about Sarah.

She picked up her notebook and added two questions to the right-hand page: *What happened at the end of November? Has Mum forgotten or does she not know?*

55

The office was packed the next morning for the 10 a.m. debriefing. Jo stood at the back, near the door. The seizure at Buckler's Hard had led to a slew of additional arrests in Manchester and London. Suspects were being questioned and the effort now was on collating all the evidence for the CPS.

Ivan Rossi's mugshot was third in the top row displayed on the screen. Jo wondered if he'd woken up yet to her part in his arrest. She hoped her cover had been preserved as she didn't fancy yet another disgruntled villain with a motive to harm her.

Vaizey introduced the briefing, but then invited other officers to fill in the details. He looked weary and dispirited, a common reaction when the euphoria following a big bust subsided. Jo suspected he might be an adrenaline junkie, so he was probably suffering withdrawal symptoms. He glanced in her direction once. She avoided his eye and they didn't speak.

Jo had already decided that she was owed some skiving time and she sloped off at the first opportunity. If Foley needed her, she assumed he'd call. As for the boss, she hoped that her behaviour had indicated to him she didn't intend to be any sort of problem and had drawn a line under their encounter.

She took the tube to Liverpool Street. Cynthia Fenton-Wright had a corner bay-windowed office in a Victorian refurb above a sandwich bar in Spitalfields. She was the CEO of a branding and digital design agency, and a quick trawl through her client list on the net led Jo to the conclusion that she was pretty successful at it. She had some big-name clients and a stack of industry awards.

The young man who ushered Jo in wore a T-shirt and Converse high tops, but offered refreshments with all the obsequiousness of a butler.

Cynthia, no longer Cyn, held out her hand. 'DC Boden. I'm so pleased to meet you. Though I'm glad to say we don't often get visited by the police.'

Jo shook her hand. 'As I hope I made clear on the phone, I'm here in a personal capacity. This is not official.'

'Yes, you're Sarah Boden's sister. You said that. She was such a lovely girl. What a terrible tragedy that was.'

Cynthia perched on one of the two vintage Ercol sofas and invited Jo to take the other. Although she must've been the same age as Sarah, Jo concluded she only looked about thirty. Hair and make-up were subtle, the clothes elegant and expensive. Her own personal brand had changed dramatically since her student days.

Jo smiled. 'Do you keep in touch with many old friends from university?'

'Social media. Not really in touch. I suppose we're all a bit competitive. We like to know who's done well and not so well. Marriages, divorces, how many kids, that sort of thing.'

'My sister wrote a journal during her time at uni and I've been reading it.'

'That must be rather bittersweet.'

'Gut-wrenching. That's how I'd describe it.'

Cynthia gave a concerned nod. 'You must've been quite young when it all happened.'

'Eleven.'

'Old enough to hurt but not to understand.'

'That's a good way of putting it.' Jo smiled. 'Sarah mentions you. You were called Cyn back then?'

The businesswoman laughed. 'Yes. I liked the double entendre, thought it made me sound cool. It's the sort of silly thing you think when you're nineteen.'

'I get the impression that you and my sister didn't get on that well.'

Cynthia raised her sculpted eyebrows. 'You mean the play? When I replaced her? It was her decision to pull out.'

'Do you know why?'

'She probably had some row with the director. His name was—God, can I even remember—Randall? Yes, that's right, Randy. He was this American on the exchange programme. When he found out that Randy had a rather different meaning over here, he insisted everyone call him that. Loved it. But then he was totally obnoxious.'

'Was Sarah ever involved with him?'

Cynthia chuckled. 'No! I wouldn't have thought so. Does she mention him in the journal?'

'Briefly.'

'He was short and fat with terrible halitosis. You'd have to be pretty desperate to succumb to his charms. Certainly not Sarah's type.'

'But you and Sarah weren't close? More rivals?'

'It was our first year. No one knew anyone. We were all back to square one, like kids in the playground again, jockeying for position, forming cliques. Sarah was an obvious star. Beautiful. Clever. I must say, you look a lot like her. That must've been a bit of a curse for you over the years.'

Jo smiled and shrugged. Cynthia had an easy confidence and a shrewd manner, which put her in mind of Sarah. They seemed strangely similar. Perhaps this is what her big sister would've become if she'd lived: a foxy businesswoman with a perfect manicure and a pile of cash.

Cynthia crossed her legs and clasped her palms together. 'I wish I had known Sarah better. I think in the long run we would've got on well.'

'Yes, I think you would.'

There was a pause as the two women eyed each other. The preliminaries were over and Cynthia Fenton-Wright seemed completely composed. Perhaps too composed. Jo was wondering if she even knew of Briony Rowe's death. Or maybe she hadn't connected Jo with Briony.

Jo crossed her own legs, mirroring the businesswoman. 'Well, you must be wondering why I'm here.'

Cynthia shrugged. 'I had heard, I can't remember where, that a film's being made about your sister's murder. Trying to get her killer off. But I'm sure you wouldn't involve yourself in anything like that.'

'You're right. I wouldn't. But Nathan Wade has been released on licence and, as you can imagine, that's very difficult for my family. Especially my mother.'

'The media can be so irresponsible.' She pursed her lips like a disapproving schoolmarm. 'They go for the shock and sensation and give no thought to who might be affected. It's all audience figures and sales. Don't get me wrong—I have no problem with the profit motive. I'm in business to make a profit. But there are ethical considerations too and lines that should not be crossed.'

'I agree. So what did you make of Nathan Wade?'

'I'm very glad to say I didn't know him.' She gave an involuntary shudder.

'You wouldn't have recognized him at all?'

'Well, I sort of knew who he was. That he was on our course. But there were quite a few of us.'

'You knew him by sight, then?'

'Yes, I suppose so.'

Jo observed the tension in Cynthia's hands. Her self-possession was cracking. Was she anticipating Jo's next question? What exactly had Briony Rowe told her when they'd met for lunch?

She laced her own fingers. 'On the night the murder took place, were you on campus?'

'I lived on campus. Most first years did.'

'But not Nathan.'

'I have no idea where he lived.'

'Is there any possibility you could've bumped into him that night?'

'Nathan Wade? No.' The reply was quick and emphatic. Too emphatic. Boden lounged back on the sofa and smiled. Cynthia Fenton-Wright was not a good liar.

The cop tilted her head. 'Do you remember where you were that night, or what you were doing?'

Cynthia exhaled. 'No. It was a very long time ago.'

'Did you go out?'

'I don't remember.'

'With some friends? When I first went to uni, we were in the bar most nights.'

'Maybe.' The businesswoman's demeanour had changed. Still in control, but unsettled. She glanced at her watch.

Jo prodded a little more. 'Nathan Wade thinks he bumped into you that night and asked you for the time.'

Cynthia spluttered. 'Well, he's mistaken about that.'

'You said you don't remember what you were doing.'

'I would've remembered that. Obviously.'

'Obviously. Well, I don't want to take up any more of your time. Thank you for agreeing to see me.' Jo got up. Cynthia looked surprised, then visibly relieved. She stood too, ready to usher her guest out.

As she reached the door, Jo turned. A standard detective trick, but worth a try.

'Oh, I meant to say, did you know Briony Rowe? She was a friend of Sarah's and also on your course, I believe.'

Cynthia's brow puckered. 'I have a vague recollection. Rather overweight, I recall.'

'Is she one of your social media friends?'

'Oh God. She might be. All sorts of people come out of the woodwork wanting to connect with you. You know how it is.'

Cynthia's anxiety to get rid of her was palpable. Jo stood pondering for a moment. She turned to face the business-woman, smiled, sighed, taking her time.

'Well, you've heard about the film. It's Briony Rowe's project.'

'I don't think I knew that.' Another lie, which was interesting. She was taking quite a risk.

'Apparently, Briony thinks there's an alternative suspect. She believes Nathan to be innocent.'

'That's ridiculous. And if he is innocent, why wouldn't he have spoken up sooner and tried to clear his name?'

'I agree. But unless you've got money for lawyers, it's quite hard to get an appeal heard. Perhaps he lost heart over the years and decided he'd get out sooner if he accepted his guilt and went for early parole.'

'You actually think he was wrongfully convicted?'

'I didn't. But since Briony's death, I've begun to wonder.'

'Briony's dead?' The shock that swept over Cynthia Fenton-Wright's face was impossible for her to conceal. 'How did that happen?'

'Suicide, accident? No one's sure. A train killed her on a level crossing outside Littlehampton. Early hours of yesterday morning.'

'That's terrible.' The colour had drained from her face. She sat down on the sofa.

Jo gave her a sympathetic smile. 'I'm sorry. That seems to have upset you. I didn't realize you knew her that well.'

'I didn't. It's just…the idea of anyone dying like that is so awful.' Cynthia put her hand over her mouth.

'Yes, it is. I suppose I'm a bit more inured to these things. Well, thanks again for seeing me.'

Under the careful make-up, the businesswoman's upper lip was damp. 'You don't think…I mean, is there a connection to your sister's death?'

'I've no idea.'

'You said you've begun to wonder. Are you looking into it?'

Jo had her on the ropes and she went for the knockout blow.

'Briony's death is a matter for Sussex Police. I have no involvement. I don't know what I think about my sister. But I would like to know the truth. My family deserves that.' Jo kept her tone as bland as possible but gave the businesswoman a penetrating stare. 'I know it was a long time ago, but if anything comes to mind, any small, incidental thing, especially about the actual night, perhaps you'd call me?' She held out her business card and smiled. 'This is where you can contact me.'

Cynthia took the card between thumb and index finger. 'Of course.'

Heading out, Jo speculated as to what Cyn might do next in response to the grenade that had just been lobbed at her. Contact Bruce? In an ideal world, she'd put Cynthia under surveillance, track her phone calls and her movements. But she had no official sanction to do that, which was a problem.

56

When Jo returned, the office was half empty. The gun-smuggling suspects were being interrogated at various locations. The clock was ticking to assemble the evidence and get the nod from the CPS to formally charge. She joined Sandra in front of the bank of monitors showing live feed from the interviews.

The analyst gave her a friendly smile. 'Looks like your boy might cough.'

'You reckon?' Jo peered over her shoulder at one of the screens. Ivan Rossi was disconsolate, seated at the interview table in a paper jumpsuit with his brief beside him. The sound was low. 'What's he been saying?'

'Blames his Belarusian uncle. Says he didn't know what they were up to. Admits he thought it might be dodgy, but claims he didn't want to upset his mum. All the others are going *no comment*, so getting him to testify against the rest could be useful.'

Jo watched him for a moment. Slumped in his chair like an overgrown teenager, he looked frightened and out of his depth.

Sandra glanced at her. 'Don't feel sorry for him.'

'I don't.'

'First big undercover job is always the hardest. You get close to them, earn their trust, then betray them. If you're a decent person, you will have some guilt. It's natural.'

Jo smiled. The truth was she'd enjoyed the duplicity. It was a carefully constructed con and the hapless Rossi was the mark. This is what villains did all the time. Jo didn't like to admit how much of a buzz it had given her. Her earlier pangs of guilt at what she'd done to Rossi seemed to be fading. Perhaps she wasn't as decent as either she or Sandra would like to think. After all, she'd just slept with her married boss. Rossi was a scumbag. He knew what he was doing. Why shouldn't she enjoy taking him down? That was her job.

'Can I ask your advice, Sandra?'

'Several large G and Ts and a couple of days off. That's my advice.'

'This is something else.'

Sitting down beside the older woman, Jo told her about Sarah's murder, then a summary of recent events ending up with the death of Briony Rowe. Finally, talking about it to someone who had professional detachment was a relief.

The analyst shook her head and took a large slug from her mug of coffee. 'Wow! That's quite a tale. No wonder you look like shit, if you don't mind me saying.' She waved the mug at the screen and the forlorn Rossi. 'I thought you had the heebie-jeebies about this.'

'You think I'm that soft?'

Sandra gave her a sardonic smile. 'Probably not.'

Jo pointed at the screen. 'I passed my sergeant's exams two years ago. I've been waiting ever since for an opportunity like this.'

'What are you going to do about this other thing?'

'I'm not sure.'

'So you suspect that this woman Cynthia knows the real killer, and after what's-her-face—'

'Briony.'

'After Briony tells her she can ID him, she passes the information down the line.'

'Yeah. But when I told her Briony was dead, she freaked. She had no idea. She's the weak link. I need to find a way to put pressure on her. That starts with a proper investigation into Briony's death.'

The analyst tapped her pen on the desk. 'Well, Vaizey can be unpredictable. Bit of a wing and a prayer man. But he's smart as a nest of vipers. And he's got political clout. Go to him, tell him about your sister and all this, and ask his advice. Why not?'

'I suppose I don't want to—' She sighed. 'It's complicated. I don't want him to think…Oh, I dunno.' Jo knew her face said it all.

Sandra gave her a quizzical look. 'You're a complicated girl. But, y'know what, Jo, you were right before when we talked about Foley: don't shit where you eat. That's always gonna get you in a mess.'

'I know that.' Jo sighed. 'You won't—'

'I mind my own business.'

'Thanks for listening, Sandra.'

The analyst shrugged.

Jo Boden had been a police officer long enough to have perfected the art of looking busy even when you weren't. She had a report to write up on her dealings with Rossi. But she'd made plenty of notes, so it was soon finished.

She continued to mull over Sandra's advice about talking to Vaizey. It was the sensible way forward. The problem was that going to him now with what might sound an outlandish story could make him think she was doing it to prolong something more personal. But she was short of other options. In the end, she decided he could think what he liked. She'd play it straight. But crossing the office, she found his door wide open. There was no sign of him and no one knew when he'd be back.

Thwarted, she headed for the basement canteen, bought a coffee and a sandwich, found herself a quiet corner and called her father.

He picked up and the noise in the background, the whine of an electric saw, suggested he was on one of his building sites. 'Jo! This is a nice surprise.'

'I said I'd keep you in the loop.' This had never been her intention, but the journal had been weighing on her mind.

'I'm glad you've called.'

'Well, I thought you should know that Briony Rowe has turned up dead.'

'Dead? Seriously. What happened?'

Jo was reluctant to go into details. The last thing she wanted was him getting involved. 'It's complicated. It could be suicide, but I'm going to speak to some colleagues. There needs to be an official investigation.'

'Presumably it means an end to this awful film?'

'Who knows? Thing is, Dad, I've been reading Sarah's journals and there are some things I need to ask you about.'

'I don't understand why you're getting drawn into all this. The past is past, Jo. Reading your sister's journals—'

'I'm not like you.'

'What on earth d'you think you're going to gain by this? She's dead. We can't change that.'

'So you won't help me?'

'Of course I'll help me. That's what I'm trying to do. I'll come down and we can talk about this properly—'

'There's no need for that.'

'I can be there in a couple of hours. I want to help.'

'Then answer my questions.'

'Okay. But you need to trust me. I'm not the enemy. If we can't talk to each other honestly and openly—'

'Just bear with me, Dad.'

There was a pause, followed by an audible sigh.

'Fair enough. What do you want to ask?'

'In her first term, November sometime, did you go down to Brighton and see her on your own?'

'You mean without Mum?'

'Yes. She wrote to me. I've still got the letter. She said you had some business down there and you popped in to see her.'

'Yeah, maybe I did.' He sounded evasive.

'Mum doesn't remember this at all.'

'Jo, the number of prescription drugs and other forms of self-medication that your mother's had over the years, I'm surprised she remembers anything.'

'Was it a secret visit?'

'Why would it be a secret? If I was down that way, I may well have popped in to say hello.'

'She wasn't having some kind of problem?'

'Not that I recall.'

'Okay, well, after this visit, there are several pages missing from the journal. It's as if she wrote about something, then changed her mind, which suggests there was something she wanted to hide. D'you have any idea what that might be?'

'No. But I do remember going there now. We went out for a meal in town. She was absolutely fine.'

'Did Mum know you did this?'

'Of course she did. She's just forgotten. I think you're making a mountain out of a molehill here, Jo.'

There was a terseness in his tone, which barely disguised his unease and behind that the murmur of something unspoken and long hidden echoing down the years. Jo felt the hairs on the back of her neck prickle. Nick Boden and Cynthia Fenton-Wright had one thing in common: they were both lousy liars.

57

Jo sat at her desk, twisting her pen repeatedly between thumb and fingers, but this was the only sign of her inner turmoil. Being a detective for any length of time, particularly on a Murder Investigation Team in the Met, had its downside. It was easy for rampant suspicion to become your default setting. The phone call to her father hadn't helped. He was lying, and this had led her to wonder what else he could be covering up. The speculation that he might be responsible for Briony's death had grown into a gnawing fear. It was a grotesque idea and yet it possessed a certain logic.

She was trying to clear her head and look at the facts. He'd been determined to put a stop to Briony's film and had mentioned talking to his lawyers about an injunction. When he'd discovered that was unlikely to succeed, could long-buried rage and frustration have driven him towards an extreme solution?

Jo would've been the first to admit that she didn't know him that well. Was he capable of murder? In the right circumstances most people were, that was her professional judgement. But the idea of her dad as a killer was impossible to process. She felt ashamed for even thinking it. Yet it was a possibility that she had to consider.

Her childhood dad had played Frisbee in the garden, taught her to swim, and explained the mysteries of long multiplication, but that man disappeared from her life long ago. He left them. Without warning. She went to school one morning and when she came home, Alison told her and Carl that he was gone. Gone where was never explained. She'd cried, because Carl cried. But when Nick Boden returned, more than a year later, she'd refused his hugs and his gifts.

The wranglings of her parents' divorce had passed her by. She'd been asked who she wanted to live with and her unequivocal answer had been Alison. In view of her mother's sometimes fragile mental state, Nick had argued for and been granted joint custody of his remaining children. But whereas Carl went to live with him, Jo did her level best to avoid even visiting. Nick hoped she'd come round eventually and adopted a policy of never forcing her to do anything she didn't want to. And this might've worked if Alison hadn't been so resolute in her campaign of vilification.

For Alison, the grief and anger at Sarah's murder melded with bitterness at her husband's abandonment of her. She could see no way out of her despair and only one person to blame for the ruination of her life. As a result, she clung on fiercely to her remaining daughter. No one would rob her of Jo.

When Nick married Emily, Jo had refused to go to the wedding in solidarity with her mother. By then she was a moody teen, who responded to all overtures from her absurdly young stepmother with undisguised hostility.

But when his new wife became pregnant, it seemed to Jo that her father gave up on her. He didn't have the energy for two families, plus a new business. There were the usual cards and presents for birthdays and Christmas. He came to her graduation, an awkward and unpleasant event for all concerned, freighted with memories of Sarah. His attention was focused on his new baby sons, his unscathed wife, and his life in Norfolk.

This was the point at which Jo moved from reflecting her mother's resentment to a more personal grudge against him. Feeling abandoned yet again, she retreated into icy politeness and indifference in all her dealings with him. Plenty of people had a parent who'd let them down and who they didn't get on with. It was one of those things. She accepted it and moved on.

Jo found herself staring out of the window, trapped in a cycle of negative rumination. The waning afternoon light gave the office a sombre feel. She needed to get up and move her limbs. In the hope of placating Sandra, she went out for doughnuts and coffee. Returning with her haul, she was distributing the sugary treats round the office when her phone buzzed.

The handsome features of her brother Carl popped up on the screen. Like his father, he had a beard; his was bushy, making him look more like a brigand. Jo had been wondering when he'd get in on the act.

'Carl, how're you?'

He was on the move, striding down some glass-walled corridor. 'Hey, babes. Just been talking to Dad. He says you've got snow.'

She was pretty sure that wasn't all he'd said.

'A bit. Probably not as much as Toronto.'

'Went up to Mount St Louis at the weekend. It was awesome. Best skiing I've had this winter. When you coming over?'

'When I can afford it.'

'I've been trying to persuade Dad to bring Emily and the boys. I'm sure he'd stump up for you, too. Make it a family trip.'

Jo tried to ignore her brother's jaunty tone.

'I presume it was Dad who phoned you?'

'Well, yeah.' Her brother sighed. 'Told me Nathan Wade's been released. And some stuff about a film. How's Mum taking it?'

'How d'you think?'

He stopped and tilted his head with brotherly concern. 'Listen to me, Jo—'

Here was the lecture. It'd taken barely sixty seconds. But then Carl Boden was even more impatient than her.

'—you cannot take responsibility for her.'

'Someone's got to.'

'She's a grown woman. She's of sound mind. Well, sort of. She's made her own choices. You can't let her manipulate you.'

'I don't.'

'She plays you, Jo. She always has.'

Jo said nothing.

'You have to let the past go.'

'And do what, Carl? Take up extreme sports, OD on the adrenaline rush. Get a new relationship every five minutes.'

He chuckled. 'Don't be a bitch. That's Mum's trick. You can say what you like, you won't shut me up. And for your information, me and Kirsty have been together now for over a year.'

'Congratulations. You're doing better than me.'

'Know what I think. You should move out here. Join the RCMP.'

'I don't think I'm cut out to be a Mountie.'

'You've lived in London your whole life, Jo. You need to do something different. Take a risk.'

She heaved a sigh. What did he know about risk? He was a Web Developer. 'What if Nathan Wade didn't kill Sarah? Doesn't that interest you?'

'Whoever did it, she's still dead. That's the thing that will never change. And it's the thing Mum won't accept. Answer me one question: do you want your life to always be about Sarah?'

Jo exhaled. 'No, and it isn't, but—'

'There are no buts. That's the decision.'

'In your view.'

They'd reached their usual impasse.

Carl huffed. 'Well. Got to get back to work.'

'Me too.'

Jo tossed her phone on the desk and bit into a doughnut. Then she emailed copies of her report on Ivan Rossi to everyone on the distribution list. Her job for Operation Grebe was done.

Steve Vaizey returned to the office around five. His raincoat was sodden, his hair wet and sleek like an otter surfacing from a stream. He must've walked a considerable distance in the rain. Jo watched him, mesmerized. He shot a penetrating glance across the office. It pierced straight through her without recognition. He bellowed. 'Sandra!'

The analyst got up, grabbed a notepad, raised her eyebrows, and headed for his office.

Any remaining inclination Jo had to ask for his help evaporated. She checked her bag; fortunately she had remembered to bring an umbrella. Getting up, she retrieved her jacket from the pegs and left.

She took the DLR to Greenwich and found her mother

with a large glass of wine and a small bowl of tinned tomato soup.

Alison looked up in some perplexity as Jo propped her umbrella behind the door. 'Oh. Wasn't expecting to see you.'

'I was wondering if I could borrow the car.'

Her mother shrugged. 'Want some soup?'

'Is that all you're having?'

'It's what old people who live on their own do. They eat soup.'

58

The drive to Norfolk took Jo close to three hours. The traffic out of London was still heavy. She opted to take the A2 out to the M25, which she hoped would be a longer but easier route than the Blackwall Tunnel. But the tailbacks at the Dartford Crossing still held her up.

She didn't tell Alison what she was doing or where she was going, opting for evasion as opposed to an outright lie. *I'm wondering if Dad murdered Briony Rowe* wasn't a conversation she needed to have with her mother. She mentioned Tania Jones and *some information she needed to check.* This seemed to satisfy Alison, who'd retreated into a bubble. Jo noticed that the old photo albums were out, but the journals, still piled in the corner, remained untouched. She left her mother pouring a second glass of wine and hunkering down for another wallow in nostalgia.

The village of Brancaster was on the north Norfolk coast and in the winter months, it was empty. The expensively-renovated second homes were deserted, leaving the place to a few birdwatchers and weekend walkers who weren't put off by the freezing fog rolling in off the North Sea.

Jo drove into the village on the main road at about nine thirty. There was still some snow on the verges and a hoar frost sparkled in the headlights. She turned the Astra into a winding lane and from this onto the narrow track that led up an incline to Nick Boden's renovated barn.

It stood on rising ground, an imposing structure, the original flint walls carefully preserved but with the addition of huge windows to take in the magnificent view over marshland and sea. Not that any of that was visible in the eerie halo of the security light, which came on as Jo pulled up on the gravel drive.

She'd texted her father, saying that he was right. They needed to talk face to face. There was a temptation to turn up unannounced, but she decided that would be too melodramatic.

As she got out of the car, the front door opened and he appeared. He smiled, but there was a wary look in his eye.

He gave the Astra a nod. 'I'm surprised that old rust-bucket still goes.'

Jo slammed the door with a forceful clunk. 'It does the job.'

'I would've come to you, y'know.'

She allowed him to envelope her in an awkward hug. He patted her shoulder. 'Anyway, come on in. It's freezing.'

'It's always freezing up here.'

'You just need a proper jumper.'

As the front door closed, the warm fug of the interior engulfed her. It glowed in muted tones of brown and beige and grey with splashes of orange and red, like a home in a design magazine. In fact, if Jo remembered correctly, it had featured in a recent edition of *Homes and Gardens* or *House*

Beautiful; seaside boltholes for those with shed loads of cash. Nick Boden knew his brand and how to promote it.

As he helped her out of her jacket, Jo noticed her two half-brothers hovering in the doorway. Jack and Oscar, she tended to forget which was which. The taller must be Jack; he was the eldest.

Her father tousled his hair. 'I bet you hardly recognize these guys. When they heard you were coming, they insisted on staying up.'

Jo stared at the two little boys in cosy pyjamas and moppet haircuts, and they stared back. 'They've grown loads.'

Then Jack piped up. 'I got a quad bike for my birthday. You can have a go if you like. But we're only allowed to ride it in the field.'

Oscar joined in. 'You have to wear a helmet.'

'Sounds like fun.' Jo painted on a smile. She was beginning to wish she'd accepted her father's offer to come to London. At least she would've avoided the sham of behaving as if she and these two little kids were in any way connected.

Nick was gazing at his sons with gentle affection. Had he ever looked at her like that? Not that she could remember.

His tone was chatty. 'Not a full-sized quad bike, of course. A smaller version.'

Suddenly Oscar grabbed her hand; it made her start, the contact with his soft, sticky palm. 'You can borrow my helmet. Mum says we have to be nice to you because you're our sister.'

'Kids, eh! They always drop you right in it.' Emily stood in the kitchen doorway, wreathed in smiles, wiping her hands on a tea towel. 'It's so lovely to see you, Jo.'

Stepmother and stepdaughter exchanged a polite hug.

Emily beamed. 'You've had a long drive. Are you hungry?'

'No, I'm fine.' She hadn't eaten since the afternoon doughnuts.

'Let me put a few bits on a plate and see if I can tempt you. Darling, open a bottle of wine. What d'you prefer, Jo? White or red?'

'Whatever. I'm not fussy.'

They sat down at the long solid oak farmhouse table and Emily ferried dishes from the kitchen. A cheese board, some slices of homemade quiche, fresh chunks of sourdough bread. Jo realized she was starving.

The two boys sat down opposite her, side by side, obedient and watchful. A black Labrador rose from its basket and wandered over.

'What's the dog called?' Jo knew, but she needed a topic of conversation.

'Rosie,' the boys answered in unison, then giggled.

'She's expecting.' Jack gave her a knowledgeable I'm-the-older-brother nod.

'Wow! Puppies. That'll be exciting.'

'Daddy says they'll be trained as proper gun dogs so we can't keep them.'

'Okay.'

Jo realized she had snippets of her father's life, but not the complete picture. He belonged to a wildfowling club and had a licence to shoot on the marshes. She had the vaguest memory of that. Could he have used one of his shotguns to threaten Briony and get her out of her car?

Nick uncorked a bottle of Merlot and poured Jo a hefty glass.

'If my memory serves, I think you like red.'

Jo smiled. The last time they'd managed a civilized

311

dinner on one of his rare trips to London, he'd chosen some expensive red that it was hard not to like.

'Thank you.' She took a sip of the wine and gave him an appreciative grin.

Emily whipped up a small salad garnished with fresh herbs from the greenhouse. She placed it in front of Jo with what looked like an elegant decanter of dressing. 'Just eat what you want. I won't take offence.'

Jo noticed the nerviness of her smile, which melted as she turned to her two boys. She was about ten years older than Jo, which made her almost a contemporary of Sarah. It occurred to Jo that this was his response to the pain of his daughter's loss; he'd gone in search of a replacement and then married her. The whole thing was vaguely obscene.

Emily adopted a tone of maternal authority. 'Right, you two—bed!'

After some argy-bargy and complaining and the promise they'd see Jo in the morning, the boys were shepherded upstairs by their mother. Before they went, they each stepped up to give Jo a goodnight kiss. Emily had them well drilled. But their silky cheeks, the soft smell of their skin, was enticing. Jo couldn't help liking them. Her little half-brothers, they were the innocents in all this.

She ate quiche and salad and the delicious sourdough bread. Nick poured himself a glass of wine and drank it down as he watched her.

His eyes were shiny and she suspected he'd had a few before she'd arrived. 'I'm glad you came. I know that, well, each time you walk into all this, it can't be easy for you.'

Jo shrugged. 'It's nice to see the boys.'

'Y'know, none of us planned this.'

'Carl's already phoned me and given me the you-have-to-move-on lecture.'

'Even so. If Sarah had lived—'

'You'd probably have got itchy feet and traded up for a younger model, anyway.'

'Maybe. I've never pretended to be anything special. I know I've been selfish, but I tried to be a good father. I realize I haven't managed it with you.'

'You want me to feel sorry for you? Poor old Nick Boden, struggling along with all this.' She threw open her palms to encompass the room, reaching up to the vaulted ceiling and exposed rafters.

'I'm sure you didn't come all this way just to give me a hard time. You could've done that over the phone.' He sounded more sorrowful than critical.

Jo fortified herself with a slug of wine. 'Okay then. Briony Rowe.'

'What about her?'

'She threw herself under a train.'

' Well, I didn't much like the woman. But that's horrible. Suicide, eh?'

'Possibly. But those who knew her best don't buy that.'

'What then? Someone killed her?'

'Did you try for an injunction to stop the film?'

'I spoke to the lawyers. But as you rightly said, unless they libelled us, no grounds.'

Jo stared at him and sighed. It wasn't the same as sitting in an interview room facing a complete stranger. The accusation hung on her lips. How could this be true? Such a cold-blooded act. Was he capable of being that kind of monster? He read her look and her hesitation.

'My God, Jo, you don't think that I would—' The tears welled in his eyes and fattened into droplets that rolled down his cheeks. He brushed them away with the back of his hand.

She looked down at her plate, rearranged the knife and

fork. Watching her own fingers move filled her with an odd sensation. She felt disembodied. And her head started to spin.

'When did this actually happen?' It seemed to Jo that his voice came from far away.

She had to concentrate. Her thoughts had become quite blurry. 'Wednesday night. Well, more early hours Thursday.'

He got up, took a tissue from a box on the sideboard and blew his nose. Then he headed across the room towards the far door. 'I'll be back in a minute.'

Being left alone was a relief. It gave Jo a chance to marshal her chaotic thoughts. She was tired, a stressful day, followed by a long drive. This was the most likely explanation for her sudden giddiness. Or perhaps it was the wine. She thought about escaping while he was gone, but she was too shaky to drive.

She got up, went to the kitchen tap, tipped her wine away down the sink and refilled the glass with water. As she returned to the table, he came striding back into the room.

He slapped an A4 envelope down in front of her. 'Take a look.'

'What is it?'

'My air tickets and hotel invoice. Tuesday night I flew to Berlin. From Stansted. I went to present a workshop at an interior design fair on Wednesday morning. I talked about incorporating modern design with traditional materials. There were about fifty people in the audience. You can see extracts on YouTube. I stayed at the Crowne Plaza in Nuernberger Strasse. Flew back on Thursday.'

Jo stared at him. She felt like a twelve-year-old caught smoking.

His eyes were boring into her. 'Go on, check it. There are business colleagues, both UK-based and from Berlin, who can confirm I was there. I'll give you their numbers. You can phone them.'

Picking up the envelope, Jo emptied the contents on to the table, not because she disbelieved him but because it seemed the only way to satisfy him. There were two combined e-tickets and boarding passes and a printed hotel bill, which had been settled by credit card.

'I'm sorry, Dad.'

'I'm sorry it's come to this. That you really don't know who I am.'

'It's the cop in me.' This sounded both foolish and childish.

'I blame myself. I let Alison win with you, because that was easier.'

'She's hardly the winner. No one is.'

'Well, I don't know what to say. Except I truly am sorry.'

Father and daughter stared at each other. They both had tears in their eyes.

59

Waking to sharp splinters of light escaping round the cracks in the blinds, Jo didn't know where she was at first. Her sleep had been heavy and dreamless, weighed down with a weariness that seemed lodged in her bones. She'd wanted to drive back to London, but Nick wouldn't hear of it. He'd taken charge, ordered her to bed and, like a small child, she'd complained but complied.

She dressed and went downstairs to the aroma of fresh coffee and warm croissants. Through the vast plate-glass window, she could see Jack and Oscar hurtling round the frosty garden. Jack was attacking his brother with something leafy and wet.

Emily was assembling coats and backpacks and kit. She rapped on the window. 'Come on, you'll be late for Taekwondo.'

She smiled at Jo. 'Sleep well?'

Jo nodded.

'Pour yourself a coffee. Your dad's in his office.'

'Thanks.'

Emily seemed about to say something else, then changed

her mind. She laughed. 'These two! They wear me out. They seem to take after Carl. Endless energy. Will you be staying for lunch?'

'Probably not.'

'Oh well. Take care, Jo. I must get on. Even on a Saturday it's a madhouse round here.'

She scurried out with some relief, Jo thought.

Jo wondered about going and saying goodbye to the boys, but decided not to. She didn't want to aggravate Emily by making them late.

She poured herself a mug of coffee and wandered through the house to the back, where Nick's home office was situated. It was light and airy, a vast marshland panorama out of the windows, plans, maps, designs covering the various walls. He was on the phone and gave her a friendly wave as he wrapped up the call.

They looked at each other for an awkward moment.

He sighed. 'Well—'

'I should be getting back to London.'

He nodded, hesitated. She sensed he was on the brink of a difficult decision.

'You know this thing you asked me about? When I went down on my own to see Sarah.'

'Yeah. In November.'

'There was a reason for me going. She did have a problem. But I've never spoken of it to anyone.'

'Why not?'

'Because I made her a promise. That it would be between the two of us. She particularly didn't want your mother, or indeed anyone else in the family, to know.'

'What was it?'

He sighed. Elbows resting on his desk, he steepled his fingers. 'We all do stupid things when we're young. I didn't want her life to be ruined by it. She'd only just started at university.'

'Don't tell me she was pregnant.'

'She met this boy at the very beginning of term. Had unprotected sex. She said only the once. My guess is it could've been more than that.'

'What was his name?'

'She wouldn't tell me. Probably thought I'd go after him. And she was right.'

'Was he a postgrad?'

'I don't know. He seemed to be putting pressure on her, insisting she was his girlfriend. And she didn't want that. She was at the beginning of everything, for Chrissake. It was a silly mistake. So I arranged for her to have a private abortion.'

'Did he know about it?'

'Definitely not. She'd finished with him by then. We saw a private doctor and the university didn't know. I didn't want her future to be affected by it in any way.'

'Could she have confided in anyone else? A friend perhaps?'

'Jo, she was—' he had to put his hand over his mouth to stop the tears. 'She begged me to help her. She was ashamed. And, well, desperate. We pretended she had the flu. She spent a couple of nights in the clinic to make sure everything was all right. But it was early stages, so the procedure was straightforward. No one at the university suspected a thing.'

'Is that why she dropped out of the play?'

'Yes.'

'Dad, why didn't you tell the police this?'

'Because it had absolutely no relevance to her death.'

'You don't know that.'

'She didn't even start going out with Nathan Wade until

after Christmas. Can you imagine what would have happened, what his lawyers would have said about her, if they knew she'd had an abortion? She was the victim, but they would've put her on trial. I had to protect her, her memory.'

'What if this other boy found out about the abortion?'

'There was no way he could have. Your mother and I met Nathan Wade and I have to say I didn't think much of him. I told Sarah that. The police thought he was involved in drugs, selling cannabis to other students. So my instincts about him were right.'

'There's a passage in her journal about wanting to run away. She had some kind of plan to apply for the exchange programme and go to an American university for a year.'

'Your mother wasn't keen. But I thought it was a good idea, get her away from Wade. I think she'd learnt from her mistakes. Unfortunately, it didn't happen soon enough.'

Nick Boden raked his hand through his hair. Jo watched him. Pain radiated from his hunched body. 'You think I don't curse myself every day for not having taken action to deal with Wade, to get him out of her life? Afterwards, when the police told me about the drugs, I cursed myself even more. If I'd done something, I could've saved her. Now he wants to prove his fucking innocence! I tell you, Jo, if I was going to kill anyone, I'd kill him.'

60

Oh, Jo, what a disappointment you've turned out to be. You must really think I'm a fool. Don't make the mistake of thinking you can lie to me and play me. That's what Sarah did.

You think this is the life I'd planned? I've suffered too. A lifetime of boredom and regret. I've done my penance.

I thought I could rely on you to ignore all this ridiculous hogwash. The media are like vultures, always seeking out carrion. They have to feed to survive. But I was sure you'd tell them to stuff it and not get involved. You're a police officer. You know justice is sometimes a fluid concept. What matters is that we have a system we can all believe in, a system that assures us we can sleep safe in our beds. Reality is about perception, and so justice depends on fast and dependable convictions. Truth is incidental and can get in the way.

But the truth is, your sister was a selfish slut who thought that what she wanted trumped everything else. Would it have helped your family, your poor grieving parents, if that had been exposed in open court? I don't think so.

And now what are we going to do? I've been forced to

act, to go back to a version of myself I never wanted to revisit in order to cover my tracks. And this is your fault, Jo. Why oh why couldn't you leave well alone?

I guess I am a fool. I did hope, dream even, that with you I'd have a second chance. Maybe you and I could've had the relationship I always wanted with Sarah. She was too young and self-centred and arrogant. But I thought you were different, that you'd appreciate what I had to offer. Seems I was wrong.

So now I have to stop you. And I will. I've got a feeling this is not going to end well, which is sad. I had such high hopes for us, I really did.

61

Jo left Norfolk in the late morning and headed down the M11. The day was damp and dull, leaden clouds threatening more snow. The engine of the old Astra was whining and she kept her speed to a restrained 40 mph. But the needle on the temperature gauge was twitching into the red. She turned into Bishop Stortford services and crawled into the car park.

A cursory examination of the front of the vehicle revealed a slow drip from what Jo assumed was the radiator. She considered opening the bonnet but found it hot to the touch. Mechanical problems always left her feeling annoyingly female, although she knew plenty of blokes who'd be as clueless as her, faced with an overheated engine.

Fortunately, she'd coerced her mother into investing in annual breakdown cover and carried the card in her wallet. She called them, got herself a takeaway coffee and settled down to wait for rescue. At least she'd made it to the services and wasn't stuck on some freezing verge beside the hard shoulder of the motorway, breathing a cocktail of toxic emissions.

Bundled up against the creeping cold in coat and scarf, Jo

extracted the shiny black journal from her bag. This was her sister's last testament; Jo had skimmed through it searching for clues, but now she was re-reading it in the light of what her father had told her.

It was clear why Sarah had cut out the missing pages. If she'd given any hint of her feelings about her unwanted pregnancy and the subsequent abortion, then she'd have risked exposure. A journal was no place for proper secrets. Alison was quite capable of claiming parental privilege and reading things that were none of her business. She'd done that with Jo.

Sarah had erased her immediate response to the situation, but in the entries from the days and weeks following, Jo discovered a subtle change in tone. Nick Boden was right; his daughter was learning from her mistakes.

It pisses me off the way we're expected to dance around them. If you fancy someone and you come on to them, you've always got to be so careful. Not too confident or too sexy or too clever, you'll scare them off, give the wrong impression, get labelled a slut and a one-off shag. Once you're that sort of girl, you're in an even worse position. A target.

You want a boy, you still have to let him think it's his idea. He gets to ask; you get to be girly and grateful. And here's the stupid thing, you are grateful and excited. He wants you, and that gives you such a buzz. Like he knows something about you that you don't. Even if you want to say no to something—for example, sex without a condom—then it's awkward. He might get upset. You have to take care of his feelings because you're the girl. Is this biology? I hope not. I wish I could be tough and different and just tell the truth. But then people won't like me. They won't like me if they find out what I really am!

Jo smiled. Not even nineteen and Sarah had a pretty mature, though cynical grasp of how the game was played.

What would she have made of a one-night stand with the boss? Jo was swamped by an overwhelming sense of regret. How good it would be to go to her big sister and ask her advice.

What would she have made of Steve Vaizey—married, chilly, domineering? And why the hell did Jo even find that attractive? Maybe Sarah could've explained it and told her she was being stupid. They might've shared a bottle of wine, moaned about Alison, compared notes on men and sex. In the absence of religion, who better than your sister, your blood sister, to hear your most shameful secrets and grant you absolution?

A yellow van pulled up in front of her. Tears ran down Jo's cheeks. She brushed them away, blew her nose and got out to greet her knight in shining armour.

He had smart overalls straining over his paunch and a jolly demeanour. Apologizing for the wait, he had the bonnet up in a jiffy and as he worked started a monologue about Astras: a sturdy workhorse of the road. Unfortunately radiators were the weak spot of many older vehicles. His diagnosis and explanation of what he was doing slid into Jo's brain and out again. Her gaze glided through the drizzle and came to rest on a grey Insignia.

The car park was busy with comings and goings; in the hour she'd waited, although she'd been focused on the journal, her subconscious had been on autopilot, scanning and noting the turnover of vehicles.

An Insignia had followed her in, a couple of cars behind, and parked in the next bay, facing away from her. The tinted rear windows made it impossible to see the occupants. Now it was one of only three vehicles remaining in that sector of the car park that had been there since her arrival. The other two comprised a Ford Galaxy with a large Asian family—the kids kicking a football around on the slippery grass—and two scaffolders in a van, who'd consumed the contents of three large buckets of KFC and were taking a nap.

Jo studied the Insignia—it looked empty—its owner was probably a salesman who was inside in the warm working on his laptop. She hadn't noticed anyone get out, but she could've missed it.

Monitoring her surroundings had become a habit. It was an automatic response to her high level of anxiety and her churned-up emotions. She'd left her father on superficially better terms, but feeling ashamed like a guilty child. To have accused him of such a crime felt shocking now, even to her. The years of resentment and self-pity had spilled over and obliterated rational judgement.

The mechanic was pouring something viscous and evil-smelling into the radiator to seal it when the passenger door of the Insignia opened. A man got out and jogged towards the building. He had his back towards her, the hood of his dark sweatshirt up and concealing his face. But the curve and tilt of the narrow shoulders as he ran, hands thrust in pockets, sent a shudder of recognition through Jo. It was Jabreel Khan; she was sure of it.

62

The mechanic advised Jo to wait thirty minutes for the gunk
—not the technical term he used—to solidify before driving
the car. As soon as he'd left, she strode towards main services
building. If it was Jabreel, she was going to confront him and
demand to know what was going on. Was he back undercover
and, if so, why was he following her? It could be a bizarre
coincidence, though that seemed unlikely.

Her head was scratchy with questions and speculations.
Were the Kelmendis still targeting her? Surely all that had
been dealt with. Had he been dispatched to protect her? Had
she been followed all the way to Norfolk or picked up later
on ANPR? But then, how did they know she was driving her
mother's car? She hadn't discussed her plans with anyone in
the office. Her thoughts skipped to her phone. She'd texted.
But the notion her phone was being tracked was absurd.
Why?

She was on a mission as she headed into the building.

It was triangular in shape, glass-fronted and airy, with the
various catering outlets and seating areas arranged around an
open corridor. The place had a vibrancy and bustle as trav-

ellers escaped the winter chill, queued for hot food and drinks, made a beeline for the toilets, or browsed for sweets and magazines. Jo scanned each area systematically, but there was no sign of Jabreel Khan.

She hovered outside the toilets. If that's where he was hiding, she'd wait him out. But after fifteen minutes of pacing and hawkish observation, there was no sign. Perhaps she'd made a mistake and paranoia was getting the better of her. She just driven over a hundred miles to accuse her own father of murder. Now this. She needed to get a grip.

Returning to her car, she saw the Insignia was gone. She felt foolish. The world was full of young men in hoodies. Jabreel had moved on to another job. He'd told her that. Perhaps she'd been wishing subconsciously for a better rescuer than her garrulous mechanic.

She drove south and on the outskirts of the city joined the belching tailback of red winking lights stretching ahead into the early encroaching darkness. Crawling through the rush-hour traffic, she finally made it back to Greenwich and parked the car. It seemed doubtful it would pass its next MOT and neither she nor her mother could afford to replace it. Nick would've probably stepped into the breach and bought something for her—quad bikes for the boys. Why shouldn't she get a car? But the idea of being beholden to him irked her.

When she let herself into her mother's house, she found the place in darkness. She called out, flicked on a couple of lamps, then saw a glimmer of light from the painting shed in the garden. Switching on the security lights at the back of the house, she picked her way down the damp and slithery path. It was composed of old brick, crumbling at the edges, and had acquired a coat of lichen which made it treacherous when wet. She made a mental note to get someone in to sort it out before Alison slipped and broke a bone, creating yet more problems.

The windows of Alison's painting shed were fogged with condensation, and a gush of warm air met Jo as she opened the door. Alison was on her feet, in front of her easel. Her face was animated and she waved her brush.

'For me, it's all about texture. The interplay of texture and colour.'

Standing beside her, arms folded, nodding, was Nathan Wade.

'I like it. It's got real energy.'

Jo stared in horror and disbelief. They were chatting, like two art buffs at a gallery opening, and beamed in unison at the sight of Jo.

'Hello, darling. Look who's come to see us.' Alison slotted her brush into a jar of white spirit.

Jo glared at him. 'How the hell did you get this address?'

He gave her a bland smile. 'From Kayleigh. It was in Briony's address book.'

As Jo stared into his eyes, she had a jolting sensation that, although he was gazing right at her, he wasn't seeing her at all. He was inside his own head, in another time and another place.

Alison shot her daughter a peevish glance. 'Don't be so aggressive, Jo. I think we could all do with a nice glass of wine.'

63

The sight of Nathan Wade lounging on her mother's battered old sofa with his legs languidly crossed struck Jo as an insult and an invasion. There were questions to be answered, but he was still her sister's convicted killer. He refused wine and asked for a cup of tea. To buy herself some time, Jo retreated to the kitchen to make it. Alison followed, went straight to the fridge and poured herself a glass of wine.

Jo caught her eye.

Alison slopped wine on the kitchen worktop. She spoke in a stage whisper. 'Don't look at me like that. I opened the door. There he was. I didn't know what to say to him.'

'Go away?'

'Oh, yeah, right? You'd've done that.' Her mother took a hefty slug. She seemed rather hyper and Jo knew that the alcohol was likely to bring her down, probably with a bump. Nathan Wade had thrown them both onto the back foot. But Alison was right, curiosity would've got the better of her. She boiled the kettle and made a pot of tea.

By the time Jo sat down in front of him, she was composed and fixed him with an impassive stare.

He picked up his mug, sipped, smiled. 'You must be wondering why I'm here. As I explained to Alison, I've come to apologize and to answer your question.'

'My question?'

'You asked where I was on Monday night, when Briony died. I was in bed at the hostel. With Kayleigh. I was still with her when the police rang and told her about Briony. If you call her, she'll tell you it's true.'

She nodded and waited for him to say more.

'You've met Kayleigh and I'm sure you've observed how upset and indeed angry she was about what happened. She was very close to Briony.'

'She wouldn't lie to protect you. Is that your point?'

'Yes. But please, ring her and check. I can give you the number.'

'Oh, I will. Is that it?'

'No. I've been doing some thinking.' He leaned forward and sighed; it was the charming, self-deprecating manner he'd adopted before and Jo found it deeply suspect.

He rubbed his palm over his close-cropped scalp. 'Look, I decided years ago to accept my guilt and serve my time. But the truth is I didn't kill Sarah.'

'That makes little sense. If you are innocent, why wouldn't you continue to argue that? Even if you couldn't afford a lawyer—'

'I said I didn't kill her. I didn't say I was innocent.'

Jo glanced across at her mother, perched on the edge of the armchair; she'd already drunk most of her wine.

Nathan Wade turned to her with a sad smile. 'I am so sorry, believe me. I was stupid and arrogant. And young. But I loved Sarah. They were trying to get to me. And they used her.'

Alison blinked at him, got up and moved unsteadily into the kitchen to refill her glass.

'Who did?' Jo shifted forward in her seat.

'I sold drugs on campus. Cannabis. I dunno, I had the stupid idea I was being cool. Made a few quid, plus paid for my own stuff. I got it from a dealer called Rigzi, and I owed him a couple of hundred quid. I thought it was no big deal. He could wait for his money. He struck me as a bit of an old hippie. It didn't occur to me he was dangerous.'

'Did you tell the police this?'

'I didn't know at that time, didn't think it was connected. In fact, I didn't know until five years later. I met this other guy in prison. He'd worked for Rigzi, and reckoned Rigzi had done it to put the fear of God into all his other street dealers. He said Rigzi put it about that if anyone crossed him or didn't pay up, they'd end up like me. In jail for life, convicted of their girlfriend's murder. Apparently, it worked.'

'You saying this Rigzi killed Sarah?'

'Or had her killed? I don't know.'

'What convinced you this story was true?'

'I wasn't convinced at first. When you're inside, you hear this kind of stuff all the time. Mostly it's rubbish. I thought Rigzi could've just exploited the situation. Used it to put the frighteners on people.'

'Did you discuss this with anyone? The prison authorities?'

Nathan shrugged. 'I had no proof. No one would've given a shit. They would've thought I was trying to make excuses. It would've scuppered my chances with the parole board too.'

Jo scanned him. It had some plausibility as a story, but she was still finding it difficult to let go of her view of him. He seemed to be trying too hard. But could she bring herself to accept anything he said at face value? This could be the truth as Nathan saw it, or an elaborate lie to get the Bodens onside. She remained suspicious.

Alison was frowning. She was already quite drunk. 'A drug dealer killed Sarah? My God, a drug dealer!'

Jo put a gentle hand on her mother's arm. 'It's only a theory, Mum. And I'm guessing Nathan can't even tell us Rigzi's proper name.'

'Oh, but I can. A couple of years later, I saw him on the telly. That's when I thought it could be true.'

He had that faraway, dreamy smile again. In his mind's eye, he was somewhere else. It made him appear harmless. A clever trick.

'I saw it reported on the news. His name is Richard Green and it was the biggest drugs bust in the south-east for years. A County Lines gang out of Lewisham. All in their teens and twenties except for one. The ringleader. He was much older with, they said, Yardie connections going way back. And there he was, Rigzi. He's in jail.'

64

Jo stood in the doorway of the office and took a moment to observe her quarry. Calvin Foley had returned from Manchester once the interviews were completed and all the suspects formally charged. He was sorting out his desk, covered with detritus from other users, and was dumping coffee cups and a stale sandwich in the bin. As she approached, he looked up and smiled.

'All right?'

She'd rehearsed her spiel and considered all the angles. At least she hoped she had. If she was about to put her promotion prospects, not to mention her career, on the line, she intended to be careful.

'Yeah. Good result, skip.'

'I think so.' He was looking her up and down, blatantly she thought. But she hoped this would distract him.

'I wasn't sure if I'd be staying with Grebe, or what. So the last couple of days, I've been following up with some-thing I was doing for my old squad. Didn't have much else to do.'

'Yeah? That's very diligent.'

'That's me. Diligent.' She treated him to her best smile. 'The thing is, I got a sniff of something. The Kelmendis beat this trafficked Syrian girl half to death. She was my chis. We've been looking for her sister. Only twelve. We think they sold her to a pimp in Manchester. I've got a name of a drug dealer. Richard Green. He's in the nick. He might know about her, if I can get him to talk to me. Mind if I follow this up?'

Foley shrugged. 'You should be asking Hollingsworth, not me.'

'Strictly speaking, I still work for Vaizey's firm.' She gave him an arch look. 'And I know the two of them don't get on. I don't want to upset anyone. You know what they're like.'

Camaraderie in the ranks, us against the bosses. That would appeal to Foley.

'Okay. You reckon you might get some traction, go for it.'

'Thanks.' She was about to walk away.

'Couple of the team I met up in Manchester are pretty good blokes. They might help you. I could give them a bell.' Foley had a smirk, as if he was dangling some juicy titbit.

Jo wondered what he was up to, though she could guess. 'Yeah. That'd be great.'

'Email me the details on this girl. I'll pass it on.'

'Okay. Thanks.'

'So, now it's quietened down a bit, perhaps you'd like to go for a drink sometime?' He was tipping his chair back like a schoolboy, arms up over his head, his barrel chest thrust out. Tough but gauche, there was something touching about it. Jo could like him, almost... But. There was always a but with Foley. He was a good DS and probably decent enough on a personal level once you got beyond the usual masculine bullshit.

He was gazing at her and she glimpsed how nervous he

was. 'Y'know, I enjoyed our trip down to Hampshire. Made me think we should get to know each other better.'

Jo sighed. It was tempting to agree just because it was easier. 'I appreciate the offer, Cal. But well, I'm not, y'know, looking to get involved with anyone right now. Especially not at work.'

He chuckled, but his face seemed to snap shut, any trace of softness gone. As he leaned forward and folded his arms, his bull-neck seemed to expand. His tongue skated over his lower lip. 'Yeah? C'mon, Boden, that's not what I heard.'

65

Jo travelled down to Winchester by train. She knew she was sailing pretty close to the wind. Her brother's assertion that she never took risks slipped into her head; it showed how little he knew about her. Using the Police National Computer for personal matters was a serious disciplinary offence. But was tracing Richard Green strictly a personal matter? She hoped she would never have to argue this point with her bosses. Her ruse with Foley, she hoped, would keep it under the radar. Technically, he'd given her permission, even though it was based on a lie.

She'd used the PNC to access Richard Green's records and the Prison Location Service to find him. She'd put in a request to interview him. He'd been convicted of the cultivation of cannabis with intent to supply and false imprisonment. His cannabis farms in Sussex and Kent and the network they supplied were extensive. He'd used enslaved Vietnamese teenagers smuggled into the country illegally to tend the crops. Approaching the halfway mark of a twelve-year term, he had one eye on the parole board and an early released. He declared himself more than happy to help Jo with her enquiries.

The prison was old and Victorian, though currently being refurbished. She faced him across a rickety table. He greeted her with a polite handshake and then proceeded to fold a square of tissue and wedge it under one of the table legs.

He beamed at her. 'Annoying, innit. Place is falling apart.'

According to his file, he was fifty-five and Jo could see from his languorous manner why Nathan Wade had assumed him to be a bit of a hippie. His face was tawny and weathered, a wispy goatee, his hair neatly braided, but the dark eyes were hard and watchful.

He laced his fingers. 'What can I do for you, officer?'

Jo wondered if she was finally looking at her sister's killer.

'I understand you were known as Rigzi.'

He chuckled. 'Not in a while. I prefer Richard. Richard sounds more businesslike.'

'And that's what you are, a businessman?'

He tilted his head and gave her a speculative look. 'Rigzi? That takes me back, I dunno, fifteen or twenty years. So, what am I being accused of?'

'Do you remember Nathan Wade?'

'Oh yeah.' He gave a throaty smoker's laugh. 'Killed his girlfriend.'

'He was convicted of her murder.'

'Lovely girl.'

'You met her?'

'Students were my best market. All these posh kids wanted to get stoned.'

'You sold drugs to her?'

'Maybe. I don't remember. I only remember wondering what she was doing with a fool like him.' He frowned and shook his head. 'What happened to her, that was sad.'

'Did he work for you?'

'Nah. He could've put some business my way. Other students looking to score.'

'Did he owe you money?'

He fixed her with an amused stare. 'I see where this is going. And I'm looking at you and I'm thinking, is this personal?'

'Sarah Boden was my sister.' Jo saw no point in lying.

He grinned. 'Sarah, yeah, that was her name.' A wistful look came into his eye. 'Y'know, if I'd kept things smallish, I wouldn't be sitting here. I'd be on a beach in Jamaica sipping rum. But ambition got the better of me, bigger operation, more risk. Y'know what I'm saying?'

'Not really.'

'It was just a business. But I was good at it, that's why they give me twelve years. Killing nice white college girls, that's not good for business. Campus full of students, that's a lush market. Cops everywhere, turning everything upside down. Why would I want that, eh?'

'To punish Nathan.'

'I wanna punish Nathan, I'd've cut off his supply. I ain't a violent man. Violence costs. Stupid kids who wanna play the big man, gangs, that's the weak link that got me here. I'm a businessman.'

Jo met his gaze. The argument made sense, but then she doubted he'd admit to murder.

Rigzi seemed to read her mind. 'They had me in at the time, local cops. Think they woulda quite liked to pin it on me. But they couldn't. It was the boyfriend.'

'Nathan Wade?'

'I dunno. Him. Some boyfriend. Your sister, she had lots of boys running round after her.' He gave a gravelly chuckle. 'Bet you do too. You look just like her.'

'So I've been told.'

66

Back at her flat, Jo reviewed her notes. She felt weary. She seemed to be going round in circles, chasing her own tail, and she wasn't even sure to what end. Had she expected Rigzi to confess to her sister's murder? He was a major league drug dealer; whatever his bullshit about being a businessman, he would never have got into such a position without being prepared to use violence.

What interested her more was Nathan's decision to confess. Was it even a real confession? It seemed to have come out of the blue. Why now? He didn't kill Sarah, he said, but regarded himself as responsible for her murder because he thought Rigzi had done it to punish him. Was he just sending her round in another circle, lying to confuse the issue?

Maybe it was Briony's death that had pricked his conscience? Perhaps he believed she had committed suicide. But then what about Bruce? What about Sarah's journals? The pregnancy and the abortion that no one knew about. Except what if they did?

Jo rubbed her eyes. Out of her window, the afternoon light was dying. A lassitude had crept over her. What was the point of any of it? Nathan killed her sister. Rigzi killed her sister. Bruce killed her sister. The ghost of Sarah had dominated her life forever. Carl was right about that. Why had she become a police officer? She thought she knew. It was a thankless job at the best of times. But was she just an adrenaline junkie like her brother, courting danger to give her the high that kept darker feelings at bay?

Like most people, she lived one day at a time, putting her best foot forward. There was the occasional high-risk burst of activity, but the job rarely satisfied her. Mostly it was a frustrating slog. The money she earned barely covered her bills. Rent in London was exorbitant. At the end of the month, she had nothing to spare. A holiday or a meal out or a new dress; they all went on the credit card, and the debt mounted. She tried to be disciplined and keep things in check while she battled for the next promotion. But too many people were chasing the same few vacancies. You had to be special, or canny enough to make yourself seem special. The Met was being cut and cut again. Nothing was expanding, and no one in the more senior ranks was about to move aside to make a place for you.

Friends and hobbies and getting bladdered on a Saturday night, this was how most people she knew got through. Until that was replaced by marriage and kids and sleepless nights and the odd trip to the pub. Love was an emotion she'd waited for, but it never arrived. Would she even have allowed herself to feel it? Men asked her out. That had never been a problem. But they were all blokes like Foley. There was always a but. And the men she was drawn to were always wrong, like Vaizey.

Jo knew she had emptiness where her optimism should be. She was young and fit and healthy. She had physical energy, most of the time, but her spirit was forlorn. One former friend had accused her of lacking a sense of humour, and they were right. The world didn't strike her as an amusing place. If her sister had lived, it would've been different. Or would it?

It was already dark when Marisa came bustling in with a bag of groceries. Her buoyancy immediately filled the flat. She switched on all the lights and dumped her purchases in the kitchen.

'Hey, babe, why you sitting in the dark?'

Jo stood, arms folded, in her bedroom doorway and smiled. Seeing her flatmate was a relief. 'Thinking.'

'Thinking what?'

'Trying to work out what the hell I'm doing and why.'

'Oh, that old chestnut. Any luck?'

'No.'

Marisa unpacked her shopping. 'Well, I'm knocking the takeaways on the head and getting healthy. Proper home-cooked food.'

'Sounds like hard work.' Jo had to smile. Marisa always had some project for self-improvement.

'Doesn't have to be. Salad and fish, simple and good for you. Fancy that?'

'Okay. Want some help?'

Marisa laughed. 'I can manage. Don't want to stop your cogitations.'

Jo went back into her room, picked up her notebook, and sighed. She envied her flatmate's endless vitality. She was wondering how she could get a dose for herself when the doorbell rang.

Marisa called out from the kitchen. 'I'll get it! You expecting anyone?'

'No.' The word was hardly out of Jo's mouth when an

overwhelming sense of dread surged through her. 'Marisa, wait!'

Jo flew out of her room and made it to the corner of the short hallway when the feral howl of pain ricocheted off the walls. Marisa was stumbling backwards as she kicked the door shut behind her. Screeching in panic, her arms were flailing. 'Acid!'

Jo grabbed her by the shoulders, propelled her into the bathroom, and turning the shower on full, she shoved Marisa's upper body under the cold water. 'Where did it get you?'

Marisa was gasping and spluttering. 'Right arm! Side of my face! Aargh!'

Jo held her friend under the torrent of water. It cascaded over both of them, swamping the floor.

67

Jo didn't wait for the invitation to enter before stomping into Detective Superintendent Hollingsworth's office. She'd been up all night at the hospital and she wanted some answers.

Marisa's own quick reflexes had saved most of her face. She'd thrown up her arm to protect it as her attacker squirted sulphuric acid from a squeegee bottle, and she'd kicked the door shut. The immediate dousing in water, when Jo pushed her into the shower, had also helped.

She'd been taken to the Royal London in Whitechapel Road, the same A&E department where she worked, and her colleagues had rallied round. Once the shock and trauma of the incident had begun to subside, it became more apparent how lucky she'd been. She had acid burns on the underside of one arm and a small streak and some splashes across her forehead just below the hairline.

Returning to the flat, Jo had discovered that what had missed her flatmate had stripped paint off the front door. She'd spoken to the local officers, who were the first responders. There was a possibility of some CCTV of the attacker from the security camera on the corner shop. They were looking into it. But she knew that there was only one place she'd get answers. And she wasn't about to be fobbed off.

Hollingsworth was behind his desk, but standing beside the window, arms folded in his usual restless stance, was Steve Vaizey. Jo felt a rush of relief. The two men didn't get on, this much she knew. So the fact they were there together did at least suggest that finally they were taking the Kelmendis' targeting of her seriously.

Hollingsworth seemed to be considering his opening gambit, but Vaizey beat him to it. 'How's your friend?'

'Traumatized. The plastic surgeon's seeing her this morning. The primary concern is her arm.'

Vaizey nodded. 'She used it to protect her face?'

Jo met his eye. It was only the second time she'd seen him since they'd slept together. 'Yes. She was lucky. But that's hardly the point, is it? Sir.' She added this for Hollingsworth's benefit.

Vaizey returned her look with a glacial stare. He slipped his hands in his trouser pockets and sighed. 'You seem to have got yourself in a pretty compromised situation, DC Boden. But this isn't a matter for me. I'm going to leave it to Superintendent Hollingsworth and obviously the IPCC to deal with you.'

'What?' Jo stared at him. What he'd said made no sense. 'I don't understand.'

'You've been very foolish.' He shook his head—sorrowfully, Jo thought—and headed for the door. 'Very foolish.' He walked out.

Hollingsworth tapped his pen on the file in front of him. 'Sit down, Boden.'

She'd used the PNC to get Richard Green's records. How had he found out about that? Had Foley twigged and started asking questions? But that had nothing to do with the acid attack and the fact she was still being targeted by the Kelmendis, which they'd failed to sort out. Now somehow they were blaming her. It was outrageous. She was determined to stand her ground.

'Thank you, sir. I'll stand. I can explain my actions.'

'Can you? Well, I shall be interested in hearing what you have to say. This girl is your flatmate, so I'm sure you're feeling guilty enough about that. But when you sup with the devil, Boden, you should use a very long spoon.'

Another glib old-fashioned cliché. Hollingsworth was full of them. She had to rein in her temper.

'Yeah, I do feel guilty about Marisa, but—'

He held up his palm and picked up the desk phone handset. 'Can you ask DC Khan to join us? Thanks.'

Jo's stomach lurched. What the hell was going on? Jabreel Khan? Was it him at Bishop Stortford services? Had he been following her?

Hollingsworth gave her a pensive look. 'You can be a little strident, Jo. But I've always considered you to be a good officer.'

The door opened and Jabreel Khan came in. He avoided Jo's eye.

'I saw you at the services on the M11. You've been following me.'

'DC Khan has been acting on my instructions. Now will you both sit down.'

Jo took the left-hand chair in front of Hollingsworth's desk, Khan the right. A sense of foreboding swept over her. He still didn't meet her gaze.

The Detective Superintendent opened the folder in front of him. 'In fairness to you, Jo, I'm going to give you a chance to explain this first, before we move to a formal interview.' He removed a sheet from the file. 'A copy of your latest bank statement. Can you check the account number and confirm it is your account?'

She took the piece of paper. The truth was she could never remember her account number exactly, but it looked close enough. Her hand was shaking. She'd come here to lambast them about the attack on Marisa, but he was turning it around, acting as if she were to blame.

'The last entry, a deposit of £5,000, dated yesterday and which we have traced to an offshore account in the British Virgin Islands. Would you care to explain who has given you this money and why?'

Jo stared at the document. After a sleepless night, the figures danced off the page. 'It must be a mistake. No one's given me any money.' She focused on the column of figures. She'd been a bit overdrawn, but now she was in credit to the tune of nearly five grand.

'You went down to Winchester yesterday to visit a prisoner called Richard Green? How does that relate to any of your current enquiries?'

'It doesn't.' She sighed. 'Look, sir, I have no idea where this money has come from.'

Hollingsworth leaned back in his chair. 'As I think Jabreel himself told you, we have known for some time that an officer or civilian employee in this building was passing information to Ardi Kelmendi and his associates.'

'You think it could be me?'

'Could it be you, Jo?'

'How did you get to this? Ever since Ardi was arrested, they've been after me.'

Jabreel turned towards her. 'So we've been led to believe. But it's bothered me from the outset. You came blundering in that morning, to save your chis, you said. What kind of idiot would do that?'

'I'm the kind of idiot that would do that.'

'We don't buy it. We think you came to warn Kelmendi.'

'That's rubbish, Jabreel.'

'This notion you were being targeted? A dead cat? Bit of roadkill you'd picked up? That's the so-called evidence you're being targeted.'

'You told me I was being targeted.'

'We think it's all a set-up. To disguise the fact that you're the informant.'

'Ardi Kelmendi is a thug. He's not that bright.'

Jabreel's eyes were feverishly bright. 'But you are, aren't you, Jo? And Richard Green, he's your go-between.'

'What? You can't find the real informant, so I'm being fitted up?'

Hollingsworth leaned forward. 'Richard Green has had a long association with the Kelmendis. You wait for things to calm down after Ardi's arrest, you go to see Green and within hours of that visit, you get your payment. You saying that's a coincidence?'

'Yes. I didn't know Richard Green had any association with the Kelmendis. I can explain all of this. If I'd known which prison he was in, why would I've—'

'Jo, I'm going to stop it there. I had hoped that, confronted with the facts, you would decide to come clean.'

'What facts? Sir, I'm not lying. Let me explain.'

'You can do all the explaining you like to the IPCC in a formal interview. You're suspended from duty forthwith.' He held out his hand. 'I'll take your warrant card. We'll also need your work phone.'

68

Expectation is a curiously human ailment, Jo. Perhaps we should regard it as a chronic disease because so many of us are afflicted by it. I'm as foolish as anyone. I have had such expectations, such hopes of how things could be turned around and the past redeemed. But we're both fools, aren't we, Jo? Both you and I.

The idea of you as a police officer appealed to me. It seemed fitting. I don't know what Sarah would've made of it. I mean, let's face it, your sister was an intellectual snob. I've got a feeling she would've regarded it as not quite the thing. Not creative enough.

She could've been an actress who played a cop in some rubbishy TV series. That would've been fine. But doing the job for real, as you have? Sarah wanted glamour, the admiration of the public gaze. But she was also young. So we'll forgive her, shall we? She would've learned, as we all do, that expectations are rarely fulfilled.

I think you'll find prison an interesting experience. But you'll be okay. My advice would be don't let despair get the better of you. And don't turn to drugs. I know a bit about that.

Plenty of bent coppers survive the experience and come out all the better for it. They learn humility and we could all do with some of that.

Bear in mind I'm letting you off lightly. Your sister let me down, badly, but I was much younger then. Emotions got in the way. I've never been a person who enjoys violence. It's a tool to be used when necessary. I take no pleasure in it. You may end up feeling that you've lost everything. Your job, your friends, your reputation. But you've still got your life. That's the important thing. And that's my gift to you, Jo Boden.

69

Hollingsworth had Jo escorted from the building by two uniformed PCs. Two seemed excessive, but Jo got it. He was making a point. They took her via the Grebe office to collect her belongings. The IPCC would contact her, she was told, with a date and time for her formal interview and she was entitled to ask for a Federation rep to be present. But Jo knew that if she was being accused of corruption, she'd need more than that.

As she went through her desk drawers and transferred the few items to her bag, she scanned the office. Vaizey's door was shut. Sandra looked up from her computer screen and gave her a chilly glance, then turned away. News travelled fast, as Jo knew it would.

But it was Foley who got up from his desk and came over. Hands on his hips, his attitude was hard to decipher. 'Well, you are one slick operator, I'll give you that.'

Jo decided not to engage with him. What would be the point?

He shook his head and she was aware of the sheer size of him looming over her. He was back to bullying, his true nature. 'So what was it about? The money? You fancied a nice trip to the Maldives, or maybe a new car?'

It didn't seem as if he was about to move out of her way, but she refused to be intimidated. 'Look at it this way, Foley, by refusing to go out with you, I was doing you a favour. Saving you from the embarrassment of being associated with me.'

'Go out with? Nah. What I had in mind was a couple of drinks and a quick shag.' The glancing blow of male bravado bounced off her. Was this the best he could come up with?

Jo stood her ground. She didn't let her gaze waver. In the end, he'd have to back off. So she waited him out.

As he finally allowed her to walk away, flanked by her two minders, he called after her. 'Be sure to get yourself a good lawyer. But then Daddy'll pay, won't he?'

She clattered down the tiled stairway. There was no way she was hanging about waiting for the lift. The shame was burning her face. It wasn't so much Foley's viciousness that stung as his disillusionment. It seemed so easy for all her colleagues, officers she'd worked with and trusted, to believe the worst of her. No one was interested in her side of the story. They'd closed ranks. She'd seen it happen before, so it shouldn't have surprised her.

In less than two minutes, she was out on the street and her escorts were closing the doors behind her. Pulling her scarf tightly round her neck, she strode away. When she reached the corner of the road, she broke into a run. Once she was out of sight of the building, she ducked behind a dumpster and the tears flowed. Maintaining a front was a matter of pride, but inside she was raw and bleeding and reeling with shock.

It felt as if she'd stepped off the edge of a cliff and was tumbling into the abyss. What made it worse was she could make no sense of it. How had five thousand pounds ended up in her bank account? There was no sensible explanation. Had her father decided to give her some money to help her out? Towards a new car? But he wouldn't be transferring it from some offshore account, would he? And anyway, he'd have told her.

Clutching at straws, she rang his number. He had her bank details. They hadn't changed since her student days. She prayed he'd pick up.

'Hello, Dad.'

'Jo. How are you? I was—'

'D'you have an offshore bank account in the British Virgin Islands?'

'Pardon?'

'I dunno, Dad, for tax avoidance, for your business, for whatever.' She knew that she must sound breathy and tearful. She had to swallow hard to stop herself from sobbing.

'No. Absolutely not.'

'Tell me the truth, please.'

'I am telling you the truth. What d'you take me for?'

'So you haven't just transferred five grand into my bank account?'

'No. What the hell is this about, Jo? Are you all right?'

'It's nothing. A mistake. I have to go.'

She hung up.

Her heart thumped, but she had to keep moving. She walked with no destination in mind. The phone was on silent but it vibrated against her hip from inside her bag; once, then again, then a third time. Nick Boden wasn't giving up.

And Foley had mentioned her father. *Daddy'll pay.* No one in the job liked a bent cop, not if they were supposedly in the pay of a scumbag like Kelmendi. But Jo never spoke of her family at work, so how would Foley know that Nick Boden could afford to get her an expensive lawyer? He'd wanted to say something nasty, that was obvious. Was he guessing she was from middle-class parents who had money? Did she come over like that, a bit posh? She didn't think so. At Hendon, she'd morphed into a streetwise cop with a slangy London accent and that had been her work persona ever since. Or at least she thought it was. In her old squad, the likes of Darryl knew about her history and her murdered sister. But could that gossip have spread throughout the whole building?

Her head was thrumming and it helped to walk. She crossed Regent's Park, the squelchy turf muddying her shoes, and ended up in Camden Town in a bar she knew on the Regent's Canal. She'd been there on a couple of dates. It was restful and affluent, London for those who could afford its pleasures and wanted the choice of forty different brands of gin. The place was warm and deserted; she took a stool at the bar and ordered herself a drink. It came in a large bulbous glass, fizzing and friendly, with several raspberries floating in it. The barman gave her a neutral smile, and she wondered if he saw her humiliation, a woman drinking in the middle of the day, needing a drink to cope. It was probably more common than she thought.

Foley had flickered in and out of her mind, as had Bruce and Briony and Nathan and her sister. It was Nathan who'd pointed her in the direction of Richard Green. Had he somehow set this up? But why? How could he know the drug dealer was an associate of the Kelmendis? Perhaps he knew Green far better than he'd let on? He could have other jail-house connections, too. What she couldn't figure out was why he'd want to harm her.

As she sipped her drink, her tumultuous emotions settled, the shock of Hollingsworth's accusation subsided and one question floated to the surface of her mind. Why was this happening? She was being falsely accused of corruption. Why? Someone had given her five thousand pounds from an offshore account, supposedly as a pay-off. How would you even arrange that?

Briony Rowe had been about to identify Bruce and she'd ended up dead. Jo had started to ask questions, and she was out of a job and facing criminal charges. Someone wanted to shut them both up, someone with determination and resources and who understood the internal workings of the Met. It had to be Bruce. He killed Sarah. And Cynthia Fenton-Wright had warned him. Bruce was real. He was out there and he was dangerous.

70

The feeling was hard to pin down: the sudden realization that it was over for her, that she was done for. There was inky darkness and she was sinking into it. It was soft and squidgy, a black quagmire sucking her downwards, swallowing her up. She was trying to speak. She was pleading, begging for her life, but the words wouldn't come. He would save her, surely he would save her? She was gasping for breath.

The hammering and ringing came from far away. Its insistence helped her surface. As she opened her eyes to blinding morning light, she realized she'd gone to bed without closing the curtains properly. Coming home tired and spent, having drunk far too much gin, all she'd wanted was to escape into the oblivion of sleep.

Jo threw back the duvet, got out of bed, zigzagged unsteadily through the flat to the front door. Then she hesitated. Marisa was still in hospital. The shock and the panic of the acid attack came rushing back. No way was she just opening that door.

There was a spyhole of sorts, but like everything in the flat, it wasn't fit for purpose. Jo peered through it. The tiny bead of glass was cracked. She could see nothing but a shadowy blur.

'Who is it?' Her voice sounded croaky and small.

'For God's sake, Jo, it's me! It's freezing out here.'

Alison? Her mother rarely visited the Lant Street flat. She hated travelling on the tube.

Raking her hand through her hair, Jo unlocked the door and opened it.

'You smell of gin.' Alison didn't wait to be invited. She barged in. 'What's happened to the door?'

'Long story.'

Alison pulled a copy of the *Daily Mail* out of her shoulder bag. 'Have you seen this?'

Jo took the newspaper. Her head was a clotted fug. It took a moment to focus. Then the tabloid headline screamed at her: *Corrupt cop named. Traffickers paid five grand to Met detective.* There was a picture of Jo, snapped on a long lens as she left the building after her encounter with Hollingsworth the previous day. They'd been waiting for her. Someone had tipped them off.

She scanned the front-page article. Its tone was hyper-bolic but the detail was there: the Kelmendis, an Albanian people-trafficking gang, also responsible for the prostitution of young children, had been fed vital inside information from within the police operation targeting them. And she was named—*Detective Constable Joanna Boden, 28, of the MPS faces investigation by the IPCC and is likely to be charged.*

Turning to her mother, tears welled in Jo's eyes. She had a pulsing headache. 'It's a pack of lies, Mum. Not true, any of it. You have to believe me.' She felt desperate and desolate, like a small child.

Alison sighed, threw her arms round her daughter's shoulders and pulled her into a hug. 'Don't be soft. Of course I believe you.'

Jo wept in her mother's arms. She couldn't remember the last time she'd done this. Probably when she was thirteen and her school bag was chucked under a bus by the class bullies.

'Hey hey, c'mon.' Alison held her close and stroked her hair.

'I'm so sorry. I just…oh, Mum.' Somehow the tears wouldn't stop.

'What've you got to be sorry about?' Alison took her daughter's face between her two palms. 'Listen to me, Jo. You need to get dressed. And we'll get a cab.'

'A cab?'

'I've been talking to Tania Jones on the phone. She and Gordon agree with me. First Briony, now this. Someone's setting you up to shut you up.'

'You've talked to them?'

'As soon as I saw it. I only went out for a carton of milk. It confirms all our suspicions.'

Standing in her pyjamas with bare feet, Jo could feel the cold seeping up through the stripped floorboards. But she wasn't alone. It was hard to believe, but her mother, her mad flaky mother, was there to protect her.

Jo wiped the back of her hand across her nose. 'And it has to be Bruce, doesn't it?'

'Yep. We all think so.'

71

By midday, Jo and her mother were sitting in Tania Jones' plush office with pictures of celebrities on the walls, balancing large cups of coffee. The film was going ahead. There was no question of abandoning it. Tania insisted they owed it to Briony, and she already had interest from a major broadcaster.

Jo didn't know whether to be worried by their enthusiasm or relieved that someone believed her. She could end up on the telly and out of a job, neither of which appealed. Cops and media were different tribes. They used each other, but it seldom turned out well. The bottom line here was money. More controversy, allegations of police corruption, another *innocent* abused by the system. It was all grist to their mill— and part of Jo didn't trust it.

Gordon Kramer roamed in and out, using a headset to speak on his phone. Jo watched him chatting and laughing. He was a trader in information and peddler of favours, a man continually in search of the real story. But what was real to him? It looked like a game and one he enjoyed.

As a detective, Jo believed she had a more principled

route to the truth, but was she fooling herself? It was tempting to feel morally superior to a journalist like Kramer and to dismiss him as a hack. But did she have any right to? Her boss, the squeaky clean by-the-book Dave Hollingsworth and her so-called colleagues wouldn't even listen to her; they'd already made up their minds she was guilty.

Hanging up, Kramer came and perched on the corner of his wife's desk. 'I've got an old mate who's a sub-editor at the *Mail*. He won't say who's gunning for you, though he admits someone might be.'

Alison gave him a stern look. 'Then how can they print these lies?'

Gordon puffed out his cheeks. 'It's a story. The interesting thing is it came to them two days ago.'

Jo frowned. 'That's before I even saw Hollingsworth.'

'Someone planned this. They won't divulge the source, obviously. But it's definitely someone inside the Met. Probably in your building.' The reporter gave her a quizzical look.

'Not the IPCC?' Jo was still harbouring the hope that it wasn't one of her own who'd betrayed her.

'Other cops like to blame the IPCC for all sorts. It's the standard get-out. But leaking to the press is rarely in their interests.'

'Two days ago was when I went to see Richard Green. But that came from Nathan.'

Kramer stroked the dimple in his chin. 'Yes, our boy wonder. I talked to him this morning. I think he genuinely believed what he told you.'

'Green denied having anything to do with Sarah's death.'

'Doesn't mean Nathan was lying to you. Could just mean that what he believed was wrong. The story chimed in with his psychology because he felt guilty about your sister. But there's no way Nathan has access to offshore bank accounts.'

'He could've met someone in jail who does.'

'What motive does he have to discredit you? He's resentful, he's angry and he hates the system. Sixteen years in jail doesn't make you a nice person. It makes you bitter.'

Tania laced her fingers. 'Jo, Nathan's been upfront with us. What he wants out of all this is money. But who can blame him?'

Jo shrugged. 'He still strikes me as devious.'

Kramer laughed. 'He is devious, very devious, that's how he's survived in the nick. But someone's trying to ruin your life, Jo. If you can think of another reason for that, fair enough. I think it's because you went to see this Cynthia Fenton-Wright. I've got a researcher doing some digging, see what we can find out about her.'

'There's also the Kelmendis, scumbags I helped arrest. My flatmate's in hospital because someone knocked at our door and threw acid in her face. I'm guessing that was meant for me.'

'Oh, God, Jo.' Alison's hand flew to her mouth in horror. 'Why didn't you tell me?'

'Because…' Jo hesitated. 'Because…' her thoughts were spinning.

Panic, fear, confusion. So much of it had been swilling around in her head. The shock of what had happened to Marisa, coupled with gnawing self-blame, had thrown everything out of kilter.

But Kramer was right. Too much noise, discordant and screeching. She had to filter it out, focus on what was essential. Sift out facts from feelings. The Kelmendis were thugs for whom revenge meant violence. Setting out to incriminate her with the use of offshore bank accounts was too sophisticated for them.

This all came back to Cynthia, and the evidence was

there, staring her in the face. *Inside the Met. In your building.* Suddenly, his behaviour made sense. Brighton. He went to the same university as Sarah; he told her that. He was the right age. He'd even tried coming on to her; she'd found that creepy but also weirdly knowing. And then there was the unguarded comment about her father. How would he know about her background if they'd been thrown together randomly as colleagues? It was almost as if he was teasing her.

Jo caught Kramer's eye; he was studying her. He was no fool. Behind the fancy shades and the vanity lurked a razor-sharp intellect. He may be an adrenaline junkie who liked to challenge authority, but he hadn't won the stack of awards decorating the wall of the reception area for nothing.

The reporter tilted his head and smiled. 'You know who it is, don't you?'

Jo hesitated. Could Calvin Foley be Bruce? She didn't want to believe it. But wouldn't it have taken a big, strong bloke, someone as big as Foley, to shove Briony Rowe under a train?

72

Suspended in an emotional limbo, Jo sat and watched in a daze as the resources of Xtraordinary Productions swung into action. She'd answered Kramer's question, given him the name he needed. DS Calvin Foley was Bruce, her sister's killer. Saying it out loud had somehow made it real. Now she seemed paralysed, unable to get up and leave as she wanted to, but also unable to join in. Her limbs were too sluggish and heavy to do her bidding.

Alison, in contrast, seemed more alive and engaged than she'd been for years. She chatted to one of the young researchers, who was jabbing an index finger at his computer screen as he explained what they were doing. Jo couldn't hear the words. They sounded like a confused babble in the general background hum of the office. But her mother was nodding like a wise primary school teacher, giving encouragement to an over-excited pupil.

Making a documentary film and running a police investigation seemed to have more similarities than Jo had previously thought. Gordon was the dynamo, tossing out ideas, theories, demanding information. Tania was the steady hand on the tiller, making sure proposals were noted ready for translation into some form of action.

The team comprised three researchers on computers and phones, a whiteboard splattered with mugshots and questions, plus, lined up on the table, an array of tiny covert cameras and state-of-the-art audio devices which, Jo reflected, would've been way beyond the average police budget. They already had Cynthia Fenton-Wright's Spitalfields office under external surveillance, with a live-feed to a bank of monitors, but they needed someone to get through the door to turn it into an effective stakeout.

The potential illegality of it all bothered Jo. As a police officer, should she even be a party to this? But was she? All she was doing was sitting there watching and trying to summon up the energy to move, to leave. Perhaps this was some form of delayed shock? Then she remembered she had nowhere to go. She was suspended from duty and under investigation. Could her situation get any worse?

The queasiness she put down to a hangover and no breakfast. But she was feeling odd. She became focused on the bobbing of Kramer's Adam's apple, up and down, with the bellow of his voice.

Then from nowhere, Phil, Gordon's cameraman, plonked down on the sofa beside her and insisted on explaining the workings of his telephoto lens, which he boasted he'd used to read text on a government report tucked under the arm of a hapless official at the other end of Downing Street. It had led to the resignation of a cabinet minister who'd been lying. He seemed very pleased with himself. They all seemed so pleased with themselves.

Jo felt hot, but also shivery and light-headed. She wondered if she was about to faint. This had never happened before, but a voice dragged her back from the brink. She felt a cool hand on her brow.

'Jo, are you all right?' Tania Jones was looming over her. And Alison. They gave her water, she took several sips.

'She's still in shock.'

Her swimming vision came back into focus. 'Sorry.' This was embarrassing. She looked up at a swirling sea of concerned faces. Then she blacked out.

73

Jo woke up on a narrow divan with a wet cloth on her forehead in what turned out to be Gordon Kramer's private inner sanctum. He was sitting on a low-slung canvas chair beside her and offered her a can of Coke.

'Sugar hit, it'll bring you round.'

Her hand was still unsteady, but she accepted the drink and managed a mouthful.

He lounged back in his chair and watched her. 'Y'know, one time in Helmand the Taliban got hold of me. Threw me in this stinking cellar. Dark, evil place. I was convinced my number was up. They left me there, no food, only water, two, maybe three days. I lost track of time. And you think about everything. Your emotions go from anger to self-pity to despair and back again. But Homo sapiens, we're survivors, we fight back. It's in our DNA.'

Jo sat up. 'I want to fight back, but I don't know how.'

'Oh, you do. It just takes some figuring out. You're in shock. That's a natural reaction to a surprise attack. But you know your world and you know how to win in it. This bastard's out to get you. Accept that, regroup, reassess. And be prepared to do what's necessary to beat him. You're tougher than you think.'

'How did you escape the Taliban?'

'My boss paid a ransom to an Afghan intermediary. That's the other thing: know who's on your side.'

After her fainting episode, Jo consumed a double cheeseburger and chips that one of Kramer's sidekicks brought her and felt better. She also decided to take his advice.

She was a cop and wanted to remain a cop. Her first concern was to gather enough ammunition, in the form of solid evidence, and take it to Vaizey. She'd have to deal with how that evidence had been obtained afterwards. But she was sure of one thing—whatever had happened on a personal level between them would become irrelevant once the boss got wind of what had been going on.

Steve Vaizey was a respected and ambitious senior officer and if one of his DSs had gone rogue, he'd want to be the one to deal with it and nail him. Jo also suspected that he'd be more than happy to see Hollingsworth proved wrong. Separate but related enquiries would be needed—into Sarah's murder and Briony Rowe's apparent suicide. Nathan Wade's innocence and his supposed suffering in prison might make a great film, but it wasn't Jo's primary issue. She still disliked and distrusted him.

In the end, it all hinged on her getting the evidence that would force Vaizey to listen.

The private stakeout of Cynthia Fenton-Wright's office was being run from a quiet booth in the back of a café-deli across the road. When Jo walked in, she wasn't too thrilled to find Nathan Wade tucked away in the corner beside Kayleigh.

They both looked up at Jo's approach and greeted her with tepid smiles.

He must've read the disapproval in her look. 'I'm here for Briony. We all are. I just want to be useful.'

To Jo's ears, his tone was disingenuous, but she just raised her eyebrows. 'Then let's get on with it.'

Establishing the connection between Cynthia and Calvin Foley was the priority. They'd both studied in Brighton. Foley was born in 1981, which made them contemporaries. But Jo knew they'd need much more to build a credible case.

Kayleigh had the kit ready. Jo sat down beside her as she fitted the covert button camera in the lapel of Jo's jacket. Nathan reached under the table to a large M&S carrier. It contained a leather briefcase with a concealed pinhole camera and an audio recording device. He slid it across the table to Jo. Tania Jones's strategy was to record everything, as much footage and, from as many angles as possible, a belt-and-braces approach.

Jo had worn a bodycam in her days as a uniformed PC, but the technology had moved on considerably. These devices were a fraction of the size, designed to produce broadcast quality footage and were a much higher spec than anything the Met had, which, as a cop, didn't please her. But they would do the job.

Kayleigh fixed her with an anxious look. 'Thing is, nowadays most people expect you to use your phone. So show her that, make a point of turning it off.'

'I know how to fool a suspect and make a covert recording.'

'Sorry.' The attempt to look contrite wasn't all that convincing. Jo got the impression that Briony's former intern didn't much like her.

She turned to Nathan. 'How long have you been here?'

'Since seven.' He flipped open a page in his notebook. 'Twenty-five members of staff in the branding agency. Most got here between 8.45 and 9.15. But Cynthia herself didn't arrive until 10. Says on her website she has two children, which probably explains it.'

'Probably.' Jo gave him a smile, but his face remained taut and sombre.

She decided not to mention that during her previous encounter with the businesswoman she'd observed an impressive platinum and diamond rock on her ring finger, plus she had a couple of felt-tip kids' drawings pinned up in her office. It was reasonable to assume her hours were tailored to her childcare arrangements.

'What about her husband? What does he do?'

'Website doesn't say. Just says married with two children.' Nathan's tone was brisk.

She shrugged. 'Okay, let's rock'n'roll. Isn't that what you telly people say?'

Kayleigh glared at her. 'No. And by the way, in case you need reminding, we're here to find out who had Briony murdered.'

Jo looked at the young film student, bristling with grief and hostility, and bit back a retort. Nathan looked sullen. They didn't get the flippancy and the black humour that the job fostered. Jo envied their certainty, their belief that, after all these years, the truth would be revealed. She had no such belief, only a vague hope that somehow she'd get something to rescue her career.

She picked up the briefcase and headed out of the door.

Dodging traffic as she crossed the road to Cynthia's office, she felt wired. A fainting fit followed by sugar, caffeine, food and adrenalin had thrown her metabolism out of whack. Her brain was nattering, telling her this was crazy but necessary; it was the only way to get Foley.

She took the stairs up to the first-floor office two at a time and arrived in the open-plan reception area. The CEO's office was in the far corner and, ignoring the receptionist's protestations, Jo steamed across the room straight for it. Cynthia saw her coming through the open door and Jo was gratified to see that her reaction was tinged with panic.

The businesswoman was quick to gather herself. 'DC Boden. I would say come in, but you already have.'

'Afternoon, Cynthia. I've got a couple of questions. It shouldn't take up too much of your time.'

'Really? I follow the news. I've seen what the papers are saying about you. You're under investigation for corruption. I think you should leave.'

Jo plonked her briefcase down on Cynthia's desk.

'I wanted to ask about an old friend of yours. Calvin Foley.'

Cynthia frowned. 'Not a name I recognize. Are you going to force me to call the police?'

'Think back. That night on campus when you met Nathan Wade.'

'I didn't meet Nathan Wade. I've already told you that.' The pitch of her voice rose. Her fingers were tightly clasped. 'What is this? Some kind of bizarre attempt to salvage your reputation?'

'No, I've figured out what happened. It's no coincidence that you and Briony had lunch shortly before her death. You wanted to find out what she knew. And I think Briony would've wanted to boast to you. She would've told you she was about to identify the postgrad who'd stalked my sister.'

'I have no idea what or who you're talking about. This is

a total fantasy. Where's your proof?' Back against the wall, Cynthia was a steely adversary.

'Murder is a kind of proof. The circumstances of Briony's death are suspicious. So there will be a new investigation. You'll have to answer their questions. In the meantime, I'd be worried if I were you.'

Jo knew she was clutching at straws, but she had to force Cynthia onto the back foot.

'What do you mean?' The tremor in the voice was slight, but it was there.

'You didn't expect him to kill Briony, did you? You were genuinely shocked. I saw that in your face, Cynthia, when I told you.'

Cynthia was shaking her head, but Jo could sense her self-assurance ebbing.

'Of course I'm shocked by her death. Who wouldn't be? But if she threw herself under a train—'

'She could identify him. And you can too. If you make a full statement, then you and your family will receive police protection. How many kids do you have?'

Whatever misgivings Cynthia had, they vanished. She glared at Jo. 'You would bring my children into this? You're despicable.'

'You need to think about them. He will.'

'Who? This...person?'

'Calvin Foley.'

'I have never met him or even heard the name.'

'What if we can prove you do know him?'

'I'd like to see you try.' Cynthia got to her feet. 'I shall be calling my lawyer, DC Boden. And he will contact your superiors to demand that you withdraw these malicious and totally unfounded allegations. You think you can walk in here and intimidate me with your threats? Dragging my children into it. I am not without resources. In fact, I'm quite a wealthy woman and if I don't receive a full apology in writing for this outrage, I will sue you and the organization you work for. But I don't think it'll come to that.'

'Why, Cynthia? Because I'm going to jail? Because someone's transferred five grand into my bank from an offshore account in the British Virgin Islands? As you say, you're a wealthy woman. Have you got any offshore accounts? These days, the authorities in the BVA can be more cooperative than people think. And the IPCC will be in touch with them. It's a theory, I'll admit, but I wouldn't mind guessing that money can be traced back to you.'

'Get out of my office!' Her face was pale, and she was shaking.

'Think about it, Cynthia. Looks to me like you've got a very nice life. A very successful business. Are you really going to put all this on the line for Calvin Foley?'

74

Jo Boden strode out of the building, with a worried frown. Had she overplayed her hand? Confronting Cynthia directly had been a high-risk strategy based on a theory for which they had not a scrap of concrete evidence. The notion that the IPCC would track the money that had ended up in Jo's account was a hollow threat. However, Cynthia's reaction suggested Jo was on the right track. Or did it? Jo was uncertain. She was being accused of corruption. Although it was untrue, she'd lost confidence in her own judgement. Dodging the traffic, she scampered across the road towards the café.

Everything now depended on what Cynthia did next. Without the luxury of tracking her phone—though Jo suspected Kramer might be trying to arrange this despite its illegality—they would have to rely on old-fashioned legwork. It was a waiting game with the hope that eventually Cynthia would lead them to Foley.

Jo rejoined Kayleigh and Nathan. 'Well, I think I got under her skin.'

'We heard.' Kayleigh didn't sound impressed.

'She had eyes on me all the time. I couldn't get a bug in her office, too risky.'

Jo unhooked the button camera and put it on the table with the briefcase. Her nerves were jangling. She wanted to escape. 'You'll have to make sure you don't lose her. And hope that she decides not to trust any communication to the phone.'

'That was the idea of bugging the office.' Kayleigh's tone was petulant.

'I know.'

'You'll have to help us.'

'I can't. I've got something else I have to do.'

'What? You're suspended from duty. What's more important than this?'

Jo was going to the hospital to see Marisa. Another part of this mess. But she didn't see any need to explain herself. 'You've got my number. Let me know what she gets up to, okay?'

'Oh yeah, right, leave it to us.' Kayleigh gave a mock salute. 'And what about Briony's Mini? They won't give it to me because I'm not a relative. Even though I was on the insurance.'

'I've explained. We've got to get Sussex Police to open an investigation. That's what we're working towards.'

'We are. You're just buggering off.'

Nathan put a gentle hand on Kayleigh's forearm. 'Come on. We'll manage.'

His gaze met Jo's. She still didn't trust him.

She shrugged. 'This could take days. Surveillance is a game of patience.'

'Oh, I'm good at that.' He gave her a ghostly smile.

'I'm sure you are.'

'Don't worry. Wherever she goes, we'll get it on film.'

'Okay. Just don't be too obvious.'

Kayleigh gave her a surly look. 'Oh, for fuck's sake!'

Jo turned on her. 'What exactly is your problem?'

'My problem? You're the one with a problem. She was doing this for your sister and if you'd only listened…'

Jo scanned the girl, still in her teens, trying to hang tough but close to tears. She had a point. But Briony Rowe had also been intent on making a name for herself.

'You know what, Briony was an annoying pain in the arse. Much like you, in fact. But I do care about her death and the probability that she was murdered. And once we get the evidence we need, I will make sure that this is investigated and her killer brought to justice. And that'll have to be good enough for you, okay?'

Jo didn't wait for a reply. Turning on her heel, she marched out of the café.

75

Marisa had been transferred to a specialist ward on the twelfth floor of the Royal London. Emerging from the lift, Jo was crossing the lobby towards an open waiting area and the wards when she caught sight of her two former colleagues, Darryl Tanner and Debbie Georghiou. They were at the vending machine and had their backs to her.

Shame and confusion swept over Jo, and she ducked round the corner. Darryl was laughing and making some comment—probably one of his dubious jokes—as he fed coins into the machine. Peering at them from her hiding place, Jo felt like a complete fool. It seemed too much of a coincidence; they must've come to interview Marisa about the attack. But at least Hollingsworth was investigating.

Jo berated herself. She had nothing to be ashamed of, why the hell was she skulking like this? It had been a knee-jerk reaction. But what did she fear? Their judgement? So what if they assumed the allegations were true? She'd come to see Marisa. She took a deep breath and stepped out from behind the wall in time to see the two DCs disappear into the lift with their drinks.

A sense of relief cascaded through Jo. She couldn't help it. What concerned her more was facing her flatmate. If they'd already interviewed her, then she'd know. Steeling herself, Jo lifted her chin and walked down the corridor and into the ward. She wondered if she should've brought flowers. She'd spaced that out.

Marisa's bed was nearest the window in one of the bays. A nurse directed Jo. She found her friend, eyes closed, dozing. Her right arm was swathed in bandages, and she had patches of white gauze taped to her forehead. Jo stood rooted to the spot. She hadn't seen Marisa since she'd accompanied her to A&E. Responsibility and guilt washed over her. This should never have happened; it was all her fault.

'Crap picture. Makes you look about forty. If the paps are gonna get you, at least it should be glamorous and flattering.' Marisa opened her eyes and smiled.

Jo sat down beside the bed. 'You've seen the paper, then?'

'A couple of your mates kindly brought me a copy. They've just gone.'

'Yeah, I saw them.' Jo had to swallow hard. She was accustomed to accidents and car crashes. She'd attended her fair share. But this was her best friend. 'Oh Mari, I am so sorry about this. It should've—'

'Hey, it's not your fault. Wasn't you that chucked the acid. But it was you that shoved me in the shower. So I've seen the plastic surgeon and the treatment plan seems fairly straightforward. Couple of skin grafts on my arm and a small patch on my forehead.'

'How's the pain?'

Marisa smiled. 'That's all sorted. I know the staff nurse. We've worked together.' She raised her left hand and fingered the gauze. 'Pity this wasn't a bit lower. They might've done me a nice nose job on the NHS too.'

Jo had to wipe away the tears. 'There's nothing wrong with your nose.'

'Don't blub, Boden. You're supposed to be the tough cop.'

'I don't much feel like it.'

'Paper says you've been suspended. But as I explained to Tweedledee and Tweedledum, you're not stupid. If you were being paid off by this gangster, what would be the point in them coming round to throw acid at you?'

'The theory is it's a set-up to distract attention from the fact I'm their informant.'

Marisa laughed. 'Seriously? You could've easily opened that door. At least a 50 per cent chance you would've done.'

'They might argue I deliberately let you do it.'

'Yeah, but they don't know you. I do.' Marisa's gaze came to rest on her. 'This world is full of nasty people, capable of horrendous things. But you're not one of them.'

Jo took her friend's hand and squeezed it. 'Thank you.'

76

Jo spent more than an hour with Marisa and by the time she left the hospital, it was getting dark. She emerged on to Whitechapel Road to join the streams of scurrying shoppers weaving between roadside stalls of stacked vegetables or bales of sari silks and the belching crawling traffic. As the drizzle started, she crammed herself on to a bus, which took her—standing room only—down to London Bridge.

It was a wintry evening with wafers of freezing fog floating across the river, but Jo was feeling more bullish. Marisa had encouraged her to make the most of the help on offer. Whatever Jo's reservations about working with Gordon Kramer and his crew, it was her best chance of fighting back. Without them, the naturally conservative institutional forces of the police would work to silence and destroy her. Marisa agreed she had to make Vaizey listen to her. Once he understood Jo wasn't angling for an affair or likely to rat him out to his wife, then he'd be more likely to do the right thing.

Jo spent most of her cramped bus ride on the draft of a text to him. Text, she decided, was better than email. It was a more personal appeal but, she concluded, distant enough not to come over as badgering.

However, it was no easy task to create a succinct summary of the events leading up to Briony's death. She also had to explain her emerging belief that her sister's killer was still at large and could indeed be a police officer, one of his officers, Calvin Foley. As she walked across London Bridge, she tried to organise her thoughts. She knew that she'd only get one chance to present him with her arguments and get him onside.

Skirting the edge of Borough Market, her thoughts turned back to her flatmate. As soon as Marisa was discharged from hospital, she was going home to her parents in Peterborough to convalesce. It would be some time before she returned to London and the flat, and Jo wondered if she would return. The experience of the attack had traumatized her, although they hadn't spoken about that. Marisa was the youngest of three. Her older sisters had children and all lived in Cambridgeshire and the edge of the Fens. Jo could imagine that, after what had happened, her family may well put pressure on Marisa to get a job up there.

This prospect left Jo feeling abandoned. They'd found the flat together and it would be bleak without her. By the time she turned from Southwark Bridge Road into Lant Street, the steady flow of passers-by had thinned to a trickle. The freezing drizzle was turning to a sleety downpour and Jo held her jacket over her head as she scurried along the wet, dimly-lit pavements towards the flats.

As she skipped across the rough tarmac outside the block, he loomed from the shadows and they practically collided. The street lamp was out, so she couldn't see his face. He grabbed her arm and she reacted instinctively, twisting free and readying herself to land a blow.

He threw up his palms. 'Hey, go easy! I surrender.'

Jo's heart was thumping. Another attack? Then recognition dawned.

Calvin Foley gave her a thin smile. 'I've been waiting ages and I'm bloody freezing. Can we go inside?'

'What d'you want?' Jo managed to keep the panic out of her voice.

'Look, I'm sorry about how I was before. I was upset. We need to talk. But I'd rather do it inside.'

'I'd rather do it here.'

'It's bloody sleeting.'

'I like sleet.'

He sighed and turned up his collar. 'I've been talking to Jabreel Khan. Found out he was the one who initiated the corruption investigation.'

'So?' What was he up to now? Some new trick?

'I've worked with Jabreel. He used to be a mate. A good officer, but then they made him go undercover.'

Jo took a step backwards away from him and towards the street. No way was he going to trap her. He was big, but she was hoping she was faster.

He slipped his hands in his jacket pockets. 'Two years is a long time undercover. I don't think it's done him any good. He's changed, gone paranoid and weird. I heard the other day that he brought one of the pool cars back with a dead cat in the boot. A dead fucking cat. And he just left it there.'

'Why are you saying this to me? Why not to Hollingsworth?' Her hair was soaking, icy water was seeping down her neck and under her collar.

'Believe it or not, because I thought I could help you.'

'How?'

'There may be a way out of this. Don't you want that? Why are you backing away from me?' His tone went from cajoling to miffed. She couldn't see his eyes, but she didn't need to.

'Take a guess, Foley. I'm not as stupid as you think.'

'What's that supposed to mean?'

Jo knew her only advantage was surprise. She had to go for it. Spinning round, she turned on her heel and ran, sprinting through the puddles, heading for the light of the main road. Only when she reached the corner did she allow herself a brief glimpse over her shoulder.

He wasn't moving, but he shouted after her. 'I'm trying to help you, you ungrateful bitch!'

77

Jo Boden ran. Within minutes, the hard glittery lights along the river were in front of her. Her chest was heaving, but she was fitter than she'd thought. There was no sign of pursuit. But then it occurred to her she was being tracked. If he knew where she was, he didn't need to run after her.

She'd altered the settings on her phone, but with the right equipment that could be overridden. It struck her as ironic that she'd asked him for permission to use the PNC to find Richard Green. She had to assume that he would have no scruples about the illegal use of resources to keep tabs on her. Or perhaps Jabreel was working with him? Or maybe he'd just lied to Vaizey. There were too many things she didn't know.

When she reached Southwark Bridge, she slowed to a walk. The sleet had turned to rain. She was soaked through. As her initial panic subsided, she tried to come up with a plan. Had he come to kill her or negotiate, or both? *There may be a way out of this. Don't you want that?* It sounded like the prelude to an offer. The corruption charge could be made to go away if she backed off? Well, he could stuff that.

The immediate priority was to find somewhere safe to hide, where she was off the grid. Going to her mother's was not an option. It was the obvious place to look. She toyed with her father's home in Norfolk. But Foley had mentioned him, which suggested that wouldn't be safe either.

She glanced over the parapet of the bridge at the inky river below. The tide was high. Shards of light danced across the ridges of the waves. She extracted her phone from her bag. It wasn't ideal, but it was the only solution she could come up with. The text she'd written to Vaizey wasn't finished, but all the main points were there. She clicked on it and pressed send. Then she tossed her phone into the river.

Using a credit or debit card wouldn't be too smart either, which ruled out a hotel. She checked her purse; all she had was a handful of coins. She was beginning to appreciate what it felt like to be a target and on the wrong side of the law. And it was scary. The winter city was no place to be cast adrift. A homeless man huddled in a doorway cuddling a mangy dog asked her for change.

She set a steady pace and headed north, cutting across Cannon Street and winding her way up through the lanes and snickets of the old City to Cheapside. She picked a route away from the busier thoroughfares so she'd have a chance of noticing anyone suspicious. When she reached Moorgate, she selected a bar, still crowded with office workers, asked to use their payphone and called directory enquiries.

Through her damp jacket and jeans, her core body temperature was dropping. The ends of her fingers were numb. The last thing she fancied was a night on the streets. She silently prayed that they weren't ex-directory.

Fifteen minutes later, Gordon Kramer pulled up outside in a red Tesla Roadster. He leaned over, clicked open the passenger door, and Jo climbed in.

The relief of being cocooned in the warm comfort of the car was overwhelming.

He gave her a sidelong glance. 'He was waiting for you?'

'Outside my flat. I ran. Chucked my phone in the river.' She was finding it hard to speak.

A weariness was creeping over her as she thawed out.

He gave her a curt nod. 'You did the right thing.'

78

The Kramers lived in a tall, three-storey early Victorian terraced house overlooking Clissold Park. Gordon slotted the Tesla into a permit-holder-only space outside. The branches of the bare horse chestnut trees overhanging the park railings created a stark, dripping canopy.

Gordon unlocked the front door. 'Come on in.'

'I'm sorry about this.' Her relief at being rescued had turned to awkwardness.

'It's not a problem.'

Tania was in the kitchen. 'Oh, Jo. Are you okay?'

'Yeah. Soaked, that's all.'

The couple exchanged looks and asked no more questions, from which Jo concluded she must appear more bedraggled than she thought.

They offered her a hot shower and a fluffy bathrobe.

The bathroom contained a large walk-in shower with power jets. She positioned herself in the midst of the cascade and let the needles of water pummel her weary body. Then she started to panic. Maybe she'd been precipitous in the text she'd sent to Steve Vaizey. Foley had his ear, and it would be all too easy for him to present her allegations as nonsense dreamed up to save her own neck.

There was a hairdryer in the bedside drawer of the comfy guest bedroom and an expensive bottle of moisturizer on the mantelpiece over the restored fireplace. It was the kind of attention to detail that Alison would've appreciated. A comfortable home of the sort Jo had grown up in until her parents' divorce robbed her of such an enviable lifestyle.

Not for the first time, she reflected on how her sister's murder had altered everything. Slipping under the plump duvet, she tried to make a plan, but exhaustion snared her and she was soon fast asleep.

When she awoke, sunshine spilled through the gap between the curtains. At first, she had no clue where she was. Then she noticed her clothes folded in a neat pile on the chair. Someone in the Kramer household, she assumed Tania, had washed and dried them.

For a few moments, she lay staring up at the white ceiling rose as the events of the previous evening seeped back into her conscious mind. Foley's audacity angered her, but it also sharpened her resolve. She would not be beaten. With renewed determination, she got out of bed and dressed.

Making her way downstairs, she discovered the back of the house had been opened up to create a large kitchen-diner with sliding doors onto a patio and the garden. A lanky youth with headphones on sat at the marble breakfast bar.

He gave her a smile. 'Hey, I'm Angus.'

'Jo.'

'Can I get you anything? Mum makes her own muesli mix. It's not bad.'

'I'm okay for now. Where is your mum?'

'They're all in the basement, looking at some footage.'

She followed his directions and opened what must've

been the original cellar door. It led to a steep carpeted stairway. The carpet also extended up the walls to create a well-insulated basement viewing theatre.

At the bottom of the stairs, she found herself in an oblong space with a large screen at one end. In front of it, there were six low leather armchairs arranged two abreast in three rows.

Gordon was at the back of the room, fiddling somewhat ineffectually with a laptop. Kayleigh was standing next to him, itching to take over. Tania was sitting in the front row and Nathan Wade was next to her.

Tania craned her head around. 'Jo! You're just in time. Come and join us. Nathan and Kayleigh have brought their surveillance footage round to show us.'

Jo sat in the chair behind. Coming to them wet and beleaguered in the night, asking for help, had left her embarrassed. It felt as if she'd lost control and been cast as the victim. She tried to adopt a businesslike tone. 'Of Cynthia Fenton-Wright? Did you get anything interesting?'

Nathan shrugged. 'Nah. She went to a meeting with clients, then she went home.'

Jo hadn't been holding out much hope. She'd provided them with a couple of her tourist snaps of Foley, taken at Buckler's Hard as part of her cover, so they could identify him. But one thing was clear about Cynthia: she had a cool head and was unlikely to do anything rash.

They spent the next twenty minutes trawling through the material Nathan and Kayleigh had gathered. It was well-shot and clear, Jo would give them that, and far superior in quality to most of the surveillance footage and CCTV she dealt with. But it contained long passages of nothing in particular. They went through in chronological order. Jo couldn't have cared less about the composition. She longed to fast-forward. She knew the only way to nail Cynthia Fenton-Wright was with a professional police surveillance team sitting on her 24/7, and tapping her phone, for as long as it took. But that wasn't about to happen.

They were getting towards the end of the footage. Kayleigh, armed with a GoPro, had followed Cynthia on foot as she took her commuter train home from Liverpool Street to Ingatestone in Essex.

Cynthia walked from the station to a substantial detached house on the edge of the village. It was set in a large plot with a high bay hedge at the front. As darkness fell, Kayleigh edged forward and concealed herself between the fence and the shrubbery.

The intern sighed. 'I stayed until her husband got home. But I was freezing. Then it started to rain. I figured she wasn't going anywhere.'

Jo sighed. This is exactly when she was most likely to slip out and meet Foley. But she was thinking like a cop. A bunch of media hacks didn't have the expertise to do this properly.

Tania gave Kayleigh a reassuring smile. 'No one can say you didn't go the extra mile. Briony would've been proud.'

This was turning out to be a colossal waste of time, as Jo suspected it would be. She was about to make an excuse and leave.

On the screen, a grey BMW pulled into the drive and the outside security light came on.

Kayleigh provided commentary, as a man in a suit got out of the car. 'This is the husband. Tried to get a decent shot of his face.'

The image was fleeting. Jo peered at the screen. Her stomach lurched as if she'd been punched in the gut.

He walked towards the front door, opened it, and disappeared inside.

Jo's brain was reeling. She was staring at the screen and willing it not to be true.

A moment later he returned to the car, took a coat and a briefcase from the back. Cynthia came out and spoke to him. As they headed back inside, the light fell on his face, and there was no room for doubt. It was definitely Steve Vaizey.

79

Jo sat on a wooden bench in Clissold Park, staring straight ahead of her. The path was muddy and slushy from the overnight downpour. A friendly greeting from a morning dog walker startled her. Her thoughts were scattered and dark.

He'd slept with her. She'd work for him. She thought he was a man she could trust.

Her brain, her whole body, was struggling to adjust. She remembered when she'd first spoken to him, standing beside the drinks machine with a broken nose. He'd offered her a job. It seemed to come out of the blue, but had it?

Could he be Bruce? She didn't want to believe it. But she'd been shown the evidence, carefully filmed by Kayleigh.

Did he know she was Sarah's sister? What did that mean to him? Why didn't he just avoid her? He seemed to have deliberately drawn her into his web. But why? It was hard to comprehend and harder to accept.

Sitting alone in the damp park, she watched her breath condense as she waited for the shock to subside.

It must've been close to an hour later, she couldn't tell,

when Nathan Wade came strolling towards her. She didn't register his presence until he sat down beside her.

He folded his hands. 'Gordon's good at this. He's been chatting up someone at my old uni. Steven John Vaizey graduated with a MSc. in psychology in 2001. Joined the police six months later.' He hesitated. 'Looks like he could well be Bruce.'

Jo said nothing.

'We also found out he married Cynthia Fenton-Wright at Chelmsford Register Office in June 2006. She kept her own name for business purposes.'

The hollow feeling in her stomach, the desolation and sense of betrayal would take a long time to abate. But the void inside was filling with anger, a white-hot rage, and the adrenaline that came with it was the stimulant she needed to bring her to her senses.

She turned to look at Nathan. 'If you didn't kill Sarah, why didn't you argue with them? Why didn't you keep protesting your innocence?'

He gave his head a weary shake. 'I was nineteen years old. The police told me I'd done it. That I was so wasted I didn't remember. I suppose I believed them. I didn't want to upset anyone. I know that sounds stupid.'

'Naïve, maybe.'

She scrutinised his face. He was thirty-five, the age her sister would've been. He looked ten years older, worn and weary.

'When they transferred me from young offenders to adult nick, I realized I had a choice: work the system and survive or top myself.'

'Did you believe the story about Rigzi?'

'Mostly. It meant I deserved it. I was being punished for something that was my fault. Oddly, it made it easier. I was just another con. I behaved like a con. Problem is now, that's how I am. That's me. But I have to learn how to do things differently. I can't treat everyone like they're a scumbag with a shiv up their sleeve. Normal people get upset.'

Jo was struck by the sourness in his tone, which, she suspected, would take a long time to disappear.

He fixed her with a chilly stare. 'D'you think anyone can change?'

'Perhaps in time. And if they want to.'

He nodded. 'Still, I've found something I might enjoy doing.'

'Film-making?'

'Kayleigh let me get my hands on the camera a couple of times. I think I could get quite good at it.'

'You two seem to get on.'

'You mean am I shagging her?'

'Well, yeah.'

A crafty smile spread over his face. 'You're not gonna like this, but she reminds me of Sarah. Not in looks, obviously. But they're very similar.'

Jo scowled. No way was she buying this. 'Perhaps it's just that you haven't had sex for a long time?'

'Same age. Nineteen. Clever. Both headbangers.'

Was this his solution? Go back and pick up his life where he left off. She doubted it would work.

'Sorry. I don't see it.'

He sighed. 'Well, I suppose Sarah was a very different person to you. Big sister, someone you looked up to.'

Jo let it go. Even if he was innocent of her sister's murder, she could never like him. But that was irrelevant. Inside she was as bruised and battered as anyone who'd had their guts kicked out, but on the surface she needed to function.

'What about going to the CCRC and persuading them to order a review of your conviction?'

'I've been talking to Harry, my lawyer. He says it'll take time. My parents are both dead and I couldn't give a toss what anyone else thinks about me. But some compensation would be nice.'

He stood up, stretched his arms above his head and gazed up at the trees, the fretwork of bare wood forming a vault over them.

'Gives me a buzz, all this. Being outside, fresh air, proper vegetation. It's what I missed all those years.' He was about to walk away. 'Nearly forgot. Reason I came out, Tania said to tell you that your mum and dad have turned up.'

'My mum *and* dad? Together?'

'Yeah. They're all having a big strategy meeting about what should happen next.'

What should happen next? Jo was well aware that she had no answer to that question. She had her parents and a motley crew of media hacks.

Vaizey had the resources of the MPS. He could still destroy her and probably would.

80

By the time Jo walked into the Kramers' kitchen, the discussion was in full swing. Nick Boden and Gordon Kramer were facing each other across the granite island and the chrome taps. Harry McNair-Phillips was scrolling through the trial papers on his laptop. Tania was making coffee and Alison was watching.

They all turned as she came in, but Gordon was first off the mark. 'Ah, Jo. An update for you. Looks like Foley's off the hook. Born 1981, he was only a year older than Sarah. That makes him a second year, not a postgrad. Whereas Vaizey definitely fits the profile.'

Jo was staring at her parents; she managed a nod. All this new information seemed to swirl around her.

Harry removed his glasses. 'But it's going to be a hell of a job proving it.'

She knew she had to think like a cop. Sort through everything in stages. Be logical. It was the only way she'd survive this. 'What if Vaizey and Foley knew each back then?'

The lawyer scratched his head. 'That would complicate the issue if this is some kind of conspiracy.'

Gordon folded his arms. 'Possible, but highly unlikely. There are two universities in Brighton. We checked and found Foley went to the other one. It's a town with thousands and thousands of students. There's no reason to connect him and Vaizey back then.'

Jo sighed. Was she clutching at straws because it was too hard to accept the truth?

Alison stepped forward and put her arms round her daughter. 'Are you all right?'

Jo glanced from her mother to her father. She couldn't remember the last time she'd seen them in the same room together. Since Nick Boden had remarried, his ex-wife had refused to speak to him.

He gave his daughter a nervous smile. 'Your mother and I agree...' he hesitated, possibly to highlight the rarity of this, 'that it would be best if you came and stayed with me for a while.'

'How would that work, Dad? You planning to hide me from the police?'

'We only want to protect you, Jo.' She noticed him swallowing and the glint of a tear.

Gordon Kramer waded in. 'I've spoken to the Deputy Assistant Commissioner and told him he's got a problem. He's agreed to see me at twelve o'clock. Once we show him all the footage and recordings we've got, I think he'll agree he has to at least investigate Vaizey.'

Jo nodded and checked her watch. 'That's helpful. Thanks, Gordon.' He meant well, they all did.

Alison looped her arm through Jo's. 'You wouldn't be hiding exactly. But until this is sorted out, we think you'd be safest at your dad's.'

Nick Boden was nodding. 'She's right. I can drive you back to Norfolk with me right now.'

Jo smiled. She studied her parents' earnest faces, and she didn't want to hurt their feelings. But why had they no real perception of who she was? Could it be the fallout from their shared family tragedy or something that would've occurred over time, anyway?

She wondered who'd called whom. The initiative must've been Alison's. She knew more of what was going on. Either way, her parents adopting a united front in order to help her was momentous in itself. She should probably be grateful.

They were all watching her expectantly. She shook her head. 'I'm afraid that's not going to work. I know you both want to look after me. But I'm not a little girl any more. Or a teenager like Sarah. I'm a grown woman. And I'm a police officer. You want to help me, Dad, lend me your car.'

'What?'

'If you recall, I qualified as a police driver some years ago.'

'Yes, but—'

'Okay. If you don't want to help me.'

Alison huffed. 'Of course he wants to help you. For God's sake, Nick, give her the keys.'

He stared at his daughter. Jo could see that her confidence and resolution puzzled him. 'I don't want to argue with you —'

'Then don't. I know what I'm doing, Dad.'

Her gaze bored into his. He pulled the keys from his pocket and handed them over.

Jo turned to Tania. 'And can I borrow some of your fancy kit plus a phone? I chucked mine in the river.'

The producer nodded. 'Absolutely.'

81

As Jo gunned her father's Range Rover Evoque up the outside lane of the A12, she reflected on the difference between driving this and her mother's Astra. It felt like some kind of caustic comment on the way their lives had diverged. One of Tania's researchers, who was taking the morning shift outside Cynthia's office, had reported that she hadn't turned up for work and Jo was taking a punt on her being at home and on her own. Vaizey would have already left for the office.

But the confidence Jo had displayed at the Kramers' was an act. Did she know what she was doing? She was suspended from duty and facing a corruption investigation. Going to confront Cynthia in her own home was an enormous risk. Was it even the best way to proceed? A formal interview at a police station was more likely to persuade her to tell the truth, but that wasn't an option.

Driving at speed in a powerful vehicle got the adrenaline pumping and the thoughts churning in her brain. They made little sense. She was still trying to process the evidence. Was he Bruce? He fitted the profile, but that wasn't proof. And was this even about her sister anymore?

A far more urgent question was could he have done all this to her? The corruption charge. Did he set her up? Someone did. Did he have sex with her, then disappear into the night, drive to Littlehampton and murder Briony? It was possible, but was she ready to believe it? Could there be another version of events that she just wasn't seeing?

I'm married and I intend to stay married. He'd made it clear he was using her. Part of her just needed to see it. The home, the family he went back to. Squirming inside her subconscious was the primal impulse to take a sniff at a sexual rival in her lair. Except Cynthia had been Sarah's rival, not hers. This made it even more disturbing. She'd spent most of her life being a proxy for her sister.

When he offered her a job, what did he want? About the only thing she felt sure of, was that couldn't have been a random encounter. Even then, he was targeting her. But why?

Kayleigh had provided the address and Jo drove through Ingatestone village and into a leafy lane of large, recently built luxury homes. Each driveway had a tall hedge, a clipped lawn and at least one high-end four-by-four or expensive sports car. This was the Essex of serious money, of City financiers and celebrity hideaways.

A small white van pootled ahead of her and pulled up. The lettering on the side advertised its business as *Jules's Doggy Daycare* and the driver opened the back doors to load two Golden Retrievers being handed over by their owner.

Jo parked in the road outside and surveyed the house. It was large, a portico with columns on either side of the front door, a double garage and a substantial garden ringed for privacy with shrubs and trees. She walked up the semicircular brick drive. There was no way Steve Vaizey afforded all this on even a senior police officer's salary. Cynthia and her successful branding agency must've paid for their multimillion-pound home.

She paused to psych herself up. This was the point of no return.

If there was a spyhole in the front door, Cynthia didn't use it. Answering while the doorbell was still chiming, she was expecting someone else and looked aghast when she saw Jo Boden on her doorstep.

'What the hell…' Her right cheekbone was bruised and mauve with a large contusion that was partly closing her eye. She had a coat and scarf on and a suitcase behind her in the hallway. 'I thought you were my brother.'

Whatever Jo was expecting, it wasn't this. She stared at Cynthia. Is this what he was capable of doing?

'Did Steve do this to you?'

Cynthia ignored her and turned back into the house. 'Sasha, put your coat on now!'

'Did he attack you? You need to go to the police.'

'The police? You think I'm stupid?' She shot a nervous glance towards the road. 'I'm hiring a security firm and a very expensive divorce lawyer.'

'You won't need a security firm if your testimony sends him to prison.'

Cynthia shook her head. Her swollen face looked painful. 'Why are you here? What do you want?' The tone was disdainful, a hint of the other Cynthia, the cool businesswoman.

'When you told him about Briony, what did he do? She was going to identify him. He had to stop her, didn't he?'

Cynthia seemed startled. She tried to bat the question away. 'I certainly didn't think he'd kill her. I swear to you.'

'What did you think he would do?'

An Audi Station Wagon turned into the drive.

Cynthia gazed at the driver with relief. 'I've got to go.' She turned back into the house and called. 'Come on, kids! Uncle Mark's here.'

Jo grabbed her arm. 'Cynthia, please.'

She flinched and pulled away. 'Let go of me. I don't know if he killed your sister.'

'What did happen that night?'

Cynthia was in a spin. She looked broken and fearful.

'Okay, it's true, we saw Nathan.'

'We?'

'Me and Steve. We were a bit pissed. Nathan asked the time. Steve looked at his watch and told him.'

'Then what did you do?'

'Steve was coming back with me. I lived on campus.'

'You were sleeping together?'

'On and off. I knew he was still obsessed with Sarah. That was pretty obvious.'

A little boy, around five years old, emerged from the house and with him an older girl, ten or eleven. Uncle Mark got out of the Audi and opened the back door for them.

Cynthia was trying to hide her panic from the children; she shepherded them towards the car. 'Jump in. Seat belts on.'

Jo watched them. They were taking their cue from their mother. Both looked extremely anxious. The girl had the hard, watchful grey eyes of her father. She glared at Jo. Cynthia's brother gave her a curt nod as he stepped into the hallway to collect two large suitcases.

'Did you know my sister got pregnant?'

Cynthia was fussing over the children, settling them in the back seat, but this stopped her in her tracks. She closed the back door of the car and stepped away from it.

Her gaze came to rest on Jo. She was shaking. 'Was it his?'

'I don't know. She had an abortion.'

A distracted look spread over Cynthia's features, a glimpse of some private torment. 'He hated condoms. When I became pregnant, I told him I wasn't sure I was ready for kids. He went ape-shit and we got married straight away.'

Jo thought back to her own sexual encounter with him; no condom. He didn't even suggest it.

She fixed Cynthia with a hard stare. 'He didn't come back with you that night, did he?'

'No. He said he was going to move his car, didn't want to get a ticket. He didn't come back.'

'How did he seem?'

'Moody. He was always moody. I didn't see him until about a week later. And then he was nice as pie.'

'But by then, Nathan Wade had been arrested. Why didn't you go to the police and tell them you'd seen Nathan that night?'

Tears welled in Cynthia's eyes.

Jo watched her. Contrition or fear? It was hard to tell. 'You knew it was Steve, didn't you? Or you suspected?'

She brushed away the tears. 'I didn't know anything. But I knew what he was like. He was angry with Sarah about something. All I wanted was for him to choose me. That probably seems foolish to you now.'

Jo met her gaze. 'No. It doesn't.'

The suitcases were loaded in the back of the Audi, and Cynthia opened the passenger door.

'I'm sorry for all of it. But you have to understand, I was in love with—'

The grey BMW turned into the drive at speed and came to a sharp stop in front of the Audi.

Cynthia froze, panic in her eyes.

Vaizey got out. His gaze zeroed in on Jo, then flipped back to his wife. 'What's going on?'

Mark came round to stand in front of his sister. He was a big bloke, thickset. He placed his hands on his hips. 'Don't make any trouble, Steve.'

Vaizey smiled and opened his palms. 'Hey, I'm not making trouble. Just asking a simple question.' He turned to his wife. 'Cynthia?'

Her head dipped. She couldn't face him. She cowered behind her brother. Jo had seen enough battered wives to recognise the dynamic. The control he exerted over her. She only glimpsed it for an instant, but it was real.

Vaizey gave his head a sorrowful shake. 'This is totally unnecessary. And it's going to upset the kids. Do you really want to do this?'

Cynthia still couldn't speak. Vaizey glanced from her to Jo. 'What nonsense have you two been talking about, eh?'

Cynthia remained behind her brother, but her voice was soft and pleading. 'Nothing. Nothing she can prove. Please just let us go.'

Vaizey sighed. 'They're my children. That's why they bear my name. You can't take them away from me. I won't allow it. You must know me well enough to understand that. Come on darling, you don't want to do this. It's silly.'

Mark took a step forward. 'She's told you. She wants to go. And that's what's going to happen.'

The two men faced off for a couple of seconds, then Vaizey shrugged in acquiescence.

Mark took Cynthia by the shoulders and steered her to the passenger seat of the Audi. Once she was safely in the car, he trotted round to the driver's seat, got in, backed up and drove round the BMW.

The Audi accelerated down the drive, brake lights flashing on as it paused at the gate, then it turned out into the lane and disappeared.

Steve Vaizey sighed as he flicked his key fob back and forth in his fingers. 'What is it they say, marry in haste, repent at leisure? It's an old-fashioned notion, but I think it's true.'

Jo scanned him. If he was angry, there was no actual sign of it. He seemed blankly indifferent. This was the opposite of her own tumultuous feelings. She knew she should get away now while she could.

But he turned to her and smiled. 'Don't look so worried, Jo. I'm not going to hurt you.'

'I've seen the state of your wife's face.'

'She came at me with a very sharp Japanese sushi knife. Believe me, when her blood's up, she's dangerous.'

He walked round the BMW and took his briefcase from the passenger seat. He held it up. 'Come on in and have a drink. I've got something on my laptop I want to show you.'

Jo stood rooted to the spot. Outside, she was comparatively safe. Her heart was thumping, her palms were clammy.

He seemed amused by her reluctance. 'Don't be put off by that little marital tiff. You've been a cop long enough to know there are two sides to every domestic. Cynthia's no innocent. Don't you want to hear my side of the story?'

'You killed my sister. All the evidence points to it.'

He laughed. 'The evidence? Does it? What evidence? I'm not denying I knew Sarah. But a court convicted Nathan Wade.'

'But you know and your wife knows that he caught that train.'

'That was the argument for the defence, tested in a court of law and rejected.'

Jo didn't know what to do. He was so charming, and so

plausible. 'When you realized she was my sister, why didn't you walk away? You came after me. Why?'

He tilted his head and smiled at her. 'You know why?'

'No, I don't.'

'This is not about Sarah. That's the past. She's long dead. This was always about us, Jo. You and me. You feel it too. The special connection. Or else why did you sleep with me? Okay, bad timing in some ways. The end of a stressful operation. We were both knackered. But you wanted it as much as me. You know that.'

He turned round and strolled into the house.

82

Jo hesitated. She never thought facing him would be easy. But what had she expected? He disappeared into the house, leaving the front door open. She felt foolish, hovering on the doorstep. He was right. The evidence against him was circumstantial. Could this all be a vast misunderstanding? What if Briony Rowe committed suicide?

She reminded herself she was a cop; wishful thinking should never trump doubt.

He reappeared with a bottle of single Malt in his hand. 'Be realistic. I'm not likely to set about you in my own home. Think of the forensics. And the neighbours round here have got more security cameras than Fort Knox. They're worried about being car-jacked or phone-jacked or someone parking on the grass verge.' He met her gaze, and the look was compelling. 'C'mon, we need to talk, because you've got yourself into quite a tricky situation, Jo Boden. And the only person who can get you out of it is me.'

That was the hook, and he knew it. His manner was friendly and unthreatening. But those implacable grey eyes were surveying her. Jo could feel it in her body, in every sense and intuition she relied on; he was manipulating her. They were playing a deadly game. She also knew she had no choice.

He disappeared back into the interior. Jo took a deep breath and followed.

The hallway was spacious with a wide glass-panelled staircase. A large abstract painting hung on the facing wall. Despite its semi-rural location, the place had a cool metropolitan feel. Using visual detail to create mood was Cynthia's business, so it seemed likely this was her taste.

Vaizey was in the kitchen pouring the whisky into two heavy-bottomed tumblers.

He opened the freezer. 'Ice?'

She nodded. 'You have a beautiful home. I can see why you want to stay married. Because she pays for all this, doesn't she?'

He plopped ice cubes into a glass and handed it to her. 'Don't be fooled by the lovely Cynthia. She's not that smart. This is all family money. She inherited it.'

Jo was doing a rapid scan of the room. She was locating the exits. Sliding doors into the garden, but probably locked. She also noticed the block of knives on the worktop near the island sink. If it came to it, she could grab one, but that would be a last resort.

'Is that why you married her?'

Walking round to the other side of the marble-topped breakfast bar, he perched on a stool and loosened his tie. 'Partly. I always wanted to be in the police. But, living on a copper's wages, that wasn't so attractive.'

He tilted his head, and a wistful look crept into his eye. 'I wonder if Cynthia would've been quite so willing to talk to you if she'd known we'd slept together? And how much I enjoyed it.'

'She didn't know?'

'Not unless you told her. Did you enjoy it, Jo?'

He was teasing her, trying to provoke a reaction. She sipped her whiskey and shrugged. 'Honestly? I found it disappointing. I should've known better. Shagging the boss? Always a mistake.'

He chuckled, but his gaze hardened. 'You wanted it though, didn't you? I gave you the chance to walk away. You didn't take it because you couldn't. And now here you are. You still can't walk away.'

Jo could feel the blood pulsing through her veins. Adrenaline. Fear. If she hadn't realized what she was dealing with before, she did now. The narcissism gave him away.

He was smiling, then, in an instant, his expression changed. He drained his glass in one gulp and put it down with a snap. 'Right. Let's cut the bullshit. I'm guessing you came here to doorstep my wife and you've recorded that encounter to use as evidence. Am I right?'

Here we go, thought Jo. Gloves are off.

She sighed and shrugged. 'You're right.'

He held out his hand like a disappointed parent.

She pulled her mobile phone out of her pocket and placed it on the counter. It was still recording.

He picked it up and clicked it off. 'Nice try. You appreciate I will have to relieve you of this?'

She nodded.

At one end of the breakfast bar, there was a tall glass vase containing an arrangement of white lilies. He grabbed the flowers by the stems and tossed them in the sink. 'Don't want any accidents, do we?' He dropped the phone into the vase of water and pushed it down until it was submerged. He held it there for a moment, a smug smile playing on his lips.

She watched him. Why had she never seen this before?

Because he was good at hiding it. The glasses. The urbane manner. But this was the real Steve Vaizey. He thought he was invincible. He believed he could get away with anything. The casual battering he'd given Cynthia. There was no remorse, or even any embarrassment.

'So are you going to get me out of this…situation?'

A glint came into his eye. He dried his hands on a tea towel. 'There's something I need to show you first.' He went to his briefcase, pulled out the laptop, and extracted it from its sleeve. 'I've been writing to you. No one writes letters any more, do they? A dying art. These are drafts. I was going to print them out.'

He opened the laptop and turned it on. 'I didn't know if I'd ever show them to you. But I thought if you understood this from my point of view…' He inhaled, shook his head. 'But maybe it's too late for all that.'

Was he toying with her?

Jo watched the document come up on the screen, but for the first time she glimpsed a hint of uncertainty, felt a zing of sexual energy. She knew she had to use it.

She dipped her gaze in submission. 'I'd like to read them.'

'Would you? Really?' The tone was tentative. He was deciding whether to trust her. Or perhaps it was just another game.

'Yeah. Really.'

She could see him scoping her for some flicker of desire, something to reassure him. She knew she couldn't fake it, but then she didn't have to.

Abruptly, he seemed to make up his mind. He clicked on another document. 'Actually, I wrote something this morning.'

He turned the screen towards her. She took another sip of her whisky—she hated whisky—and read:

I think of my unborn baby often. I wonder if it would've been a girl or a boy. I wouldn't have minded. I think Sarah would've made a good mother once she'd put all her nonsense away. And you would've grown up in very different circumstances with a little niece or nephew to spoil.

She gave him what she hoped was an understanding look. 'How did you find out about the abortion?'

'How do you know about it?'

'My father told me.'

He grinned. 'Yeah. When your old man turned up out of the blue, that's what alerted me. I am quite a good detective, y'know. She'd been behaving oddly, tried to dump me. He arrived. That's when I smelt a rat. I watched him. He was definitely upset about something. She skipped a couple of seminars, pretending to have the flu. But she was fine. Then she dropped out of the play. I knew how much that'd meant to her. And I had a hunch.'

'When you slept with her, did you use a condom?'

'I hate those things. Unnatural. Well, I think you already know that. But you're on the pill, aren't you? Which is sensible in your position.'

Jo wondered what he thought her position was. A woman, not virginal, approaching her sell-by date, who should be grateful for any casual sex that came her way?

'So you guessed she was planning to have an abortion? Why didn't you try to stop her?'

'Oh, believe me, I was going to. I was following them when my car broke down. It was knackered; all I could afford back then. The clutch went. The next time I saw her, she'd done the deed.'

'Didn't you ever try to talk to her about it?'

'She said she just didn't want to be with me. Which more or less confirmed it. So I went into her room, read her journal. It was there in black and white what she'd done and how it was none of my business. She was unhinged. I don't know, perhaps it was the hormones. I was in love with her, Jo, and I would've married her.'

'Maybe she didn't want that. She was only nineteen, just starting university.'

He shook his head. Now the anger was emerging. 'But then she took up with that idiot, Nathan Wade. It should've been me, not a stupid boy. She was only interested in him because she could control him.'

Jo watched him. He was still seething with resentment after all these years. He hadn't let it go.

'Was that why you killed her, Steve?'

She'd said it. It was out there. She had no idea how he'd react.

He glared at her, got off the stool, removed his tie, and huffed.

'Look. I need you to understand this, Jo. Then we can move forward, you and I. That's how we get out of this stupid situation. I know it's what we both want.'

'Understand what?'

'Sarah. It was an accident, pure and simple. I went round because I decided to give her another chance. But she insisted on being difficult. I never intended to hurt her. She fell, hit her head.'

'That's not what killed her. She was asphyxiated.'

'I had no choice. She would've ruined my life.' He reached over to the laptop. 'Here, read my earlier letters. I've explained it to you.'

'What about Briony Rowe?'

He sighed. 'What about her? That's not something you and I need to discuss.'

Jo took a careful breath; in this deadly game of poker, everything depended on her holding her nerve.

'Why not?'

He started to pace. 'Bloody media! You know what those vultures are like. We do an important job. We've seized an arsenal of weapons. Put some serious criminals away. How many lives will that save? But along comes some meddling hack with an agenda.' He shook his head wearily. 'She was a loose end.'

Jo tried to imagine the fight, the brute force required to push another human being into the path of a speeding train. He was strong enough to do it. But the most shocking thing was his cold indifference. He was pitiless. *A loose end.* Why had she not seen what he was? How had he beguiled her so easily? Was she this feeble-minded?

'A loose end you failed to tidy up. Briony Rowe had a dash-cam in her car.'

'What?' A look came into his eye that she'd not seen before. Not fear or even anger, more petulance.

'You should've guessed. She was a film-maker, into all that.'

He frowned. 'You're right. I was in a hurry. I should've checked.' His tone implied an annoying omission, like forgetting to collect the dry-cleaning. But Jo could see the calculation going on behind the impenetrable gaze.

He poured himself another whiskey. 'Right, but we can sort that out.'

He continued to pace, his restless energy brimming over, planning his next move. Jo watched him; the confidence was riveting.

'What about me, Steve? I've been set up, accused of corruption. You said you're the only one who can help me.'

He gave her a considered look. 'You put me in an untenable position. The point had to be made.'

'Believe me, you've made it. I just want my job back. Can you do that?'

He smiled. 'I knew you come round. So we have a deal, do we?'

'I don't know. Do we?'

'I'll speak to Jabreel Khan. Explain that I've received further intel from my source and the transfer to your account was a computer error.'

'The money was from you?'

He reached out and brushed her hair with his fingers. 'You should've left well alone, Jo. But I think you understand that now, don't you?'

'My life would've been simpler.'

'And it can be again. You're a good police officer. I've always thought so.'

'I hope you're right. Steven Vaizey, I'm arresting you for the murder of Sarah Boden.'

He stared at her in disbelief. 'Don't be ridiculous. I thought you understood.'

'You do not have to say anything, but it may harm your defence—'

He was across the kitchen in two strides. With explosive speed, his right fist flew straight at her head. It was a boxer's move, a lethal punch designed to do serious damage. She jumped backwards and it missed her by a whisker. He followed with a jab in the stomach that knocked her off her feet. She slid backwards across the shiny tiled floor and slammed into one of the kitchen cabinets.

He towered over her, hands on hips, hatred in his eyes. 'This is your fault. It didn't have to end like this.'

The pain in her abdomen was excruciating. She couldn't breathe.

Grabbing her by the lapels of her jacket, he hauled her up to her feet. As he did so, the small camera concealed in her lapel came loose and clattered to the floor.

Jo fixed him with a stony gaze, although she hardly had breath to speak. 'Button camera…live streaming… to a remote computer—'

'Rubbish! You're bluffing.'

He flung her onto the floor, reached over to the knife block and pulled out the longest blade.

She tried to scrabble to her feet. He loomed over her.

A crash and thump of boots in the hall; Foley burst through the door like a charging bull. He grabbed Vaizey from behind and threw him against the wall. A phalanx of uniformed officers followed him in. They seized Vaizey.

Foley helped Jo to her feet. 'You okay?'

Vaizey was cuffed, but his unremitting gaze bored into her. 'This is nonsense. Your word against mine. It'll never stand up in court. You realize that.'

She glared back. 'I told you. They've got it all, audio and video recording, broadcast quality, too. You think you're so smart, boss?' She pointed at her phone in the vase of water. 'But you fell for the oldest trick in the book. Misdirection.'

EPILOGUE

It was 5 a.m. and the sodium-yellow drenched streets were deserted. Jo Boden and Cal Foley stood side by side in a dark patch of shadow on the rain-slicked pavement. The eerie silence was broken occasionally by the staccato crackle of the comms in the nearby van. They were in Rusholme, South Manchester, waiting round the corner from the target premises while the armed response team and the local officers all got into position.

They'd driven up from London and arrived in the early hours. Foley had suggested a curry, and they'd gone to one of the late-night establishments on Wilmslow Road.

Jo had been amazed by how much the DS could eat. He'd consumed his own meal, then hoovered up what remained of hers.

With the arrest of Steve Vaizey, Operation Grebe had been put on ice and its officers redeployed. There was a good deal of shock amongst the team. The Met's press office was engaged in a battle with the media to present it as a case of one rogue officer and not an indication of wider corruption.

The Deputy Assistant Commissioner had defended this position in an interview with veteran reporter Gordon Kramer, which had been broadcast on *Channel Four News*. The fact officers like Jabreel Khan and others had inadvertently assisted Vaizey had been glossed over. Khan was on sick leave.

Foley had been the first to work out that Khan and Hollingsworth himself had been conned by Vaizey. He took his suspicions to Dave Hollingsworth and helped to expose the set-up that his former boss had put in place to discredit Jo.

The Major Crimes Unit in Sussex was investigating Briony Rowe's death. The retrieved dash-cam footage from her Mini showed her being pulled over by an unmarked police car, hauled out of her own vehicle, brutally coshed and dragged towards the railway line. Her assailant was identified as Steve Vaizey. He'd used his position on Grebe to put an ANPR tracker on Briony's car, so he knew where to find her.

They'd charged him with her murder, and he was also being questioned by the team set up to review the safety of Nathan Wade's conviction for Sarah Boden's murder. In both cases, the CPS thought the evidence strong. Cynthia Fenton-Wright had reconciled with her husband and hired a top-notch legal firm to defend him.

Sipping his beer, Foley had smirked at Jo across the table. 'So when all this stuff goes out on the telly you're gonna be the Commissioner's blue-eyed girl. You solved your sister's murder. Your career'll go into the stratosphere.'

'I doubt it.'

'Hope you remember who your friends are.'

'Are we friends?' She was teasing him. It had become the unspoken strategy they'd both adopted to get over the awkwardness between them. But Foley wasn't the sort to bear a grudge. He also harboured the hope that Jo Boden would come to see him in a different light.

He'd been as good as his word and used his Manchester contacts to add some weight to the search for Razan's missing sister.

So they were present at a dawn raid on a crack house and brothel. As usual, much hanging around and waiting was involved. Jo rubbed her hands, Foley stomped his feet. It was the end of February and still bitterly cold. Finally they heard the thwack of the door going in, the splintering of glass and wood.

Foley nodded. 'Let's go take a look.'

By the time they reached the house, a nondescript Victorian semi, several of the occupants were being marched out in handcuffs. A uniformed officer directed them up the stairs to the front bedroom. Officers were everywhere, turning the whole place over. Evidence was being bagged.

There was a shabby divan on the floor, and a female detective was kneeling beside it. On the divan were three girls, all barely teenagers. The detective was trying to reassure them.

Jo pulled out her phone and checked the picture on the screen. She looked at the three petrified faces. Cowering in the furthest corner was a girl of about twelve, the youngest. She was clutching a ragged blanket around herself to cover her nakedness.

Tapping the detective on the shoulder, Jo Boden knelt down beside the divan in her place.

She gazed into the child's dark, terrified eyes. 'Amira? Are you Amira Midani?'

There was a tiny nod of the head.

'I'm Detective Constable Jo Boden. I've come to take you back to your sister. Your sister Razan.'

Amira's lips moved, pronouncing the name, but there was no sound. Her whole body was trembling.

Jo held out her hand and smiled. 'We're going to get you out of here. You'll be safe now. Come on.'

NEXT IN THE SERIES
SHE'S GONE

Prologue

He throws her into the back of the van like a sack of rubbish. Her shoulder slams into the metal wheel arch. She hears the bone crack as she rolls away from it and across the hard floor. She ends up on her back. The pain is excruciating. Her lungs are still screaming for air after being held in his throttling grip. She's dizzy from lack of oxygen. Now she feels sick.

Her stomach clenches with fear. If she loses consciousness now, then it'll all be over. She must focus and fight back. But her head is swimming with random thoughts. She's spiralling downwards. The pain is fading. A bad sign. She remembers her mother's smile.

Is this how it ends? Slipping away. What do you think of in your last moments? Is it easier to let go, accept the inevitable?

* * *

Chapter 1

Friday 7.15am

For the first week after Phoebe left for university, Marcia Lennox couldn't pass her daughter's bedroom door without opening it, taking a peek at the unnaturally tidy interior and thinking: she's gone. But as the days pass, the sense of loss is becoming more muted. Getting on with things is the solution, obviously. Moments of desolation still hit her; the smell of coffee in the morning. She always took Phoebe a cup to encourage her out of bed. Teenagers need their sleep. She read it somewhere. Quite natural.

Now it's just the two of them. But that's fine.

It's all as it should be. She's done the job she set out to do. She keeps telling herself that.

She wrinkles her nose as she flips the sizzling bacon with a steel spatula. The enticing aroma floods the large, airy kitchen. But it doesn't entice Marcia. To a vegan, it's disgusting. She turns on the extractor fan. It reminds her of what? The shrieks of pigs being dragged to slaughter. Is that a genuine memory or some TV documentary she once saw?

Hard to tell.

She forces her mind back to the now. To her easy-wipe induction hob and her task: making breakfast for her husband.

A grey dawn filters through the full-length windows. The screen of shrubs covering the garden wall is heavy and dank. London in October.

Dull and depressing. Summer's gone. The worst time of the year because there's nothing to look forward to.

Rain patters on the skylights. It'll be a miserable journey to work.

Marcia wears a navy and white apron reaching from her neck to her calves. The name of a French Michelin-starred chef is embroidered in the top corner. A Christmas present from her daughter. As she turns to the granite-topped kitchen island, where a sourdough loaf sits waiting on the breadboard, her husband heaves a sigh.

Harry Lennox is perched on a stool, elbows resting on the breakfast bar. He peers through his glasses at the laptop open in front of him. Picking up his mug of coffee, he takes a sip and huffs again.

Marcia scans him. She doesn't speak. She cuts two slices of sourdough and transfers them to a plate.

Harry glances up. 'Can I have butter?' he says.

'No,' says Marcia.

'Ketchup?' He has the pleading look of a small boy.

'No.'

'Tomato's a vegetable.'

'It's loaded with sugar.'

Marcia transfers the cooked bacon to a square of kitchen paper to drain.

'At least leave some fat on it,' says Harry.

'It's the fat that's the problem. For heaven's sake, Harry, I'm trying to take care of you.'

'Maybe just a little mayo then?' He tilts his head and gives her his trademark cheeky grin.

That grin. How many women have fallen for that? How many are still falling for it?

'Rocket and some sliced tomato,' she says, returning his smile.

'Okay,' he says. 'You win.'

Harry is fifty-seven, over six foot, loose-limbed and rangy. Even though his cholesterol is way too high, he'll never look fat. He has a full head of hair with a floppy grey-blond fringe, the rom-com good looks of a breakfast TV host.

He returns to his laptop and continues to scroll. Endless columns of figures. Dow Jones, FTSE, Nasdaq, Nikkei, Hang Seng. Marcia is familiar with the main stock market indices, but she doesn't know what he's looking at, only that every morning he checks the markets. Harry is the number two at a major equity hedge fund in the City. He could be number one if he wasn't so lazy.

One wall of the kitchen is covered with floor to ceiling

cabinets. Marcia's fingers slip into the carefully engineered side groove, and she pulls open the fridge.

The hand-built kitchen is one of the delights of her life. It operates like a machine. Never lets her down or surprises her. She opens the salad drawer at the bottom, takes out a tomato and a packet of rocket.

Harry puffs out his cheeks. 'Bloody ridiculous,' he says. 'We've just taken a huge position in Chinese telecoms and now the US is having another pop at the Chinese. I warned Tom it was too risky. The price'll tank.'

Marcia washes and slices the tomato, assembles the bacon sandwich, cuts it in half diagonally, and places it next to the laptop. He seizes it in his right hand and takes a large bite.

The stink of roasted flesh pervades the room. She turns the extractor to full blast.

'That's unfortunate,' she says.

'Damn sight more than unfortunate,' he replies with another sigh. He demolishes half the sandwich in three more bites, wipes his mouth with his fingers and says, 'It's not that bad with tomato.'

She takes off her apron. 'Glad you like it.'

She's wearing the silk pyjamas he bought her on his recent trip to Dubai. Oyster grey. A colour she likes. Not that he knows that. She can imagine him diving into the airport shop and grabbing the first thing that looked expensive enough.

But he's not looking at her. She wants him to look. But she won't beg. Never, *never* beg. His eyes are back on the screen as he devours the other half of his sandwich.

Eventually he turns and says, 'What're you up to today?'

Marcia is Head of Account Management at an awarding winning advertising agency in Notting Hill. But Harry has the knack of making her feel as though this is just an interesting hobby.

'Oh, you know,' she says. 'Whatever's in the diary.'

'Bit wet out there. Is that why you're not running this morning?' He finishes his sandwich. He's making conversation. Ticking the communicate-with-the-wife box. Ask a question and pretend you care about the answer.

Harry smiles. Now he's waiting. Caring about the answer.

She smiles back.

Marcia is forty-three but as lithe as when she was twenty; she runs through nearby Richmond Park three times a week to keep it that way. Her hair, cut in a neat bob, is without a trace of grey. She has a manicure, pedicure and facial once a week.

'It's Friday,' she says. 'I've got my personal trainer at lunchtime.' Why does he always forget?

'Oh, yeah. I always forget.' He nods. He's preparing to leave. His thoughts are already up and off.

She feels a surge of panic. Such an old reflex.

'I was thinking,' she says briskly. 'On Sunday we could drive up to Cambridge and take Phoebe out to lunch.'

He shakes his head and sighs. 'Darling, leave the poor girl alone. It's her first term at university. She's only been there two weeks.'

'Three, this weekend.'

'Whatever. She needs time to settle. And she'll have so much to do. People to meet, parties to go to. She's eighteen. You remember what it was like. Let her enjoy it.'

Marcia remembers the damp basement flat she lived in and the two jobs she had to work to pay the rent. And the scabby landlord who tried to… but she's put all that behind her.

'I thought she might be homesick. Or a bit lonely.'

'I doubt it. Not very Phoebe, is it? She'll be in the thick of it.'

'But—'

'Take my advice,' he says, 'and wait to be invited.' He closes his laptop and looks at his watch.

Marcia has a stabbing pain in her chest; acid reflux from the anxiety twisting in her gut. She should eat. She thinks about her daughter, her beautiful golden child. Since she left, the house is like a mausoleum. No awful music with a thudding bass-line vibrating the floorboards, no laundry all over the bedroom floor, no coming down in the morning to find strange young people asleep on the sofa.

The large Edwardian villa on the edge of Richmond Green has six bedrooms and a sizeable extension at the back. When they moved in fifteen years ago, she knew it was the perfect family home. Harry's sons from his first marriage visited every other weekend. Lively and full of laughter, it was the hub of all their lives, that's how Marcia remembers it. Back then they knew the neighbours. They even had a dog, a scrappy terrier that barked at everyone.

'I know you miss her,' says Harry. 'It's only natural.' He tucks the laptop under his arm and smiles.

She can hear the but, although he doesn't say it. He must think she's stupid. Their daughter is eighteen — *only eighteen!* — officially an adult. Marcia wants her to have a wonderful life. And freedom. Especially that. And not to waste her opportunities. And to watch out for men trying to spike her drinks. And to look both ways when she crosses the road. And... and... She sounds awful and preachy, even in the confines of her own head.

It's easy for him; child-rearing's done. Pack up your feelings — the fears, the regrets, losing that bouncy little person, who always adored you — and get on with the next thing. What is the next thing?

'Will you be home for dinner tonight?' she says.

He frowns. His gaze slithers away and he sighs. 'Not really sure. Tom's got a new client he wants me to meet. Just drinks, but you know how these things drag on. Don't go to any trouble.'

'Fine,' she says.

'I'll text you.' He's still avoiding eye contact.

'Okay.'

He smiles, gives her a peck on the cheek and disappears through the kitchen door. World's worst liar.

Does he not realise how transparent he is? Perhaps he doesn't care.

Marcia is left standing alone at the centre of her beautiful kitchen. She strokes the cold granite with her fingertips. Her thoughts are blank. She feels at a loss. Why doesn't he look anymore?

The tears prickle.

This is no good. She gives herself a stern reprimand. The kitchen she'll leave for the cleaners. They come in at ten.

She goes upstairs to shower and dress for work. It's a blip. All relationships have them. She'll soon turn this around. She always has. And she will see Phoebe. She'll text her.

LEAVE A REVIEW

If you feel like writing a review, I'd be most grateful. The choice of books out there is vast. Reviews do help readers discover one of my books for the first time.

Scan QR code to review

tiktok.com/@susanwilkinsbooks

bookbub.com/authors/susan-wilkins

facebook.com/susanwilkinsauthor

instagram.com/susan_wilkins32

x.com/SusanWilkins32

A MESSAGE FROM SUSAN
PLUS A FREE BOOK TO DOWNLOAD

Thank you for choosing to read *It Should Have Been Me.* If you enjoyed it and would like a free download, plus keep up to date with my latest book releases and news, please use the address below.

susanwilkins.co.uk/sign-up/

*Your email address will never be shared, and you can unsubscribe at any time.

Scan QR code to go to Susan's sign up page

Do get in touch and let me know what you thought of *It Should Have Been Me.* I love hearing from readers. You can message me at: susanwilkins.co.uk/contact/

Scan QR Code to go to Susan's contact page

BOOKS BY SUSAN

Detective Jo Boden Case Files - Prequel.

It Should Have Been Me 2nd edition

Detective Jo Boden Case Files:

She's Gone

Her Perfect Husband

Lie Deny Repeat

See Me Fall

You Left Me

Other Books by Susan:

The Informant

The Mourner

The Killer

Buried Deep

Close To The Bone

The Shout. Free when you sign up to Susan's newsletter

A Killer's Heart